Praise for

DANCING NAKED AT THE EDGE OF DAWN
A Book Sense 76 Bestseller

"What a delightful story . . . Kris Radish's book offers a refreshing, often humorous, view into making changes in order to live life to its fullest. The writing is eloquent and packed with fascinating characters. Kudos to Kris for her vibrant read!"
—roundtablereviews.com

"Radish sings the praises of sisterhood by creating an enticing world of women helping women to become the empowered individuals they were meant to be."—*Booklist*

"Radish again features powerful friendships and zeroes in on female longings and liberation in this novel."
—*Milwaukee Journal Sentinel*

"Radish's . . . characters know how to have a good time on their way to matriarchal Nirvana."
—*Kirkus Reviews*

THE ELEGANT GATHERING OF WHITE SNOWS
A Book Sense 76 Bestseller

"I wish I could buy a copy for every woman I've ever met. I am so in love with this book, the women's stories, and their relationships with each other."
—Susan Wasson, Bookworks, Albuquerque, NM

Also by Kris Radish

THE ELEGANT GATHERING OF
WHITE SNOWS

DANCING NAKED AT THE EDGE OF DAWN

And coming soon from Bantam Books

THE SUNDAY LIST OF DREAMS

Annie Freeman's

FABULOUS
TRAVELING FUNERAL

Kris Radish

BANTAM BOOKS

ANNIE FREEMAN'S FABULOUS TRAVELING FUNERAL
A Bantam Book / February 2006

Published by
Bantam Dell
A Division of Random House, Inc.
New York, New York

Book design by Karin Batten

Library of Congress Cataloging-in-Publication Data
Radish, Kris.
Annie Freeman's fabulous traveling funeral / Kris Radish.
p. cm.
ISBN-13: 978-0-553-38264-8
ISBN-10: 0-553-38264-0
1. Funeral rites and ceremonies—Fiction. 2. Inheritance and
succession—Fiction. 3. Female friendship—Fiction. 4. Loss
(Psychology)—Fiction. 5. Women travelers—Fiction.
6. Bereavement—Fiction. I. Title.
PS3618.A35 A85 2006
813/.6 22   2005053176

Printed in the United States of America
Published simultaneously in Canada

www.bantamdell.com

BVG   10   9   8   7   6   5   4   3   2

This book, which some might think is about dying, is really about living. It is for any woman—every woman—who has ever lost something or someone she loved and then grieved, touched the sorrowful edges of her own soul, embraced the heart of loss—and then moved forward.

Acknowledgments

Writing a book is often a solitary expedition that consumes so much of a writer's soul, mind, body, heart and thus her life that it's impossible to communicate with such a person when they are on this perilous journey.

On my journey through this writing expedition, the usual suspects were always there—my family, my editor, my glorious agent, the remarkable people at Bantam Dell who make a jumbled manuscript into something pretty and sellable, and the guy who sold me all that coffee, and the other guy who winked when I rushed in for another bottle of red wine. "It's a funeral," I kept telling him. And it was.

Then there are the women who read my books.

The women who send me letters and e-mails and come to listen to my wild writing tales. The women who get what I am trying to share and say and who see a part of themselves in one of my characters—the way she said something, the time she finally did something, that one conversation on that one page.

Just so you know, I am terribly grateful and I think of you—each one of you—when I write and growl and worry and cry and bend over the words that eventually move you to connect with me.

Thank you. Just thank you for giving me your own thoughts, sharing your intimate stories of survival and change and for fueling the flames of a passion I have had since the day I was born. It's a wonder I do not explode.

I am nothing without the booksellers, small and large, who

carry my books from box to table, who read my stories, who then tell customers and clients and friends and anyone who cares to hear about this Radish book. From Duluth to Las Vegas to Seattle and Los Angeles and through all the little towns and communities and back again through Albuquerque and into Florida, up the entire coast and into the heartland—every single one of you make a difference in my life.

Thank you.

Thank you.

Thank you.

My writing may help some of you reach for your own dreams, see something in yourself that is a bit dusty or motivate you to think, do, be, act—and just so you know: because of you my dreams come true also.

I get to write and spread my passions throughout the pages of a book—how lucky am I.

Annie Freeman's

FABULOUS

TRAVELING FUNERAL

1

There is a hole the size of a golf ball in the right side of Katherine Givins's black Bali bra.

This is the one article of clothing that has made her feel sexy for the past 3.6 years in a row, and even though the straps lie at half-mast on her fine shoulders, the elastic exploded last summer and the hooks have been pulled so many times she has actually used a needle-nose pliers on them, Katherine cannot bear to throw the bra away.

"Shit," she says, turning into the mirror and then leaning so her nose practically touches the glass to make certain there really is a hole. It's there, and getting wider every second, as she puts her finger in the middle and realizes that one wrong move could explode all of the seams and send her breasts into orbit.

Just as she grabs them and begins laughing hysterically at the long-held notion that the bra, like her lost marriage and her fabulous mother and the man she thought she loved two men ago or even the one she loves now, would last forever, the doorbell rings and makes her scream herself back into reality.

Her scream, the kind you might make when something

normal—like a doorbell—flushes you from a very far-away place—reaches the UPS woman on the front step who is glad as hell that someone is home so she doesn't have to leave a note and come back the next day. In the UPS world, screams, especially those coming from anywhere in front of the brown trucks and not under the rear wheels, are very good signs. So the UPS woman waits.

Katherine does not care who is at the door immediately because she is already in mourning about the loss of her bra. The bra that held her up and saw her through when her daughter announced that she had her first kiss (3.1 years ago) and then snapped the back of her mother's Bali bra instead of performing the regulation high-five; when she found out her ex-husband Michael was about to be married (2.8 years ago) as she was sorting wash and the bra moved from her fingers and into the black depths of a dark load; when *finally* a man emboldened by vodka martinis put his hand down her strategically placed low-cut sweater and ran his fingers very slowly past the elastic top and curved his hand around her left breast; when her father came to her one night (2.1 years ago) and said that he could no longer care for his wife, her mother, and could Katherine "please, please, please" help him find the right place, and then leaned into her, clutched her shoulder, his sad and tired arm thumping against the metal hook; when she let Alex finally make love to her (1.8 years ago) and he turned her around, lifted her blouse and took his sweet, sexy and fabulous time unhooking the Bali and then replaced it with hands that spoke seventeen languages; when she leaned over her mother's coffin (.8 years ago), the metal from the underwire tapping against the edge of the coffin as she ran her hands through her mother's hair one last time and then wept so long and hard that the funeral started almost an hour late, and just now the hole emerging like an omen of age and change slapping her upside the head and making her wonder, "What next? What in the hell is going to happen next in this life of mine?"

The doorbell.

Katherine, angry at the unseen intruder who had startled her, miffed about the meaning behind her disintegrating bra, and half-naked, lunges for the door as the terrified blonde woman drenched in brown is reaching for the doorbell for the third time.

"Jesus!" she shouts as Katherine falls into her arms the very moment the door opens.

Katherine, still angry about the intrusion, has managed to grab a kitchen towel on her run from the bedroom. It is a small towel but a towel it is and when she falls into the arms of the UPS woman the towel drops and they both watch it descend to the floor as if it may break and shatter the instant it touches earth.

Anyone lucky enough to be watching would be breathless. What next? Who will move first? Will the UPS woman find this incident funny or humiliating? Will Katherine begin screaming again? And the package . . . what in the hell is in the package?

The UPS woman, who just happens to be a kind and gentle soul who lives alone and keeps notes on all of her customers, has her arms wrapped around Katherine to steady herself. Katherine has a brief moment of clarity when she feels the warm fingers of the woman on her shoulders and this resurrects a historic moment in her mind.

She remembers that her friend Reva took her shopping the day she bought the bra. Reva stood in the center of an old-fashioned department store, hands on hips, moving from foot to foot, and said that her mother had sold bras door-to-door in rural Nevada and it was a simple gift that a woman could give to herself—the proper fitting of a bra. This was said to Katherine P. Givins, attorney at law, who had purchased every undergarment in her entire life on the fly, cups too small, elastic tight against her back, tiny dents under her rib cage from wires that should never have been put into women's clothing in the first place.

And then, the moment the saleswoman fitted her—the measuring tape sliding to the floor, her aging fingers gently lifting her breasts into this bra—this very exceptional bra—and the look on the older woman's face, a look of kind satisfaction, as she watched Katherine move and realize that "Yes, damn it, a good bra can change everything."

Their eyes meet then. The UPS woman asking with her soft green eyes what she should do next, and Katherine, not moving away, holding her there, for one, two, three seconds while she lets go—just lets go.

"It's the bra," she tells Ms. UPS. "Have you ever had a bra that has taken you through so much and held you in place like nothing else?"

The UPS woman, who was a woman way before she was UPS, does not flinch. More than once in her twenty-six-year career, a man has answered the door naked. She has walked in on clowns dancing on tables, a wife throwing meatballs at her husband's favorite television show, and so many drunk people she cannot even begin to remember them all. Katherine in her favorite bra, holding her in her bra on the porch, is nothing.

"I love jogging bras," the UPS woman begins. "In my business there is quite a lot of bouncing and jumping and although I am far from voluptuous, I need a good, solid foundation for the kind of work I do."

Katherine falls right into the conversation, wearing her favorite undergarment, a pair of faded green cotton shorts that have another story to tell, and absolutely nothing else. The UPS woman, with more than a hint of subtle and gracious poise, motions for Katherine to step back inside of the house, but the women do not stop talking. They dance backwards and Katherine, hands flailing idly as they always do when she is excited, continues to talk about the demise of her Bali.

"Well, how about just getting a new one?" Ms. UPS asks.

"I've written and called and stopped at every department store in the United States and in three foreign countries. They do not make this bra anymore."

"How sad is that."

Katherine, who is usually gracious and poised herself, has this ridiculous urge to invite the UPS woman into the kitchen for a glass of wine or a cup of coffee so they can talk about undergarments all day, but she's also a practical and usually wise woman. She knows there's a good chance Ms. UPS has to finish working but she can't quite stop herself. Undergarments, she thinks to herself, surely do strange things to one's inhibitions.

Later, when days and weeks have passed and she has time to backtrack to this very moment, she will remember it as one that she should have paid more attention to when she was asking herself about why the hole in the bra was spreading now and why she was standing in her underwear in front of a stranger and why none of it seemed out of the ordinary.

"That thing," she will eventually say to herself, "that inner voice that was tapping against my heart and asking me to pause— Damn, I should have listened. I should have paid attention because that's when everything changed."

Everything changed.

But first a wave of laughter rising from the two women who visually embrace each other as women do who can talk at the ring of a doorbell about underwear, and breasts and menstrual cycles and the way women connect and can fall into each other's lives and arms so quickly.

"This must seem ridiculous," Katherine says as the two women tip their heads and the sound of their laughter mixes and rises to the edge of high windows in Katherine's very old but lovely home.

"Well, as you can imagine, I've seen everything. I'd much rather be greeted by a woman in a black bra who has a great story than a man in black underwear who has no story at all."

Then Ms. UPS reaches inside of her brown pants pocket and she pulls out a small, soft stone that has been worn smooth and shiny by one ride after another inside the cotton pants pocket.

"You have a lucky bra, something that I imagine has carried you through some challenging and tough nights and days, and I have this rock."

She lets Katherine take the rock into her hand and feel how just holding it, like wearing a fabulous bra, can be a comfort. They don't talk about it because they are women and they know. They know about comfort and the loss of it and they know about sacrifice and change and that the ring of a doorbell, a wild call at midnight, the scent of something new, the touch of a baby or a lover's fresh face, can change everything.

They know.

"I see," Katherine says and then she gently hands back the stone, understanding its importance, but also not able to stop herself from saying, "You'll understand if I don't hand over the bra."

They laugh, which is the perfect thing to do, and then Ms. UPS says, "The package!" and goes back to the front door where she set down her clipboard and the box, wrapped in the requisite brown paper with one single and simple label.

"This is for you if you are indeed Katherine P. Givins."

"I am."

"Expecting this?"

"I have no clue."

"Well, this is your surprise and you were mine then," Ms. UPS says, smiling as she dips to pick up her sign-off sheet.

Katherine signs the metal-backed ledger and then Ms. UPS bends to pick up the box. The transfer is swift and easy and the package passes from woman to woman in a ceremony that is completed only when Katherine, who has always been way to the other side of spontaneous, bends to hug Ms. UPS one last time.

"You are a sweetheart," she tells her new blonde friend.

"Well, that's nice but it's all part of the job. I never know what is going to happen or what I might see when I ring someone's doorbell."

"I imagine you've seen more action than a pile of undergarments,"

Katherine says and then pauses for a second. "There's something new and exciting behind every unopened door."

"Sounds like a book title," Ms. UPS responds just before she turns back toward her waiting van. "Time to go see what's behind the next door."

There is a quick wave and then Katherine finds herself alone in the foyer of the home she has spent twelve years restoring. The home she bought with the proceeds from her first fairly huge lawsuit, which netted her $69,283 and allowed her to move from a two-bedroom apartment with her daughter Sonya following her divorce from a man whom she had once loved a great deal but had come to realize she should have never married for a variety of reasons including the not-so-obvious fact that he had never gotten over the love of his life—a woman he still saw three times a week at places like hotels, nice restaurants, and the back seat of her husband's car.

The package.

Ms. UPS is stepping into the brown van when Katherine looks for just a second at the package that is wedged against her own chest, just where the Bali touches the top of her last rib, and wonders if the shape of the box does not hint that there may be a pair of shoes inside. Her mind stops there as Ms. UPS turns, shouts, "Bye now," smiles as if she knows a wild secret and then disappears behind a sliding door that sounds like a smooth and even gunshot.

The door closes as Katherine turns to tap it with her heel, because ever since she has owned the home that is what she does to make certain that it really is closed, and when she turns she can see her reflection in the oak mirror by the door. She sees the bra hole—which is now wider than a golf ball, maybe even a tennis ball—widen to the shape of an almost ripe grapefruit.

"Damn it," she says, even though she is not prone to swearing and loathes the societal turn of events that makes a word like "fuck" commonplace. "Just damn it."

The package is wedged under her bra and Katherine does not realize that it is the package that is now holding the bra in place. She does not see that there is a dwindling span of threads the size of three toothpicks that is holding together the left side of her bra and that the minute she sits or moves too fast the bra will fly open and be lost to her forever. She doesn't see this but she is thinking about it. She is thinking about the miles of highway that the bra has seen her over and the heartaches and the laughs and then, because she harbors a secret, a very old and almost forgotten desire to write children's books, she wonders if anyone has ever written a story about a girl's first bra. She is also thinking about the mysterious box and the who, what, when, where and why of its existence.

Katherine settles into the rocking chair just beyond the edge of the front hall, the box pushed tight against her chest, and rocks for one, two, three minutes wondering if Ms. UPS will race home and call someone to tell the story of the wild woman with the ancient bra who answered the door just past noon.

"No," she answers herself the same way we all speak when we are alone or working and need to just hear a word so we can validate our own precious thought. "This probably happens all of the time."

She imagines then just for a few moments what it would be like if she had the UPS woman's life or anyone else's life but her own. She wonders about delivering packages with unknown contents instead of drafting law briefs; she wonders about changing an entire career just like that, like the snap of a bra, for something new and maybe not so ferocious and seemingly arbitrary like distributing little pieces of the law. She wonders about skipping a beat, about missing an appointment, about maybe running down the road naked or doing something impractical like not even wearing a bra anymore. Something. Anything. She wonders and as she wonders she is astonished to realize she is tired. Physically tired and mentally tired. Tired of routines and all the expectations of her own life that she has so carefully designed and now scrambles daily to keep in place like one of those ridiculous plate-balancing acts at the circus.

Then it is time for the package.

Wrapped in a brown paper bag that has been cut with scissors and then taped so the edges touch perfectly. A package that comes to Katherine's house on a Wednesday when she is rarely, if ever, home, but because of a scheduling mix-up and a sick clerk and the desire to breathe in some rare quiet for just a few hours, Katherine, who considers herself beyond predictable and north of reliable, slips from her assistant district attorney's job and into her favorite nasty clothes, in which she expects to read a pile of old magazines until her daughter comes home for dinner from her third year of high school, track practice and a Spanish IV study session.

Her hands on the brown paper feel nothing but the smooth skin of old trees. The heart of a seedling turned into a cover sheet, she thinks, that is now wrapped around a mysterious package in the arms of a semi-naked woman in Northern California who is about to push aside its opening embrace and see what has certainly become part of a very interesting stolen afternoon.

No return address.

Printing neat and slanted, the hand of a woman, Katherine thinks, because there is something familiar and feminine in the way the letters turn and slant. She has seen this writing before. Someone she knows sent the package—but who?

When she moves to open the package, spreading apart the sealed edges, this is when the bra finally and forever snaps open and when everything changes.

Katherine does not feel the bra give way because from the moment she sees the note, from the moment she smells the rushing scent of sage that has been sprinkled across the top of the box and sees the two red tennis shoes inside, nothing else, not even the glorious bra, matters.

The note, folded in half once and written, Katherine thinks, by the same woman who addressed the outside of the box, tells half of the story before she even begins to read, and she gasps in astonishment because what she is holding is something spectacular, unforeseen and frightening.

Katherine,

It had to be you because you see the rough edges of life and death every day and because you were always in charge and because you touched my heart all those years ago when I needed it so badly with your fine friendship and a love that saw me through days no woman should have to know.

Packed in these red shoes, the ones I loved to wear without socks and through every season, are my ashes. You know that I am dead. You know how I suffered to get to that spot and you know my heart just as well as the women whose names rest under these fine red shoes.

So here, baby, are my bones and the pieces of my life that remain here while the rest of me has sailed on to a place I longed so to touch when I was so very, very ill. The whole idea of being dead pisses me off but as we always said, "It is what it is"—and I just happen to be dead.

Katherine, I never asked much of you after those first months when you held me up so that I would not fall away into a dark space unlike even this death, but this, this last wish, is not just for me, but also for you and for every woman on this list.

Do it. Just fucking (I know you hate that word!) do it. And in the doing, you will find that in my death, that in letting go of the others who have died and who are dying, and seeing this period of your lives for the rich, deep time that it is, you will feel the remains of my love for you all.

The instructions are under the shoes.

Be ready. I am asking a lot but then again, I always gave you, and them, the same.

I love you now as I always did and will. You are the sister I

*never had and you know that I loved you in a way I never loved
anyone else.*

*Do this for me and in the end it will be the greatest gift you
ever gave yourself.*

Annie G. Freeman

Katherine does not cry or move. She sits for five, ten, and another
five minutes after that. Then she moves both hands across the tips
of the red shoes and bends over to kiss them and that simple,
lovely, beautiful movement snaps the bra in half.

2

It takes 6.2 hours and one fairly expensive bottle of Shiraz for Katherine to open the shoebox again and read the instructions that have been whispering in her ear since the moment the box arrived and her bra exploded. She has been unable to eat, told her office to hold her calls, has not returned even one personal phone call and has stared at the shoes so long she can now describe in detail every scuff mark, the way the laces fold the wrong way, how three eyes are loose and the edges of the top frayed with miles of wear and tear.

There is absolutely no reason for Katherine not to open the instructions that were placed under the red shoes after Annie's death, by whom? A son? Her last lover? Another best friend? Or, as impossible as it might seem, by Annie herself. No reason except the idea that she may be asked to do something hard. Hard but remarkable, Katherine assumes, because she knows Annie, she knew Annie, she'll always know Annie.

"Damn it," she finally says to herself, tapping the shoes as if she were slapping someone she loved. "Just damn it."

It is now beyond late on a Wednesday night and Katherine has begged off a dinner date with Alex, agreed to allow her daughter to sleep overnight at her friend's house on a school night, and handled every other possible distraction, including a messy kitchen, wash, wild thoughts, a pending case that could end up in the state supreme court and a tiny whisper that extends beyond sorrow and leads into a field so wide it is almost more than Katherine can bear to lift her eyes to see what is around the next turn.

Almost.

Before she opens the sealed instructions, Katherine flips through the files in her mind that she has lined up in a row that points to her heart, files from the week Annie died. She remembers the electrifying feeling of knowing that Annie would die before she ever saw her again. She remembers the flash of that moment in the high school bathroom all those years ago when their friendship was cemented forever, the way Annie held on to her hand when they came to get her and that second when her fingers slipped from her hand and then the months and months before she saw her friend again. The last days of high school, the summer they decided they would one day live in California, the night they climbed onto the roof and drank beer when their parents were at dinner and then all those years until now—kids, and lovers and weekends in the city and paths that crossed at intersections rimmed in sameness even though they had different roadmaps. And there was also Katherine's schedule. The trials, the workloads and always this nudge, that she continually ignored, in the back of her mind that told her maybe she was spending way too much time on justice and not enough time inside of her own life.

"Damn you," Katherine says, holding whatever is in the envelope to her breast in the same way she might hold Annie if she was sharing a sorrowful moment, maybe the loss of a love, the struggle through any avenue of life's often messy streets. And even though she has already mourned the loss of her friend for weeks, she is wise enough to know that grief and remembering and loss cannot be predicted or held at bay. She knows and she lets her anger at the missing, at what must be in the envelope, at all the time she let slip away, spill from inside of her.

"Damn you for leaving me. Just damn you," she says, wishing for just that second not to be as strong and as wise and as wonderful as Annie believed she was. Wishing that she could erase all her valleys of loss, fill them in with butter and cream and wine and walk across them like a bridge to an ocean as blue as the California sky.

Katherine thinks then for just a moment about her mother and she has the same pangs of regret, of missing, of loss, of suffocating sorrow. She allows herself to slip an inch down the wall, humbled even now, all the months, eight of them, following her mother's death. The grieving, she knows, never ends, and all that will remain is the miracle of love. And she holds on to that miracle as if to save her life for the time it takes her to steady herself, to smell, without the reality of it, her mother's scent—a fine mix of Dial soap, some ancient Avon product, garlic and Tide—her mother always used Tide.

"What you remember," Katherine reminds herself, "is not what they think you will remember. It is often not."

Before she opens the envelope, Katherine fingers a well-worn piece of newspaper she has retrieved from the kitchen counter that she has read so many times she could recite it from memory. She reads it one more time leaning against the edge of the fieldstone fireplace so she can look out into her backyard, the place she always imagined would be where she'd sit to write the same ashes-inside-tennis-shoe note to Annie as Annie wrote to her.

Her place. Her happiest space. The view into the garden, across a small hill and into the yard of her neighbor. No rooflines. Pure green dotted with flowers and a stretch of lawn that she has let go wild. Just this one spot no one else in the entire world dares to touch. Katherine looks and then she reads to prepare herself for the reading of whatever is under the damn red shoes.

San Francisco Chronicle

DEATH NOTICE

ANNIE G. FREEMAN—Local historian, English professor at San Francisco State University, founder of the Brighton Adolescent Suicide Prevention Network, Survivor's Poetry Coalition, and Words on Wings Youth Summer Program; lively friend, mother, and the first woman in Northern California to successfully challenge the discriminatory hiring practices of all of California's school systems, including the university system, has died of ovarian cancer.

Ms. Freeman, known by her friends as someone with a fiery spirit, endless compassion, and a laugh that "could be heard a mile away" died April 21 at the age of 56.

She moved to the San Francisco area from Milwaukee, Wisconsin, in 1968 with her family. She lived in the San Francisco Bay area most of her life but graduated from the University of Wisconsin–Madison with a PhD in English and immediately returned to her much beloved Northern California.

Her work, first at San Francisco State University and later at Sonoma State, gained her international prominence as an advocate for teachers' equality, a proponent of the use of writing as a therapeutic tool, and a developer of numerous young adult programs throughout California and the United States.

An adolescent survivor of a suicide attempt, Ms. Freeman was an outspoken advocate for treatment programs for young people battling depression and loneliness. Her unique and sometimes controversial programs, which have been used at clinics throughout the world, involved the use of teen mentors, wilderness settings, and writing to help heal what she called "the empty hearts" of young boys and girls.

Ms. Freeman was also a social and feminist activist who worked with a coalition of young academics to restructure the university pay system and institute gender awareness training at every California university system campus and at public schools throughout the state.

Although the majority of her writings were used to help others and in therapeutic settings, she also authored numerous articles and books on the history of Northern California, especially the small communities near Sonoma.

While her professional life undoubtedly helped thousands, Ms. Freeman said the single most profound act of her life was raising her two sons and making certain that they were exposed to as many thoughts, places and people as possible. Married briefly to an Italian painter in 1971, she never disclosed the identity of the father of her sons.

"She was a remarkable example of a woman who embraced life, fought stereotypes and helped so many people," said Jill Matchney, retired president of the California State Teacher's Union and a longtime friend of Ms. Freeman. "No one, not one single person, knew the breadth and scope of who Annie was, what she did, and how many lives she touched."

When she was first diagnosed with cancer, following a routine exam, Ms. Freeman immediately became a regional spokeswoman for a variety of women's cancer organizations, authored a book of poetry for those fighting "unlikely happenings," and personally answered every letter or phone call from anyone who needed help or wanted to help her.

"My mother, once she decided that she wanted to live all those years ago after she tried to kill herself, loved life in a way that was beyond contagious," said Nick Freeman, her son, who is a social worker at the Walons Family Clinic in Milwaukee. "Mom's gone, but believe me, she is not done—not done at all."

Ms. Freeman died with her two sons, Donan and Nick, her hospice caregivers, and her sister-in-law at her side, in her yard facing the edge of the mountains and her beloved ocean.

As part of her last wishes, Ms. Freeman asked that no formal funeral services be held but that well-wishers spend their time and money helping others and that any woman or man who has ever been touched by her life, writings, or one of her organizations reach out to help someone else.

When at last she opens the envelope, Katherine knows there is no way to really prepare herself for what request might be hiding inside. She knows that she owes the world nothing and that her dearest friend would ask her only for something that she deemed possible, and she knows, too, that in Annie Freeman's world anything and everything was possible. The request, like Annie, could be astounding. It most likely is.

The letter is handwritten and when Katherine sees the first word, when she sees her name—*Katherine*—sitting there at the top of the page in the slim writing style from one of the fine black pens that Annie loved to use, she knows that this must have been done toward the end, toward the time when Annie knew she had only a few weeks, when this idea, whatever it was, had come to rest in a place that was ready to be put onto paper. The letters are shaky and for a moment Katherine closes her eyes and sees the trembling fingers of her friend, moving deliberately across this very sheet, focusing with every ounce of her remaining strength to just keep the tip of the pen against the top of the paper.

As wild and free as Annie was, and remained, she was also exact. Annie seldom hesitated. She would have hesitated in writing this only because it took her breath away to simply move her fingers.

While she reads, Katherine imagines her friend sitting in the wicker chair that faced the long backyard at her home. Annie would look up occasionally just to check the sky, just to see if it was still there curving above her, just to make certain that she could do just that—look. She would be thinking of Katherine and would maybe laugh out loud as she imagined Katherine, at this very moment, drinking her wine and filled with intense waves of wondering. Yes, Annie would definitely laugh.

"Shit," Katherine said out loud. "You *so* knew who I was."

The instructions, however, were filled with nothing laughable except the seemingly sheer impossibility of the desires placed after her name—"*Katherine . . .*" The instructions to the untrained eye might seem as hilarious as anything so difficult to accomplish that the only, the real, the natural response—must be to laugh.

> *Katherine, Laura, Rebecca, Jill and Marie——*
> *I sure as hell would never have wanted a traditional funeral. You can all figure out how to get along without me. You can figure out that this makes sense and that at this time in your lives—Katherine, your mother; Laura, your daughter; Rebecca— everyone, so much loss and now me too; Jill, whatever loss you hold against your breastbone: all those students you no longer have to love and to help sustain your energy and direction; and Marie, all those lingering souls—all that loss needs to be colored in and then held to the light and you need to get rid of me, celebrate me, allow me this one last wish and here it is:*
> *I want a traveling funeral.*
> *That's my wish.*
> *I've spent weeks and weeks thinking about this, planning it, making the arrangements, and it has given me the great and extraordinary opportunity to take a remarkable journey back during the planning so that I can now move forward and so that you—and the women I have loved most—can honor me, grieve me and also prepare yourselves for what is coming down the road in your own lives. You are also allowed to have some fun. You all work too damn hard.*
> *Do not—even one of you—say that you cannot attend my*

traveling funeral, because you are the procession. Do not one of you make an excuse why you cannot share this time with the women whose names are with yours on this list and do not think that this will be entirely painful. It will be fun. You will share stories and remember me and in that remembering you will also remember a part of you that may have become buried under all the damn layers of life that accumulate day after day until they have lined up like a brick wall to prevent us from seeing—really seeing.

You may not always get along, especially if Katherine is always in charge (Katherine—I'm kidding—remember what they said about you in high school?) and it may not be easy for you to arrange your schedules and families and the timetable in your own heads, which were not prepared for something like the traveling funeral of your friend Annie. But I am asking each of you to try. Please try and do this.

The tiny little details of this trip are not set in stone—however, the tickets, the reservations, the days you will travel are unchangeable because some of you will think of a way to back out, will make excuses, will think of something to detain you. There is no stopping Annie Freeman's traveling funeral—it may even end up to be fabulous.

Katherine is the leader because she was the first. She saved my life in many ways and allowed me to see the true value of female friendship in a way that set the tone for all of you—for the way each of you entered my life and hollowed out your own place there and then stayed no matter where the road took all of us.

I have spoken to each one of you during these last months of mine and have tried very hard over the years to let you know how much I love you and how I have treasured your place in my life. I choose no formal service because I know that death does not erase my memory in your life and I suspect that you will not be gone from my lingering spirit either. Those damn funerals have always driven me crazy—celebrate, I say—life, death—living and this process of dying that parallels our lives every single moment.

Honor me now and you will honor yourselves. Honor me now with this one last gift of a traveling funeral no matter how impossible the asking might seem when you first hear it and I promise that you will find something that will secure you a place in your grieving, in your other losses that will set the tone for the days and nights that are lined up and waiting for you—maybe not so patiently and maybe not so far away.

I have given great thought to this adventure because I have been given a tiny gift of time to ponder that and so many other things as well. I have selected six locations for you to spread my ashes—places where something grand and remarkable passed into and through my life. Places—one where I made love for so many nights in a row we almost had to send for help (you guess the location), one where I let go of something so old and heavy that I almost flew without wings . . . Well, you get the pattern and you five women will now set the pace for this trip and see what happens. Just see.

For if people could see—if women especially could see—what is real and true and how the elegant possession of what is in each of our individual hearts is what matters more than anything—well, oh, please just see—always see.

This is what you will see next:
California—my beloved Sonoma County.
Albuquerque, New Mexico.
The Florida Keys.
New York City.
The North Shore of Lake Superior.
A small island close to Seattle.
Those were my places. That is where each and all of you will spread my dusty bones. Every single one of you has already met

through me though not necessarily in person—I can tell you now which of you will notice what, who will become best friends, who will sit in the front and who will order first and that's what pisses me off the most.

I want to fucking be there with you.

So Katherine, Jill, Laura, Rebecca and Marie—be there for me. Think about me. Throw not just my ashes, the dust of my life, into the wind—but throw a bit of yourself too and enjoy this time, these places, each other—as my final gift of thanks to you for all that you have given me, for the love we six women have shared, for the degrees of fineness that you added to a life that was as rich and full as anything I could have dreamed or made up.

I love each and every one of you. That will never fade.

Never.

My traveling funeral better be grand.

Now go.

I am the whisper of the wind at every stop. I am there—with you.

Always,
Annie G. Freeman

The tickets fall from the envelope like heavy chunks of wet, late-winter snow. A car rental slip for each city is pulled from its binder with the weight of the tickets and then a long list of hotels, a check for spending money and food, and one last note—handwritten—describing the best wine that is available in each location.

Katherine laughs because Annie could always make a party out of death and then sprinkle her love of wine and song and fine friends all over it. Then she gathers up all the tickets and notes into a pile as if she is in Las Vegas and has just won the last deal at a blackjack table. She pushes all the papers in between her legs and she finishes up her glass of wine knowing now that perhaps the damn bra snapped loose for a reason and that no matter what happens in the next hour or day or week, she is now in charge of, and going on, a traveling funeral.

She is.

But then she looks down and the instincts of a mother, woman, attorney to get the detail in the midst of an emotion rise as fast as a bullet, and she sees that time is of the essence. Can she really do this? How can she do this? A flash of her own schedule makes her stomach clench. Her daughter. Work. The man in her life. The possibility of the seemingly impossible makes her beyond nauseous. Was Annie insane when she wrote out this request?

The first plane leaves in nine days.

"Shit," Katherine says, rising to search for a phone. "Nine days? I'm going to kick your ass, Annie."

And then she stops because Annie G. Freeman is dead and Katherine P. Givins realizes that the traveling funeral Annie has requested will be no picnic. Who knows what will happen when a group of grief-stricken women who have never even been in a car together embark on a traveling funeral and bare their hearts and who knows what else to one another?

"How in the hell," she whispers to herself, "can I make this happen?"

Katherine keeps moving and then her hand moves instinctively to touch the side of her bra—the lovely Bali—and she's so accustomed to its support that she gasps as she remembers that the bra too has died.

"Damn it," she says probably for the fiftieth-plus time in the last ten hours. "The bra is gone."

Gone and now lying like a trophy on top of the dresser near the window in her bedroom.

And there is barely time now for more than that quick thought of the bra before her mind explodes with the dozens of details that must be handled before tomorrow, as fast as possible, in a hurry, this exact moment. Schedules. Meetings. Plans. What should she erase? How should she erase it?

She starts at the beginning, with the first name on the list, the list of other women who are about to have their own lives and schedules collapsed as if they were made of air. When Katherine makes the first call she does it braless.

And the traveling funeral begins.

3

Annie and Katie

Milwaukee, Wisconsin, 1963

The long halls at West High School are barely light at noon, so when Katie Givins finally figures out how to sneak into the school through the gym door at 7:16 P.M. there is just enough light to see her way past the locker room and toward the far side of school.

Katie is not scared to be in her own high school walking alone from one dark room to the next without a flashlight or a friend. She is not afraid of what her mother will say when she gets home from the store and finds her note—*"Gone to find Annie"*—lying next to the telephone. She's not afraid of being suspended or getting locked in all night. Katie is only afraid of one thing. She is afraid that she might not find her best friend in the girls' bathroom near the science lab where Cheryl Swanson said she saw her just after the late bell. Her best friend since first grade. Her best friend who is in a mess of trouble.

"She was just sitting there on the window by the register, you know the one we throw our cigarettes into, and I tried to talk with her but she was just sitting there—like she was there but she wasn't. Do you know what I mean?"

Katie knew.

For the past six months Katie had watched her best friend dip in and out of a depression so deep it was as if Annie had surrounded herself with a brick wall. Annie talked about things, horrible things, and Katie had worked hard to know where she was twenty-four hours a day, to alert her parents—well, at least her mother, because no one knew where Annie's father was half the time—and she talked to a counselor herself so she could try to understand what was happening. All big stuff for a fourteen-year-old who barely knew how to keep pace with her own inner emotional turmoil, let alone try to save her best friend from falling off the face of the earth.

She didn't see Annie in the bathroom at first. Annie was lying against the far wall, back behind the garbage can, with her feet up against the wall. She was barely conscious.

"Shit," Katie said as she ran to pull her upright. "Annie? What did you do?"

Annie would say later that she remembered only that she reached up to put her hand on Katie's face and that she wanted her to say something nice, just one nice thing before she died, and then she slipped away to the edge of a place that was just a breath away from what she thought she really wanted.

It wasn't the end, and it was barely the beginning, but Katie didn't let go and Annie held on at first to her smallest finger and then to two more and then to her entire hand until she was in a place where her mind could heal and where she could see the light, the trees, the wisp of air off the lake in the morning, the sincere words from the mouth of her mother, everything in her world for what it really was and not what the thin ledge at the bottom of her brain tried to tell her it was.

She lived and Katie helped her live and the salvation of their friendship—of two girls becoming women and ascending the next mountain and the one after that—became a bond that lasted through forty-two more years and to the moment when the sudden arrival of a brown box filled with red shoes launched Katherine Givins to the edge of one more mountain and made her remember the bathroom floor, the power of caring, and the love she felt for a lifelong friend who apparently had one more thing to say from the depths of a pair of shoes that were now resting comfortably on the dresser and screaming every second of the day for attention.

4

Jill Matchney gets the first call.

Sitting outside, not more than a mile from the backyard of
Annie Freeman's back porch, with her feet propped up on the edge
of her deck, she can see stars bounce like fireflies against the bank
of clouds that open and close just long enough to expose the tiny
planets she loves to watch.

When the phone rings, Jill is right there in the clouds, all those
hundreds and thousands and millions of miles away, floating
through this day and the one before it and the one she anticipates
tomorrow. Jill watches herself and her life like she would watch a
movie—pushed back against the side of her house, legs dangling
off the edge of her porch, a glass in her hand, imagining in the center of her analytical mind how the end will match the beginning
and the middle.

"The smell of roses, someone singing at the end of a long hall,
all my papers in order, a small dinner party after the ceremony . . ."
she says to herself, planning her own funeral as she watches another cloud bump into another set of stars and then swallow them.

Jill, the retired educator, is like this and she has no intention of ever changing. She always had her papers graded before they hit her desk, loved committee work, swelled with the challenge each new student brought to her table, and each time a new and naive faculty member blew into her office she would look them in the eye and promise herself that she'd turn them into a diamond, a living promise, one of her own stars.

That's what she vowed when she first saw Annie Freeman— wide-eyed and naive but far from quiet. Annie Freeman who galloped, not walked, into her office and shared a litany of excited prose about her classes and her own promises and a dozen other wide-eyed calculations that made Professor Jill Matchney close her own eyes in eager astonishment at the abrupt appearance of her protégé—the successor she had been searching for ever since she had been appointed the head of the English department.

Annie G. Freeman.

"Damn her," Jill grumbled, pushing herself away from the wall and toward the end of her deck so that her voice would spread out across the dark, empty yard and into the sky, toward one of the stars where she imagined Annie G. Freeman was even now holding court.

"Damn you, Annie."

The phone rings then, splinters this thought, and every one that might have come after it. Thoughts that someone like Jill craved like sugar to keep her existence in line, to adhere to her patterns, to keep her knowing what might come next.

"Is this Jill Matchney?"

"Yes," Jill responds, knowing that only the chosen few who have this number would dare to call her past 10:30 P.M.

"My name is Katherine Givins. We've never met but you sort of know me."

At this, Jill smiles and then looks at the stars, selects the one she imagines is now inhabited by her fine friend Annie Freeman, and then she listens, grabs the edge of the tall banister to support herself while she hears the entire story about the funeral, minus the bra, and realizes that something fierce has unexpectedly grabbed hold of her fairly empty appointment calendar and is about to swallow it whole.

Jill, who should have been the hardest sell, did not seem to hesitate.

"I'll be there," she told Katherine, and "Yes," with a slight chuckle, "I know who you are and I imagine I know everyone else you are about to call."

And call she did.

Jill first. The retired professor who knew there had been no formal funeral. Jill who talked softly and who quickly but surely promised to be at the San Francisco airport in nine—wait, now only eight—days with equipment for something that Katherine has already begun calling The Traveling Funeral.

"Well," Katherine says, thinking as she speaks because she is shooting from the hip or really from the knees because she is moving so quickly she can barely pick her words off the ground— shooting from the hip would be way too late. "I suppose you need to bring something for hiking, something for sitting in the car we rent, something for sleeping—if you sleep in something—a bathing suit . . ."

Katherine stops.

Jill Matchney laughs.

"What's so funny?"

"She knew this would happen."

"What?"

"Annie knew we'd have this discussion. And she would have laughed and then told us we were predictable."

There is a short pause. Both women have jumped into the same track. They almost talk at the exact moment but Katherine, edged with coffee, gets there first.

"She thought about this for a long time, didn't she?"

Jill speaks in a kind of whisper when she talks about her friend.

She misses Annie so much sometimes that she drops to her knees because the burden of sorrow, the empty shadow of what once was is too much for her to bear. She really drops to her knees.

"I don't know you, but I know you because of Annie," Jill says slowly to Katherine, who is listening with her eyes closed, her fingers wedged on either side of her temples, her mind focused on this memory of Annie speaking about this woman, this teacher, this Jill, with such respect and love that Katherine felt jealous because she had not yet met her. "She's already linked all of us and she knows that we may end up loving each other, not like we love her, but in new ways that take us to places she went to before she left all of us—"

Katherine cuts her off. "Maybe."

"Maybe?"

"She was dying. Remember that. Everything changes when that happens. I think she simply planned a funeral and that she wanted the women in her life to be her traveling attendants. Call us the moving female pallbearers. That's what we are—this is our duty because we loved her and she loved us."

Jill leans forward and moves her eyes off the horizon. She thinks that maybe she doesn't really know what will happen in eight days. She thinks that maybe she should stop thinking so much. She continues thinking anyway because she cannot stop herself from thinking after all the years of school and classes and schedules and students—oh, the students!—that set her days and weeks and months and years into such distinct and precise patterns. She thinks that maybe her intellectual inner guideposts may need to be retired for a while, just like the rest of her life. She thinks that the loss of her friend coupled with the loss of her students, her administrative post, all the patterns in her life that gave her comfort and something to spread out in front of her to see day after day, has dimmed everything she thinks she knows.

Everything has changed.

Everything is changing.

"You don't know?" Katherine finally asks, snapping Jill back to the present.

Jill moves her eyes back to the horizon, where they belong, she knows, but looking there, toward what is to come, is now sometimes frightening. Too much has happened. So much loss. All the empty hours.

"I don't know about this traveling funeral she planned, perhaps one of the boys knows, but my guess, knowing Annie the way I do, is that no one knew and that you, lucky you, Katherine, were the first to know."

"You were so close to her though."

A swell of grief rises from Jill's stomach and passes directly through her heart. It is a fast wave that catches her off-guard and changes how she speaks and thinks and moves and talks.

"Oh God . . ."

"Jill," Katherine whispers. "We all loved her so goddamn much. I don't really know you but I am certain of that. Are you okay?"

Jill answers in short sentences. She tells Katherine, a woman she has never met but knows through stories and tales and clippings from newspapers and from the voice of her dead friend, that the loss of Annie has knocked her flat. She tells her about the days and nights following her recent retirement and how she struggles to see—after years of knowing—where all the pieces will now fit from day to day. She stops once or twice to gain control of her own voice. She stops again because she simply cannot speak. Then she admits to Katherine Givins and to herself: "I want right now to just lie down on this porch and not wake up for a very long time."

"Oh, sweetheart," Katherine says. "Do you want me to drive up there?"

Jill smiles again. She grabs the blanket off the wicker chair behind her, wraps it around her shoulders, and slides to the floor of the porch. Then she laughs.

"Are you laughing?" Katherine asks, bewildered, and worried that she may indeed be crying.

"Yes, and now I am lying on the porch floor all tangled up in a blanket."

"Should I come?" Katherine offers again, immediately worried.

"You are already here, Katherine. It's okay. I have to ride this until it's just a whimper. I didn't think about this happening. I wasn't ready for all this change. In my wildest dreams, which were pretty damn tame—this right here—me lying on the porch and preparing for a traveling funeral, Annie's death, the emptiness I feel now that my career has ended—it never felt quite real. I'm also terribly used to being alone, although alone without Annie won't be the same. You will probably get heartily sick of me in the first three seconds on this funeral trip."

Katherine thinks for a moment about changes and chance. She thinks about loss and movement and how in a million years she could never have dreamed of this set of circumstances that has rocked her world in a new direction, and then she thinks about her mother.

Katherine closes her eyes while Jill positions herself and asks her to please hang on, and in that dark spot, just behind her eyelids, Katherine seeks something sacred and true. She finds a memory that resurrects itself with just the simple closing of her eyes.

This is that moment. This one moment just weeks before her mother's death. Katherine was sitting in her mother's room at the hospice center. There had been hours of silence as Katherine monitored the twitches in her mother's face, the graceful way her mother's hands remained folded on top of her chest, the fine lines that moved from the corner of her mother's eyes to reach for her silver hairline, the way her mother turned to greet every single person who came into the room no matter how much pain she was experiencing, the way—even when the drugs had grabbed hold of her—that she tried to rise off her pillow to make certain that Katherine was still in the room with her, standing guard, protecting, making certain—as she always did—that everything was taken care of and that everyone was moving in the proper direction.

Katherine moved her chair to the side of her mother's bed and as soon as she did so, her mother felt her there and raised her hand so that their fingers were touching and then something moved inside of Katherine that she had never felt before. A startled cry came from her throat and she rose to her feet so abruptly she pushed the chair over when she stood up. Katherine, without thinking, turned down the covers to her mother's hospital bed, slipped off her shoes, and climbed into bed with her mother.

Her mother stirred for a second and then moved into Katherine's arms—her daughter's arms—as if she were a baby. Katherine held her with such fierceness she wondered for a moment if she might be hurting her mother, her dying, terribly ill mother, and then whatever was passing through her exploded in a shock wave of grief, in the acknowledgment of the finality, in a burst of knowledge that made her moan and cry like she had never cried before in her entire life.

"Oh Mommy," she moaned. "Oh Mommy I love you so much."

Somehow her mother found the side of Katherine's face and she moved her fingers in small circles on the skin of her cheek and then she slid her fingers into her hair. Katherine could feel her mother's labored breathing in her ear, she could feel her heart beating against her own heart and she felt a surge of love so fierce she almost willed herself to die with her mother—almost.

Katherine's mind then moved throughout all of the cycles of her life, back to her earliest memories, and into only the fine and wonderful things that she could remember about her mother. She remembered the soft feel of clean sheets against her legs every Friday night and the smell of freshly baked cookies on Saturday mornings. She remembered how her mother packed her lunch and often left notes in the folds of her sandwich wrapping. She remembers how she once viewed her mother as weird and different because she never worked and how her mother held her gently but firmly against the wall one afternoon and said, "Don't you ever, *ever,* the rest of your life make fun of someone else's choices." She remembers her first period and how her mother took her to dinner to celebrate and brought her a silver bracelet that she still wears to "honor all the female parts of her life and the glory of being a woman." She remembers moments like all of these as if she were on fire and through her sobs and her mother's tormented breathing she thinks she will explode with the seemingly endless positions of grief.

Katherine remembers her mother backing off when she was growing up and needed to be alone and then slipping a note under her bedroom door the afternoon her first boyfriend dumped her. She remembers how her mother always waited up and would kiss her without thinking twice in front of friends, in department stores, in the middle of a conversation at a family party. She remembers the day she married and how she found her mother crying softly in the bathroom and how she went to her and said, "Thank you for always being there, Mom." And how her mother told her that she was the most wonderful daughter a mother could ever hope to have.

When her mother stirs and then moans out loud, Katherine still remembers. She remembers giving birth to her own daughter and how her mother stood at the window in the hospital and told her, "Now you know," without ever saying a word. She remembers how just after the baby was born her mother would simply show up on the bad days without a call—and how on those days they would enjoy a small glass of wine with lunch and then maybe another glass in the middle of the afternoon and how Katherine thought she was losing her mind because she had no idea what she was doing, how to raise a baby, how to some days even rise off her own bed. She remembers how her mother walked through the reception line after she received her law degree and leaned to say, "I never ever doubted you for one moment since the day you were born."

She remembers the day her mother came to her to tell her that she was dying. The way, even then, her mother was there so she could lean against her and how then suddenly, everything changed in the next sentence.

"I need you now," her mother told her. "I need you like I have never needed anyone, and you have to help me. Be who you are now, baby, be who I taught you to be. This is not going to be easy and I am going to have to lean into you."

And she did. Katherine remembers that the leaning began immediately and she remembers every second of the doctor visits and then the day her mother could not eat and the day her mother could not walk and the day her mother could no longer talk and they brought her to the hospice, and then she knows that she will remember these last moments with her mother every single day for the rest of her own life.

"Katherine . . ." her mother choked into her ear, just the word "Katherine . . ." and it is enough, it will be enough to get her through the next day and the day after that and the day her mother died and the funeral and the months and days after that and then this—this remembering as Jill finds her own safe place on the porch floor.

Always remembering.

They talk then, Jill and Katherine, about the traveling funeral and just a bit about loss and making plans and how bizarre it will be to finally meet each other in person and how they hope they can find their way and Annie's way and how they hope everyone else can go, and then when Jill is settled, it's time to make the next call.

Jill reassures Katherine that she will be fine, eventually she has to be fine, that something inside of her has slipped loose and that perhaps the traveling funeral will help her move the knots of her life a bit tighter—or not.

"Maybe not," Jill says, pushing the blanket around her own face. "Maybe that is not what will happen at all."

Katherine knows what she means. She knows that women who have climbed through a large chunk of their lives are always wise enough to realize that certainty equals uncertainty.

"You know what they say," she says, looking into the edges of the night that have come to rest outside her own porch.

"What's that, Katherine the great attorney who saved Annie Freeman all those years ago? What do they say?"

Before she answers, Katherine bends down to pick up her bra. She throws it over her shoulder and then hangs on to the end with her left hand like a baby would hold on to a blankie that was tattered and had been dragged through grocery stores, libraries, Grandma's house and thirteen neighborhood backyards.

"They say funerals are for the living."

The calls to the three other women continue at odd intervals because of time zones and Katherine's need to rush out at the crack of dawn for fresh coffee and then her realization that she has to quickly call in sick, which she has done only twice in the past two years, and have her clerk reschedule everything on her calendar that day. Maybe more—but first just this one day. And maybe the world will fall apart because Katherine Givins missed a day of work, was late, turned left instead of right. But Katherine manages to make the calls anyway.

What is remarkable, beyond the fact that she does every single thing without her Bali bra, is that there is no hesitation. None. Just delicious movements of precision because there really isn't that much to do—Annie has done almost everything as Annie has always wanted to do and she surely wants to do this more than anything she can remember or imagine. It is as if there is no choice. As if someone or something else has decided and Katherine is just filling the order like the fine waitress she was back in college when she worked until two A.M. and dreamed of calling her clerk—this moment—and saying, "I won't be in."

"I won't be in."

5

Jill and Annie

Sonoma, California, 1978

Jill Matchney hears the new assistant professor coming before she sees her. Boots clicking against the tile floors in the long hallway outside her office door. Hesitation. The sound of someone breathing quickly—deep breaths from that spot just below a breastbone. A longer pause. She must be looking out the windows, thinking about what to say, what it will be like, what this next step into this next part of her world will be like.

"Perhaps the protégé I have been waiting for all these years," Professor Jill Jacobs Matchney says to herself while she waits for the required knock. "Perhaps."

Hand selected, recruited, interviewed ad nauseam, Annie G. Freeman was the number one choice of every single member of the interviewing committee, and she was offered a salary and a position higher than anyone her age, anyone with her years of experience and surely anyone with her saucy attitude—which is precisely why Professor Matchney wanted her.

"If we want to move forward, if we want to attract the dollars and the attention that a university needs to bring in the top students, leaders, community support and faculty members, then we need a dozen Annie G. Freemans," she declared, standing with her hands on the oak table in the chancellor's office and her mind stretching to the future. "This woman has drive, talent, charisma and fabulous academic credentials."

Professor Matchney got her Annie Freeman and now—now—would be the true test. Could Annie Freeman carry it off?

"Lock the door," Matchney told Freeman that very first day, "and please come into my private office."

Professor Matchney had dismissed her assistant early and had notified the switchboard to hold her calls. She had canceled her evening appointment with her friends at the bookstore and she was willing to stay as long as it took.

Assistant Professor Annie G. Freeman moved past her mentor quickly and then stopped suddenly, which surprised Professor Matchney. The two women faced each other, close enough to kiss, and Annie G. Freeman put her hand on the professor's arm, in that long stretch below the shoulder and before the elbow, and she grabbed her firm and long.

"Thank you for hiring me," Annie Freeman said with such directness that the professor was startled and lost that place in her mind, her bookmark, that would have allowed her to see the next page, the next thought, the next word that she must utter clearly.

"Thank you?"

"Oh, yes!"

Jill Matchney cannot speak. She already knows she has made the proper decision. This close to Annie Freeman, she sees a spark the size of a boulder simmering behind the younger woman's eyes.

"I wanted to work with you," Annie Freeman tells her. "You are the reason I am here."

"Just me?"

"I didn't apply anywhere else. I have read everything you have ever written. I've interviewed your students, talked to former professors, examined every thesis and document produced by the department in the past three years, and I've made myself physically ill worrying about this meeting, this first day, my professional introduction."

Professor Matchney smiles. She wants to laugh out loud but she imagines her new protégé would be frightened, even with her obvious bold spirit, by a laugh just now. She can feel a tremble right where the assistant professor's fingers touch the edge of her shirt and nudge into her skin. "I'm flattered."

"Thank you."

"Please, then, sit down. We have much to discuss."

"Wait, please."

The professor has turned away but when she hears the request, she turns back to face the assistant professor. "What is it? Are you all right?"

"I need to ask you something. It may seem ridiculous but I have to ask it. The question and several following it—well, I just have to ask them."

Jill Matchney is now perplexed. She cannot imagine what this bright, wise, attractive, challenging young professor could be worried about. She cannot imagine what is keeping her from moving from the spot on the floor of her office where her own feet have become frozen. She cannot wait to hear the question.

"Of course," she responds. "Of course."

Annie G. Freeman drops her hands. She grabs them, one holding the other as if she were holding something delicate that still needed to breathe.

"Will you help me?" she asks.

"Help you?" Jill Matchney responds so quickly she barely realizes she has spoken.

"Yes, help me. It may sound foolish but I want you to help me. I do not want to be challenged irresponsibly like I have been at other universities by self-righteous, pompous senior professors. I do not want to be tricked. I don't want to have to stand on my head to get promoted or to get stuck teaching only the night classes. I want to be mentored and trained and I'd like to stay here forever."

The negotiations continued for hours. There was no begging or pleading, only an honest and raw discussion between teacher and student, mentor and trainee, soon-to-be comrades, focused talents.

In the end Professor Jill Matchney agreed to help Assistant Professor Annie G. Freeman, and the agreement, an unwritten set of directions, an intersecting diagram that covered parallel and yet totally distinct ways of life, became a shared heartbeat, an enlarged passion, and a bond between two women that lasted until the very day one of them died and then beyond that moment, even beyond that moment.

6

Laura has had one of those feelings all day. It's that "looking over your shoulder because you think someone is watching you" kind of feeling. It's that "something's going to happen" kind of feeling that has her remembering what she looked like in the morning and how she felt after lunch and the face of the man at the last corner before the post office, because one of those things, maybe two or three or fourteen of those damn things, will be a significant reminder for whatever is winging its way toward her on this particular day when her hands and mind and every single thing about her will not, could not, cannot stay still.

When she was young, Laura knew things. She knew the exact time—almost—her father would arrive at home each evening, and she would always be there, sitting on the steps—even in the dead of winter—to greet him. She even knew his ever-changing seemingly startled response: "There's my baby" or "Look, someone left a package on the doorstep," or "Wow, someone is shooting a commercial and there's a model on the doorstep" or mostly just, "Hi, baby doll."

Not just that for all these years, but other things too. Important things. Knowing when to stop just before an accident occurred at the bridge. Staying home and then the call comes. Turning left to see that sunset—waves of light, brilliant colors that make people stop and rush into Kmart to purchase a camera. Touching the woman in line at Albertson's who came to the grocery store wearing her loneliness like a new hat just so someone would do that— simply touch her. Closing her eyes and seeing people she has never met, does not know except for the certain feeling that they exist. Seeing their faces, the color of their hair, the way they walk their dogs, how they forage for food, the way they tilt their heads slightly to the left just before a kiss—in places so distant they are barely dots on the international maps she keeps in her small bedroom office.

"Crap," Laura says to no one in particular at 8:29 P.M. when she steps into her dark kitchen and hears the phone ringing.

Laura has to answer it. It doesn't matter what the caller ID says. The ID could be wrong. It may not be Wells Fargo but instead some voice from the past that connects her to a lost fortune of feelings. It could be a wrong number that turns into a conversation that is as enlightening as anything she has ever experienced. It could be her wayward and often missing prodigal daughter Erin reporting in from Belize or Kentucky or Tokyo or wherever in the hell she has landed this particular week. It is most likely not her husband or the neighbor who is tending to her dying father. But it could be anyone else. Absolutely anyone. Laura has this feeling, this twinge in the center of her quivering stomach, that tells her in a warm rumble that moves there to the center of her mind to the edge of the hand that she must pick up the phone, that to not answer the phone would be beyond a mistake.

It is a woman's voice. One that she has heard at only a distance as an echo behind another voice. One that has paced through her mind constantly for the past three days so that Laura was certain she was about to see or meet or in some way encounter the very woman who owned the voice. One that she would not recognize until she hears the voice say the name "Katherine Givins" and

Laura can then recall a long-ago conversation, the mention of this name many times, and that echo of sound.

"It's Katherine Givins," the woman says, then hesitates, and Laura Westma, forty-nine years old, who lives in a tiny bungalow in a suburb just barely north of downtown Chicago with her husband, a cat and all of her wandering and often missing daughter's possessions, sits down abruptly because she is suddenly lost in a swirl of memories, vivid, wide, and so consuming that they make her lose her balance. Laura who has hair cropped so close to her head she is often mistaken for a short man who likes to wear pressed jeans and turtlenecks well into summer and who refuses to wear makeup and who walks with such determination people who don't know her think she is perpetually angry. Laura with her eighty-hour workweeks as the director of the women's center and her fund-raisers and the very old and increasingly heavy weight of the knowledge that there is never going to be enough time, enough money, enough anything to save everyone, including herself and especially her daughter.

"Annie."

She forms the name with her mouth but she does not say it out loud. Instead she begins a conversation that she knows is taking her someplace. She knows that already but she does not know where or how but only the why just this moment. It is because of Annie Freeman. It is because of Annie's death. It is because of some unique and marvelous connection that she and Katherine Givins shared for years and years.

"Katherine, how are you?"

"You remember me?"

"Annie talked about you all of the time. Once, I think we were just a few minutes from actually meeting each other as you were coming in from the airport in San Francisco and I was leaving," Laura said.

"I remember. The boys were young. Annie had a mess of friends and relatives on a very unique schedule so we could all help her that year she was so sick."

"So sick. Have you thought about that now?" Laura asks and then keeps on talking, already feeling certain that she may be onto something. "I have wondered if that illness all those years ago wasn't the beginning of what happened to her when she got sick again. I have wondered if that kick started something inside of her that never left."

Laura always talks as if she is in charge. She is used to phone-wrestling and to talking people up and down and to making certain that she is believed and trusted even if her own hand is on fire and she's lost in an alley. It's her job and it's also her inner core.

"I think about things like that also. All of the time. It's hard not to."

"Are you okay?" Laura asks Katherine. "Can I do something?"

Katherine cannot help but laugh and the laugh startles Laura back into a standing position.

"What's so funny?"

"Well, you can do something but you might not believe what I am about to ask you to do."

The conversation turns a corner into lightness as Katherine reads the letter from Annie. Before the end of the first page Laura is also laughing. She wants to tell Katherine she is laughing because she has already imagined this moment or one so similar that one thought, one sentence, one echo on the phone could be mistaken for another.

"Stop," she finally tells Katherine. "Isn't this just like Annie? We should have seen this coming. It made sense that she didn't want to have a formal funeral. She hated that shit. I imagine she wanted the boys to spread her ashes around the backyard of that house she loved so damn much. But this? This is classic. It's perfect. It's . . ."

Laura stops. She has already spread out the traveling funeral in her mind. She's already formed pieces of the trip that stretch like banners into the lives of the other women, the people they meet, their conversations after midnight, the way they fall into each other without hesitation, the way some of them don't like each other at first or wrestle for attention, the way they manage to finally fit the curves of their personalities into each other so the puzzle is complete, the way they will change. She feels the emotional water of the traveling funeral washing over her and she knows, she thinks she knows, why Annie wanted them to do this. But she stops herself. She doesn't want to know everything and she has that power also. She can let it ride.

"Hey . . ." Katherine says, a little puzzled by Laura's silence.

"I'm okay. Just thinking about what this is going to be like."

There is another pause and Laura thinks that there are so many things that she doesn't know for sure. She doesn't know when she will see her daughter again. She doesn't know if she can save every woman at the shelter. She doesn't know how she can afford to take a short leave of unpaid absence, because she and her husband live on such a tight budget that one unplanned trip, one traveling funeral, one real funeral, and the whole budget is shot to hell. But she also doesn't know how she could not go. It is an impossible possibility, but possibility to Laura is everything.

"Let me finish reading first," Katherine says. "Then we'll discuss the rest of the details."

Laura listens and then, right after Katherine begins speaking again, she remembers the spiral notebook that Annie kept with her the last time they saw each other. It was not so long ago, just four weeks before Annie died, weeks ago—just weeks ago when she saw her last.

The notebook never left Annie's hands. She placed it on her lap the few times she managed to sit outside on the deck, set her fingers on top of it, resting her palms on the metal spiral edges when it rested on her chest while she lay in bed, moved it under her elbow when she managed just once or twice to shift to her side, pushed it under her pillow each and every time she fell asleep.

"What is it?" Laura had asked Annie. "Are you working on something?"

Annie looked at Laura as if she were trying to see right through her. She moved her hand so two fingers rested on the side of her leg.

"I'm always working on something, you know that. Right now I'm trying to figure out a way to forge a gentle exit but I'm having a hell of a time, sweetheart. This wasn't part of the plan. Not at all."

"Can I do something?"

"If I could laugh I would," Annie had said, smiling just a little. "You've already done enough and when the time comes you will know if there is one more thing that you can do. You'll know. Just having you here now for this time is good. It's good, sweetheart."

Laura had looked hard at Annie then. She saw how her dark eyes were rimmed with even darker circles. She reached over and brushed Annie's brown hair, laced with occasional loops of silver, away from her weary eyes. She noticed how the lines across the top of Annie's mouth and under her eyes and descending from her lower lip had suddenly grown longer, wider, deeper. She saw how the arms and hands and fingers and legs and every inch of her beloved Annie had melted away so that her bones had become dominant features.

"Goddamn cancer," she'd said to herself. "Goddamn fucking cancer."

Ovarian fucking cancer. Such a secret disease. This tiny pain in Annie's stomach. First quiet, and then more and more insistent. Then one day when Laura finally pays attention Annie is by the fountain in the center of campus, doubled over with the constant pain, and she cannot move. Annie eats an apple and feels as if she has swallowed a turkey whole. Pounds dropping away as if she has been injected with Mr. Atkins personally. Blood, tiny drops the color of a Wisconsin sunset in early fall, moving from her vagina when she is not even close to her period and then days of it and then the look on the doctor's face when she tells her all of this, when Annie G. Freeman lines up all of her symptoms and the doctor says nothing for a moment, then calls the hospital, and

Annie G. Freeman does not go home that night or for many nights after that.

There are quick calls from the hospital. The network is alerted. Katherine, Annie's two sons, Jill, Laura, neighbors, the assistant who will cancel classes. Quick calls and the feeling that the doctor already knows something.

The doctor with the gentle eyes and hands that glide like only a female doctor's hands can glide. A female doctor who knows what it is like to have objects the size of a toaster oven inserted into a vagina. A doctor who knows that the soft placing of a hand on a knee or arm or even on the side of a worried face before an examination can make a woman feel safe and protected. The hands of a doctor that take their time and move slowly with the orchestrated sounds of a female voice. The assurance and that kind voice of knowing because she has been there, felt that, winced at the exact same moment when something so unnatural moves into a natural place.

The doctor who tells you, "Yes, I will be honest." And "No, there is no way to know for sure," and "Maybe it will be okay," and then, "Maybe it will not."

The female doctor who tells her secretary, "Please hold my calls and cancel my last three appointments." The doctor who says this because she gives a damn. The doctor who gives a damn beyond what the HMO tells her to do and the doctor who knows it takes more than fifteen minutes to tell a woman she may have a form of cancer that will kill her. She may have a form of cancer that has already pawed its way past her absolutely fabulous ovaries. The same ovaries that helped her generate two of the most remarkable sons on the face of the earth. The same ovaries that pelted her with cramps and made her drop to her knees in bathrooms throughout the continental United States and in five foreign countries. The same ovaries that she doubted when she was thirteen years old because half of her friends already had their periods and her menstrual cycle was just getting cranked up. The same ovaries that claimed her as "woman" and made her want so desperately to feel things she would never have felt without them—rising tides, the glance of a handsome man, the yearning to touch the tiny hairs on the head of her own baby, the salt from the tears of her best woman friend, the warm ashes from a fire that kept her warm for days and nights along the shores of Lake Superior, the scent of lust rising from inside of her own skin, the desperate need to always say yes.

The doctor who will hold on to you as tightly as you hold on to her and who will place you without letting you go into the arms of another doctor who will do another test and then whisk you off into the arms of yet another doctor. She will not let you go because she is yours and you are hers and your malignant tumors are now a shared part of a relationship that is a mixture of grief, sadness, anger, longing, zeal, panic, hurt, wondering, more longing and something else indescribable.

Annie's tumors started out as cells that found her ovaries such an inviting, warm and friendly place. So friendly that they multiplied like those late winter beetles she remembered from the Midwest that collected on her window screens and then crawled into her bedroom to form puddles of soft red and black on her light blue bathrobe like moving paintings from some science-fiction movie. The tumors multiplied, and then as if the ovaries were not enough, they started looking around and then saw another warm place and jumped, one by one, to that warm spot in her abdomen and the other warm spot just below that and from there to the next spot until that day when the doctor put her hands there, at the spot where they were about to jump to next, and said very loudly so Annie could hear it, "No."

"No, damn it. No, you have had enough of her."

And then Annie knew what her doctor did—that it was the time for miracles and the trying and the wanting to live. Just simply wanting to live.

And then the next part, which necessitated keeping a spiral

notebook with her so that she could plan what happened after this. So that in the end when she knew she had so very few choices left, when she knew that her commands and wishes were buried beneath the tangled mass of the cells leaping over each other to get to the next spot, when she knew that to dare to wish for anything but for the pain to go away for just five seconds or maybe, maybe just one second—one quiet heartbeat of a second—was asking too much, then all she had left was the notebook and this plan. This idea. A reason to keep sailing to Tuesday just one more time.

The notebook never crossed your mind again because that very day you had to call the ambulance because it was impossible for you to know what Annie needed next and which pill was supposed to cap the pain until the next pill and then when you said goodbye you knew that she would never remember and that it would not have mattered if she had remembered anyway.

What mattered had already happened and you, her friend Laura, hold only what you remember in the palm of your hand—a friendship which had turned into a deep love and respect and admiration that carried you through years of richness with a woman who came to you once, just once, for help, and then opened her heart so wide that you slipped inside without ever knowing your feet had left the earth.

"So," Katherine says, waking Laura from her memory. "Is this all too much to do?"

"Too much to do for Annie Freeman?"

"Ridiculous question, but all I really know of you is how you rescued her that one horrid night and how your connection with women's centers has never been broken. There are so many things that I don't know. So I have to ask: Is this too much?"

"It's not too much for a friend, for what we all had with her, for this one last thing that she asked of us, whatever her reasons."

Then a quiet descends and at the same moment Laura and Katherine are imagining what Annie's reasons might be, what might happen, who they will become or what they will know of themselves.

And one more thing.

"Katherine," Laura says, her voice dipping just below her level of normal command, "when I was there, those days before she died, we talked a lot and one thing we talked about for a very long time was that she wanted me to think about buying her house and moving to California."

Katherine finds nothing surprising this day. A traveling funeral? Here we go. Jill sobbing on her back porch? Seems normal. Laura and her husband moving to California? Why not.

"If you come on the funeral," Katherine tells her, "I'll help you end that part of your story and then we'll all go back to Chicago and help you pack."

"There, that was easy," Laura laughs. "We'll see. I don't and can't see everything about that issue clearly, especially with the news you just dropped into my lap, but we'll see about this. Annie got me thinking about it for sure and then toward the end when she was so sick we let it go."

"Will you need anything before we meet at the airport?" Katherine asks finally to move them on, because she is in charge of moving the flock, at least for now. "Will you need anything at all?"

Laura wants to leave for the airport right away. She wants to run from her house wearing only what she has on and get to it. She is already seeing vistas across a New Mexico plateau and the mist rising from a stand of tall grass near a Seattle island. She is already holding the hands of her traveling funeral comrades and she wants to see it all, do it all immediately. She cannot wait. She wants to hurry. Somehow, she knows, she'll figure out how to escape her job, her husband, the cold Chicago spring.

"I want to write while we do this," she says spontaneously.

"Write?"

"This is going to be remarkable," Laura says. "Not just for

honoring Annie, but also for what will happen to us and what we might discover. So I want to keep some kind of diary, journal, design a movie script—whatever in the hell it turns out to be."

"She'd love that," Katherine almost screams. "She'd love the writing part."

"I have no clue but let me start now. I'll start with this conversation and see what happens and I will move a truck with my bare hands to get to the airport."

"Can you do it?" Katherine asks again.

"I can do it, baby."

Laura does not know how. It will seem impossible in just a few moments, in an hour and for several days and even after the funeral procession has changed direction. But she is certain, totally certain, that she will be at the airport in seven days.

Then the conversation ends quickly because the time is moving from one zone to the next fast and two more women are waiting and Laura Westma needs to go to the bathroom, unpack her groceries, and make plans for a traveling funeral.

One thing at a time. One thing at a time.

7

Laura and Annie

Chicago, Illinois, 1987

Annie waited 43.8 minutes before she called. Minutes, all 43.8 of them, that were the longest she had ever spent in her entire life.

Almost as long as the minutes when a man once tried to kill her.

A man she remembers having seen only during a lecture on political activism she was giving at the University of Chicago during her four-month sabbatical in the fall semester. She remembers him because he paced constantly during the lecture, rising and falling in the back of the auditorium like one of those moving targets at a carnival that you get to keep if your quarter lands inside of its head or you pop out its eyes with the air gun.

"How strange," she remembered telling herself during that lecture and again later when she was safe, when it was over and when one part of her life was forever changed. "Why doesn't he sit down? He's driving me crazy."

Driving her crazy.

And then without knowing who or why or what was happening, strange objects began appearing on her car window and outside her office door where she had been given research space, where students lined up every day to see her for just a few minutes, where she spent so many hours each day she considered moving out of her campus housing unit and sleeping on the ancient office couch.

Rubber knives. A glass of wine. Slippers. Then the notes started.

"I could tell you about killing. I could show you."

"We know what you really mean."

"Three times and once times 100 and then the end will flatten us like nothing. You will see."

At first it was funny but then the phone started ringing when she was in the office at 12:30 A.M. or at 5 A.M. when it should not have been ringing. There would be a voice on the line, a man's deep cough, a rough whisper, the sounds of something—metal maybe—and then fear rising in her throat as she began to think that maybe none of this was random. Maybe none of this was random at all.

Annie G. Freeman was no campus kid the year she took her four-month sabbatical. She was thirty-eight years old and her two boys came with her and were plunged into the city/university life and when they were not complaining about missing their friends they were busy making new ones. They may have known something was amiss. They may have known that their mother began staying up too late, making too many quiet phone calls, had too many male friends sleep over on the couch just so someone would guard the door. They may have known she looked too tired all of the time.

They may have known something but no one knew everything.

No one knew how he watched her and followed her. No one knew he sat in the back seat of her car the days she forgot to lock it. The nights when she did not work late he was often in the unlocked office down the hall listening, waiting, thinking, wondering and hoping. Sometimes he slept in the bushes underneath her bathroom window. He knew exactly how long she stayed in the shower almost every morning.

Annie was no fool. She eventually called the campus police and they called the Chicago police. The police took the notes and the slippers and the rubber knives and then they made their own notes and said—as if they were simply warning someone about crossing a street—"Be careful."

Then they left and then one night he came.

Even with this man—whom she came to call the Cat Man because he often mentioned during his late night phone calls how he would love to touch her pussy—stalking her nights and days and mornings, Annie often became lost in her work. She was desperately trying to write a high school counseling book and she was teaching writing classes at the university, and raising her two sons. Sometimes in the middle of all that living, she completely forgot about how she needed to be guarding her pussy.

But he never forgot.

He came for her at a strange angle, and lost in her life thoughts, Annie G. Freeman was taken off-guard. His arms shot out at her at 37 minutes after 6 P.M. when the campus was strangely quiet and on a Friday when no one was coming in, everyone had left and only Annie on sabbatical was determined to work.

When he pulled her down in the deserted hallway that led to her office, she went willingly because she was so startled and unsuspecting. He wore no mask. There was no disguise and as he climbed on top of her and worked to push her into the restroom she studied his face in that moment, the moment when something horrible is just beginning and you do not yet realize it, you are simply curious, you are just on the early side of not yet knowing enough to be terrified.

His eyes were blue, not black. He was handsome, not grotesque. He smelled of musk and soft soap, not sweat and danger. He had on a denim shirt, jeans, a belt with a silver buckle. When she looked at him for those five seconds, before she noticed how large his pupils were, that his face twitched endlessly, that he rolled his neck every few seconds, she had no idea she was about to fight for her life. Five quick seconds. Seconds that fled faster than any seconds she had ever before held or seen or dared to imagine.

It took her a while to fight because she was not sure what he wanted. Rape? To simply see her pussy? To put his hands around her neck and watch her slip from one world to the next? To beat her senseless? To make small cuts on her writing fingers and across the ancient scar on her wrist that already marked her as a survivor?

Suddenly it was all of the above and all she could see were the tiny fingers of her boys when they were babies. An image that came from nowhere like a mysterious stranger in a dark hallway. The tiny fingers all lined up on the piano keys in their living room in California feeling the smooth top of the ivory keyboard as if they were playing in the sand on the beach back at Grandma's cabin on Lake Superior.

"Oh," she screamed. Then again. "Oh."

The sight of those invisible fingers made Annie do something strange and remarkable. Not unlike the woman near Omaha who lifted the car off her eleven-year-old daughter who had gone underneath it to retrieve a baseball only to have it crash down on her legs. The woman could never do such a thing again. She should never have been able to do it in the first place but there was her daughter, with the fingers from her right hand waving silently for help and the woman simply lifting up the car as if she were picking up the edge of the curtain in the living room to discover a lost tennis shoe.

That's what Annie Freeman did. She went nuts. She raised herself up off the hallway floor, with those baby boy fingers in her mind, and she slammed the man in the denim shirt into the side of the stall door in the men's john on the first floor of the English wing as if she were tossing a scarf over her shoulder. She tossed him and then she ran.

He grabbed her ankle on the fly but she kept her balance—eyes on the baby fingers—and she ran into her temporary office, slammed the door, locked it and then in another show of mother's might she managed to push an ancient wooden desk up against the door and wedge herself under it for extra weight. Then she waited.

Annie waited for those long 43.8 minutes and she listened paralyzed with fear and unable to reach out for the phone. She heard rattling at the end of the hall. She heard him come close, breathing hard, she heard him whisper—because he knew she was there— "I'll get you." She heard fingers tapping across the door. His breath separated from her by the thickness of a wall.

And then she thought she heard him leave.

She reached for the phone from under her desk breathless, shaking, unable to think. Her fingers dialed a random number that came up empty. She could not even remember a simple number. Dialing 911 was an impossibility. She waited for a fast miracle, mind blank, hands trembling, a line of dried blood from gashing her head into the metal belt buckle streaked across her left cheek. There on the side of the office phone was a number—1234. The campus crisis line—twenty-four hours every single day of the year. Just dial those numbers and someone will help you.

"Help me, please."

"Who is this?"

"Professor Annie Freeman. On campus. He's in the hall. Jesus. I don't know what to do. Please help me."

The voice was so calm, so kind, so wonderful.

"What building are you? Can you tell me that?"

Annie G. Freeman who has conquered foreign worlds, salvaged her own soul, given birth to two large-headed babies, faced a Board of Regents as if she were looking into a gorgeous sunset, changed the rules in dozens of books—that Annie Freeman surrenders to that voice.

She will do anything, any fucking thing, for that voice.

When they come it is not too late to save Annie but too late to save the man from doing it to someone else.

"Hey," she hears the voice say to her from just beyond the door, where he must have been, was, may be again. "Hey, Annie, are you there?"

Annie waits before she answers. She is in that place where she thinks this might be a trick. She holds her breath to make certain and the voice sounds again. It is strong, safe, wise.

"Hey, Annie, it's Laura from the campus crisis line, the women's center. You called me. It's safe now. There are police here. He's gone. It's okay."

Laura. Oh, wonderful Laura.

It did not happen overnight. It was not easy. It would never be forgotten or forgiven. Annie fell into the arms and heart and talents of Laura and her women's center and its many causes and concerns. It was an embrace that transcended the incident where they first met, an embrace that blossomed into friendship, fine love, and passed the test of time and place that often triggers a distance that makes friendship cloudy and forgotten.

But Annie never forgot.

Laura never forgot.

They forged a bond of hope, of change, of memorable moments that covered the night they met and moved them both to a place of shared strength, talents and friendship that lasted until the day Annie died.

And even longer than that.

8

"Shit."

This favorite word that passed across the lips of Rebecca was like dessert to her. No matter where she was or what happened, just saying the word "shit" made her somehow feel better.

"Some people think it's filthy because someone told them it was a dirty word," she told someone at least twice a day. "But 'shit' gets me through. I say it and it makes me smile. I can't stop it or help myself. I love 'shit.' "

That made her laugh too.

"I love shit."

"Say it," she would tell people, some of them people Rebecca had never met but happened to be sitting next to, or sharing a meal with at a convention, or parked next to at a busy intersection. "Just say it and see what happens."

Mostly people laughed too because a fairly attractive, kind-looking and gentle-speaking—well, except for that "shit" word—woman who appeared sort of harmless, looked her age (which was fifty-three), was talking to them about a word that most people perceived as being from the Swear Family.

Rebecca was swearing when the phone rang. She was saying something worse than "shit." A word that has become as acceptable as part of everyday verbiage in many cultures but a word that even she was loath to speak out loud. Except when the phone was ringing when she did not really want to answer it. Except when she was wanting to lie down and sleep and yet was seemingly waiting for something else to happen. One more thing. One more shitty thing.

"What?" she asked herself out loud as she picked up the phone and then asked it again without waiting for some kind of reply or question in return.

"What? What the shit do you want?"

Katherine laughs. She should have expected this. This is Rebecca. Katherine knows this. She does. She knows about the "shit" and the somewhat messy life, like shit itself, and the way Rebecca often talks in questions because she is always going someplace and she is always in a hurry and in a shitty mess. She imagines Rebecca who just about always wears flip-flops, has refused to dye her hair, loves huge earrings and men's tailored shirts, dressed just like that and with her hand cradling the phone between her chin and chest.

"Hey, Rebecca, it's Katherine Givins. How are you?"

"What the hell?"

Katherine laughs again. She can't help it and then her mind launches into one of those tired, kind-of-hysterical places because she has been up now for a very long period of time and she is manic at best and getting worse. Rebecca's predictableness makes her laugh and she quickly stops herself from sketching out the rest of the conversation.

"Just hearing your shitty voice makes me want to laugh. Annie would like that."

Rebecca laughs, too, just hearing her response, and then quickly flies into a place that brings her out of orbit very fast. It is their connection. How they know each other. Why they may be speaking on the phone this very second.

Annie.

How she misses Annie.

"Katherine Givins," Rebecca says. "Of course I know who you are," she adds, acknowledging a name, then a woman, then a parade of memories that come marching toward her before she can think to get out of their way.

"Oh my God . . ." she manages to say and then Katherine gives her a minute.

She gives her a minute because she knows who Rebecca Carlson is and was and always will be. She knows how Annie moved in next door to Rebecca in 1993 following six months of heated and sometimes hilarious and frequently shitty debate about the price of the piece of the land—money which Rebecca needed desperately but would never admit so—and the location of the house that was to be built and its height and the landscaping until Rebecca was about to suggest and then demand the placement of stones up the driveway and Annie finally said, "No, damn it, no. You let go, woman. You let me be your neighbor and take my money and let me share your view."

Rebecca let go. She had no choice. Depleted resources. A mother and a father who gave her everything and then took it all back and then some as she nursed them over and through and then way beyond a valley of sickness so dark and thick and wasteful that it was a wonder Rebecca could wake and walk and breathe in the morning.

Then she dragged herself through a succession of funerals. Father. Mother. Aunt. Then her sister. Her lovely, young beautiful sister, who bounced against the steering wheel and then flew out of the car window as if she were trying to grab something off the top of the tree she hit. An endless succession of improbable loss.

And then there was Annie G. Freeman with her wide life and her damn earthmovers and those young men of hers and Rebecca could not help herself. She could not keep from falling into the arms and life of her sassy and sometimes shitty neighbor who had the gall, the goddamn gall, to die.

"She died too," Rebecca whispered into the phone, thinking that maybe Katherine would not hear her.

But Katherine was ready. She knew this story and she was ready to stretch her arms across the miles from where she was standing in her kitchen and fool this woman, this Rebecca Carlson, into thinking that her own fine limbs could substitute for the limbs and heart of the neighbor who had turned into family—solid, true, loving, forever lasting.

"Give me a minute," Rebecca says. "Don't go. I just need to catch my breath. To sit."

Rebecca sits. Grief had exhausted her. She sits where she can see Annie's house, dark and quiet and nestled against a small hill that she had always imagined, since the house was built, was put just there to help support a home where a woman lived who could hold up the entire rest of the world. A house where Rebecca learned how to keep moving and to allow herself to feel and to love again. A house where Annie pushed her fingers against Rebecca's not-yet-healed scars of loss and grieving that had barely disappeared when she had to do it all over again. And again and then one more time.

And the day Annie told her. Rebecca moving from the gate and garage toward the house and then catching a glimpse of Annie walking slowly, her hands tucked inside of her blue down vest that she wore so much it had faded three shades up so that it was more white than blue. Annie walking with her eyes on Rebecca's face, a face covered in an ocean of wetness, and then a cry of anguish that came from a place so far away that it was not real, could not be real, was nothing more than an imagined echo from an ancient time and place.

"Honey," Annie cried. "Oh, honey."

They moved from the walk to the porch to the living room couch where they had spent so much time, so many hours of talking and solving and sharing and getting on about every aspect of life that it had become their four-legged oasis, a harbor, a place to nest and heal before they threw themselves back into the orbit of the real world.

And now the real world would never be the same. Everything would change and for once Rebecca knew, she knew exactly what would happen next and what she could do and could not do and she knew, too, that her heart had healed just long enough to be severed in half one more time.

"Oh, Rebecca, I'm sorry to do this to you again. I'm so sorry and I'm so damned scared."

They talked after that with Rebecca holding on to her as tightly as Annie was holding on to Rebecca. Hours of touching and talking that set them on a course that took them to a place that was not and could never have been imagined.

"Rebecca?" Katherine asks.

Katherine asks this question because she imagines that Rebecca, like Jill and Laura, has fallen into a place of remembering, into the heart of her grief, into that place where when you close your eyes you can still feel the faint breath of your friend when she kisses your cheek, the warm fingers of her hands supporting your arm when you scurry up the hill during a hike, the call at one A.M. when you see her bedroom light still flickering through the trees at the edge of the lot line, the waving hand on your way to work, the six-pack of beer on a Friday night that she leaves on your doorstep, the edge of laughter that has been pounded like an ancient drum against your own laugh line.

"I'm here," Rebecca responds, lifting her head and then turning so she moves away from the view, that shitty shared horizon.

"These have been tough weeks. I haven't called in a while and now I have something else to tell you."

Rebecca laughs and the laugh, which is raucous and bold— almost something you could lift over your shoulder it is so real— makes Katherine laugh too.

"This isn't really funny," Katherine says through her own machine-gun giggles. "But we both know something else had to happen. We both know that Annie would have to do something else."

"Please do not tell me you are dying," Rebecca begs in all seriousness.

"No, Rebecca, that's not it. We should all have known that Annie had one more request up her sleeve for us. Something she wants us to do. One last thing."

"Nothing, so it seems, is ever really over."

Rebecca is thinking of her own divorce when she says that. The painful throb of the mere word makes her laughter shriek to a halt, and the last laugh, for now, the last laugh lingers while she pauses to hold that anguish from his leaving, her wanting him to leave, the idea that was once an eternity will now be locked forever at 7.7 years and that the one daughter they have managed to create will now become a tool, a pawn, a poker chip that he will choose to throw on the table, take back and then throw again so many times it almost blinds Rebecca with anger.

"Should I go?" the tiny voice of her daughter Marden asked her so many times when she was eight and then nine and then twelve and then finally when she was sixteen and said, "This is enough. Now I know I should go."

The phone calls about insurance and who pays for what and the screams of his new babies in the background and the unmistakable pounding of the new woman's hands on the table as she locked his eyes with hers and most likely mouthed, "Hang up on the bitch," while Rebecca waited for an answer about the band trip, summer vacation, a car, college tuition, the rest of their daughter's life.

Even now, random phone calls: "Did she move?" "How can I get hold of her?" "Did you take my name off of her insurance?"

You think it might be over and then something turns up in the basement boxes that throws you into a place of swift agony. The shitty photos from the trip to Mexico the year before the divorce. Remembering things now that should have been a tip-off. A phone number on the bill that he said "must have been a wrong number." The way he looked away when you asked him to make love to you on the beach, "Too much sun," he'd said and added, "Maybe tomorrow." Tomorrow there was the fiesta and then the bus tour and then in six months the fighting and what you considered trying without knowing that he was already gone, that he had left so long ago it would be impossible to remember back that far.

"Rebecca, she wants us to do something," Katherine says again, shaking loose the divorce memories for just a moment.

"God, yes, it was always one more thing with Annie. This project. That project. A party. Another party. Another article. Rounding up protesters this week, getting them ready for the week after that. What am I telling you this for? You know all of this. It was constant and endless and I miss every damn minute of it."

Katherine misses it too. She misses the phone calls and the wild trips north to attend a party or rake a yard or plant a new row of trees or bail Annie out of jail again.

"How many times did I end up on your couch because there wasn't enough room at her house?" she asks Rebecca.

"Was I supposed to count?"

They laugh again, which is the entire point. It's the laughing that they need to hold on to and they talk about that too. They talk about lining everyone up on the porch that one day in July and spitting watermelon seeds into tin cans. They talk about running naked through the sprinkler the night they drank a case of champagne when Annie got an article accepted into a prestigious journal; they talk about the road trip to the ocean where they ended up getting kicked out of the resort for "not acting their age." They talk about Annie's boys watching them all the years and learning things about women that made other boys jealous and other girls want to just be in the same room with them. They talk about daughters and the boys and girls that weekend from hell when they realized that their kids don't necessarily have to be friends just because *they* are friends. They talk about being together in ways that are unique and should not be and how the word "family" is not something you can easily define, and Rebecca stands with both hands on her thin hips as she often does, still looking out across her yard and into Annie's yard. She wears her silver hair down to her shoulders and just long enough so that she can put it in a ponytail and stick it through the baseball hats she loves to wear when she is not at work. Worry and life have kept her thin—you can stay thin lifting sick and dying people, driving to the hospital, and planning funerals.

Rebecca wonders, as Katherine talks and she splits her mind in two, if it will be something hard that Annie will ask of her. Will she have to beg off work, her position as a marketing specialist for a real estate development company, again? Will they let her? Will they even believe her? Will Annie's boys feed the cats and pick up the mail and do the 267 other things that might be asked if she has to go away from what is left of her life without Annie?

"Please let it not be too hard," she whispers to herself as Katherine asks her if she is ready for the request, and then she lies and answers, "Yes."

Then Katherine tells her about the traveling funeral. She reads the notes and tells the story of the UPS woman, which is already becoming, in one short day, the thing legends are hatched from, and she puts her hand right on top of the red tennis shoes as she says how no one could be more astounded than she is to have to be doing something like this.

This makes Rebecca laugh even louder and say, "Not."

"What do you mean, 'Not'?"

"It all makes sense. She was into place and capturing moments and my guess is that if I went over there and went through the house I would find detailed diaries about exactly what it was that happened in each one of those spots . . . where the hell are they?"

"Here, Santa Fe, New York City, Florida Keys, Lake Superior, some island near Seattle."

"Jeezus. How many days?"

"Ten."

There is a quiet moment while Rebecca adds it all up in her

head and subtracts those days from her remaining sick leave—none—her remaining vacation days—none—her remaining personal days—none—and the remaining days for the rest of her life when she will regret not having gone, not having seen what Annie wanted her to see. Everyone is dead and she cannot remember the last time she went on a retreat, spent more than a handful of hours with a group of unfamiliar women. Took her clothes off in front of anyone but the cat. Stayed up talking for hours. Told someone everything. She's suddenly just a bit terrified.

"Shit."

"Well?"

"What happened in those places she wants us to go to? What could possibly have happened that we don't know about? Where the hell did she come up with this idea? What if we don't get along? What if I need to be alone for an hour?"

Katherine starts laughing again and they launch into a discussion about the possibilities of the trip. The possibilities of five women mixing hands and hearts and pouring their grief on top of it all and then waiting for the whole damn thing to come out of the oven. The possibility that someone will be in menopause and crabby as hell, that someone will not be in menopause and be crabby as hell. The possibility that it may ruin the casual relationships some of them already have. The possibility that some or all of them might not want to come back. The possibility that it may be an impossibility to even think about going.

"She's paying for it all," Katherine says, as if she were reading Rebecca's mind.

"It's not the money. It's the time, and I—"

"Think about the word 'time,' Rebecca," Katherine interrupts. "Think about that shitty word right now and tell me what you see when the word flashes across that screen in your mind."

Katherine is pacing now. She has turned into the assistant district attorney. She needs to sway this conversation fast. She has her left hand on her hip and with her foot she is pushing her toes up against the side of the red shoes so that they move back and forth like the ticking hands of a huge clock.

"Here's the deal," Rebecca finally says, surrendering to Annie, doing it for Annie, thinking it's just for Annie. "I'll ask for a short leave of absence. They are used to me doing this at the real estate company. For God's sake, I've been gone more in the past ten years than I have been there and I'll promise them something. I'll develop a new marketing plan. When we sell Annie's house I'll donate some money in their name to some hospice group or to cancer research. They'll do it. They loved her too. They'll do it and you know I'll do it. You knew that before you even called me on this shitty phone."

"Are you sure?"

Rebecca is sure of many things. She is certain that her daughter loves her in a way that will last forever. She is sure that she has this moment, this day, and maybe a few hours after that. She is sure of the past and of what might linger on the horizon only as far as she can see. She is certain that if you take your grief and you hold on tight to it, it multiplies and divides and soon conquers you so that it wins a war that was never meant to be started.

She is sure that she loved Annie G. Freeman in a way that many times made her want to cross a boundary that she was sure she was not meant to cross. She loved this friend, this woman, this neighbor in a way that opened up a world to her that changed her very heart, what can fit inside it and where it was meant to go.

She is sure that tomorrow is not guaranteed and that too many women and men wait so long to say something, feel something, or go someplace. Too damn long.

She is not sure she could live with herself if she didn't go, if she didn't do one last thing for Annie. She is not sure she will ever love again the way she loved Annie. She is not sure about looking out into Annie's backyard for the rest of her life and seeing someone who is not Annie running through the sprinkler in August. She is not sure she will ever be done grieving.

"Oh, baby, you know me," Rebecca tells Katherine. "No matter how hard it has been and remains—I have to do one more thing for Annie. I'd do anything for Annie."

"I do know that, but in this case we are reading the same book but on different pages. I have things, you know that, that place me in the 'undecided' category. I could use a flipping traveling funeral. I have not stopped to take a breath in a long time and to take it for Annie, well, that seems like it could be grand."

"I suppose she knew that too."

"What didn't she know?" Katherine shoots back.

"She didn't know it would be so quick. She didn't know it would happen to her. She didn't know that it would be as easy as it was in the end. She didn't know what she would see from the last turn."

"Stop, please stop," Katherine says, bending to touch the tips of the shoes with her fingers. "We'll get to this. We'll get to it all but I need a breath now."

Rebecca thinks that what she needs is to take a walk and get the blood moving into her face and she needs to move fast so that she doesn't linger in the impossibility for more than just a few minutes.

"Is there anyone else to call?" she asks Katherine.

"One more woman."

"Who is it? Anyone I know?"

"Marie Kondronsky."

"Shit."

"Her hospice nurse. I have no idea how this is going to work with her and her patients. We have to figure that out this week, too. Can you help me do that, Rebecca? I think I am going to have my hands full."

Rebecca thinks for a second. Marie has a schedule that would cripple a young and healthy pope. She has four half-grown kids, a husband who runs a huge construction company, and she's the hospice nurse in Sonoma County for at least eight dying neighbors, friends, butchers, bakers and candlestick makers.

"No problem," Rebecca tells Katherine. "If there is one more thing that I know it's that we can pretty much do anything. I'm thinking about lifting up the edge of the house with my bare hands before I go back to work in the morning. I'll figure that part out. What else is there? Is there something else I can do?"

Katherine gets up again. She feels woozy, as if she is about to spin into a place that is just a bit frightful.

"I'm just a little, what? I don't know . . ." she confesses.

"The word is temporarily 'overwhelmed.' Don't worry. You know we'll all be fine but we had better bring along a shitload of Kleenex."

"Good idea. I think I may just be a bit tired."

"One more thing," Rebecca tells her. "We have to call this something. You know she loved that shit. Naming things. Putting headlines on her papers."

"You're right. I can see it now: T-shirts, hats, we can put logos on cars and buses. You won't have to sell her house now and we can run tours through the damn place."

"I have it," Rebecca admits.

"Hit me."

"Let's call it Annie Freeman's Fabulous Traveling Funeral."

Katherine tilts back her head so far when she laughs that she almost tips over and lands on top of her dear friend's ashes. When she speaks it's a raspy whisper because the laugh feels so damn good she does not want to let go of it.

"It's perfect."

"Well, it's something. Perfect is in question," Rebecca adds, ready now to get to it. Ready to put all the pieces of the funeral train in motion. Ready to keep laughing and then maybe pause occasionally for a remarkable cry.

"I do know this," Katherine tells her, "it will be fabulous."

Rebecca laughs even louder. Laughter is her new fuel, what she will use to get her through the next seven days until she has to get to the airport. What she will use to help her get a leave for yet another funeral. What she will use to finish sorting through the rest of her dead friend's clothes and the yard and about two thousand boxes in the garage.

"No shit," she finally says.

"No shit," Katherine promises.

9

Annie and Rebecca

Santa Bonita Estates,
Section 38, House 42, 1993

It's past midnight when Rebecca Carlson throws back the first sip from her fourth beer and breathes a sigh of relief that would fill up one of her three empty beer cans and knock the teeth out of anyone in recovery.

"She's done," she tells herself, still not willing to leave her post by the living room window. "Maybe she'll leave."

Rebecca has been watching her new neighbor pile rocks in the soon-to-be shape of a house. A new house. The house Rebecca has decided she will hate the rest of her life.

"Damn it. Damn the house."

Rebecca has not noticed that her soon-to-be-neighbor has been watching her. When Rebecca moves to the kitchen for another beer or to skip to the bathroom, the neighbor woman wishes she'd stick her head out the door instead and invite her over for a beer. She'd just about kill for a beer after hours of hauling rocks so the construction team can at least try to get her house in the spot where she'd like to see it built.

Annie G. Freeman has spent hours outlining the shape of the

house that will soon throw a late afternoon shadow across the side garden of Rebecca's yard. The garden that doesn't really need the sun that late in the day and would welcome the new fingers of a fine woman to snap dried leaves and pull the tall grass off the tired roots.

Mystified by her neighbor's reluctance to forge a neighborly partnership, Annie has surrendered to the silence that erupted following the final negotiations for the sale of the land. She knows of her neighbor's losses, her struggles—both financial and personal—and yet she also knows that once they cross the trenches of the invisible war that has been declared, Rebecca will see and know for certain that everything is going to be just fine.

But this day, this first day after the signing and when the wings of change have brushed against her life yet again, Rebecca Carlson just wants to be pissed off.

She wants to be angry at the woman who on one hand saved her from financial ruin and the loss of her own house, and on the other changed her view, disrupted the quiet of her hillside life and made her somewhat angrily step into rhythm with a world that seemed to shove her into places that she had no desire to see, feel or experience.

"Shit," Rebecca said, moving the word through her mouth as if she were about to swallow something that tasted just as nasty as the word itself.

Annie catches Rebecca's shadow dancing close to the window and she smiles. She focuses for a while on the struggle often associated with the word "change." For her, for even this woman next door, she thinks, that sure thing that brings comfort is not really sure at all.

"Come on," she says out loud to Rebecca. "Come to mama."

The rocks have made Annie's hands sore. The tops of her knuckles are bleeding and she'd love to run her hands under some warm tap water and then rest them gently in her lap. She'd love to sit out on the back step of Rebecca's old house and swig a beer or two and memorize the shapes of the trees, the flow of the sky from west to east, the way the far house—barely visible—looks like a ship about to fall into the deep side of the square earth.

Rebecca does not know if the woman she is about to call neighbor has a family. She has not seen anyone else come to the land. She has not asked the woman about relatives or sons or daughters or a husband. Annie signed the papers alone. She owns the land now. But Rebecca wonders. She wonders how long she can hold out and what she will do if she needs one more egg for the cake or what she will do if her car won't start and she sees that Annie is home. She wonders what it will be like the day the walls of Annie's house go up and then the roof goes on amidst the constant drum of hammers and trucks and the sideways glances of the construction crew. She wonders as she drinks her beer standing up and leaning against the window and then shutting her eyes for just a moment to see it all.

That is when Annie places the last rock in place, wipes her hands on her jean-covered thighs, and takes a step toward the back door of Rebecca's house.

Rebecca does not see this. When she opens her eyes Annie is no longer in the yard and it's about to get dark, and she murmurs, "What the hell." And then she hears the knock.

"Shit."

Annie looks exhausted and Rebecca, who has a heart that is truly a flower, melts instantly when she sees spots of blood on Annie's knuckles when she raises her hand to push the hair out of her eyes.

They both just look at each other for one of those moments when words would be meaningless. One of those moments when someone should say "Hi" or "I'm sorry" or "Please come in." One of those moments that erases everything bad and opens up a door into a place that is hopeful—awkward for another inch or two—but still hopeful.

Annie speaks first.

"I don't know what I need more: a beer, a kind word, or some warm water across the tops of my hands."

Rebecca cannot help herself. She can no longer be angry at this woman who is in the process of saving her from financial ruin, who needs something now that Rebecca is perfectly capable of giving her.

"How about all three?" she answers, opening the screen door so that Annie can come inside.

"Beer first?" Annie asks.

"A woman who understands priorities," Rebecca answers as they waltz slowly into something as new and fresh as the stone outline of an unbuilt house.

The beginning stretched into hours. There was more beer, the rewarming of yesterday's pasta dinner, a tour through every room in Rebecca's house, and then a pause long and sorrowful in front of the photos that lined the wall going into the kitchen.

"My parents, my sister, my aunt, the wild daughter alive but gone to seed," Rebecca whispers as she shows her photo gallery to Annie. "All gone. Now you know why it was so hard for me to let go of one more thing."

"The land?"

"The land, the view, a sense of something, one thing just staying the way I thought it should be."

"Control."

This word stops Rebecca. It stops her and she wants suddenly to lean into this woman with the strong voice and bloody hands. This woman who will most likely become the best neighbor in the world and who will lend her books and sleep on her couch when she is lonely and never lock her door and open her world and life to Rebecca in a way that changes everything—every single thing.

"I'm tired," she tells Annie. "Tired of losing ground, of losing control, of losing so many people that I love. I fought this sale because of that, losing control, which is ridiculous because in the end selling you the land will give me something back. I'm so sorry."

Annie does not want Rebecca to be sorry. She does not want her to take back her words or her actions or how she feels inside of her wounded heart. She puts her hand on the side of Rebecca's face and Rebecca does not try to take her hand away.

"It's going to be okay, you know that now, don't you?"

"I know there will be something else but I also know that it will be okay, it has to be okay, you are right."

That first night turned into a second day and the beer turned into wine and the wine turned into breakfast after a night on the couch from the beer and wine and a conversation that launched a friendship and gathered strength as the walls of Annie's house went up and then the damn slanted roof came into view and a garage that was scaled back so that Rebecca could look out of her kitchen window and still see the top of her favorite hill.

Strength as the daughter and sons came and went, as one job became a struggle and the other job a delight. Strength as the grass took hold and the trees grew and as one romance soured and another erupted like a well-tended fire and then burnt out at the mere hint of a strong breeze.

Strength finally to the end. Through that day when Annie slowly crossed the yard and cried in Rebecca's arms and beyond that, those months beyond when it seemed as if Rebecca had moved in and without knowing it passed a notebook into the hands of her dying friend so that she could design a traveling funeral.

Annie Freeman's fabulous traveling funeral.

10

~~~⤜⟳⤛~~~

John Richardson started tapping his fingers on the dining room table a good forty-five minutes before Marie Kondronsky was due to tap her own fingers against the back door window every night.

It was not a game to him, this tapping. It was a way to try and push his mind away from the pain in those last few minutes before his medication arrived. Marie was John Richardson's medication for many, many reasons—the least of all being the morphine. Mostly it was just the knowledge that she would come. It was knowing that she would ask how his day went and the night before the day and that she always touched his arm, sometimes his face, and sometimes she sat for a while because he was her last stop and she was always exhausted. Sometimes, just after the medication began climbing its way through his exhausted veins and toward the place where the pain lingered like lions waiting for dinner, she sat with her fingers on the veins below his wrist pretending to take his pulse. He knew she just wanted to touch him, to be sure. He knew this for certain.

John Richardson, terminal lung cancer patient just off of the Benton Way highway turn, would be John Richardson, terminal cancer patient at the Fenton Valley Care Center if it were not for Marie and her extraordinary talents as nurse and friend to the dying.

"Marie," he said just before she turned to leave that first week. "What would happen if you couldn't come?"

"John," she said, making believe she was going to slap his hands for talking naughty, "I'll always come. You know I love you. When I left last summer didn't I send the nicest woman to fill in?"

John liked the other woman but she wasn't Marie. He needed Marie. He did.

"I won't leave you, John. I'll be here. It's okay."

Marie always made certain he had her cell phone number taped to the edge of the counter. She made sure his wife knew to call and she made sure that as he got worse, nothing, not even her precious family time, would interrupt those last days, the last week, the last anything.

It was what she did, who she was. Marie the hospice nurse. The director of the entire valley program and the woman who had held the dying hearts and hands of more men and women and way too many babies and boys and girls during the past seventeen years.

And the phone was always ringing.

Three teenagers still at home. One in college. A husband with a construction business. Marie always on call and the phone never stopping.

It rings almost on cue after dinner, three hours past John's goodnight, "I'm going to sleep now" call, dishes are done, everyone is reading or doing homework, and Marie finally curls into the chair by her bedroom window. It's her place, her only place, and she has the chair turned so that she can look out from the second-story window into the hands of the trees. She sees the long limbs of the trees as an extension of the earth and all things that grow and flourish and she likes to see them reaching, moving, growing every single day. And this time, these few minutes every night, is when she puts her world back together.

During this time, her children would call for her only if the house were on fire. Her husband would wet his pants rather than come in to use their bathroom and disturb her during her alone time. Her sisters hold back from picking up the phone until morning or later in the night. Some friends forget and call, but her second-oldest daughter often catches the call before the first ring has finished and takes a message.

Only someone who didn't know about these sacred seconds would bend the unwritten rules and call asking for Marie at this time. Only someone who didn't know that these moments were the ones Marie needed to keep the tears and gashes in her own soul from washing her out to sea. Only someone who didn't know would dare to interrupt the time when Marie fanned back through all of them. George, Mitchell, baby Jessie, Cynthia, the Hernandez brothers, Tom and Brad Zimcheck, Grandpa Harley. All the faces of the men and women and boys and girls and aunts and uncles and mothers and fathers Marie has helped to ease from one world to the next.

A life of dying, Marie calls it, and how and why she came to do it astounds her every single night just as it does this night when she places one hand on each arm of the rocking chair and feels the wood beneath her fingers. The wood is solid and real and she can feel it. She holds on to the rocker's arms as she prays. She prays first for each person under her care who has already died and then she prays for those who are dying tonight and those who will die tomorrow or next Friday. She prays during these precious moments only for her people—"clients," some nurses call them, but she calls them "her people." She does not pray for her family—not her four daughters or her husband or her sisters. Those prayers are for the morning or for the drives to see her people or for every other moment of the day when she is not in her life of dying.

The phone rings and there is a scramble downstairs that Marie hears and it makes her laugh out loud just a little to think how well her family knows her and understands this space that she has to protect to keep on going, to tell herself, "Yes, I'm alive and I can do it again."

A tap at the door startles her because it has been so long since there was an emergency at this hour. So long since someone called and needed her now, just like that, during this time, *her* time.

"Mom, I'm sorry," whispers Sarah from behind the door. "She says she needs to talk to you right away."

"That's okay, honey," Marie whispers back, not wanting to break the spell of her own prayer service with a loud voice. "Who is it?"

Sarah is a good girl. She is really a young woman who is only months away from handing over the reins of this very important job to her younger sister when she graduates from high school. But for now, maybe for the last time, she is the one who whispers first one name and then another from the other side of the door. Sarah is the one who will stop her mother's beating heart with the names of two women. Sarah, who will eventually go on to become a doctor and who will be remarkable not only for her healing powers but for remembering the kindness and grace that she witnessed every single day in the actions and life and breath of her own mother, Marie Kondronsky, the hospice nurse from Sonoma County.

"Mom, she said her name is Katherine Givins and that she needed to talk with you about a funeral for Annie Freeman."

Marie cannot move for one, two and then five seconds. The weight of Annie Freeman's hands on her arm is still so fresh in her mind that she cannot think to speak to her daughter who is waiting to be dismissed, to know for certain that her mother is going to know what to do next.

"Mom?"

"I'm fine, sweetheart. I'll tell you about it later. Can you hang up down there?"

"Of course."

Of course.

Katherine Givins and Marie Kondronsky spoke on the phone often during Annie's illness. They met twice during Katherine's visits but they have never gotten past the graceful discussion of the medical world. They have discussed cancer and medication and efforts to comfort the dying, but they have not balanced over the edge very far to explore the potential possibilities of common denominators. Life beyond dying has danced around them even as they have embraced and cried together and then turned to get on with it.

This is the launch of something new. This is where those "How are you?"s move quickly to the heart of the call.

"How are you, Marie?"

"Fine, Katherine."

Then Katherine Givins begins her tale of the traveling funeral while Marie rocks in her chair and imagines, in between sentences, that she is gliding across the tops of the trees and that she will never fall and nothing can stop her from floating as if that is all there is to do. Float and be in the now with the living. That is all. Just that.

"Did you know about this?" Katherine asks her. "The traveling funeral?"

Marie does not answer Katherine's question. Instead, she tells her a story. She tells Katherine about how she falls in love with every single patient that she cares for and how her heart breaks every single time one of them dies and that they all die.

They all die.

Marie did not know. She did not know that Annie used the pen and notebook to plan her own funeral. A traveling funeral. She did not know that the pages she'd found folded over when Annie fell asleep were the directions to all the secret and wonderful spots that helped make a remarkable trail. She did not know that Annie's writing was a simple journey back to reclaim a portion of what was once alive for those who remained, for those she loved, for those she loved beyond all the others. She did not know that while planets of grief and sorrow started swirling around the sons and friends and colleges and the young boys and girls in Memphis and Orlando and Princeton who had read about Annie's own brush with death years and years before and who knew that she was really, finally dying again that Annie was smiling and laughing at what she was planning.

Her traveling funeral. A place beyond the yard she loved to watch and the faces she memorized with all the photos she asked Marie to help her line up against the front of the dresser. Marie did not know that she was a key player, that her placing the pen in the perfect spot and never reading the notes and holding open the covers and making certain that the medicine and the baths were just the way Annie liked them—all these things, she did not know.

"What did you think she was writing?" Katherine asked.

"I never thought about it. It was not my place to imagine or intrude. It was not my place to look over her shoulder or to dare to read even one word that she had written."

"I understand."

"I respect them, you see, Katherine. I know you get this because Annie talked about you, because I have met you and looked into your eyes. I know when to ask some things but mostly those who are dying . . . they have so much to think about, so much to remember, so much to imagine. There is no time for questions."

"I see, I do see."

Silence guides them for a few moments while Katherine imagines Annie and Marie sitting just this way, in the quiet. Marie is monitoring some bodily movement, the flow of the medicine, the way the IV drips from the machine into Annie's thin arm, and Annie is swept away with her writing, her planning, her traveling funeral.

"I'm wondering now why you are calling about this funeral,"

Marie says. "Annie would know there is no way for me to leave without weeks and weeks of preparation. She would have known this even as she was planning it."

"You know what you meant to her. You know what you must mean to all of them."

Marie knows. She knows as she watches a brave slice of wind bend the hands of her favorite tree into what she thinks looks like a graceful prayer, hands moving to windy music, the music of her aching heart.

"Of course. I am the last resort. I am the one last stop before they have to start all over again. I know. I do know."

"Marie, she wants you to come on the traveling funeral but she knows you would have a hard time leaving your patients. She wrote about it. She called you the Mother Teresa of Sonoma County. The living gift to the near-dead. The heartbreak before the pills. Well, she had a list of names for you. I will send them all. But she also had this idea."

Marie starts laughing. She sees Annie as she was the first days, when they were getting settled into people they would become. Laughing. Everything was funny. The tubes and bottles and the way she turned for the shots and how she made everything seem light, at first so easy and even at the end there was always something positive.

"What's so funny?" Katherine wants to know, laughing just to hear Marie laugh. Then adding hastily, "Does this seem weird to be laughing when we are talking about Annie's funeral?"

"It would seem funny not to laugh."

Then they laugh together and Katherine catches it first. The irony of this laughing, which she is sure Annie would have predicted and wanted and hoped for during this very conversation.

"She was always full of ideas. This plan and that plan and what she wanted to do and how she never missed a chance once she got her life back."

Marie pauses, remembering. She pauses and her mind flies back to a soft moment when Annie had laughed so hard and for such a long period of time Marie was worried that she may have crossed over some invisible physical line that would make her die sooner. Annie turned to her in the middle of the coughing and the laughing and the serious question about whether or not she would be okay and said, "This is where the term 'die laughing' comes from," and then of course, yes, they both laughed some more and then that was the first and only time she ever gave Annie extra medicine, unprescribed, but she did it. She did it so Annie would not die laughing.

"So," Marie finally asks Katherine, taking a deep breath. "How is this plan going to work?"

The details are simple. The plan is simple. Marie's involvement in the traveling funeral is essential for its success and survival.

"I don't know if I can go," Marie says, standing up in her bedroom so that she can now see over the top of the tree. "She knew it would be close to impossible."

Katherine thinks maybe she should have hopped in her car to travel to Sonoma County to tell Marie how this would work. She thinks that maybe she should have pulled an all-nighter since the red shoes arrived, should have driven to Marie's backyard, climbed her favorite tree and talked to her through an open window.

"Well, here's the deal. Annie knew you, above all others, might struggle with the idea because of your patients. Can you try? Can you think of a way? And if you can't come, if you can only come for part of the funeral, Annie thought of that also. She told me to buy you a cell phone."

The plan is simple and Katherine tells her that Annie has suggested a cell phone purchase with unlimited hours for a very long period of time so that Marie can attend the traveling funeral virtually if she cannot attend all of it in person.

"What?"

"You will call us and we will call you. She wants you to be a part of this, and this phone thing was a way for her to make it happen if you cannot leave, a way for you to help us with this funeral, for us to maybe help you and for you to keep on doing what you need to do for all those other people that you take care of every day. But it would be best if you could come along."

"It sounds easy so far," Marie says, whispering again as she sits back down, putting her hands back on the arms of her chair, settling in, thinking. "Maybe I need this too. Maybe I can figure this out. Annie would like that. Annie *deserves* it."

"Maybe, Marie. Maybe it will be some kind of interesting break that really isn't a break. Don't you get tired?"

"Are you trying to make me laugh again?"

"No. I'm serious. How do you keep doing this?"

Marie wants to tell Katherine about the day the first man died in her arms. She wants to reach her entire body through the invisible phone line that magically connects her world to Katherine's world and rest her head in Katherine's lap while she talks and while she cries.

Ron Smith. His name was Ron Smith. A simple name for a man who had been born in a time when men do not cry or ask for help. A time when a man who is sixty-six years old and dying of inoperable lung cancer from smoking three packs of Camels a day is brought to the hospital because his sons can't help and his wife is also ill and no one else can handle it. There was no one else.

Marie wants to tell Katherine how everyone was afraid to touch him because he was big and swore and because they had never seen anyone from his family touch him. Marie touched him. That's what she would say and she will say if she makes it on the virtual funeral. She will say how one day she just reached over and put her hands on his head not to see if he was feverish or to move his face for some medicine but just so she could feel his skin under her own fingertips. She wanted to touch him as Marie, the kind woman, the mother, the wife and sister, and not Marie, the hospice nurse who had to touch him because it was part of her routine, part of her job.

"He raised his hand slowly and he covered my hand," Marie thinks she will eventually tell her traveling funeral companions. "He held my hand for a very long time and then he moved it down so that I could feel the tears running from his eyes. He cried and he cried and the entire time he cried I willed no one to come into the room and I moved my other hand to his shoulder and then I put my lips to his ear and I told him that it was going to be easy now and that he could let go. I can still feel his hair, how it bunched under my fingertips and how warm his tears felt and how something in me gave him something to trust." But she does not say this now.

Katherine can tell Marie is thinking. She gives her the moment, waiting for the release of a breath, the voice she will hear for all the days of the traveling funeral on the end of the cell phone.

"It's who I am," Marie tells her. "It's what I am supposed to do. Every night, just like this, I sit in my chair and I release my sorrow into the arms of the tree outside of the window. Annie knew this. I told her everything, and except for the funeral she was planning without me, I imagine she told me pretty much everything also."

Katherine knows Annie must have shared all the corners of her world with Marie or she would not be invited to the funeral. She runs her eyes down the list of women—Jill, Laura, Rebecca, herself, Marie. All women who had somehow earned and maintained a special place in Annie's life and heart. Katherine, because of the suicide attempt and the bond only youth and beginnings can command. Jill, from the university, and because she was the professional center and mentor of Annie's world. Laura, who at first was the voice on the phone during the attack and then later the steady arm of friendship and support through dozens of causes and concerns. Rebecca the neighbor, the family, the unending light of calmness in the window. Of course, Katherine tells herself, Marie would have to be invited on the funeral trip. Marie was the gatekeeper. The one who held her hand until the very last moment. The fresh and kind face of trust that helped ease Annie through a tornado of pain and sorrow and to the moments just before her death.

"She talked about you," Katherine tells Marie. "I know she told you what you meant to her but she told me, too, and I am sure she told the others who were invited to the funeral also."

"She was very grateful. Not all of them are. Some of them are so scared and angry they cannot let go. It makes it harder but Annie was not hard."

Marie starts to cry. She doesn't want to cry. But she cannot stop herself. She does not cry easily and her tears are always genuine, always deep, always filled with the salty realness of a heart that knows only one true direction.

"I miss her, Katherine. I miss her."

"I know. We all miss her and she's giving us this one last gift. I keep thinking about funerals. How we all have them and we hate them and how for years Annie and I have talked about throwing some kind of big party or doing something to honor a life and not mourn it."

"That's tough because look at us," Marie said, wiping her hand across her nose. "We are mourning. Because it's sad. Loss is sad, but I see where she might be taking this."

"She *so* lived. Do you know?"

"Yes. I knew it right away."

"Marie?"

"Yes?"

"Are you okay?"

"Sure. But maybe I should come for part of the funeral. Maybe I can make it a few days. Arrange someone to fill in for just a few treatments, for two days or something. I should try and make this happen for Annie."

Katherine thinks that already some kind of traveling funeral magic has taken hold and she looks up toward the sky, where most people believe that souls float and linger before flying on to the next realm, where she imagines Annie smiling like crazy at the notion of her own traveling funeral and what will happen now that it has begun.

"She'd like that. She probably knew you could work something out, that you'd try."

"You know, in some countries they mourn for weeks and months. They hold lavish ceremonies and they keep the bodies propped up in living rooms. Tradition. But maybe there is something to that. Maybe celebrating with a fine mixture of tears and laughter is the way to go. Maybe what you said is true, Katherine."

"What? Did I say something meaningful?"

"Funerals are for the living."

"That's probably the whole point of this. It's a funeral. A traveling funeral, but if we don't have a hell of a good time mixed in with all the tears, I am sure she'll rise up and haunt us the rest of our lives."

"Or until we planned our own traveling funeral," Marie added, smiling because she is sure that is exactly what Annie would have said.

When they hung up a few moments later Marie and Katherine knew they were already on the traveling funeral. They knew that Annie G. Freeman had planned a party to beat all parties and that in just a few short days when the band of women who had formed a tight ring around Annie's heart merged into one long hearse at the San Francisco airport the world would move and sway in a way that had never before been seen or felt.

"I'll make it happen somehow. I will do what I can," Marie promised. "I owe it to myself, to Annie, to my family—to everyone that is waiting in the wings to hold my hand."

After Katherine said goodbye, Marie stayed in her chair a long time. She heard one set of footsteps come to her door and then another but no one dared interrupt her time. When she got up to move downstairs, to help finish making dinner, to push back the hair in her daughter's eyes and to tell all of them she loved them, which was also part of her ritual, she first opened the bedroom window, leaned across the frame and touched the edge of the nearest limb.

"I'm going on a traveling funeral," she told the tree. "Just for a few days. I'll be back. Save my spot."

11

Marie and Annie

Annie's bedroom, California, 2005

The light before dawn fades through so many shades of darkness that Annie cannot bear to take her eyes off the horizon.

She has placed her bed against the far wall so that she can look out across the yard, her yard, and into the rolling hills that move like waves toward the Pacific Ocean. She loves the view so much—the way the colors dance against the horizon, the way she can see one time of day turn into the next, the way her already irregular sleeping patterns have been blasted in a thousand directions because the light pours in from every window at brilliant angles and distracts her from necessary sleep. Morning, afternoon, evening—she loves to study this sky, this view, this living palette she calls her personal parade.

But it's twilight that wins her heart. It's the last hurrah, she calls it, every day no matter how dark or light the sky has become, no matter if it's raining or cloudy, no matter what has happened in the world—war or peace or another damn election—no matter what it is, there is still this twilight moment of surrender that she has honored her entire life and refuses now to give up even as she lies dying in her own bed.

Marie knows this. Marie, the hospice nurse, who comes every

day and sometimes twice a day depending—depending on the pain and the nightmares and Annie's need to ask for help. Marie knows not to interrupt when Annie lies quietly, which was once a rarity, and watches her sky unfold. Marie knows to step from the room and watch from another window because she has already learned to love the same view, the same daily routine, the same act of contrition and panorama that Annie has cared to share with her during this time of dying.

"It's my time of dying," Annie sings to Marie as she gets out of the car and walks toward her house. "It's my time of dying and I would be lying if I said I was not pissed off."

Annie sings in a twang. She refuses to close her windows and she can hear Marie drive up every afternoon and she waits—how she waits!—for the sound of her tires on the unpaved highway and then turning into the gravel driveway, and then the footsteps walking toward the house. She sings as loud as she can. She sings to keep, some days, from going insane from the pain and to make Marie hurry.

"Hurry, Marie," Annie whispers while she hears the door open. "Please hurry."

Marie always hurries. She knows what Annie needs, why she waits with the window open, why they have this twilight ritual, but she is also waiting for Annie to let go. Anne has to let go. She has not let go yet.

Annie is rarely alone. She has a parade of friends, her sons, her fine neighbor. She has women from the university and at least three thousand friends who would sell everything and move into her garage if they thought they could help her for one moment.

But she has only one Marie.

Marie with the wide smile and hands that speak of medicinal things but do so in a way that also offers hope, the promise of something wonderful beyond all the horrible days. Marie, who lines up the photos of her own daughters and cares to share not just her skills and license but also her own self and life. Marie, who will lift a bedpan, dress a seeping wound, wipe something off the inside of a ravaged mouth with the hum of kindness seeping from her pores.

There is only one Marie.

This is the day Annie will tell her. This is the time, during the twilight, when Annie will ask Marie to stay with her and hold her hand and maybe, maybe lie next to her in the bed because she knows there are not so many twilights left.

"Marie," Annie finally says, firm and bold. "Please now, please, stay with me through the twilight."

There is a rainbow of light at twilight that not everyone notices. It is the signal of glorious color, of lust and life, the last breath of every day that pushes through clouds and storms and even the darkest day. This rainbow is precious because so few see it. Those who do see it rarely talk about it. Annie sees it and so does Marie and now Annie asks and the asking is surrender. A beautiful, kind-of-soft pause where everyone knows but someone finally has to say it.

Marie stays without saying a word. She sits with her feet propped up on the heater just below the ridge of the rise before the long sill. Annie had windows installed wide and very long so that she could see as much and as often as possible. Marie can tell. Anyone can tell.

"Marie?"

"Yes, Annie."

"You've done this before. How many times?"

"I don't count, honey."

"Why not? Really?" Annie is leaning as much as she can, which is not very much anymore, toward the chair where Marie sits with her feet propped on the heater.

"Because each time is important. It's always the first time. The one. I honor every one, Annie. I can't, I just can't keep count."

Annie laughs. It is not her trademark laugh but a slow and

steady line of laughter that would be much, much louder if she were well.

"Marie?"

"Yes, baby?"

"I love it when you call me baby."

Marie turns and smiles. She calls everyone baby. It's like Annie's "sweetheart" or her dad's "honey."

"Oh, baby," Marie asks, "are you okay?"

Marie knows that Annie is not okay. She knows that now is the time for her to come over to Annie's bed and sit on its edge and take Annie's hands in hers and listen. Now is the time to listen.

"I'm scared. Marie, I didn't think of this. This is the one thing that passed me by, that I never embraced, that I could simply not imagine."

Marie puts her hand to her throat. She pauses. She takes a quick glance out of the window and she asks the God she prays to, she asks this God—whom she has always seen as a fine woman with soft hands and a heart that can be molded to love and honor every single person alive—to help her know what to say.

"Annie . . ."

"You don't have to say anything," Annie answers. "I can do this . . ."

Marie stops her by placing her hand across her mouth. She stops her by bending low to show Annie that she means business and that, of course, Marie has something to say. She stops her by moving over an inch on the bed so that their hips are touching through the layers of blankets. She stops her because Annie is now surrendering.

"You can do it," she tells Annie. "We all know that but you don't have to. I am not going to leave you, baby. I am going to be here until the end. It is going to hurt like hell but only for a little while and that's part of what I do, why I am here, what I can do. So stop worrying. I have you covered."

"You have my sweet ass covered?"

"I had your sweet ass covered from the day you called, baby."

Annie smiles. It is a weak smile, but she smiles. She has one more thing to say.

"Marie . . ."

"Yes?"

"Oh, Marie, I'm scared. I'm afraid to say it but I am scared."

Marie says nothing else. Not a word or a whisper or a false movement. She leans down and scoops Annie into her arms and holds her against her chest. Against any rule of comfort and love that may have been written before she invented her job, she holds Annie G. Freeman. She holds her and she feels Annie's heart beating and she promises her with just that gesture that no matter how hard and long the next month and the one after that might be that she will be there and that Annie, alone as she may have to be, is really not alone at all.

"Let it go now," she finally says into Annie's right ear. "Let it go now."

And Annie lets it go. She lets it go as the fingers of the day tug at the night sky, stretching it long and hard until there is nothing else to do but let go. Let go.

When Marie leaves, it is way past dark. Hours past dark and Annie is asleep and she is breathing in a way—labored but firm—that will last her about 3.2 months until that one night when the sky coughs up what seems like two sunsets at the same time and she knows at last that she has had enough.

And yes.

Marie will be there.

12

The proper way to engage a traveling funeral, Katherine decides, is at the airport bar lounge. She has selected the largest bar, the one before Terminal D that fans out into a corral of loose tables where a small funeral procession can gather for its inaugural send-off.

Her lawyer's eye for detail has thought of just about everything. Jill, Laura and Rebecca have maps of the terminal with a black *F* for "funeral" in the exact spot of the Capistrano Bar & Lounge that has a lovely view of airplane wings, parents running after screaming toddlers, two drunk salesmen, a kiosk where you can purchase all the junk you forgot to buy on your vacation for the neighbors who are watching the dog, and a bartendress who looks as if she was born to serve five-dollar glasses of beer, four-dollar shots, and advice for everything from an airplane hangover to how to purchase stocks from the fast-rising stars of the business world.

In the past eight days Katherine has been a flurry of activity. Calls to the pallbearers—check. Arrange time off of work—check. Make sure daughter Sonya can stay at her best friend's house—

check. Explain this trip to friends and boyfriend—check. Tell yourself over and over again this is for Annie and it's totally justified—check. Worry incessantly about what this will do to an already regulated and schedule-driven life that makes no allowances for free time, change or levity—check. Reservations for all the planes and trains and automobiles and hotels and at least two restaurants that probably have never had anyone call and ask if they can make a reservation—check. Pick up a mysterious package from the post office that came from Annie's boys and that is now riding in the bag next to her at the airport rendezvous—check. Worry about what Annie wanted and didn't want for the traveling funeral—double check. Convince her boyfriend Alex that she has not lost her mind—sort of check. Allowed herself to fall into the funeral, enjoy it, honor Annie and their friendship—about to check.

While she is running through the real checklist that she has pulled from her backpack, the phone rings. It's Marie. She's in between patients and trying out her first call with her fine new telephone. Marie will not make the first leg of the journey. Marie will keep trying to find replacements. Marie hopes to make it to Florida. Marie, the grief counselor, has not even been on the traveling funeral and she is already missed.

"Hey, baby," Marie tells Katherine, with one hand on the steering wheel and the other on Annie's cell phone that is painted in bright red. It's nail polish. Little dots here and there. The polish Marie used to put on Annie's nails when they talked and waited for the medicine to grab hold of her veins and whip them into submission. "Is the funeral procession about to begin?"

"Marie. Where are you?"

"Somewhere between Jessie Franklin and Bob Greiese."

Katherine laughs. This is a good start. This is how it's supposed to be, she thinks. Funerals do not have to be long crying jags and people leaning into walls—well, not all of the time anyway.

"It's a bit early. I'm having a Bloody Mary, pacing myself you know, and trying to remember what I have probably already forgotten to do. I'm just a little nervous. What if we all get here and there's a catfight or someone immediately doesn't like someone else?"

Now Marie laughs. Through several phone calls she has come to understand why Annie picked Katherine to be their Girl Scout leader, the head of the class, the funeral director.

"You kill me, pardon the pun. Baby, it's women. You won't ever forget anything because between all of you there will be one of everything in the entire world. And getting along? There will be something. There's always something, whatever it is won't last long. I've heard Annie talk about all of you. I can't imagine too many rough spots."

Marie recounts the time she went on a retreat of hospice workers and all but two were women. "There were almost fifty of us," she explains to Katherine while she maneuvers down a road that was meant to be driven with two hands and not one. "By the end of the weekend even the men were walking around in their bathrobes asking us if they could borrow deodorant. I have this hysterical photo of one of the women blow-drying this one man's hair while a woman standing next to him is putting on lip gloss."

"You're right, Marie," Katherine acknowledges. "Once when all the flights in Atlanta were grounded because of a freak snowstorm, I spent two nights in a hotel room with a woman I had never met before in my life and within twenty minutes we felt like twin sisters and I still talk with her a couple times a year."

"So," Marie admonishes her as she takes a curve way too fast, "don't worry. With this group you could probably regear a jet, turn a hotel inside out and come up with a spare toothbrush, enough Tampax to supply an Army brigade, and coupons for free oil changes. There's bound to be something, there always is. Stop worrying. It will work out."

Katherine cannot stop worrying. What if something happens at work? What if her daughter needs her? What if she discovers something on the trip that is a huge secret that Annie has kept hidden from the rest of the world? What if, in spite of all of the good intentions, one of the women turns out to be a total pain in the ass? What if there is a glitch in Annie's plan?

"Stop it," Marie says, reading her mind. "You've thrown enough guilt into the wind to last a lifetime. Don't forget Annie wanted you to have a good time and toss her ashes into the wind."

"Oh, that."

They discuss the first leg of the trip—the ominous and pending initial flight to New Mexico. The drive after that in an already-too-small Jeep toward Santa Fe. The drive west from beyond the other side of Albuquerque to a place neither of them can remember or pronounce. A hike on a trail that right now might as well be in the Amazon. Marie explains the terminal complications of her next two patients and shares an update on her daughter's spring dance dress ensemble and then they talk about how glad they are to know each other.

"Marie, you are remarkable."

"Wait until I show up and start bossing everyone around. You may never speak to me again."

"Are you kidding? I'm moving in. I hear you have a vacancy coming up what with one of your twenty-one daughters off to college and all," Katherine banters back.

"Baby, this is wonderful news. She cleans the downstairs bathroom."

"On second thought, I'm canceling this cell phone service."

Katherine glances at her watch. Ten minutes until the official funeral, minus the hours of planning and worrying and racing around trying to connect the women in Annie's life.

"Marie, when can you call back? Do you really think you can make it to Florida or New York?"

"Depends on what I find under Jessie's shirt and behind Bob's feeding tube. I'm trying, Katherine. I want to be there."

Katherine has imagined Marie's life beyond their phone calls, the insanity—so she thinks—of all the dying, all the loss, and mingling that with the living she must do with her own family and her own life. It is not the physicalness of her life's work, the bandages and tubes and the obvious evidence of the demise of skin and bones and limbs and organs on the inside that you cannot see but that you can feel melting away centimeter by centimeter. It is not the way, day by day, she sees the skin shrink and the body begin to curl into positions fetal and birthlike. It's not what you might find with the woman who refuses to move for five days in a row. It is not the slow wail that starts as a whisper and then moves through the throat of a patient who can no longer summon words to express the degree of pain, the way it feels as if someone is standing on her shoulders with an ax and hammering it into the center of her chest—at that perfect spot between her two breasts. It is not that. Not at all.

It's the pressure on Marie's heart.

"How in the world do you do it, Marie?" she's already asked her a dozen times in the past week. "How do you keep standing upright?"

Marie knows how she does it and she explains it as if she is reciting a poem, as if she has died herself and seen something unlikely and yet terribly beautiful just as she crosses over the boulder of burden and sacrifice into the river of light and color.

"It is my call to life," she tells Katherine. "It is my gift and to ignore it, to walk away from the rising passion that needs to be emptied out of me with each patient and then refilled with the next, well, that would be my call to dying."

Katherine tries to imagine her work as the assistant district attorney as her own call to life. Mostly for the past several years it has been her ball and chain, the way she pays for the mortgage and a way to get health insurance. The legal lines under the nerves in her head have become dull and stagnant by what she sees as the ridiculous rules of life and justice that often result in no justice at all.

No justice for the woman she represented who was blinded by an ex-husband who kept her locked in the trunk of his car for three days and then bashed in her head with a baseball bat. No justice for at least three men she knows who were in prison for crimes they did not commit. No justice for all the kids she had to send to juvenile jail who maybe just needed a warm meal, someone to say something to them besides "fuck you," and no justice for the helplessness she often feels when there is nothing she can do, absolutely nothing she can do.

When Katherine thinks like this, she realizes that there is a heavy hand on her heart. When she stops to think about her life, closes her eyes and tilts her head back in the terribly uncomfortable office chair that does not accommodate her long legs, the length of her five-foot-ten-inch frame, what she realizes is that she is on automatic pilot and that perhaps it is only the speed of light, the direction of her travel, the air that is holding her up. Perhaps she needs a change.

While Marie hangs up and tends to her dying patients, Katherine waits in the bar for the rest of the funeral procession members to arrive and she tries to imagine what would bring her passion at this point in her life—excluding, of course, the magic hands of her lover Alex and that first sip of wine after a twelve-hour day. What would she do if she erased every mark in her overworked Palm Pilot? If she cleared through the trash of her timetables, what would really be left?

"I'm stumped," she tells herself out loud as a school group on an airport tour parades past her making more noise than the airplane she will board in two hours and she turns just in time to see the bartender balancing something on her head. "What's become of me?" Katherine asks, putting her own head in her hands and laughing. "Airport bars. Waiting for a traveling funeral to begin, kids in jeans trying to see who can make the loudest burp. This is living."

She says this with a smile and with the budding hope that something she has missed, something she may have forgotten, something she desperately wants to see again is just behind her left shoulder.

Katherine thinks of her mother for a moment, how the simple routines of her mother's life were the grounding points that kept her balanced. How her days unfolded in seemingly uneventful moments—waking her children, making breakfast, volunteering in the school library, staying up until Katherine waltzed in at one A.M., which was two hours past curfew, folding towels while she watched the noon news, driving to the city to have lunch with her father twice a week, balancing a checkbook on one fairly modest income. The routine of her mother's life had always mystified Katherine.

Once, when Katherine had been particularly snotty about how other mothers had real jobs and how she would never be caught dead ironing a man's shirts or how her life would have much more meaning than scrubbing floors every Friday morning, her mother sent her to her room and then summoned her out an hour later with something that Katherine still considers remarkable but surely did not at the moment it was happening.

"Sit down," her mother ordered after she led her back to the kitchen table. "Sit down, Katherine, and listen."

Katherine listened. She listened while her mother told her that the kitchen table was her office desk and that everything she saw in the house was her business territory. She listened while her mother rolled out a piece of paper that was her associate's degree from the local business college and she listened when her mother talked about life choices and how everyone's call to service was different.

"My mother was a drunk," Katherine heard her mother say. This was something so distant from what she had been led to believe about her grandmother that she dared not breathe. "I never told you this. I never told you how she locked me in my room and how I saw her crawling across the floor spattered with vomit or how I never once when I was a little girl had a hot meal, or clean clothes to wear, or someone to hold my hand and read me a story at night."

Katherine remembers crying softly during the telling of this story so that she would not make a sound, so that her mother would go on and unwrap the secret that she had kept locked inside of herself for such a long time.

"Once," her mother told her, looking out the window that was above the kitchen sink, "once when I was locked in my room by an outside bolt that she had installed during a brief moment of sobriety, I heard my parents fighting and I stood on top of my dresser. I looked out my bedroom window and I saw our neighbor holding her daughter and twirling her in circles in the side yard. I saw that the little girl had on a new jacket and that her hair was braided and that her mother couldn't stop smiling. Her mother was smiling and I dropped from the dresser into my bed of dirty sheets and I cried for so long that my eyes swelled shut."

Katherine sat still and silent when her mother then produced a resumé. It was handwritten. It was precise. It was a listing of all the skills her mother needed to run a house, to manage a family, to perfect a budget, to steer a ship through the shoals of childhood and adolescence and into the harbor of adulthood. When she was done reading off her list of developed skills—financial manager, career counselor, strategic planner, literary assistant, chef, time-management specialist—Katherine heard something that continued to ring in her ears even at the San Francisco airport as she was embarking on her first-ever traveling funeral.

"I just want to be a good mother," she told Katherine, holding on to both her hands in a way that would have hurt at any other moment. "I want to show you how love can mean everything, how the comforts of a home where you are safe and where kindness matters above everything else are what really is most important. I don't want you to have to worry about how you will look when you go to school, what it will be like when you come home, how your friends will feel to know how you live. I want you to be happy. I love you, Katherine. I love you with a fierceness that is the driving force of everything I do. I am a mother. That is my job and my legacy and whatever you choose to do, whoever you become, make certain that you can put your hand right there, right on your chest and feel the flames of the fire of life's passion that will change direction, surely change direction but will never go out."

Katherine has both hands pressed against her chest, feeling for the fire, when she feels a tap on her arm. When she turns, Dr. Jill Jacobs Matchney is standing at attention by the airport bar table that is decorated in a color that can only be described as something close to what you might see after sampling the delights of a tequila commercial. Dr. Jill has on hiking shorts, a T-shirt that says, *Why eat when you can read?* a baseball hat and a pair of red, high-topped sneakers just like the ones now cradling the ashes of Annie G. Freeman. She is a wispy, thin woman with hair the color of dark sand. Jill looks kind but stern.

"Jill."

"Oh, Katherine."

The women embrace and there is a mixture of laughter and tears for what they are about to begin, for what they already know, for the places they are about to examine. They could also be tears of fear for the uncertainty of this moment and the ones that are coming up right behind it.

"You look fabulous," Katherine tells her, leaning back and holding on to her shoulders. "The sneakers are a nice touch."

"I thought they were mandatory. It's about all Annie ever wore. I can see why she wanted to be flung around the country from inside those things."

Katherine, Jill, Laura, Rebecca and Marie have all talked often during the past week. All five have exchanged phone numbers and bits and pieces of their lives as they scrambled to do Annie's bidding. They have all confessed uncertainty. They have all hinted with a quick laugh or a loud sigh about the difficulties of arranging and rearranging lives for days and days when sometimes rearranging a minute is as impossible as bringing Annie back to life. They have made no pacts or promises beyond the commitment to be part of the traveling funeral and by participating, agreeing without saying a word, to splitting their hearts into pieces to do what you do at funerals—grieve and celebrate.

"This is something," Jill confesses as she sits down and orders her own Bloody Mary. "I've never thought of a funeral as fun before and I sure as heck can use a little fun these days."

"My father used to say that a change is as good as a rest," Katherine responds, leaning in to take a bite out of the pickle that is attached to her own drink that looks more like a garden than a beverage. "You've had a lot of changes in your life this past year and sometimes a distraction is a good way to push through things."

"And what a distraction this is," Jill says, laughing. "I need this distraction. I do."

Katherine leans across the table, touches Jill's hand and says, "Welcome aboard."

There is that second and ten more after it when Jill sizes up Katherine and Katherine sizes up Jill and they wonder how far they will charge into each other's lives. They wonder if one of them will whine too much, if one of them takes a long shower or has to spend too much time in the bathroom in the morning or has some unsolved crisis that will annouce itself during lunch one day and startle onlookers, astound passersby and bewilder the waitstaff.

The women bump glasses just as Laura and Rebecca turn the corner and spot them, glasses in midair, drinking without them at the beginning of Annie's funeral procession.

"Hey!" they both yell, running toward the bar. "No fair."

The introductions almost seem unnecessary because of their connection to Annie, because of what they are about to do, because they are four women whose lives have hugged the various landscapes of life with equal doses of certainty and uncertainty and even though none of them has been on a traveling funeral before they are determined not to be afraid to jump aboard and see where their common love for Annie G. Freeman will take them.

Before the bartender can be summoned for another round of drinks, all four women look down at once to discover that three of them, everyone but Katherine, have on red high-topped tennis shoes.

"Do you have any idea what I went through when I dragged my daughter with me to find these damn shoes?" Rebecca asks. "She actually took photographs of me walking through the house with them on in my bathrobe last night when we got back from the shoe store."

"Katherine, where are your shoes?"

"Fire me," Katherine responds. "I have a pair right here. I just don't think it would be a good idea to put them on yet because they are full of Annie's ashes."

"Annie would definitely be pissed," Jill says. "She'd laugh but she'd still be just a little pissed."

"Well, it's a good thing, then, that I have on tennis shoes even if they aren't red," Katherine replies. "Who wants to see the maps?"

First, before the maps, before the discussion of how this came to be and where it might lead and how they will all cohabit for the next ten days, they all look at each other. They each do it carefully and with the sly idea that no one will see them doing it, but they all catch each other and no one says a word. Already, their secrets could blow apart a gold mine.

And here is what they see:

They see a rainbow of life and in one fast glance they see pieces of themselves scattered all over the faces and hands and feet of the woman next to them. There is the instant look of sorrow. The tired lines of ache and loss on each face because of Annie and because of all the others. Because of the mothers and fathers and sisters and lovers who have died.

They see the way a woman sits to shift the weight from her back. The way one of them crosses her arms and occasionally looks out the window, perhaps wondering if she should have stayed home with the kids and the husband and the job, wondering if the guilt of leaving will overtake her, consume her and obliterate anything positive that may prance into her life. The way another one laughs so spontaneously it is like a breeze off the ocean in the middle of hot July. The way they are all skirting around the issue of how the giddy fun of the moment and the weight of their loss can be balanced. Or should it be balanced? Should they put it out there or dance slowly into what has started, at what will surely be memorable and remarkable and something that they would never have imagined doing or being a part of just four weeks ago?

Four weeks ago.

Four weeks ago when the flowers they each picked and placed in their bedroom windows caught the early morning wind to remind them that Annie loved to do that—just that. Four weeks ago when the ache of her loss was a fresh wound that needed dressing and attending and a glance every few hours to make sure that yes—it really was there and Annie had really died. Four weeks ago when they each held on so tightly to their routines and their men and their children and to other women who called them when they heard because they knew Annie too. Four weeks ago when they were wondering, every single one of them, what Annie might have in store for the world without a funeral, without some wild exhibit of her retreat from this universe to the place she had designed in her head as her next adventure. Four weeks ago when some of them called each other and no one wanted to hang up because at least they had one connection, that voice that they had heard once or twice in the background when they'd called Annie, that woman she also knew and loved, that person, that friend, that female soul who loved Annie G. Freeman maybe, just maybe in the same way that they loved Annie G. Freeman.

They look and they decide for just a few moments on nothing but to be. Each one of them says it with their eyes. Katherine, looking first to Jill and then to Laura and then to Rebecca, and then everyone else taking a turn to say, "Let's do this. Let's have this damn traveling funeral and follow her instructions and spread her fine dusty bones from California to New York and let us do it with the style and grace and the command that Annie used to shape and monitor and guide her life. Let's laugh into the wind and let's cry, too, if that is what we feel like doing. Let's try very hard not to be sorry for what we are doing or to feel guilty for doing it. Annie would hate that," they all say with their eyes. "Annie would want us to move forward and to do this without caution for a while and to remember the important things about her. Not what she did but who she was. Remember who she was and take all the parts of that—the mistakes and the growing and the openness and the courage—take it and throw it back into the universe. Let's do this for Annie."

By the time the first boarding call for the plane to Albuquerque is announced, the four women have all touched each other and recognized details of their common-denominator lives. Wives, mothers, daughters, lovers, friends—they begin to discover each other with small hints of hesitation and with their red shoes tapping quietly in anticipation about what is now starting to happen, and then Laura rises before anyone else to make a short presentation.

"Ladies, just a second, please," Laura says, with her feet spread and her hands on her hips and the flaps of her denim vest whipping back and forth as she shakes her head. "You know how at funerals when you get in your car and drive from the church to the cemetery they put little flags on all the cars so no one can break in and traffic stops and everything?"

They know. They have all been to dozens of funerals. The mere mention of the processions makes fifteen stories rise between them but they bat them down, pressing hard, so they can focus on what Laura is about to say.

"Well, this traveling funeral of Annie's already has the red-shoe thing going on and by the way, Katherine, first stop, you get a pair."

"Yes, ma'am," Katherine responds with a salute.

"So our traveling funeral needs a flag. I have red bandanas, kind of the do-rag of the funeral set, if you care to think of it that way. We can wear them any way we like or keep them in our pockets but it will be our little funeral flag."

The women whistle and clap as Laura hands each one of them a red bandana and then they tie them to necks, heads, arms.

Then they rise from their chairs, past the bottle-balancing bartender and elderly women who point to them and say, "Aren't they cute?" and toward the waiting airplane where they have been booked into first class by Annie G. Freeman for the very first time in every single one of their lives.

13

Laura finalizes her writing idea in midair as she is stretching her legs like she has never before stretched her legs on an airplane flight. She pushes her legs out in front of her to their full length, looks at her own hands to see if she is really alive and flying first-class, and then turns to Jill and realizes at that second that some-one has to take notes.

"What are we thinking?"

Laura looks at her as if a bird has just flown out of her left ear. She's spent so much time alone the past several months that human spontaneity comes at her as if she is being sucked into some kind of wild vortex. The immediate intimacy of spending all these days with women she barely knows, twenty-four hours a day, almost every minute, pretty much constantly, has upset what she has left of her life's balance.

"Laura, are you talking to me?"

"Of course I am talking to you," she says, gesturing with her hands as if she is holding an invisible basketball that she doesn't know what to do with next. "I just got this idea."

"Why does this not surprise me?" Jill asks, placing her hand on top of the imaginary basketball. "But aren't you the one who is supposed to know what we are thinking?"

Laura laughs and drops the ball, resting her hands on her lap and smiling as if she has just won the game.

"It's not quite like that, Jill. I'm intuitive. I can turn it on or off or not talk about it or see things. It's dicey. It depends on where my mind is."

There is a moment of silence. Both women, both fine minds, are thinking.

"Jill, don't worry. I can't get inside of your head if you don't want me to get inside of your head. What the hell is in there anyway?"

Jill laughs and realizes that this may be the first time she has bantered intelligently since the beginning of her retirement and she feels as if she is back leaning against the hall outside of the administration building and immersed in one of her much loved intellectual discussions. She loves Laura's quick wit, the way she talks in circles but jumps back to something remarkable just when you think it may be time for another dose of medication, the way she just says whatever pops into her head as if there was absolutely no way at all to do anything else.

While Laura begins to outline her plan, they can hear Katherine and Rebecca behind them talking nonstop. Their conversation floats across the top of the seats and hovers around them like the very airplane they are riding inside on the way to New Mexico. Jill thinks of it as a tight cocoon, a weaving together of the voices and the bodies and spirits of the women who formed an important lifeline that kept Annie tethered to the reality of where she had been and where she was and where she was headed. Jill wonders if Annie knew how their lives and voices would blend, what they would argue about, who would listen and who always wanted to talk.

"Listen," Laura explains, grabbing the ball again and running with it at full speed. "Annie was a writer and a teacher and she'd love it if we did some kind of funky memorial as part of the traveling funeral that included our own funeral thoughts."

"Funeral thoughts?" Jill asks.

"Funeral thoughts, yes. Like remembering moments and how you felt and what happened because of a funeral, any funeral, a death, something funeral-like. Or not. It could be about Annie or anything."

"Do you remember the first time you thought about death?" Jill asks her, pulling back through the weeds of her life and memories to try to find her own earliest funeral memory.

Laura pauses. She sets her ball down between her legs for a moment and rests her hands on the top of her legs and says the words "My grandma."

The story is a little girl's story. A phone ringing late at night and a father driving off to a hospital.

No one sleeps and then another call so late in the night Laura remembers it as the first time she saw daylight breaking across the sky and shedding streams of light from horizon to tree to house to street in a way she had never imagined or seen it before.

"I had no idea what was going on, something bad, I remember thinking, and when I saw the sun coming up I ran to find my mother and told her something like 'Mom, the sky looks like it's crying light,' and my mother was crying. She was crying and she took me into her lap and held me close like she did, or I imagined she did, when I was a baby and rocked me back and forth for what seemed like a very long time for a little girl."

Later, Laura tells her, when she found out her grandma had died and she was caught up in a swirl of tears and baking and phone calls and people coming and going, her next memory came from the funeral home.

"It smelled horrible," she said. "I remember putting my little white gloves up to my face to smell the perfume I had on them and then sitting on a long, hard bench. I lifted my head and saw that everyone was crying. My aunties, my mom, my Uncle Bart. Some of them were crying hard and loud and I thought that I was supposed to cry too. So I cried, but I had absolutely no idea what any of it meant."

Jill tells Laura it is hard for her to push back through the sixty-plus years of her memories to recall the first time she remembers a death, someone dying. An uncle, maybe, she shares with Laura. Jill holds her thoughts still, afraid just a bit, that even though Laura claims not to be able to get inside of her mind, she really can.

"I can't remember much," she says shrugging her shoulders and turning away to look at the seat back in front of her. "Grief gets worse, you know that, as you get older and you actually have a relationship with someone."

Eventually they waltz their way back from childhood funerals to Laura's great idea. Instead of the usual "I was here at the funeral and no one really cares" book that rests close to the front door of funeral homes, she suggests something more "Annie-like."

"Like what?" Jill asks.

"I was thinking that we'd create a kind of roving funeral book. Like right now I would write down whatever I am thinking about and then write something that Annie would have thought or felt or a memory of her that might be passing through my mind at the same time."

Jill thinks for a second and then says, "I like it. She'd like it too."

"So let's do it," Laura says, making believe she has dropped her invisible ball and is now writing with a fine, soft pen. "Tell the girls."

Jill tells Rebecca and Katherine, who agree it's a grand idea and they also think it's a grand idea to have Laura write the first installment of the funeral booklet. Rebecca throws a notebook over the top of the seat and a pen and when Laura opens up the book, she sees *Annie Freeman—Born to Live* already etched at the top of the page. Laura laughs and sends her unopened pack of pretzels,

now considered a light meal in the airplane world, over her shoulder and announces that she is about to make the first entry.

And then she does.

LAURA THOUGHT: *I am thinking now of Annie and then the
next thought is of my blossoming friendships with these other
women who also loved Annie and then I am thinking why didn't
anyone think about something like this sooner? Why can't we
have a funeral the way we want to have a funeral? Why don't we
have a funeral to celebrate the way we lived? Tradition be
damned. The sadness of the loss needs to be honored and embraced, but for now I want to focus on celebrating. I sure as hell
need to celebrate—and what better way to do it than with the
women Annie loved the most?*

ANNIE THOUGHT: *Why aren't they singing out loud? Why hasn't
someone ordered another Bloody Mary? Why haven't they recruited three more members of the funeral procession? Why are
they not dancing in the aisles? Live large, ladies, live large.*

When she finished, Laura passed the notebook over to Jill. Jill
laughed, looked over at Laura, grabbed the pen, and then began
writing her own first installment. The book made the rounds and
came back to Laura, who thus became the official keeper of the funeral booklet.

"Whenever you want it, holler," she hollered herself. "And no
fair cheating!"

The airplane moved through a small storm, bucked and swayed
just a bit and then glided into a safe spot, a warm stream of air that
took the women from the edge of their real lives and into the heart
of Annie's traveling funeral. When they had been into the trip almost two hours, everyone switched places. The noise from their
intimate conversations was a slow rumble itself that quickly became
the foundation for the funeral—kind, open, wide and honest.

They talked mostly about time during their first long conversation. Time for themselves, time away, time that might have to be made up later if such a thing were possible. They reached in and felt around the edges of their new friendships, or what they hoped would be friendships, and they all marveled out loud at the way age sets you free instead of ties you down. Age, Jill said, relaxes you with the ease of the past, for when something like this happens, it allows you to dip back and to recall a time when you have already done this—mixed your life with someone who wasn't a stranger but who was close to it. Age, Katherine said, gives you a cushion of knowledge, of knowing how grief will ride its hands along your spine, how something new does not have to be fearful, how whatever it is that the person you are sitting next to does that drives you a little batty cannot be as bad as that one time when something with someone else was really bad.

They promised each other to try not to worry, to try and lean into the traveling funeral in a way that would be honest, not too offensive. To try and let go as much as womanly possible in the midst of a traveling funeral when the world was hovering behind them waiting, always waiting, for each of them to return.

The Albuquerque airport was quiet at noon on a Monday. Business travelers had already landed and were by now halfway through their morning meetings, vacationers were already sipping beer at the hotel swimming pools, and the airport personnel were busy trying to look busy. When the four women paraded through the airport in their red tennis shoes and bandanas, they looked as if they were headed toward a funky Santa Fe women's retreat and they blended in with the New Mexico crowd as if they knew exactly where they were going and what they were doing.

Annie had ordered them a red Jeep Cherokee. Limited luggage space, a sunroof, room for four—barely—and a spot to put Marie's cell phone right between the passenger and driver and Marie, too, in case she happened to show up. It did not take them long to throw their luggage into the Jeep—one bag each—and drive out into a new landscape, a stark hunk of desert that made them all take a deep breath and exclaim, "Oh my God, this is beautiful."

And it was beautiful, especially as they drove past the sprawling city of Albuquerque, where time and people had taken up one section of bare earth and then another and another, transforming it into a mass of clay roofs and patches of green and gated communities to protect what they thought was their private piece of serenity.

"I haven't been here for like twenty years," said Katherine. "I can't believe how much this city has grown and reached outside to cover all these hills and mesas and every piece of flat land up to the river, over it and to the edge of the mountains."

"Does anyone know when Annie was here? Does anyone know what happened to her here?" Rebecca asked in response.

"Not me. I saw old photographs in her house of some desert scene, someone in the background, but I don't remember ever hearing her talk about Santa Fe or New Mexico or anything about this part of the world," Jill said. "She did keep a red rock on her desk. Sometimes when I knew she'd had a particularly tough day or student, she'd pick up that rock and hold it in her hand, rub it between her fingers, sometimes put it to her lips. It's a clue. Maybe it's a clue."

"Well," Katherine responded, "here's something."

She's holding up a cassette tape. It is black and has red writing on the front.

"What is that?" asks Laura.

"I have no idea. It was part of a package that was delivered from her son Nick last week. It was delivered with instructions that I not open it until the night before the trip and what was inside was a tape for each step of the journey."

"What the shit," Rebecca says, using the word "shit" like someone else would use the word "heck." "Was there anything else in the package?"

"No," Katherine says, making a wide turn into the freeway that will take them from Albuquerque, past miles of row houses that look as if they all came out of the same cereal box and sprawling neighborhoods pointed toward Santa Fe. "But I wouldn't be surprised if other packages show up along the way. Remember she has everything planned and picked out. Which is exactly what I intend to do for my own funeral the second we get back."

Laura laughs before Katherine can put in the tape. It is infectious, a wild virus that latches onto each one of them and refuses to let go and so they all laugh, not certain why, but the sound of gorgeous laughter distracts them from the tape for just a second.

"What," Jill finally asks, "are you laughing about?"

"I'll have to cancel my life and spend all my time going on these goddamned traveling funerals. I can see it now. A whole cottage industry springing up for travel agents and writers and all those people in Hawaii who plan those weddings that everyone thinks are so special but are really just like every other wedding in the whole world. It will be a whole new career opportunity for someone."

"The tape, for crying out loud," Jill shouts above the new laughter. "Put in the damn tape."

Katherine obeys and slips in the tape quickly even though they are still laughing. She keeps her fingers on the edge of it, as if she were holding on to the fingers of her daughter who is leaving for the very first day of school. Katherine holds on and keeps her fingertips on the dashboard as they hear Annie Freeman's voice and they drive toward Santa Fe on the first leg of her fabulous traveling funeral.

At first no one can move or speak and Katherine considers pulling off to the side of the freeway so she can focus on every word, every syllable, every sound from the voice of her dead friend that she hears coming from inside the radio.

"Shit," Rebecca finally says as Annie Freeman welcomes them to her funeral.

Hey. Did you all make it? I bet you did. I know Marie is probably holding someone's hand right now but I hope she made it, but I know I can count on you all to have the kind of funeral for me that I want to have. This came to me fast. I would have had my own damn traveling funeral but there wasn't time. I needed my strength to just breathe and so I am counting on you, counting on all five of you.

My boys helped me plan all of this. It was their penance, I told them, for all the times they were little shitheads when they were growing up. Everything should be in order and there are enough tapes in here for every stop to help you figure out what happened and what I need to have happen now—this one last time.

And women: Please do not be too morose. That would piss me off. I know it must be weird to hear my voice now, to have me lecture you one last time, but think of this as many things and one of them should be to have a damn good time and to get to know the women I loved, the women who you may also come to love during this interesting assignment. And for godsakes try and get along. Katherine, don't be too damn bossy. Jill, get on with it and don't sulk. Laura, it's way beyond time to get going and move—and I mean really move on. Rebecca, I'm sorry, honey, about all the loss and death but you can do it, you can. Marie, if you are there, it's okay, baby, as you would say, to stop and give the baton to someone else once in a while.

Annie does not talk long during the first tape but every second of her short speech leaves each one of the women speechless.

Katherine manages to keep the car on the road until they get to the part about why they are in New Mexico, and then she does pull off the freeway, turns into a gas station parking lot, and turns up the volume. No one asks her why.

After I tried to kill myself when I was in high school, after Katherine saved me, or gave me the chance to save myself, after I had reached into the black pit of a place that was a breath away from death, my parents sent me to a ranch close to where you are headed. It was a residential treatment program for adolescents in a secluded portion of the desert—like there isn't a secluded portion of the desert—and that is where I first chose to live, to really, sincerely live as wonderfully and wildly and boldly as possible for the rest of my life. Too bad the rest of my life was so damn short but I did live it and each one of you helped me to do that.

Annie briefly describes the place where she stayed and the people who flowed into her world all those years ago to show her a new way to think and who remained a vital part of who she was about to become.

"Did anyone know this?" Jill asks, leaning forward from her position behind Laura in the passenger seat.

"She went away," Katherine answers. "I knew that much because when I went to find her a week after she tried to kill herself her mother told me that she was getting help and that she would contact me when she was ready to come back. I just assumed 'come back' meant from the psych unit of the hospital, and when we talked about it later, a long time later, it never came up. Once she decided to live, as you all know, she moved quite rapidly."

"She apparently never forgot—how could you?" Laura asks without expecting an answer.

"Maybe none of us knew her as much as we thought we knew her," Jill, the professor, adds quietly. "Maybe she wants us to put all of our knowledge of her together and form this whole new Annie. Maybe it's like a puzzle."

That's when Rebecca passes the funeral book over to Jill and suggests that as they get closer to their first drop-off zone they forge ahead with another journal entry. Jill would rather throw the book out the window. She'd rather sit on it or pass it to Laura, but she also understands the importance of the written word, of getting it down, of leaving something for whoever might need to discover the intimacy and unexpected adventure that can be found in a traveling funeral or so she hopes.

She writes with her eyes occasionally moving toward the fast-moving landscape and the edge of her heart on the voice she just heard coming from the tape.

JILL THOUGHT: *How strange to hear your voice. How strange to imagine you alive again, riding in the front seat, making us stop at every landmark, roadside curio shop or for every broken-down old pickup that has pulled over to wait for spare parts. I am trying hard to paw through my own memories to see if I can find any hint of this or of what might have happened here to give you back the flame of your own life. And just now I am thinking about how if someone would have told me a month ago that I would be driving through the New Mexico desert with a group of strangers on a funeral I would have had them enrolled at the same place where we are now headed. Guilty too. Guilty, because in the midst of all this remembering you and missing you, I am falling into this trip and these women . . .*

ANNIE THOUGHT: *How many years ago would it have been? Thirty-eight? Who was I back then? Scared. Tentative about life. Terrified. Uncertain. When I drove down this same highway, my hands were in my lap, my heart flinging itself from one side of my chest to the other in anticipation of something that seemed beyond anything that I might be capable of handling. Now, these women, each one of them traveling into a section of the desert that called to me, changed me, made me as whole as possible—what are they thinking? What will this trip do to them, for them?*

*And I hope to hell they lighten up when they put in the tapes, be-
cause this is not all that serious. I did the hard part. I was the one
who died.*

The funeral book makes the rounds and then miles and miles
north of Albuquerque when the Jeep has grown silent and its four
passengers have lapsed into their own private memories of discussions with Annie about suicide and her programs and the definite
joys of moving forward, it is Laura who finally brings up the question that has ridden shotgun with each one of them since they arrived in New Mexico.

"How do we do this?"

"What part of the doing do you mean?" Katherine asks.

"The actual funeral part. I know we are headed to some small
roadside hotel but when do you actually want to spread her ashes?
Do we do it at sunset? Do we do it at sunrise? Should we do a
drive-by? Do we need to plan a ceremony?"

These questions leave everyone with their mouths hanging
open because no one is certain. No one knows what should happen next, which is what Laura decides is the best way to deal with
their uncertainty.

"Annie was the queen of spontaneity," she says. "Sure, she was
organized and directed, but how many times did she call one of us
from someplace like Spain or Canada to say that she 'just had this
idea' and then took off running?"

"She did it a lot but this is a funeral, for crying out loud,"
Rebecca objects. "I'm kind of a free spirit myself but maybe we
should put a little more thought into this."

The pallbearers banter then. It seems, so they decide, that Annie
did most of the necessary planning and that their portion of the
project should be whatever moves them at the moment—as long
as the ashes get flung or spread or dropped where Annie wanted
them to end up or in whichever direction the wind blows. As long
as there is not too much arguing.

By the time they pull off of Highway 44 and follow Annie's map down a winding road past two tiny towns and east toward the Bandelier National Monument signs, they are not only into the heart of New Mexico but realizing fast that the first ceremony will have to wait until morning.

"It looks like we have less than two hours of daylight left," Jill says as they see the first sign for the Ranchero Skyline Inn and Restaurant. "By the time we get there, unload, and eat—if the joint is even open—it will be dark."

"See how things work out," Laura tells them. "Apparently we are supposed to get up and do our funeral business in the morning."

"You could have saved us a lot of time by getting out your magic cards and just telling us this two hours ago," Katherine chides as they come over a rise and see their inn, a glorious sprawling set of buildings perched on top of a small plateau. There are just a handful of cars and four trucks spread out in the parking lot.

Annie has reserved them the most remote cabin. It is in its own world, several blocks from the restaurant, at the end of a thin dirt road that loops around piles of boulders. It is surrounded by low patches of sagebrush and a few hearty-looking scrub pine trees.

"It's beautiful," Rebecca says for each one of them.

Without saying another word, Katherine, Rebecca, Laura and Jill walk around the side of their cabin and move past their parking spot and walk in a line, their funeral procession, and follow a path that takes them to the very tip of a mesa that offers a view of a sweeping valley between two embracing mountains, a long and winding dry riverbed and a sun that is turning the sky the color of a California orange.

"Oh my gawd," Laura moans. "This is breathtaking. I've never seen anything like it."

"The Southwest is amazing," Jill tells them, standing with her foot on a rock and turning to face her friends. "The light here, it must make artists weep. This is Georgia O'Keeffe country. She lived not so far from here. I think she almost went insane from the colors, the light, everything that you are seeing right now."

"Look," Katherine says, pointing down the trail and toward another mesa. "Is that a bench way over there or some kind of sign or something?"

They all squint into the setting sun, leaning like flowers toward the spot on the horizon that Katherine has discovered. They all see it and in an instant they all know. It is just a speck, so small it could be a mile or more away, but it is out there and it has a view and something beyond the view is calling them to go there.

"That's where we'll go in the morning," Katherine decides. "That's where we must go."

14

By dawn the light streaming through the cabin window has illu-
minated Annie's red tennis shoes and it looks as if they are on fire.
Katherine has placed them on the window ledge facing toward the
canyons and valleys and mesas that stretch in front of their cabin
in endless ribbons of colors and shadows.

Jill is the first one awake and she has the coffee going. She has
one foot up on the coffee table and has leaned so far over the edge
of the chair a whisper could make her tip over but she is mesmerized by the unfolding of morning in the desert and does not want
to miss one blink of a cloud or moving shadow. Her mind is also
filled with thoughts of Annie and what is about to happen and
how she will feel when it is time to spread her dearest friend's ashes
into the desert dirt that looks as if it whips and blows constantly.

Soon, Rebecca, Katherine and Laura are awakened by the ringing of Marie's cell phone. Jill grabs it first and Marie, already posted
outside of her first client's house, wants to know where they are
and what they are about to do.

"I'm watching the sunrise, Marie, oh, Marie, have you ever been to the desert?" Jill asks, scooting back into her chair and stretching both legs out. "It's amazing, absolutely amazing."

Marie is standing behind her car, her knees pressed against the bumper and her eyes on the still-dark sky over Northern California. She wants to be there. There is a mild wind blowing cool air off the top of the hills directly outside of Willard Mantavani's backyard. Willard, who even in his dying moments asks Marie to wheel him outside so he can smoke a cigarette during this early time of the day and watch the clouds rumble east.

Marie, always the caretaker, thinks of Willard first and of his lungs with its holes the size of eraser heads and all the hundreds and hundreds of cigars and cigarettes he must have smoked to turn the inside of his body black and dark as the death that is slowly climbing its way toward the rest of his body. She lets him smoke. He loves to smoke and that is all he has left now—the smoke and the morning sky that he watches as if he were monitoring a parade, breathing through his mouth in between puffs and holding on to Marie's hand as if she were his mother.

"Tell me," she says to Katherine. "Let me close my eyes and tell me what it looks like, please. I want to think about it this morning as I take care of Willard."

It is Jill who tells her as the other women rotate to the shower and grope for coffee cups. She hears a bit of an argument between Rebecca and Katherine about the order of the use of the bathroom and smiles. She steps outside the door, closes it, and lets the morning air touch her face and hands and arms, and then she tells Marie about the wind shifting off the mesas and the way the light bounces but never seems to stop as it pushes from one landmark to another. She tells Marie that she has never seen anything like this and she could understand, standing in this one spot, how a vision like this could make you want to alter your whole life. Jill tells Marie about the countless hues of reds and oranges and how suddenly a swatch of green will appear and then vanish into a small shadow. She tells Marie that in New Mexico the sky is so huge that it's blinding and the stars look like gigantic buildings.

Marie listens and she thinks she can see exactly where Jill is standing. She bows her head, and she sees.

"Tell me about the cabin and everything, tell me everything," she begs.

Jill tells her and Marie puts it all inside of her mind. The winding road, the creaky narrow beds, the scrubbed floors, the cowboy decorations and the six-pack of beer in the small refrigerator. She tells her about the few petty arguments, discussions really, and about how everyone is staking out their territory and trying not to be terrified about what they are doing. "Oh," Marie sighs when she is certain she has it all. "It sounds challenging and lovely all at the same time."

Jill laughs and tells Marie how they have not planned a thing. She says that they are letting it happen because that's what they have decided Annie G. Freeman would have wanted.

"In the words of our Rebecca, I would have to say 'No shit,' " Marie tells Jill, laughing and then turning to see that Willard has spied her and is pointing at the California sky with great determination. "Willard needs me now," Marie tells her. "I am going to have to go and I won't be able to call back for a while."

"Is there something you want me to say?"

Marie stumbles around inside of her heart for a moment. She thinks about the bright red shoes and about the traveling funeral and of everything she has already said to Annie. She isn't sure what she would say if she was standing on the mesa, if she was actually there, if she was a physical part of the funeral. She's trying hard to make it to Florida. The other women know that but not being there is surely not the same.

"Listen, Jill . . ."

"It's okay, Marie, she would have known. She did know."

"I'll say something from here. But can you do one thing for me?"

"Name it. Anything."

"Bring me a rock or a small branch of sagebrush or something like that from each stop until I get there. Can you do that? It's silly, but can you do it?"

"It's not silly and of course I can do it."

Nothing will ever be silly again, Jill realizes as she goes back inside to round up the rest of the funeral procession.

The first Annie G. Freeman traveling funeral procession starts inside the cabin when Jill picks up the shoes and tucks them back into their cardboard shoebox home.

Before they leave, everyone straps on their red high-tops, including Katherine, who picked up a pair at the very last mall at the edge of what at the time seemed like nowhere, on the way to the cabin. Their red handkerchiefs are wrapped around heads, arms and necks.

"Ready, funeral warriors?' Katherine asks as she turns to face Jill, Rebecca and Laura.

"One second," Rebecca begs. "Let me do my entry. It's driving me nuts. I just want to get it out of my head and onto the paper."

The women wait outside while Rebecca sits at the small table near the refrigerator and writes as quickly as possible.

REBECCA THOUGHT: *If there was ever a time to say "shit," this is the moment. We are about to throw your ashes off a cliff, throw your brittle bones to the wind, and I am a bundle of remembering, remorse, sadness, happiness and expectations. Last night when we all stayed up, drinking the beer and talking about you, it reminded me of summer camp, a great adventure, and that is what I am thinking about now as my new friends pause out in the morning sun and wait for me to carry my share of a casket that does not exist.*

ANNIE THOUGHT: *I was scared, too. Fourteen years old, just out of the hospital, still thinking about death. So alone. A kid from the Midwest startled by the sudden brilliance of the Southwest. Do they see what I saw? Do they know how important this place was to me? Will they laugh as well as cry? They had better. Go, Rebecca. They are waiting.*

The women, unaccustomed to the fast and furious heat of the desert, quickly begin leaving a trail of clothes as they march in line, down the dusty trail they imagined a young Annie treading years and years ago.

They are silent, their eyes scanning the horizon and watching as the sun gets higher and then hotter every single second.

Katherine stops every few minutes to shift the box from one hand to the other and then she announces that it would be good if they all took turns carrying the shoes to the edge of the cliff.

In the desert, they quickly realize, one mile is really probably two, and they walk for a long time on a path that snakes its way past clumps of bushes, rock outcroppings, and enough sagebrush to make Martha Stewart happy the rest of her life.

"This is one long-ass trail," Laura says about halfway through the trek. "I hope my shoes hold up."

They all laugh and they walk on, trudging through their own memories and occasionally thinking that if they have to go to a "regular" funeral ever again they will never be able to sit still through it.

When they come to the cliff edge, the trail passes off to the left and they can see it winding for what they assume, now that they have walked two miles, is about another three thousand miles right to the edge of a blue range of mountains that are off to the west and most likely in East India.

"Jeezus," Katherine announces. "You could walk forever out here."

"Yes, you could. I suppose some people have," Jill says. "I bet there are bones all over this desert."

"Knock it off," Rebecca shouts from her position at the end of the funeral procession. "We are in church, for crying out loud."

This gets everyone thinking for a second and in an unrehearsed ballet they all raise their heads about an inch higher and look around.

"This is what a real church should look like," Laura announces. "Open, beautiful, a simple yet absolutely magnificent place for your soul to air itself out—or whatever it is you care to air out."

"You sound like Annie for the good goddess," Katherine shouts back. "You know how she felt about organized religion."

"Really," Laura adds earnestly. "Some of the most glorious and moving experiences I ever had were in places that had to be created by something or someone who had a power that I have yet to comprehend."

"Get ready for one more," they each say silently as Katherine leads them off the path and onto a ledge that would have room for only tiny Marie if she had been with them.

"What do you think?" Katherine asks.

"Perfect," Jill and Rebecca say at the same time.

The women wait silently for just a second and then Laura talks first. She thinks they should honor the girl/woman who was Annie when she stood right in this same spot, or close to it, all those years ago when she was deciding who she was and what she wanted to do with the person she would be.

"Clearly, Annie came here and decided to live, to let go of whatever it was that was holding her in place, or trying desperately to drag her to a place that was darker than anything I have ever known," Laura explains, speaking not just to her friends but to the world of spirits and ancient voices she imagines still inhabit the world where she now stands.

Katherine talks next. She recounts the month when Annie returned and how it was clear something had happened because it seemed as if even the color of Annie's eyes had changed.

"They were light, she was light," Katherine remembers out loud.

"She had lost a great deal of weight, her hair was streaked with strands of blonde that I now know came from this wild sun, but she was also peaceful, so peaceful."

They all imagine Annie as a teenager who had just tried to take her own life. Annie standing on the very edge of the world and still having the capacity to make that choice, to dip backwards and not fall forward, to slip away and never come back, to hike to the far end of the trail and mingle her bones with the bones of everyone else who had done the same thing.

"The view would have blown her away," Rebecca said. "She would have dropped to one knee, then to the other, and she would have been breathless for a while."

Something had happened to Annie then. Maybe, they all imagine, maybe an eagle—a bird of greatness and hope—flew from a hidden nest and whispered in her ear. Maybe one of those magical desert rainbows paused in front of the closest mountain and Annie thought she could touch it, or maybe she simply saw that the world was filled with endless choices, endless places, endless opportunities.

"She cried," Katherine states as if she is talking about herself. "She would have cried quietly after she made the decision. It would have been like a bath, a cleansing moment, and after that she would have had a burst of energy that launched her back into my life and toward each one of you."

They are all silent then as they imagine Annie G. Freeman in 1968 with her tattered jeans, long dishwater-blonde hair and the somewhat ratty green sweatshirt that she wore constantly. Hiking boots, the hint of musk on her neck and the weight of the world on her shoulders.

When the moment passes, Jill asks if they think she really might have been at this same spot.

"Shit, yes," Rebecca says. "She knew that we would follow her scent. She stood right here. And something wonderful happened here, just like something wonderful is happening to us now."

"Katherine." Jill takes a small step forward because to take a larger one would send her off the cliff. "This is your spot too. This is where you played big in her life and I think you should send her off here. Can you?"

"Can I?" Katherine asks herself softly but still out loud. "Can I?"

Before she does anything, Katherine asks each woman to touch the shoes, "Just like they do in church before they take the casket away," she explains to them and as they do this Jill bends down to pick up a long white stone for Marie. They touch the red tennis shoes and they each have a thought of Annie, young, beautiful, alive—*alive*.

Katherine unlaces the red shoes and unties the tidy plastic bag full of ashes that rests inside one. Jill tips the shoe slightly so that the ashes flow into the palm of Katherine's right hand, ashes as soft as the desert air. Without asking or saying a word, each one of the women dips her fingers into the ashes, takes a little, and then as Katherine turns and throws her hands into the soft morning wind, the women, Annie's friends, her female family, do the exact same thing.

The ashes move fast. They dip for just a second and then a gust of wind, the breath of the very desert itself, takes them and scatters them into every direction.

"Yee-ha," Katherine shouts.

Jill raises her hands and smiles. Laura weeps quietly. Rebecca drops to one knee and simply looks into the sun. Marie, just then, at that exact moment, turns her head toward the window in the middle of Willard's twenty-eighth cough and blows a long kiss toward New Mexico.

15

The six cowboys, two trailer-park refugees, a seventy-eight-year-old bartender named Buck, and Melissa, the nineteen-year-old waitress from Bernahillo, who is saving every tip so she can move to Denver or some other large city that has green grass and trees to block her view, have never quite seen anything like these women with their red tennis shoes, red bandanas, sunburned noses and tear-streaked faces.

"You at the far cabin?" Buck asks them as they literally fall into the Ranchero Grill.

This after a day spent spreading ashes, hiking more than six hot miles, debates on staying near Albuquerque or bunking one more night at the cabin before an early flight, several phone calls from Marie, numerous entries in the funeral log, a terrific argument between Katherine and Laura about directions, Rebecca hauling out her hidden bottle of vodka just after two P.M., and more than a few hilarious stories about other trips, Annie's life and the interesting set of circumstances that brought them to a bar that looked from the outside as if it had been dragged to New Mexico behind a stagecoach in 1895.

"Let's corral a table," Laura says, shaking hands with Buck and introducing herself as she passes him near the cigarette machine. "The cabin is almost as lovely as the view."

Melissa brings them a round of beers, four menus and word from Jake Hasdorf, the cowboy at the edge of the bar, that he is sending over a round of whiskey shots because they looked as if they need it.

"What?" Jill asks, looking from left to right as if she has never heard of such a thing.

"The guy in the brown felt hat, red shirt, jeans, at the bar is buying you each a shot of whiskey."

Melissa says this slowly as if she is talking in a foreign language, then she watches Jill patiently to make certain that she understands what a free shot of whiskey might entail.

"He is?"

"Yes, ma'am, he is."

Jill looks as if someone has slapped her. Katherine starts laughing because she realizes that the often isolated university world that has cradled Jill Matchney for most of her life most likely did not include traveling funerals, vodka tonics after lunch, and whiskey shots from cowboys before the buffalo burgers were even served.

"What's so funny?" Jill asked her.

"The look on your face," Katherine answers, reaching over to put her hand around Jill's wrist. "Quick—tell me what you were doing a year ago right at this very moment?"

Jill gets it and as the shots make their way toward the table she stands to greet Melissa, slides the whiskey in front of her friends, and throws back the first one before anyone can move.

"That was for Annie."

The women instantly launch into a wild discussion about other nights in bars that included Annie. The cowboys and the husband and wife from the trailer park watch them as if all four of them have tuned into a movie that has them mesmerized. Melissa wants to sit down and join them. The waitress can't stay away from them.

"Where are you from?" she asks them, anxious to hear of anything besides what she considers to be the end of the earth where she has spent the first two decades of her life.

"California and Chicago," Laura tells her. "Big places, lots of people."

"Not like this." Melissa looks past them and out onto a stretch of dark desert that makes her want to vomit. "I can't wait to leave."

"It's a big world and this is a lovely part of it too, you know. Well, you don't know but you will someday."

"You sound like my mother," Melissa says, leaning from the waist and putting both hands on the table. "Why did you guys come here?"

The question stops everyone. Do they tell her? Do they look into this young woman's eyes and just say it? Do they say, "We came to spread our best friend's ashes off the edge of the cliff"? Do they tell her they are a traveling funeral? Will she run screaming from the room? Will they have to go someplace else to get more beer? Will the revelations change this woman's life so that she never leaves home and ends up waitressing until her legs give out?

"Well," Jill finally says, "it's kind of complicated."

"Complicated?" Melissa repeats, finally pulling up a chair and forgetting that the women have not even ordered.

"Let me ask you a question before I answer that," Jill continues. "Okay?"

"Sure," Melissa says, elbows on the table, hands on her chin, looking at Jill as if she is about to hear the greatest bedtime story of her life. "Ask away. You are the only eating customers in here and the customers always get what they want."

Jill has this idea. She's thinking about the history of a place, how the people in that place are the keepers of the past. She knows this girl has a story. Melissa is part of this arid desert place and she always will be, no matter where she ends up, and she knows something. Even if it's one tiny thing, one slice of information, this young woman knows *something*.

"Is your family from this area?"

Melissa laughs. She immediately launches into an oral recitation of her family's past and Jill knows even before the story ends that they are all about to learn something that has to do with Annie. Melissa's ancestors founded one tiny community after another along this entire section of New Mexico. Land-rich and money-poor, they struggle to this day, Melissa tells them, to do things like help put a daughter through college, buy a new pickup truck, or move beyond the limits of a land that has captured their hearts.

Jill is patient but her foot is tapping under the table. She wonders if anyone has ever bothered to ask Melissa what she wants or thinks or cares about. Melissa needs to talk. The older women squirm and finger their tiny shot glasses, as the waitress unloads.

"I understand why they love this land but my heart isn't here, it never has been," she tells them softly. "When I was a little girl my father took me with him when he drove and drove and drove through all these canyons and I sat in the back reading, all the time I was reading. I didn't care about the blooming sagebrush or the way the damn sun rose over the far mountain."

The women smile, put down their glasses, and listen. All mothers but Jill, who was a mother to hundreds of college girls and boys, they see the strain of yearning in Melissa's face, in the way she bends toward the window, how she rushed toward them, their lives, their purpose in what she perceives as her tiny corner of the world.

And then there is her age.

Annie was a teenager when she stood at the edge of the canyon just blocks beyond this restaurant's windows. Melissa is nineteen. Suddenly this common denominator grabs all of them and they wait for Jill to do whatever it is that has come into her head and heart.

Jill is kind but it is a struggle for her to be still while Melissa talks. She can barely sit quietly with her questions rubbing against the bad nerve on her left leg but she waits and then she asks a question she knows someone must have asked Annie—maybe in this same restaurant, maybe at this same hour, maybe, maybe, maybe.

"What do you want, Melissa?"

Melissa rises off her chair, pushes her hands against the edge of the table as if she is fending off a stampede, and speaks slowly and very clearly.

"My own life," she says, looking directly at Jill. "Not their life or my grandma's life or whatever someone else has planned for me. A life of books, words, learning. A life that shows me more than one way to look at things. All the horizons, hundreds of them, not just this same one over and over again. Choices."

She hesitates for a moment and then begins again slowly as if she has memorized what she is going to say and is afraid she will miss a word.

"Mostly, mostly," she says, closing her eyes for a moment and then opening them again, "I want just a chance to see who I am beyond the invisible fence-line that has been constructed around the horizon they all seem to think is endless and free."

Melissa steps away from the table then as she remembers that she is a waitress and should probably not be splitting herself in two like she has just done. But Laura gently grabs her wrist and keeps her in place.

"Wait," she tells Melissa. "The saying that customers are always right is a crock of shit but wait. We'll order eventually. You need to stay here for just a little while."

Katherine looks over at Buck asking him with her eyes if it's okay for Melissa to sit for a while, before they order, before she gets them another drink, and he smiles, gives her the thumbs-up, and starts pouring more beer, including one for Melissa who has been drinking beer since she was a baby.

"Hey," Rebecca says. "It makes sense to me. You should leave.

Once you find out who you are, you can always come back. Some people never know that. Then again, some of us are still trying to find out who we are. It's pretty much a daily event in my life."

Something has clicked into place inside of Jill. It's like a slipped gear that has suddenly grabbed hold of its correct position and helps the entire machine leap back into motion. Jill knows that Melissa needs to hear that she is not alone and that hundreds and thousands of other young women in places that are not even half this remote know and feel the same things but Jill cannot hold back any longer. She is on the edge of something that she knows must be there and she has to see if it really exists.

"Melissa . . . ? Before we get into this any more I have to ask you something."

"What?"

"Your family has been here forever, right?"

"Before forever. Why?"

"Was there ever a treatment center around here? A place where people from other places sent their kids? Or came themselves to heal or see the light or save their dreary and lost souls?"

Melissa laughs. The soft growl from her throat is sweet and kind. When she finishes she sits up again and moves her eyes from Laura to Rebecca to Katherine and then to Jill.

"It's been a while," she says. "I should have asked right away but you all threw me off. Maybe it's the drinking or your openness. It all threw me off. No one has asked for a while."

"Tell us, please," Rebecca urges, leaning across the table to touch Melissa's arm just as Buck brings over a round of beers and sets one down in front of Melissa with a wink.

"He's my great-uncle," she tells them. "Around here we are all related. He's sweet. I love him."

"Was there a center or something around here?" Jill presses.

"The place was called Desert Dreams."

"The place?"

Melissa tells them as she drinks her beer and realizes that her local knowledge is a golden commodity with these women. A commodity that she clearly sees as a sudden and fun gift exchange. She tells them. She tells them because even with her rural and wide-open heart she senses that they must have kind hearts and that there is something sad that has brought them to her desert and they might help her. They might help her find her own non-desert dream. Everyone, she thinks, is looking for something. That's one thing she has learned from her nineteen years. The one thing she knows for certain beyond knowing that she has to leave the very place where she is now sitting. These women with their eager eyes and soft smiles want an exchange of information, kind of a knowledge barter, Melissa thinks, and Melissa, who has a soft smile and a young but equally kind heart, cannot stop herself. Even without the exchange, Melissa, Melissa from Bernahillo, New Mexico, would do it anyway because her southwestern life is rooted in giving and she knows another true heart when she sees one or four of them.

She tells them about a place founded in the late sixties by psychologists from California who thought that adolescents needed to remove themselves from a world that was often nasty and cruel. A world where children were groomed to be and think and act like all the other children and where someone like Annie G. Freeman would be paralyzed.

"My mom worked there," Melissa tells them, closing her eyes to help her remember a story, any story, the dozens of stories her mother recounted time and time again.

Kids from everywhere. Many of them not much younger than Melissa's mother. Wild. Savage almost. Lonely and lost souls who gathered in a place that had the power, the potential to heal them if they came to the ledge with the same feelings.

The four women are entranced. They look at Jill as if she has just discovered a cure for cancer. "How did you know to ask this?" they want to say. "Will you make some unique discovery everywhere we go? What do you know that we don't know?"

They press toward Melissa without knowing it, shifting hands and legs and arms and heads as if they were all trying to catch a cool breeze in the middle of July.

"Melissa, look," Jill finally reveals. "We came here to celebrate the life of a woman who was probably here when your mom was working there. She was young like you then and we all loved her and now here we are to remember whatever we can, to try and know her even better, to understand why this place was so important to her."

Melissa wants to say "wow," but she can't. A thousand stories are flashing through her mind and she wonders which one they want to hear and she wonders, too, about their friend who has died. Should she tell them about the girl who could only walk backwards? What about the boy who killed all his pets? How about the family who stayed in their car at the edge of the gate for three days because they were afraid their son might be eaten alive? The wild dogs? The survival walk? Or the way so many of the "kids" came back year after year to just stand at the cliff edge so they could try to remember who they were and how they had survived?

Melissa turns and looks slowly from one woman to the other. Her secluded world has given her the grace and ease and the poise of patience, respect, the ability to truly see. She sees sweet doses of wisdom and intelligence in each face as she turns from one woman to the next, smiling and grateful to know them in this small space.

"What if," she says out loud, "what if one of you is about to give me something and I am about to give you something?"

Laura smiles because she has sensed something like this from the moment they walked into the bar. Rebecca, Katherine and Jill frown as if they are about to answer a tough question on an SAT exam. They wonder how this young, attractive and wise-beyond-her-years young woman has entrapped and entranced them in such a short period of time.

Jill's heart has never beaten so wildly. For the first time in many months she knows exactly what she is supposed to do and what will happen, but she does not know how the pieces of information that Melissa holds in her hand will fit into anything—past or present.

"Melissa," she says, looking into Melissa's brown eyes. "Where was the facility? What can you tell us about what it was like? Would your mother come talk to us tonight? Are we asking you too many questions?"

Melissa smiles. She remembers rolling over in her tiny bedroom hours ago and thinking she would die if she had to stay in New Mexico one more day. And then rolling over to look out of her window and say to the late morning sky, "Help me. Faster, please. I want it faster. Three months until college starts. Give me something to hang on to until then. Please."

"Eat or talk first?" she asks the women.

"Would your mother come here?" Katherine asks impatiently. "We could go get her. You tell us. We don't want to be too much of a pain but anything would help us right now."

"Here," Melissa says, standing and taking charge. "Order your food and then I'll call her and come back and talk to you until Mom gets here. She'll come. I know she'll come talk to you."

Jill finds Melissa remarkable. The young woman's thirst for challenge and change has sparked something inside of Jill that has been frozen. While Melissa takes their orders Jill watches every move and she gets an idea that suddenly changes everything. It is a whisper at first that grows into a tiny scream and then a snarl that bangs at the back of her throat. Jill bites it back, holds it there for a while, and waits, which is not easy. In the waiting, in the minutes she watches Melissa hand over the order, make the phone call and come back to the table, Jill imagines a change coming toward her like a rifle shot. She imagines something that is a possibility of promise for herself and for Melissa of New Mexico. Jill, the pensive professor, can barely sit still. Laura notices it. She reaches over to place her hand on Jill's knee, to let her know that whatever it is must be good, to keep her still for just a few more moments.

"Mom will be here in less than an hour," Melissa tells them, hands on hips, the new commander of the Ranchero Grill, captain to funeral-goers, women in mourning, and eager ears awaiting word from the front.

"So?" Rebecca asks.

Melissa smiles. She knows there must be more to their story but she has already agreed to surrender everything she knows to these wild women from places that she has only glimpsed through her computer screen, on television shows and in magazines.

"So," she begins and launches into not only the history of Desert Dreams but into her own history and that of her family.

The women fall into Melissa's stories. They search through every word for pieces of Annie, a sign that points in her direction, a hint of who she was and what happened when she passed through the open desert door.

"The buildings are still there," Melissa tells them. "Too bad I didn't know sooner, I'd take you down there and show you around. It's like walking into a different world, kind of spooky. Some people even think they can hear voices when they are there."

"Voices?" Jill asks. "What kind of voices?"

"The place was shut down about thirty years ago when some parents filed complaints after their kids claimed they had been restrained against their will, tied onto stakes in the sun and forced to march for days in the desert without food or water."

"What?" they all exclaim at the same time.

"Some of the accusations were true and that's why the place closed down. The owners vanished and the voices, so they say, are from the kids who were tied to the stakes."

Everyone is leaning forward, four sets of hands are gripping the table's edge, eyes focused on Melissa's lips—the pallbearers are poised for action.

"What the hell happened there?"

"It was sort of funky experimental psychology. Some of it was just normal stuff. They had dorm rooms and a few psychologists who worked with people, probably like your Annie, who were basically good kids but just a bit off-center, but some of the kids who came needed to be slapped upside the head and so the people in charge designed their survival programs kind of like outdoor shock therapy."

"Jesus," Laura murmurs. "No wonder they folded. Was anyone ever hurt?"

"More people were helped, I think. That's what my mom tells me anyway. She was there right from the start. She worked in the kitchen and part-time in the office and she pretty much knew everything."

Rebecca is fixated on the part about kids being tied to stakes in the open sun. She needs to know more. In her mind she's already planning a trip back to New Mexico so she can hike through the canyons and see Desert Dreams.

"Were there really stakes in the sun?" she asks.

"Yes," Melissa tells her. "Some kids were tied to stakes there. My mom said it really happened but she also said it worked. Well, she said it sort of worked on some of them, but it sure doesn't make sense to me."

Melissa tells them about the first time she saw the Desert Dreams Ranch. It had been abandoned for years by the time she saw it but she remembers each detail of that first journey.

"It was like walking into a dream, because my mom had told us so many stories about it and then there it suddenly was, this cluster of empty buildings, pieces of old furniture still scattered around, in one building the table was still set. It was so weird and I never let go of my mom's hand as we walked from building to building and then out to the creek where I saw the stakes in the ground," she tells them. "I kept thinking I heard voices too."

"They were probably the screams of those kids who were tied to the stakes." Rebecca crosses her arms and pushes back from the table. "Would they have tied someone like Annie to the stakes?"

"Ask my mom. She knows more about stuff like that. Unless your Annie was totally wild, probably not. Your food is ready. Want to take a break to eat?"

They eat through a storm of questions, all the while imagining what it must have been like for Annie to be yanked from her high school world which may as well have been on the other side of the world, and thrown into the desert winds.

"Maybe it wasn't bad," Katherine shares. "She made the decision to *live* here, because she came back alive and moved forward after this experience; she sent us back here, it was clearly an important part of who she became. It sounds beyond freaky now but something good must have happened here for her."

Just after they finish eating, Melissa's mother flies into the bar, embraces Buck, and then kisses each one of the cowboys. She's a much older version of Melissa, gray hair tied up in a bun, jeans worn white from actual wearing and not a chemical that was applied to make them look as if they came from New Mexico, her face creased into long tunnels by years of sun and desert wind, a wide smile and an openness that is immediately perceived as inviting and kind.

"Hey," she says as she grabs a chair. "I'm Pat, Melissa said you needed me to make a house call."

Pat is as gracious as her daughter and the vision of all the women together entrances the cowboys so much they order more shots and Buck also brings them another round of beers which makes everyone's eyes bulge just a little but they begin drinking anyway.

Before they can begin talking, however, Melissa comes to say goodbye. She's off-duty and anxious to see friends in Santa Fe. Jill slips her a twenty-dollar tip, her phone number, and a note that asks her to call in a few weeks. Melissa takes the gift without question, smiles and does not ask why Jill wants her to call. She stuffs the money and note inside of her jeans pocket and is gone with a wave and a short hug for Jill.

Then they hear Pat's story. She wasn't much older than half the young people she worked with all those years ago and she recalls being astounded by their damaged hearts and souls.

"This is my world," she tells the four women, scanning her hand around the restaurant and bar, palm up.

She does not remember Annie.

"I worked there two years and then I took off, I had to leave, just like Melissa has to leave. I had her very late, as if you can't tell—I was forty-four years old when she was born," she says, laughing. "People thought her father and I were nuts. I thought the same thing for a while myself, but as you can see she is magnificent."

Pat reassures them that most of the work done at the ranch was good work. She said a few counselors went too far and the survival behavior modification work was way too close to the edge but she swore that many young lives were changed and saved before the ranch closed.

"At least once or twice a year someone comes back," she tells them. "Lots of the families stayed here before they dropped off their kids, so the first glimpse of the real desert and Desert Dreams they had was right from the edge of the cabin you are staying at tonight."

The women talk for another two hours. Pat shares her stories as if she is passing out Christmas presents one at a time and the women take notes on napkins and in their heads and then just as Buck looks as if he's ready to fall asleep on top of the bar and the cowboys throw them goodbye kisses and head back to their own ranch, Jill asks to see Pat alone for just a minute.

"What?" the women ask each other when Pat and Jill disappear. Laura knows but she also knows this is Jill's story and she will wait patiently for Jill to tell it when she is ready.

After Jill comes back, they each say goodbye to Pat. Back at the cabin, they struggle to stay awake while the beer and whiskey shots flood through their veins like a stampede of wild alcohol.

"I just had this way-out idea that felt perfectly normal as

Melissa talked to us," Jill explained. "What I have missed most this past year is the contact with the students, the mothering, I suppose, that I never had through real kids. So here's this bright, exceptional young woman whose parents struggle to make a living and there's me with a nice house, a fine retirement plan, and access to one of the most wonderful universities in the country. Stack that on top of my missing passion and it was as if something clicked inside of me."

"So, what?" Rebecca asks her. "Are you opening a halfway house?"

"Well, I'm opening my house. That's the first step. I offered Pat the chance to bring Melissa to California to see where I live, to find out I am not some kind of nut and to maybe have Melissa move in with me, so that I can help her find her way. I've never pulled one university string in my entire career to get a student admitted and I'd like to see what that feels like."

"Really?"

"Really," Jill says. "It'll change her life just like this place changed Annie's life, and it will change mine, too. I can hardly believe it myself. In fact, I'm beginning to wonder if an alien has taken over my body. We've only been gone what—one day?—and already I'm a changed woman."

"I bet Annie planned this whole thing," Katherine says. "I bet she knew exactly what would happen when we went into that bar and met Melissa. I wouldn't be surprised if Annie's ashes aren't out there smiling and clapping their dusty hands right now."

"Are you sure?" Rebecca asks Jill, frowning. "It's one thing to leave them at the edge of the classroom every day. It's quite another to bring them home and look at them another twelve hours."

"Why the hell not? I already feel as if I've been reborn. The way I see it, I don't have much to lose."

"Which is exactly what Annie probably felt when she stood at the edge of that cliff and decided to live," Laura points out. "Why the hell not indeed?"

"Why the hell not indeed," each of the women repeats as each falls into her own bed with their boozy words leaping over each other and the thought that Annie would have indeed wanted Jill to take Melissa home, wanted for them to plunge into the desert world, wanted for her ashes to be spread at this remote place that she saw as the beginning of everything.

16

The airplane leaves so early that each of the women feels half drunk when it takes off and the plane dips quick and seemingly fast toward the east. Below them the desert disappears under clouds the color of fresh snow, and when they blink, the shaded browns and dark greens of New Mexico in spring have vanished.

Katherine has the box of ashes on her lap, her hands folded over the top of them as if she is saying a prayer, and her fingers holding lightly on to a small piece of paper that she usually keeps neatly folded just inside of the box. It is her mother's obituary, her last physical link to another woman who helped form the soul of who she was to become, who she remains, who she will always be. Katherine has read the obituary so many times that it looks as if the piece of paper has been through the wash a dozen times. She wonders if she will ever stop reading it.

Katherine holds it, as she held her mother, *finally* held her mother, once she crossed over the threshold of adulthood herself and realized the power of a mother's love for a child, the sacrifices her mother made that she never appreciated, and that great gift of patience that can only be learned through becoming a mother.

Sacramento Bee

DEATH NOTICE

LEVENS, Frances A. (Frannie)

Passed away at the Fonera Hospice Center while resting quietly in the arms of her daughter on January 5 following a long and brave struggle with cancer and Alzheimer's disease. She was born on Dec. 13, 1931, in Milwaukee, WI, grew up in that area and later moved to California with her husband, Thomas, where she thrived in her roles as a loving mother and wife. Her maternal instincts and kindhearted ways extended beyond her own family and out into the community and neighborhood that surrounded her. Frances never locked her door and it was not unusual for her home to be filled with friends, organizers of a local charitable cause, or a stranger who needed a little help. A consummate volunteer, she was active in the Girl Scouts, various parent and teacher organizations, Planned Parenthood, was an original member and lifelong supporter of the National Organization for Women and participated in many activities at St. John's Presbyterian Church in Rosemont. Besides her family, her greatest joy was the volunteer services she offered at the Canyon County Women's Shelter. There her loving spirit helped countless women find the focus and direction that they needed. She will be deeply missed by her family and friends, who carry on the peaceful spirit that covered a life well lived. Frannie is survived by her husband, Thomas; daughter, Katherine P. Givins; son, Joshua; sister, Gloria; granddaughter, Sonya; and countless friends and others who were all touched by her generous heart. Donations to the Canyon County Shelter in her name are appreciated. In a letter written several months before her death, Frannie asked that instead of a traditional funeral service, a party be held in her honor to celebrate her life and the lives of everyone who touched her life as well. The party will be

held January 15 at the Girl Scout Service Center complex in
Carol City from 7 p.m. to midnight. Refreshments and music
will be provided.

Jill catches Katherine crying as the plane levels out and they
head east toward the Miami airport and the next phase of the traveling funeral. She pulls Katherine's face away from the window and
close to her so that they can talk and wipes Katherine's tears from
her face with her fingers as she asks her, "What is it?"

Katherine hands her the obituary, watches as Jill reads it, and
then tells her how Annie's funeral has her thinking about her mother.

"It took me forever to understand why my mother lived the way
she did," she shares with Jill. "There is so much of her inside of me,
yet we were so different, so very different. Sometimes the guilt I
feel because it took me so long to appreciate her and love her for
who she was and what she did for me almost consumes me."

"I didn't know, Katherine," Jill says, taking her hand. "Annie's
death on top of what happened with your mom, that's a lot."

"What's a lot though?"

"Whatever you can or can't handle, I suppose," Jill tells her.
"Everyone has a different level of 'what's a lot.' "

Katherine thinks about that. She thinks about having a baby
when she wasn't sure if she wanted to have a child, about marriage when she wasn't sure she wanted to be married, about filing
for a divorce when the entire world seemed to be pounding at her
back window telling her not to do it. Katherine thinks about how
her mother moved against her in her small hospice bed and the
smell of her hair—lemon and lilac—the final time she turned to
lie against her and then the hour that her mother died and everything, every single thing changed forever. Katherine thinks about
making love after she has not made love for a long time. She thinks
about the weight of that release on her heart and also on her pelvis
and how she thought she might die if she had sex and she might

die if she did not have sex. She thinks about how she felt when she learned that Annie was dying and then how she pushed that away to focus not on her own aching heart but on Annie and her life and needs and wants. She thinks of the void of missing her when the call came and while she wondered if she had done or been everything she could have been.

She imagines that Jill has thought of the same things. And she realizes, in the newness of their friendship, because they have been so focused on the loss of Annie and the ashes and what they are supposed to do, she has failed to ask her. Katherine turns in her seat and she takes Jill's hand off the top of hers and places her hand over her long, slim fingers.

"Jill, what has been a lot for you?"

Jill looks at Katherine and smiles. She wants to tell Katherine everything. She wants to pour every secret and scared thought into this woman's other hand and then watch her as she sifts through them to learn about the mysteries of her heart and life. She wants to say things she has not said in a very long time.

"Do you really want to know?" she asks, hoping with a fierceness that stops her heart for just a second that Katherine will say yes.

There is a pause but it is not a hesitation. It is a pause of surprise because Katherine cannot imagine that Jill would not think that she would want to know. Katherine cannot imagine that Annie would have picked each of them if they were not the same in so many ways, if their hearts had not twisted and bent and danced in similar directions.

"Yes," Katherine says firmly and watches as Jill lets out all the air she has been holding inside.

"Oh, so much, Katherine. I suppose I have my own things to let go of, too."

Katherine smiles and lets her right hand fall open onto the shoebox. She squeezes Jill's right hand with her left and leans over to kiss her on the side of the face in a spot that she finds precious, where her hair meets her ear.

"So much, I suppose, so much that I have kept so close, too close to the edge of all that I could have been," Jill says, thinking aloud. "Sometimes, I think I missed too many chances, that life was slapping me right in the face and I just looked the other way. Sometimes I was so damn busy reading the map to get directions that I forgot to look up and see what was outside the window. Do you understand?"

Katherine doesn't answer right away. She just looks at Jill, and holds her hand a bit tighter and waits for whatever it is, the one thing, the small secret that will link them forever.

"I know," she whispers. "We all have our lost directions. It's okay, Jill. Whatever it is, it's okay. It doesn't mean you can't start a new road trip."

Jill tells Katherine about a lost love that would not carry into the university life of a woman who was destined to govern the entire campus. A woman loving a woman all those years ago was not so easy and Jill tells Katherine a story of a choice that changed everything.

"I could have had it all, I could have loved her and lived with her but I never knew that, I never felt that and so I let her go and part of a life I wanted so desperately I let slip away," she explains. "One day I simply went away on one of those long walks that I still love to take and I sealed off my heart from romantic love, from the kind of feeling and life that lust and passion can bring to you."

Katherine wants to make the pilot land the plane so that she can grab Jill up in her arms and take her to a place where she can see that she can have everything. She wants to run with her naked through a women's festival and through a dozen major cities and show her how a woman loving a woman is possible. She wants to sit up, slap Jill and tell her that she knew better, that the world, even all those years ago, was more accepting and open than she might ever have imagined. Katherine opens her mouth to speak but Jill guesses what she is about to say.

"It could have worked," Jill tells her. "I know that but I wasn't strong enough, I didn't have the years and power behind me that I have now," she explains. "It was too much then but maybe it's never too late. Maybe I can start lots of things over. Maybe if I can get off my damn porch and go on a traveling funeral I can do a lot of other things."

Katherine smiles. She wonders if Jill would have ever thought this or felt this if she had stayed on her back porch and mourned the loss of Annie's life and her own life. Death, she will tell her, opens a door into more than just the life of the person who has been lost.

Jill goes on. She tells Katherine it was too much to keep up all the walls of her world and too much when she refused to cross the lines with students who would have made remarkable lifelong friends and too much when she turned down other chances to love.

"Too much, too many times," she finally admits, sitting back into her chair and placing her face in her hands. "And this was supposed to be your time to grieve for your mother, to grieve for Annie. And here you are listening to me."

"This is a part of it all." Katherine is trying hard to stay in her seat when she wants to run through the plane shouting, "Live, goddamn it, live every damn day and stop being so afraid." She wants to shout it, to say it to Jill, so that she can listen to it herself.

Instead she keeps talking. Instead she throws a wild question to Professor Jill.

"Do you think she knew this would happen?"

"What?" the professor asks, looking just a bit stunned.

"Look at us, for crissakes. We are all hungover, I'm carrying around a box of human ashes as we fly to an island we have never heard about, you've just invited a virtual stranger to live with you, and we all keep going to confession to each other. It's like a new reality show, 'Annie Unleashed' or something."

The professor laughs. It is a loud snort that whips like a wild scarf that has just caught the end of a breeze that was designed to screw with humans who think everything should be just a certain way.

"Hey," Laura shouts. "No spitting."

"Sorry," Jill explains, "but I'm having an Annie moment."

Of course Annie knew this would happen, the professor finally admits. Of course Annie knew I needed a kick in the ass and that we all needed something to fuel our lives for the next stop. Of course she knew that the common bond of her friendship with all of us before and after her death would live on because of this trip and then beyond. Of course she knew. Maybe.

"Maybe it was just supposed to be a funeral too," Jill says. "Maybe just Annie's funeral."

A ringing phone, a tiny chorus of chimes, startles both Jill and Katherine until the good professor remembers she forgot to turn off Marie's cell phone when they took off from the airport.

"Shit," she says, turning to grab the phone and answer it.

"Good answer," Rebecca whispers through the split in the cushions.

"Marie!"

"Where are you?"

"Probably about twenty-five thousand feet and climbing."

"Can you talk to me?"

"Yes, unless the stewardess comes past and tries to bust me."

And so the two women talk about patients and patience. They talk about halfway houses for retired professors and about the way change sometimes leaps up to bite people in the ankles and they talk about sorrow and how it comes to every woman in different shapes and sizes.

"Not just in death," Marie explains. "It can be so many things."

"Where are you now?"

"In my backyard. I came home for a small break. My feet are killing me and I'm going to throw on some coffee and sit for a minute before I have to run into the office and write out three thousand reports."

"I remember," Jill says, turning to watch Katherine fold her hands over her mother's obituary. "There's something comforting about regularity and things like forms and agendas and plans and promises kept."

Marie laughs and tells her regularity's also a royal pain in the ass and that she'd rather just hop from patient to patient and never fill in another form the rest of her life.

"People can get so tied to the regular agenda that they think that's how life is supposed to be. Do you have any idea how many of my terminal patients retired just a week before they found out they had cancer? Or how many of them fell and broke a hip or just wore out before they got to travel to some exotic place they have always dreamed about visiting? Why do people wait? It's not always the best thing to do."

Marie needs to sit but she can't. She's suddenly caught up in her own conversation, which has quickly turned into a confession of sorts.

"Sometimes I wait and then when I think about Annie dying and everyone else along with her I scream," she says, walking as if she is in a marching band, back and forth, back and forth in her own front yard. "I need to be more spontaneous. If I could pick one thing—that would be it. Spontaneous."

Katherine can hear parts of the cell phone conversation and she has quietly folded her mother's obituary and placed it back inside the shoebox. When she hears the word "spontaneous" the second time, she grabs the phone from Jill.

"Hey, you," Katherine says. "Are you looking for a good time?"

"Like a traveling funeral?" Marie laughs into the phone. "The people I deal with can actually lean over the edges of their beds and tell me what it's going to look like the day they die. A traveling funeral? I'm not so sure. I'm trying hard to leave. I am. I have calls in to three subs. I should know something by this evening."

Katherine thinks for just a few seconds. She thinks about the routines of her own life that have swallowed her up and kept her locked into places that she no longer finds comfortable and she realizes this for the very first time because she is on a traveling funeral. She can also not let go of the feeling that her mother would be telling her something important, something like "Make more time" because that is exactly what her mother did.

"Spontaneity is good for the heart and soul and whatever else you believe in, Marie," Katherine explains, trying to convince herself and Marie at the same time. "That's what my mother would say anyway. This whole thing has already, in what—not even two days?—turned into something much more than a funeral. Remember what I said? These things are not really for the dead but for the living and you have to decide how you want to do that. I suppose I do also."

"Do what?" Marie asks quietly, halting her march, placing her hand over her heart to still the beating blasts that propelled her to say things she already thinks she may regret.

"Live. How do you want to *live*?"

Marie cannot remember anyone ever having asked her this particular question. She cannot remember when she stopped long enough, beyond her moments of silence in her bedroom, to consider such a notion. She worries and talks about how everyone else lives. Her patients. Her children. Her husband. But her? She feels a hard ball forming in the pit of her stomach.

"Marie?" Katherine asks after a long pause when she thinks the cell must have gone into hibernation as they passed over some kind of invisible communication wall thousands of feet above the rest of the ringing phones and loud voices of the world.

"Isn't this supposed to be about Annie?" Marie asks softly.

Katherine laughs. She'd love to push back the seat and become hysterical for a good week.

"About Annie? Oh, yes, I suppose that's what she wanted us to think, but you know Annie—always pushing toward some secret and wild conclusion. Maybe this funeral will end up to be more about us, each one of us, than about Annie."

Marie doesn't skip a beat. She tells Katherine that at least she doesn't have to finish thinking about her own life or what she wants for a few more hours.

"Not for long," Katherine warns. "Wait until you get here. You are in big trouble."

"Katherine," Marie says suddenly because something large has roared to the forefront of her mind. It is something she has never told anyone, not even Annie G. Freeman.

"What?" Katherine asks as the Miami-bound plane hits its fly zone and she can hear Rebecca snoring softly above the pilot's description of the flight and the temperature and the glorious fact that anyone who needs to can now use the bathroom.

"I've always wanted to learn how to ride a motorcycle."

"A motorcycle?" Katherine says back with a smile that could probably ignite three cycles without the use of an electric starter.

Katherine knows that Marie is serious and out of all the possibilities life has to offer, how interesting that the kind nurse would choose two wheels and an open road as her most pressing secret desire. When she closes her eyes and listens to Marie describe how being alone and in control of her time is so foreign to her that she can only imagine this dream where she is wearing a leather vest and riding into a sunset on two wheels, Katherine decides that it makes perfect sense.

"Do it," she urges. "Where is the closest Harley dealer up there? They have classes."

Marie starts moving in the yard again, then slaps herself in the head. "Here we are in the middle of a funeral. We shouldn't be thinking about ourselves. What is wrong with me?"

"Look," Katherine explains, "here is what I think. There's a wound that opens when someone you love dies. It's a raw emotion that needs to be revealed every now and then."

Silence.

Marie is thinking, "Of course," just "Of course that is exactly true" and she tells Katherine it almost makes her want to go to a bar and open her wound except she has too much to do and so many people waiting on her and—

Katherine cuts her off just as Rebecca tosses the funeral book into Katherine's lap and the pilot gives them the okay to turn on some computer devices but surely not a cell phone.

"Hey, take a breath."

"A simple breath, one at a time," Marie responds quietly. "That's good advice, always very good advice."

They hang up after that without saying another word and Marie breathes deep and long and she drives to her next hoping heart and desperately ill patient with the windows, all of them, rolled down so that she can feel the California air on her face, imagining the entire time that Annie could have touched some of the air that has lingered long and wild in the swirling and very friendly winds of Northern California.

Katherine glides while Marie drives.

She turns to see that Jill is asleep with her head tilted against the two pillows and her hands open, palms up. She doesn't have to un-strap her seat belt and lean forward to see that Rebecca and Laura are also asleep, because she hears them snoring not-so-sweetly in the seats ahead of her and that is what she writes because it is her turn.

KATHERINE THOUGHT: *How lovely. Women at rest miles above the mostly sleeping world. We take turns, it seems, trying to imagine why we are here and what this really means and in the quiet moments that none of us seem to have during the rest of our* *lives, we think of ourselves. Where we are now, who we are when we knew you, Annie, who we would have become with or without you in our lives. I feel weary and then exhilarated. I feel confused about my direction and the fear that seems so real that has me treading in place. One minute I am there and the next I see something fuzzy on the horizon that is a desire I have yet to identify and then I think of you. You. Annie Freeman.*

This is long because everyone is sleeping. So, too bad.

Remember that day when we were seniors in high school and I leaned over and told you that I had always wanted to skip school? Remember? Remember how we ran into the bathroom and waited until Ancient History had started and then we bolted out into the parking lot to your car and skipped last period?

Remember how fifteen minutes into the gig we turned to each other and both pretty much said at the same time, "This is goofy?" and how we got back in time to not even be missed during class?

I've always been torn that way. I've always wanted to skip the whole damn class and go behind the grocery store and smoke some weed and then head for the Hawaiian Islands and never come home. But then I think about something like the way my daughter still calls my name the second she walks into the door and I think, "Well, maybe this—being here—is paradise."

So this is it. This is what your loss has me doing. I'm confused and I miss your sorry ass, Annie. Come skip class with me again. Hurry.

ANNIE THOUGHT: *You could always have skipped class. You could have but the real problem for you was wondering what you'd miss while you skipped class. Maybe something really wonderful was happening that day and then you missed it for what? A fast ride down the highway? The thrill of escape? Here's what I know now dear Katherine. It's very cool to skip class once in a* *while because you can copy someone's notes the next day. Follow your own advice sweetheart. You told Marie to breathe and that's what you need to do now too. Run from class. Do it. Take a breath and then stop and listen to the sound of your own beating heart. This minute is yours. Grab it hard.*

17

Rebecca's airplane dream is a breezy affair that has her singing in a kitchen that looks like something from an art deco film at the Sundance Film Festival in 1987. She is naked and thinks nothing of it as she watches herself prepare to leave the house without even considering putting on clothing.

She's leaving on a ride to pick up someone or something when she spies a tiny, very, very tiny sign posted at the side entrance of a white house on the corner of a quiet intersection. Rebecca does not know why she turns her head to look at the house she has ridden past hundreds of times but she does. The wind blows her hair across the tops of her breasts. She can feel the sun beating against her arms, the back of her neck, the tops of her thighs. No one passing by mentions her nakedness and she turns the car into the slanted driveway, gets out, leans over to grab a towel and starts walking toward the house.

Before she walks more than a few feet she stops, throws off the towel, puts on a white polo shirt—nothing else—and then wraps the towel back around herself again.

Rebecca knocks but no one answers the door. She boldly walks inside and a woman quickly hurries from somewhere inside the house and greets her in the kitchen. They do not know each other but they embrace and the woman is eager to show off what she has for sale. Just a few things. Really, maybe just four things. "It is a very tiny sale, like the sign," the woman explains, pointing toward the items she has spread out for purchase.

Rebecca picks up one bottle. It is a small mustard jar and it is full of pills.

"Vitamins, I think," the older woman tells her eagerly. "I'm sure they would be safe."

Suddenly, Rebecca thinks the woman must be mad. She does not want to startle her so she looks at the bottle, then sets it back down and without thinking further turns sharply, leans in close to the woman's ear and whispers, "I'm naked under these two things."

That's when Laura shakes her gently awake and Rebecca screams, crosses her hands over her breasts to cover herself as if she is really naked, and looks as if she has seen Annie's ghost.

"Shit," she tells Laura. "A dream. It was crazy."

"Are you okay?" Laura asks her, sitting back down as the rest of the people file past them to get off the plane.

"It's just a dream. I thought I was naked."

Laura laughs. Rebecca laughs too and they decide the bizarre dream is a combination of the hangover, airplane food for break-fast, being with a group of women whom you know but don't really know, a pile of guilt from not being where everyone else thinks you are supposed to be, and the intensity of not knowing what is about to happen on the second leg of the traveling funeral.

Even with that boost of knowledge, Rebecca cannot forget the dream. She talks about it as the two women walk off the plane, and she decides, speaking mostly to herself, that the half-naked towel thing must mean she is hiding something that needs to be uncov-ered. Rebecca always embraces her thoughts, even though they have mostly been filled with anguish and loss and so much grieving time that it has been hard to recover all these years and see a side of life that is not covered in a shroud of black. Dreams, she knows, always lead to something and maybe—maybe—something is shaking itself loose and she'll be able to walk naked everywhere and only need an occasional shawl and nothing else to protect herself from the evils of the world and insane and corrupt rummage sales. Maybe.

There is little time to linger on those thoughts of glorious recovery because as Katherine, Jill and Laura are standing near a Cuban coffee vendor and shouting about the vibrant colors and the warm late morning air, Laura suddenly decides she knows the name of the older woman in Rebecca's dream.

"What?" Rebecca asks. "How could you know that?"

"The same way I know other things. I think our dreams may have crossed over. I was dozing while you took a nap. Hang with me here. I know a woman who used to do what you said the woman in your dream does. Before my neighbor got sick she did that. She'd try and sell a jar with stones in it and she'd always tell you a story about them in broken English like they were gold nuggets or something. She looked like the woman in your dream. She was the woman. We—you and I, Rebecca—just have some interesting connection that is about to get richer for many reasons."

Rebecca gets it, sort of. She knows Laura's wild mind is a gift and she believes that Laura can and does know things. Some of those "things," she should probably just keep to herself. But she can't help it. She wants to know. She has to know who it was but beyond that, she'll wait a bit. Is there really something else coming to connect her with Laura beyond this trip, Annie's death, what they already know?

"Who the hell is she? Your neighbor?"

"Jencitia Chalwaski," Laura shouts to her startled friends.

They look at her as if she really is naked like Rebecca was in her dream.

"What?" they all ask, sipping their tiny cups of coffee that is strong enough to lubricate the bearings on the airplane that just dropped them onto Florida soil.

"She's a who, not a what. Jencitia Chalwaski."

Just as Laura gets the last letter out of her mouth, her cell phone rings. This is only amazing to everyone but Laura because her phone was not turned on and has not been turned on since they touched down in Miami.

"Magic," she tells them as they freeze in place, white cups to lips, afraid to move, wondering if Laura has not already had several conversations with Annie during the last twenty minutes that only she can hear.

Laura turns away, covers her ears, and they hear bits and pieces, Jencitia's name again, the word "maybe," lots of questions, and they watch Laura shaking her head up and down and then leaving it down as she dances a bit from one foot to the next and then after a long time and another cup of powerful coffee that could fuel a rocket to Mars, she turns back to them and says into the phone: "I'll ask them and call you back soon."

"What?" they demand again in unison as she disconnects the phone, and Laura looks at them, smiles, and thinks how wonderfully lucky Annie was to have known the three women she now sees standing against an orange wall in the Miami airport.

"You are all beautiful," she says sincerely, taking one of her mental photographs of the trio and loading it into the slice of space behind her right eye so that she can look at them, reserve the space and place of the moment in the Miami airport when her new friends were sipping coffee roasted from the bark of coffee plants that smelled of tar and she stood in front of them, one hand on her hip, smiling.

"What?" they ask again, just a bit louder.

She tells them. Laura tells them about her neighbor, Balinda Chalwaski, who has been taking care of her terribly ill mother, Jencitia, for the past eight years. She tells them that Balinda is forty-six years old, never married and has put her entire life on hold to nurse her mother. She tells them that last night Balinda finally took her mother to a long-term care facility and is now in the process of having a mild nervous breakdown.

"I'm like part of her family, I've helped her do simple things and not-so-simple things like go to the grocery store and pick up a newspaper because her mother can't be alone for five minutes or even a minute at a time," Laura tells them, watching as their cups stop moving and their minds focus on what she is telling them, what she is about to ask. "They are from Poland. Her mother speaks very little English."

Chicago, Laura explains, has the largest population of Polish people in the United States and the Chalwaskis came to follow a cousin, to start a new life just like Laura's grandparents before them started a new life from that same country.

"What does she need?" Jill asks first, speaking for all of the women. "This Balinda."

"A break, just a small break, because it may be the last time she can leave until her mother dies," Laura tells them, repeating what Balinda has just told her. "There is a Polish-speaking nurse at the home where she took her mother. The nurse is leaving in one week. After that, unless she finds an interpreter, Balinda will be back to her schedule and unable to leave especially if her mother comes home. It could be months and months or even years and years, depending on the health of her mother."

All of the women understand schedules. They understand sacrifice. They know what it feels like to never sleep, to always get up first, to wonder in the middle of a day that seems as if it stretches to forever what was the initial question and they know that they all have many more miles to go, more hands to hold, more, so much more yet to give.

And to receive.

Katherine steps forward and simply says, "Yes."

Rebecca and Jill nod and Jill says that Marie would understand better than any of them that Balinda needs them now in a way she can't need them when she is the constant caregiver for her mother.

And even if they find Laura's premonitions a bit strange, even if they are hoping that Laura cannot see so far inside of them that she spots something even more horrible than the death of Annie G. Freeman, they do not stop her.

Laura quickly calls Balinda back and gives her the name of their hotel in the Keys, tells her she can arrange a shuttle from the far terminal at the airport and lets her know that there will be a cold glass of dark beer waiting for her the minute she walks into their arms.

"Come join the traveling funeral," she invites Balinda. "We'll be waiting for you."

The conversation surrounding the word "sacrifice" never quite ends. The women talk nonstop as they load up the van and wish out loud that it was a red convertible. Their words cross over each other as they throw their suitcases into the car, drive out of the terminal, then back, and then Jill hops out because they forgot the map and directions and they talk as they stop to buy a Styrofoam cooler, beer, several bottles of wine, snacks and Tampax for Rebecca who got her period fifteen minutes after the last cup of coffee.

"Praying for menopause," she shouts through the back of the open van door as she flings her bag of supplies on top of their luggage, adds, "Damn it," and climbs back in for the ride to the Keys.

Rebecca, they decide unanimously, still talking as Laura wheels them past the edge of Miami, is the queen of sacrifice. The deaths of her parents, her aunt and now Annie have devastated Rebecca financially, emotionally and physically. Rebecca accepts the title but swings the conversation to other kinds of loss. She tells them she's had ample time to think about loss in all shapes, sizes and forms as she's waltzed through hospital stays, caregiving and so many other funerals.

"Relationships. Animals. Jobs. Retirement," she tells them. "Loss and then the grieving that comes after it arrives in many ways and forms. Think of it."

Jill, the spouseless spinster, tells them about the dog who broke her heart. Eland, an Irish setter, was her hiking companion. They walked through the California hills together for nine years until Jill detected a slight limp in her companion's front paw.

"Cancer that had driven a stake into her bones," she recalled, turning her head to look out of the window as the city flashed by. "They tell you so many things to keep you thinking it will go away, that you can have another month or so, but it isn't true and I didn't think it was fair either."

Sometimes, Jill tells them, her dog comes to her in her dreams barking wildly at a bird in a tree or dancing outside of her door because she knows they are about to go for a walk.

"I put her down fast," Jill says as Rebecca reaches over to take her hand. "The second she could not do the one thing she loved to do more than anything—run—I knew that her heart was broken."

Everyone has an animal story that brings them to tears.

Katherine's mother's yellow canary that sang every single time her mother put her fingers on the cage, and when the tiny bird died and they buried her at the edge of the tomato plants it was the first time Katherine saw her father cry.

Rebecca's family dog who slept by the kitchen door and followed her to school so many times the principal finally let the dog come into the classroom, and when Sparky ("Really, we named him Sparky," Rebecca said softly, as if she were sharing a secret) was hit by a car chasing a deer, Rebecca's mother threw herself onto the living room couch and wept for so long that Rebecca ended up calling her aunt who drove fifty miles, wrapped Sparky in an old blanket, put him in her trunk and took Rebecca with her to bury him in her own backyard, because her mother had no yard, so that her mother would always be able to visit.

Laura's cat, Pinky, who was actually black, and who she left behind when she went to college. When she called home, her mother would make Laura talk to the cat on the phone and the cat would wail for hours after hearing her voice. When the cat died, her mother cremated her and put the ashes into a ceramic bowl that still sits on top of Laura's piano.

"Well," Jill philosophizes, "I know what Annie thought about euthanasia and a person's right to choose what to do with his or her own body and life, and I agree with Annie that throughout the course of a lifetime there is enough suffering. Enough is enough. Why do we make each other suffer? Why isn't marijuana legal? Why do we plug people into machines who have no hope of ever doing a crossword puzzle again or reading a fabulous book?"

Why indeed, the women agree as Rebecca flips the conversation and asks everyone about their first great loss of love.

"Isn't this a conversation for the beach tonight?" Katherine asks, realizing as she says it that the loss of her first love is almost as painful that moment as it was the day it happened.

"Ha!" Rebecca mockingly laughs. "Apparently you should go first."

"She doesn't have to," Laura says, rescuing Katherine from a memory that surprises her with its intensity. "Maybe we should continue with the pet stories for a while."

Quiet erupts for just a moment while the women tuck their love stories back where they came from and think about the burden sorrow often brings to its bearer. They think about how all those years ago they wondered how they would breathe, get up in the morning, live until the end of the week when what they thought was a major tragedy had struck them. They think about the weight of loss and how age has given them a view of life that is so much different than it was when they were 18, 28 or 38. They think about wisdom as being a gift from time but they also know that often time skips a beat because no matter where you are in your life pattern, sorrow can cripple and maim the hearts and hands of anyone—14 or 45 or 105.

"It doesn't matter sometimes, does it?" Katherine asks and then continues to talk almost as if she is alone. "You look at yourself in the mirror, see the laugh lines getting longer and think that you can handle life now, you can handle what it brings and where it takes you and that nothing, no pain, will ever be as great as the one before it.

"But . . ." She trails off and begins to cry.

Jill reaches over to place her hand on Katherine's cheek. She lets Katherine's tears fall into the folds of her fingers and then she says, "But what? Tell us, Katherine. It's okay."

"This trip, Annie dying, my damn favorite bra falling apart, the loss of my mother—I feel as if everything has changed and it's unsettled me in a way that I am having a hard time understanding."

Jill takes her hand away. Katherine swallows and searches for what she wants to say because she isn't certain. She doesn't know what she wants to say. All she knows is that the day the red shoes arrived everything changed. Or maybe everything just started to change *faster*.

"This traveling funeral has made me think about everything, every aspect of my life, and I am wondering now how happy I have been or could be," she confesses. "It's not like I've ever even focused on what I want or where I am going. It's like life has been driving me and I have not been driving my life."

As she says it, Katherine realizes that is exactly what has happened. She realizes that her life has become a pattern of routines, routines that she always thought were necessary, have turned her into a person she no longer recognizes when she bothers to stop and look.

"I think maybe we are all feeling like that," Laura shares. "I mean it's not like my life has had rich consistency to it except for always hoping my daughter will come home again, but how often do we get a chance like this to stop and fan through things to see if we've become a damn zombie? I've got my job at the women's center and a husband but what does any of that even mean anymore?"

"I suppose Annie thought about all of this," Rebecca whispers from the back seat. "I suppose she knew we'd go beyond honoring her and find out where the empty spaces in our own lives have been hiding. It's good. It's all good."

They decide to think about the traveling funeral as a pause, like a chance to take an extra breath, and then they each say what they would have been doing at that exact moment if they had not disrupted their life patterns.

Work.

Crying on the porch.

Work.

And more work.

Grieving for Annie.

And all of it, every single part of it okay, they decide, until this moment or one last night or the one when they decided to go on the traveling funeral when they opened up a chasm of thought, of time and thinking about not only Annie's life but their own lives with and without her.

"Listen to us," Jill says softly. "I think we all thought about this trip as our last gift to Annie. That's what I thought, anyway. But it seems as if there are other gifts exploding all over the place."

No one says anything. No one can say anything.

"Katherine, didn't you say once that funerals are for the living?" Jill asks.

Miami disappears into the flat Florida horizon very quickly then as Annie Freeman's pallbearers drive toward a long bridge that leads them deeper and deeper into a conversation that centers more on living than on dying. Which, they all agree, is exactly the kind of conversation Annie G. Freeman would have expected them to have.

18

John Chester is looking underneath the side of his wooden pier, his glasses tucked into his buttoned front shirt pocket and is busy untwisting anchor ropes and fishing line when he looks up, spots a blur of red moving toward the pier, realizes it's a group of women and mumbles to himself, "Jesus, what the hell do they have on?"

By the time he drops his lines, fishes his glasses out, stands, and realizes it's the Annie G. Freeman gang, the four women are rocking the pier with so much movement he's afraid he's going to go ass-end-first right into the bay.

"Hey, ladies!" he shouts as they move toward him to the end of what is the longest and best built pier in Islamorada. "Spread out a little bit and slow down or we'll all be going swimming."

Laura, Jill, Katherine and Rebecca have been in a trance for the past hour. Their conversation trickled into short sentences as they drove through the top of the Florida Keys, past Key Largo, Tavernier and Plantation to the front door of the Harbour Haven Bed and Breakfast. Their serious conversations about life and love and what death does to both those glorious elements tapered off as they started focusing on the glorious spot where Annie's traveling funeral had delivered them on the second part of their journey.

None of the women had ever been to the Keys before—Miami, Tampa, the sandy and college-student-filled beaches along the Atlantic, maybe, but never to the dark green land meshed against sky the exact same color as the ocean that now seemed to be seducing them in waves that called their names constantly.

"Oh my gawd," Laura had said so slowly as they drove earlier in the day toward the Keys and the other women wondered if she'd ever get it out as they crossed over a long bridge that seemed architecturally impossible and then dipped down so close to the water it looked as if the van would end up as a submarine. "I had no idea it was this gorgeous here."

"Paradise, from the looks of things," Katherine agreed, pulling over at the edge of the bridge so that everyone could get out and put their toes in the water. "Let's go feel the water."

Rebecca says it first, daring to break their moment of delicious nature loving. She bends down to splash the salty water on her face and to run her fingers in the sand and then she asks, "Does anyone know why we are here? Does anyone know what this place meant to Annie?"

The other three women turn to look at Rebecca as if they are waiting for her to answer her own questions. Rebecca doesn't move. She lets the sun warm up her face and her closed eyelids but she doesn't speak.

"Until the trip I didn't even know she had been down here," Katherine says, verbally deepening the idea that none of them knew as much as they thought they did about Annie. "That doesn't mean anything, I don't think, because there are those gaps in all our lives when we were doing things like having babies, going to graduate school, trying to decide what was up and down. I'm not sure when Annie would have been down here and why."

"Something romantic," Jill suggests. "Look around. Everything reeks of romance. Either that or you'd come here in the dead of winter to get away, especially if you grew up someplace that was cold."

Laura tries to act like she doesn't know anything. But dozens of images have seeped into her mind. She looks at each one of the women as they wonder about Annie and this place and she trails her hands back and forth in the soft waves until Jill realizes she hasn't said anything.

"What?" Jill demands to know, throwing water from her fingertips onto Laura's face. "What are you seeing when you close your eyes that we don't see?"

Laura braces herself for the way her mind floats as if it is suspended when she sees something. From her perch at the edge of her own mind she can see the past and present in frames that present themselves like old movies—dark shadows, swift movement, the cloudy film of white gauze hanging over faces and places and tiny pieces of the future. This is how she sees. This is how worlds come to her. This is how she is able to know some things and parade into places that she is certain others could see if they would only try hard enough.

She doesn't know everything about Annie's Florida wanderings but she tells the other women that it feels to her as if it was definitely romance. She tells them she thinks the details will fall into place when they get to where they are supposed to stay and she thinks that is going to be someplace where Annie once stayed, too.

"How the hell do you know these things?" Katherine asks her, more than slightly astounded by her often-perfect perceptions. "Do you have psychic blood?"

It is hard for Laura not to tell the others everything. It is hard for her not to tell them things they do not even know about themselves. It is hard for her to explain how she has worked to place her own hands on the inside of herself, like continuous fingerprints on the kitchen walls, so that she can feel who she is all of the time. It is hard for her to explain that yes, some of what she has was passed down to her from wise aunties and a great-grandmother who loved to tell fortunes by reading the lines on the palms of people's hands. It is hard to tell them that she knows there are worlds close to them that they cannot even see as they sit at the ocean's edge and ponder the mysteries of Annie's life.

It is hard, but she tells them in a way that does not make her sound as crazy as she sometimes feels and her fellow pallbearers rise as she finishes her story and then they want to know more. More about Annie and what it could have been but then she rises, too, and tells them that she doesn't know everything. She tells them that the rest of the story, if it even matters, is theirs—all of theirs—to discover so they'd better hurry and get back into the van and get there.

That's why Annie Freeman's entourage is in such a hurry to get to the edge of the pier on which John Chester is now standing. It looks as if they are trying to locate Annie's body floating off the shoreline when they charge poor John. That's when Jill points out they have an entire day to figure it out and to grill the living hell out of him, so they back off and John is relieved but also terribly happy to see all of them.

John introduces himself as half the owner of the fine establishment they are in the process of taking over. The other half, his work and life partner Ben Cluskey, attorney-at-law, breakfast cook and fisherman extraordinaire, is scheduled, he tells them, to man the pontoon boat at 5:30 p.m. for a cocktail cruise, hors d'oeuvres and conversation that could last all night.

"One of those men knows something," Laura whispers to Rebecca as they climb the stairs to their rooms on the second floor of an old beach home that has been renovated to look as if it is a wild Italian villa. Laura has seen a musty version of something dangerous, emotional and a bit saucy.

"Wow," Jill tells John as he opens the door to her room and

her vision explodes with colors that have been blended to match one of the sunsets she expects to see outside of her window in just a few hours. Her room is a kaleidoscope of oranges. "This is lovely."

"My sister did it," he says, laughing. "If I decorated this place it would look like the inside of the storage shed, which is kind of a neat idea, now that I think about it. My grandfather built half the houses in this town and this is where my parents lived."

Jill knows right away by the way he looks at her that John is the one here who knew Annie. John and Ben maybe both knew her but John surely knew her if she'd been at the house, stayed here or close by. She was dying to ask him but didn't dare to do so without the other women in the same room to hear all the answers.

He tells her without her having to ask. He stood by the door as she dropped her bags on the bed, then asked her if she was the retired professor.

Jill smiled and he confessed quickly. "I knew Annie," he admitted. Maybe it was because they were the same age or maybe it was because she was letting him do it in his own way and in his own time but he told her that yes, he had known Annie G. Freeman and they had stayed in touch for years and that he had indeed helped her arrange this part of what he had just learned from Jill was now a traveling funeral.

"Can you wait a few more hours until Ben gets here and we take our boat tour and I'll tell you the entire story?"

"Does anyone else know that you knew Annie?"

"Laura. But then again Laura knows everything from what I hear."

"I'll just tell the others that you knew our Annie because if I don't I'll burst and yes, yes I can wait and we can wait but it won't be easy."

The women have captured the entire bed-and-breakfast, much to the delight and relief of John, who throws them a bone with the words, "Annie would love to know that you are in there messing the hell out of Ben's kitchen and every other room in the joint. So go. Do. I'll be on the dock where I belong."

They each have their own rooms and while John goes back to his fishing lines and his whistling they descend on the house in pairs—Katherine and Laura and Jill and Rebecca following a fast call from Marie, and another from Balinda to ask them to keep a light on and the door unlocked because she is going to get there terribly late. Marie has missed the last possible flight and will now try and surface at the Miami airport or during the next leg of the funeral.

Katherine decides to take over the kitchen and make them a late lunch but Rebecca shoos her outside with the funeral book and reminds her she is way behind in taking a turn. Rebecca joyously embraces the refrigerator and the yellow dishes and the huge wine rack as if she has just bumped into a long-lost friend. "Alleluia," she shouts as she opens every single drawer and touches every hanging pan in what is obviously a kitchen manned by a real cook.

While she writes, Katherine is surprised that she feels so tired. She grabs a pillow off the wicker chair, slides it under her head and begins writing with the funeral book propped on her chest.

KATHERINE THOUGHT: *I suddenly feel exhausted. It's odd almost and close to overwhelming to have this much time to dissect emotions that I did not even know I had. Well, I knew I had them but they've been sleeping quite soundly for a long time. And Annie—such remarkable and wonderful women you have picked for this funeral, which is loaded with surprises, like the two gay men and now this woman from Chicago who is joining us and the guessing games we play about the probable reasons for these funeral service locations. The Florida Keys. Why have I never been here and what did this place mean to you? Were you on this porch? Did you lie on this couch and look out across this bay? It is astonishingly beautiful here and I had no idea I was this tired. Come take a walk with me, Annie.*

ANNIE THOUGHT: *Oh, Katherine, you are tired because you never stop. You are exhausted from planning and working and sharing and taking care of half the world. That's okay—just remember once in a while to stop and purchase new underwear. Watch the sky here, Katherine. Let go of something. Listen and for crissakes have fun. Do you hear me, girl?*

Katherine hears but what she hears is their kind host whistling and Rebecca moving through the kitchen as if she has just won the lottery and Jill and Laura talking while they dangle their feet at the edge of the pier. She turns so that she can wedge her back up against the seat cushions on the couch and catch a piece of the breeze that is slipping around the corner of the house and she thinks for just a moment that she hears her daughter as she drifts into an easy and sweet sleep.

Sonya, who balances a schedule and a life that would make two racehorses tired and who has in her seventeen years already witnessed through life with her own mother the stress and hurt of the loss of love and the death of a grandmother whom she saw disappear in every possible way right before her young eyes.

"So much," Katherine murmurs, rocking in and out of sleep and finally allowing herself to fall into a slumber that only deepens her thoughts about her daughter. Thoughts that turn into a raging dream that she will later describe as a memory of something that must have really happened once.

Her daughter, hair dangling in braids and small enough to be clinging onto her knees. Katherine has her hand resting on top of Sonya's head and she is winding her fingers in and out of her braids. They are watching a parade that seems to grow larger and larger with each item that passes.

First there is a truck and then there is a tank. First there is one boy playing a trombone and then there is an entire band. First there is a small float being pulled by a bicycle and then there is a float that goes on and on for so long they cannot see the end of it and Sonya looks up at her mother and says simply, "That's enough, Mama."

That is what Katherine will remember and toss around in her own head after Rebecca shakes her gently and tells her that she has been sleeping for nearly two hours and has missed lunch. "Wait," Katherine begs, grabbing Rebecca's arm to wriggle up into a sitting position. "You have to hear about this dream. . . ."

Rebecca smiles and then she sits next to Katherine and they rock together on the couch that can also be used as a swing and they share Katherine's dream.

"Katherine." Rebecca turns to swing her legs up so that they are touching Katherine's knees. "What do you think about the dream? Do you get it?"

"Don't let the parade pass me by?"

"Like that would happen."

"What?"

"There are so many things to grieve. Think about it. We all did the animal thing—all those dogs and cats and birds and snakes we have loved and lost—and we're all supposed to talk about old lovers sometime while we are here. But what else?"

Rebecca rocks them back and forth after she puts her legs back down on the porch floor, she rocks them and she tells Katherine about the day she was shopping at a grocery store near her house and she stopped, to this very day not knowing why, and looked out of the huge front window that faced a small café that was right across from the grocery store. There was a group of women sitting outside of the café drinking coffee and Rebecca watched them, thinking the entire time what a beautiful group of women they were.

"It took me forever to see that one of them was my own daughter,"

she explained to Katherine. "One of them was Marden, my baby, a young woman I thought of only as a girl, a child, and there she was suddenly a woman and I felt this ache gnaw at me as if I had not eaten in a year. I stood there in that grocery store, watching my daughter gesture and laugh and move with the grace of a grown-up and I just started crying like a baby. It was not unlike the same type of sorrow we all feel when we realize that something we once had that was very precious is no longer there. That it's forever lost, changed, deceased."

"Like a baby," Katherine repeats, finally getting the heart of the story. "Gone, except in your memory and now in my memory. Like my own baby is gone."

Katherine quickly recites a line from a book by one of her favorite authors, Eudora Welty, and she shares it with Rebecca and she touches her hand at the same time. It is a sweet phrase about the treasure of human memory and how at one moment it has the possibility of joining together the past and present, the living and the dead.

"My own daughter is now a woman," she tells Rebecca. "I get it. Another passage, another form of loss. Another reason to grieve. Another part of this life process. That's my expanding parade."

"Maybe," Rebecca agrees, pulling Katherine to her feet. "Or maybe it was just a nasty old dream because you haven't had anything to drink yet today."

Rebecca, who is so used to being the caretaker she does not even blink, leaves quickly and comes back to the porch with two bottles of beer and a plate of lunch for Katherine. Then they keep talking. Their conversation roams and races into relationships and through jobs and loves and as they rock slow and sweet they dredge a foundation for a new friendship—"as long as you aren't too bossy," Rebecca half jokes, and "as long as you don't try to take care of me all the time," Katherine fires back.

Late afternoon and several beers later, Jill comes around the side of the house to tell them that the boat driver, cook, house attorney and man-about-the-bed-and-breakfast is about to take care of the next round of drinks.

Ben is too beautiful to be a man. That is the first thought that crosses the mind of all four women as he turns the corner and they see his blond hair, deep blue eyes, tanned face, and graceful walk. He's wearing cutoff shorts, a button-down shirt and he's barefoot. He embraces John first, kisses him on the cheek, says, "Hi, baby," and then hustles over to meet the traveling funeral entourage who have been breathlessly waiting for the boat tour and the answers to about five thousand questions. They guess he is fifty-plus even though he looks ten years younger. Just like his partner, he is a consummate host. He kisses the hand of each one of them.

It takes just minutes to load the boat with plates of the food he'd prepared earlier in the day—crackers and cheese and dips and finger foods that look like tiny pieces of art. Everyone agrees that white wine should be the drink of the night and John loads up a cooler with wine but not before he opens a chilled bottle and makes certain each of the women is handed a glass as she boards the boat.

Ben captains the ship but it is John who talks as they move out into the bay about the history of Islamorada and its way of life when its residents are connected to the rest of the world by the cement bridge pilings and lengths of highway that can easily be licked up for dinner by an angry storm or a hurricane. He tells them about his family and how his grandfather helped put in the original rail system and yes, Ernest Hemingway really did stop at the Chaucer's Bar all of the time and yes, Ernest did sign the book that's in the front window and yes, Bob did meet him and has a photograph to prove it.

"He was a great drunk, not unlike my own father and his father," John shared, pointing to a hotel that Hemingway often stayed at when he couldn't make it farther down the Keys and into Key West. "The stories my father told me were something else."

Annie Freeman's traveling funeral quartet wants to hear another story. They want to hear Annie's story.

The boat is moving slowly about a mile off-shore and the night lights are blinking on one by one all along the shoreline. It's a breathtaking display that goes well with white wine, budding friendships, and grieving.

John turns to Ben and before he can say anything, Ben places his hands on his shoulders and says, "It's time, John. It's time for the story."

Not even Laura knows what to expect. She has felt the hint of romance and a desire from the past that has burnt a hole in the palm of her own hands but she has not been able to center her heart on anything specific and she is about to find out why.

"Annie didn't tell me what to say when she set this up," John begins, motioning for Laura to pour him more wine. "She told me what she had planned for this funeral tribute of hers and knowing her the way I do the entire thing makes sense, but she never asked me to say anything or do anything special other than let you stay here and treat you like the goddesses that you are."

He stops to look past all of them, even Ben. He is resurrecting a tale that he has not told in a long time but a tale that is a very important part of who he is and where he came from.

"I'm fifty-nine," he tells them. "When I met Annie, I was young and struggling with the notion of homosexuality and coming from a family where a manly man drank, swore, drove railroad spikes, and made as many babies as possible. It was beyond exhausting."

John was determined to be the kind of man his family expected him to be. He met Annie at the university, dated her and loved her and then he tried, how he tried.

"I was the first man Annie loved and I turned out to be this gay man who could do and be everything for her except, well, there was this problem of physical intimacy that I could never quite conquer," he explains. "Annie didn't know and I agreed to let her come visit me here during the last year of graduate school because I thought—well, I thought something magical would happen on the beach and with the moonlight. Romance and all, you know."

So Annie had flown to Florida and met John's parents at the very house where the women are now staying and on the second night of her three-day stay John took her to a beautiful sandy beach, where he fully intended to make love to her and ask her to marry him.

"We were perfect together," he said. "I had just finished my graduate work in sociology and had been offered a position in San Francisco. It would have been perfect to be with her too because I loved her so much, I'll always love her."

John starts to cry then and Ben moves from behind the wheel, lowers the anchor and comes to stand behind him, resting his hands on his shoulders. John moves one hand to touch Ben and then continues.

"I think she knew by then, that night on the beach. I think she knew, but we both played it out until I bent to kiss her and she stopped me," he says, still crying and looking off into the dark distance of the ocean away from his beloved Islamorada.

Annie had hushed him gently and told him it was past time to tell her whatever it was he had to tell her and so he did.

"My God, I would have died or killed for her," he explained. "I never wanted to hurt her. I loved her."

Jill and Katherine and Rebecca and Laura know he loved her. They know he loved her in ways they could not love her and they see the pain of his own loss shadow his face as he bends weeping into Ben's arms and finally lets go of something precious, tender, and terribly sad. They all want to pick him up and hold him in their arms as he finishes his story but no one can move. No one can breathe.

"We sat there all night talking," he tells them. "Annie was remarkable and yet honest about her life path. She told me that she would never marry. She told me that I would have been a wonderful father and now I can tell you that I am the father of both of her boys. I am their father."

John cries so long and hard after he tells his part of the story that the sky turns dark and the shadows of the moon begin to float across the edges of the boat.

"John . . ." Rebecca finally says, with great tenderness.

"No," he insists. "I have to finish. This is my part of her funeral. The part I need to do. For her. You have to let me finish."

They do so without hesitation.

That night on the beach Annie told him that she was sealing off a part of her heart. She told him that section of her heart would always belong to him and she asked him to let her go until she contacted him, until she knew she was not going to die from a broken heart, until she could understand how she could honor their love in a way that would never really totally fulfill her.

"What happened here in Islamorada was that Annie G. Freeman found a level of love within herself that was pure and nonjudgmental and lasting," John said. "She gave me the courage to be who I needed to be, who I was, and she taught me that love can take many forms."

They did not speak again for years, he explained. When they reconnected, they designed a relationship based on a kind of love that not everyone understands, and he agreed to father her children after months of planning and great thought and they also agreed that someday, perhaps when they were an old man and woman, one of them would tell their sons.

Katherine interrupts. She cannot help herself. It is as if someone else is speaking from inside of her body.

"Do they know?"

"They're coming here next week. They don't know, but I am sure they may have guessed by now."

"Why didn't anyone tell them? Why keep it a secret?"

"It was her idea," he answers. "Ben and I have been together twenty-seven years. He was part of this. You know Annie. She had other relationships after me, before me, for crying out loud she was married for a while, and the decision not to tell them who their father is was not made or accepted lightly by any of us."

John admits that he would have been a lousy day-to-day father. He admits that his academic life that had him moving every two years and then his decision fifteen years ago to move back to Islamorada would not have been the best fit for fatherhood.

"Annie was competent, caring, gentle, brilliant," he explains. "Look how those boys turned out. She did it alone. She told me women are doing it alone all the time. It was a life choice, a lifestyle that I supported and that most of the rest of the world could or would not understand. They could accept her having an affair and getting pregnant and keeping the baby but for her to have a baby on purpose, that she wanted and loved and cared for with all of her heart even though she was not married—well, society isn't prepped for that scenario."

When they head back to the dock Ben is back behind the wheel and John is standing at the bow with his hands on the railing watching the boat dip in and out of waves that descend like tiny waterfalls.

When they tie up the boat no one wants to go to bed. Ben makes hot buttered rum and passes out afghans and they all settle in on the porch and tell Annie G. Freeman stories until it is past midnight and they hear a car turn into the driveway.

Balinda rides into the traveling funeral with tired eyes and a heart that is as heavy as the night sky. Exhausted from travel, her caregiving life and the uncertainty of her own future, she falls into the willing arms of Annie Freeman's friends as if she has been along for the ride from the beginning.

Three hours before dawn, when the house is finally quiet and the whispers have faded into sleeping sighs, the Florida horizon is

suddenly streaked with a long ribbon of white that looks as if it is a trail toward the heavens.

Katherine rises suddenly as if someone has pushed her arm to waken her, looks out the window and imagines the streak of light as a path for Annie's ashes. "How absolutely beautiful," she whispers out loud as the clouds suddenly fill the space, hiding it and keeping it safe until morning.

19

The smell of coffee is like one of Ben's favorite fishing lures and one by one, and not very early at all, the traveling funeral brigade makes its way from the upstairs bedrooms and into the dining room off the kitchen that has a view of the bay that seems to change every single time one of them looks at it. This morning there is a low mist hanging off the shoreline and above it there are long clouds being pushed out to sea that look as if they are being herded by an invisible cowboy.

The women arrive in a variety of costumes—two bathrobes, boxer shorts and a T-shirt and two long summer nightgowns— and Ben, who is cooking a heap of scrambled eggs and something that smells as if it came right out of the oven at the best bakery in town, immediately thinks of them as a parade and he wants them all to walk past the kitchen divider at least three more times which they do gladly.

"What time did you and John go to bed?" Laura asks, signaling with her hands that the parade has come to an end.

"Oh, we don't keep track of things like that down here," Ben tells her, setting out breakfast. "See?" He holds up a wrist without a

watch. "If I have a court appointment or someone coming into the office, my secretary calls but otherwise we just kind of amble around here."

Ben sets breakfast down on the counter, tells the women to dig in, then stands watching them as they fill up their plates. He fills his own plate, hollers out the window to tell John breakfast is ready and joins the women at the table that is large enough, so it seems, to fit half an army at any given moment.

"Well . . ." he says. "Does anyone need anything? Is everything okay?"

"I need to say thank you for letting me join this intimate gathering," Balinda says first. "I am very, very grateful to be joining you."

Balinda is a small woman, scarcely over five feet tall, with dark hair that cascades down her back, and when she speaks it is with the tiniest accent that automatically makes her sound elegant, foreign, and just a bit on the sexy side. She also looks exhausted and has dark circles under her eyes and would probably be happy to stay in bed for the entire day or maybe the rest of the week.

Katherine replies that they would have it no other way and begins talking about the day's most important event just as John enters the room. Because it's close to noon already and they have to get up before five A.M. to drive back to Miami the next day, she thinks they should make plans for the "funeral of the day," as she now prefers to call it.

"I've talked to each one of you about this, and, Ben and John, we'd all like to invite you to participate in the ceremony today. Actually, we'd like some input and your help in directing us to the best location for this," she explains, then raises her hand as if to stop any oncoming words. "Let me tell you that we all agreed that the ceremony probably should be at the beach where you talked with Annie all those years ago, John, unless that would be too difficult for you."

John smiles shyly, sits, and pours himself a cup of coffee before he answers. Ben is looking at him, waiting for his response, and clearly knowing the entire time what it will be.

"I was hoping you'd ask and at the same moment was thinking what marvelous women Annie chose to do this, to be her friends, to help her through the other tough passages," John says. "I'd be lying if I said it was easy and that I never worried about her, but I worried less as the years passed and she told me about some of you. You were all beyond important to her. You became her family."

They settle on sunset, that sweet time just before it's truly dark, as the lightness of day falls into the arms of evening.

Ben suggests they walk to the beach and then down the coastal sidewalk to the men's favorite restaurant, the Bay Breeze, following the ceremony. He thinks a "celebration of life" will be in order and he promises to make certain they don't close the place down so they can get up early and get to the airport. "I'll be the mom," he volunteers.

Then there is a storm of activity. Katherine announces she needs to run an errand, asks directions to the closest and largest department store, and takes off so fast she almost forgets to remove her nightgown. Laura and Balinda invite Rebecca to go for a swim with them off the pier so they can find a treasure for Marie and Jill lingers in the kitchen to talk to John about the funeral book.

"You need to write in it and we'll have Ben do it, too. She'd like that. I'm sure you know that," she explains. "It's been kind of helpful for all of us as we travel through our own emotions. You'll see."

John wants to talk. He wants to know if Jill thinks he's crazy for having given Annie up, for having fathered the boys, for living a life in a way that doesn't fit the mold.

"Absolutely not," Jill replies, firmly. "You are who you are and I know for a fact that Annie is the first person in the world who would embrace that. Love comes in various sizes, we all know that, and damn the people who judge, just damn them."

John tells her stories then. He tells her how his family would not speak to him for a dozen years and how his mother refused to visit and how it was the local mechanic who finally helped his father and eventually his mother learn to love him for the man he was and always would be.

"The mechanic? Whatever did he say or do?"

"His daughter was a lesbian and one afternoon while my dad was waiting for the oil in his Chevy to be changed, the mechanic came over to him and they talked." John turns to look out of the window and into the bay where the women are swimming. "He told my father that he had felt the same about his daughter as my father did about me."

"What changed? What happened?"

"His wife got ill, really ill, she had cancer and it was two things really," John tells her. "His daughter came home right away to help and he walked in on her giving her sick mother a bath. He saw his daughter gently talking to her, helping her wash her hair and back and as she was doing that tears kept running down her face."

Jill closes her eyes and she imagines what the mechanic saw. She sees the young woman holding up her mother as her mother once held her up. She imagines the daughter's heart cracking as she realizes her mother is going to die, as she sees that her mother has turned into a frame of brittle bones to support her dwindling weight.

"Then, just a few days later, his daughter called him at work. She said he needed to come get them as fast as possible to help her get her mother to the hospital," John continues. "He rushed home. He found his daughter in his bed, with his wife, holding her like she was a baby and telling her that everything would be okay."

"When he looked at his daughter then, he saw how extraordinarily beautiful she was. He saw that she was kind and gracious and giving. He saw her as a woman of courage and strength and he realized he had made a terrible mistake in judging her on one aspect of her life.

"He stood in front of my father and he told him not to wait until it was too late. He told my father to look beyond his own limitations, to see that I was a man of great worth who loved him no matter how I lived or how I had been treated."

John said his father told him this story only once. Before his father died, he took John's hand, told him the story, and said, "John, you are a fine man and you must never forget I am proud of you."

Death brings forgiveness, John tells Jill, but real forgiveness, before the dying, is a gift that is immeasurable.

"Sometimes I feel as if I have spent half my life hoping that people will forgive me for who I am," he continues. "My family . . . Annie . . . friends who I lost when I came totally out of the closet . . . Knowing who I am and how I have to be true to myself—Annie helped me get to that place as the years passed and we talked."

John took the book, as Jill left to swim, and he wrote. He cried as he wrote and as he remembered what a precious gift Annie had given him and was still giving him.

JOHN THOUGHT: *Oh, my sweet, lovely, wise Annie, what gifts you continue to bring into my life. Your honesty and forgiveness. Years of friendship and understanding. The confidence to move forward without second-guessing who I am, who I was, who I always will be. Thank you for letting me love you the way I loved you and for staying a part of my life, for being there in the ways that you could. Thank you now for this gift of the traveling funeral. Did any of us even know how important this was going to be? Did we know how much we needed to talk about what we thought we could not live without? Living—that's what it's all about. That's what you were trying to tell me all those years ago and through the very way that you lived. I love you, Annie—deep and rich and strong, like I have never loved anyone else. My heart beats stronger because of you and my life has been a sea of joy because of what you gave me.*

ANNIE THOUGHT: *Oh, you ass. I know you loved me. I know that I could have made it even easier and I know that you wanted so much to be a part of the boys' lives but it couldn't work that way. Be strong and good, John. Do not linger over my death too long. Do not look back any longer than necessary and be there for our boys—no longer boys but always boys to me—if they ever need anything. And for crying out loud—did you ever learn how to properly tie a damn necktie?*

An hour before sunset, everyone gathers on the front porch of the bed-and-breakfast and Katherine passes out red tennis shoes and bandanas to Balinda, John, and Ben during an informal ceremony that launches the evening's events. Her early afternoon shopping trip had taken her on a scavenger hunt that led her to five stores but triumphantly helped her produce three sets of shoes and the bandanas.

Only Balinda can wear the shoes. John and Ben's are inches too small, so they tie them together and hang them around their necks and then the group forms a line and they all follow Ben as he leads them out past the driveway and to a path that they would never have seen themselves even in the best light of day.

Katherine is carrying Annie's ashes. The red tennis shoes are tucked snugly into the shoebox, which Katherine has placed under her arm, protecting it with her free hand as if she were keeping a tree branch off of a baby's tender face during a hike through the forest. The path is wide and edges at first along the water and then narrows as it moves inland and courses through a stand of trees that Laura thinks are probably called groves in Florida.

The traveling funeral pallbearers are quiet. Red sneaker bottoms over the sand and a tight breeze off the lip of the ocean that nudges treetops and creates a swishing sound—these are the only sounds.

This does not include the beating hearts of the men and women who loved Annie G. Freeman.

This does not include the occasional deep breath from the open mouth of a pallbearer who is desperately trying not to burst into tears.

This does not include the sighs of longing and loss that seep from the limbs of every single person who is walking toward the beach.

This does not include the private whispers of stories and songs and conversations that each one of them is remembering as they pass by a private home and then move to the beach where they will take turns throwing some of what's left of their friend Annie, the physical Annie, but never ever their memories and never ever the sections of their hearts that Annie filled and will always fill.

In what can only be considered a cosmic and wonderful gesture the sun slips into the ocean as they come onto a beautiful wide beach and Jill, astounded by the moment, breathes, "Oh my God" and stops right where she is standing.

"It's so beautiful," she exclaims. "No wonder people who lived by the water thought the world was flat. They just turned around and saw that sun come up the other side and imagined that the sun and moon slipped under the edge of the earth and came up the other side after resting for a few hours."

"It is always like this," Ben says. "I thought I would hate this musty, humid part of the world but it is breathtaking. It's a marriage of earth and water here. Absolutely stunning every single moment."

They pause to watch the fading edges of the day come together into the darkness of the horizon. Laura raises her hands because she thinks she can touch it. She places one hand out to the right, the other to the left and it looks as if she is pushing the sky into place. Everyone watches her and forgets about the skyline.

She dances in place, closes her eyes and she imagines—without speaking—the spirit of Annie moving like a fine piece of silk in a breeze above the top of the ocean. She imagines Annie turning into the wind and grazing her fingers across the waves and smiling as she feels the air lift her and carry her further out to sea. She imagines Annie singing softly as the cool night air moves against her skin and the sun dances eagerly on the other side of the world. She imagines Annie at peace and never wondering if she did the right thing as she flows into the next world on the wings of her own angels and under the power of her own beautiful energy.

Everyone else somehow knows what Laura must be thinking. They think of Annie—each thought a secret that captivates them so deeply that no one can speak, no one can move anything but their eyes as Laura's hands grow closer and closer together while the sun's last few pieces of light disintegrate in between her fingers.

Everyone knows that every single person there—even Balinda, who only knows Annie through the words of her best friend Laura—loves Annie in ways that no one else did or even could and they know, too, that Annie loved them in return uniquely. They know that sometimes Annie was a shit but so were they. They realize that Annie gifted them with each other and with this moment and with a life that not only inspired but transformed them. And they know, too, that they will never forget her or each other or this brilliant sunset that has wrapped itself around Laura's fingers and is now making its way across the entire world.

They know.

"Hey," Katherine says to snap them out of a trance that threatens to make them all plunge naked into the ocean so they can swim after the sun. "What do you think?"

John steps forward. He says that he'd like to say something. He wants everyone to be a part of the entire ceremony and he asks if that is okay.

The women all look at him as they have been looking at him ever since they realized his history with Annie. And they know why she loved him so. They know that even as he could not love her the way she wanted, no one could ever love her the way he did. They know that he is kind and generous and considerate and bold and graceful and each one of them feels as if they have won the lottery to now have John and Ben in their lives.

Yes. They all say yes.

First they take off their shoes and they place them in a neat row above the row of rocks that sit above the tide line. Then Katherine takes the shoes out of the box and she carries them and walks to stand among her friends. Everyone holds hands and then walks into the water.

They walk into the water until their knees are covered and they can feel the wind on their faces and they can see why Annie would have wanted to stay on Islamorada with John. No one is ready. No one would ever be ready for this, but they all take great courage in the presence of one another, in realizing for the first time that they will do this again for maybe Laura or Katherine or Ben.

Katherine cannot stop crying but she keeps the funeral in motion. She is strong and she knows that this is exactly what Annie would have wanted of her. She is also crying because something has without warning shifted inside of her. Something that has been pushed unexpectedly out of place and that needs immediate attention and is now lashing against her lungs hard enough to make her cry—it is her own life, her very own life. She knows this and she does not repress it and she embraces the moment, which she will later discover is the first step in a whole new journey.

"I'm going to step in front of each one of you and have you take some ashes. And then I want you to hold them in your hand and when I am back in place, whenever you are ready, throw them, place them gently into the water, do whatever you want with them. And when you are done squeeze the hand of the person to the right of you and when my hand is squeezed I will know that we are done."

The hush of this night is stunning. A mischievous wind kicks up the scents and sounds from the day and blends them into a soft hum that sounds like someone is singing. They all hear it and they smile, thinking, of course, that Annie had something to do with it.

One by one Katherine distributes the ashes.

The ashes.

They are impossibly soft. Pieces of silk that touch their skin like wands of elegance.

One by one, they let the ashes sift from their hands. It is not possible to see where the ashes land and it does not matter.

It doesn't matter where they land or how they are released. It doesn't matter that each one of them loved Annie in a unique and glorious way that has branded each of them for the rest of their lives. It doesn't matter that their sadness and their joy mingle in such interesting ways that they all feel as if they are stoned. It doesn't matter that every single one of them is crying and deeply grateful to have known Annie G. Freeman and to be holding the hands of someone else who knew her and loved her.

And when they turn to grab their red shoes something happens that is astonishing and wild . . . and surprising to absolutely no one.

A shooting star moves from left to right, dipping once, like a woman might dip her head if she saw someone she loved and it was not the right moment to say "I love you."

The shooting star dips and then it disappears and at that exact moment in California, Marie puts her hand on her heart, feels a surge of movement—swift and sharp—and says, "Oh, sweet Annie," and then turns toward her east window, opens her arms and embraces the invisible sunset she imagines is crossing toward her at that very moment.

20

There are clues everywhere.

This from Balinda the newcomer as the station wagon taxi, stuffed with perhaps the first and largest traveling funeral this city has ever seen, makes its way through a snarl of traffic that appears to stretch all the way back to the Florida Keys. A flight delay from a lovely late storm that kicked up tornadoes along the east coast has landed them in New York City's rush hour traffic and they are still without Marie.

Five days into the traveling funeral, two legs of the trip and twelve funeral-book pages later, close to half the ashes flung, secrets flying as if there has been a massive explosion, enough tears to float a good-sized speedboat, dozens of phone calls from Marie, lots of phone calls home, and with two stops left after the New York funeral, Annie Freeman's traveling funeral is focused on what their newest member has to say.

"She's left you clues everywhere, you know that, don't you?"

This from Balinda who came to them for a small slice of salvation and who has ended up being a feisty, open, exhausted, and wonderful new addition to Annie's funeral brigade. Her petite frame is a lovely camouflage for the rods of steel that hold up her spine. Balinda, who has shelved her own life and the dream of moving to a small town and opening up her own restaurant using recipes that she has been collecting for twenty-three years from women she meets who are above the age of sixty, has dropped into their lives and this funeral adventure as if she has been scheming to come along since the moment she was born.

And her stories of caring for her mother, of watching her own life stand at attention while the rest of the world marches past, have given their own aching hearts permission to focus on the greater world of sorrow and a wiser role model.

"You don't plan on putting your life on hold, especially when you are in what the rest of the world considers the prime of life," she told them. "But is there a choice really? And did my mother plan on becoming so ill, of having me care for her as if she were the infant and I were the mother? Did she know that her mind would slip just a bit every day until it wandered so far from home it became totally lost? Did she sit and plan for me to give up all my months and years? How could any single person ever wish to be so ill that their own daughter has to empty their bedpan, pick their legs up off the floor so they can roll into bed, remind them of their last name and tie them to the goddamn bed so they do not walk out the front door and into the headlights of an oncoming bus?"

Sometimes, Balinda told them, she wished for her mother to die. She told them this as she struggled with her emotions so she would not weep, sitting with her hands in her lap at the Miami airport when the plane was delayed. She told them that caregiving made her at first hard and angry and hateful, and then how it changed her.

"Once, before this happened, I was in a huge park in northern Illinois and I was hiking," she told them, closing her eyes to remember, to feel something that was lost the instant it began. "I felt free and light and as if I knew exactly who I was and where I was going and what was going to happen every moment for the next fifty years. I stopped with that thought in my head. I stopped as if

I had hit a brick wall and I dropped to my knees, closed my eyes and rolled over into the grass."

She rolled over, she told them, and opened her mind to look into her own future, thinking she would see brilliant lights, a stairway to success, the bright blue eyes of her lover and the footprints of tomorrow running up and down the side of her left leg. She did see a swirl of light and a parade of dreams marching to the tunes of soft Hawaiian music and the melodies of old Broadway show tunes. She also saw shadowy figures, faces that she could not quite discern, and colors—deep shades of blue—that seemed to get deeper and darker as they got closer, just the opposite of what she expected to see.

Lying in the grass that day she never saw her mother crawling through the living room on her hands and knees at two A.M. because she could not find her way to the bathroom and was lost. She never saw her boyfriend standing in the driveway with his hands on his trunk as he told her it was too much and that he could no longer deal with a half-ass girlfriend who spent more time with her hands on a bedpan and not on him and he was sorry but he could never see her again. She never saw one year turn into the next as her mother's needs swelled and her own desires folded their hands into submission and agreed to be led around by the familial bonds of life that tied her right in one place so she could no longer move.

"I'm so tired," she shared with the traveling funeral brigade. "I need for just this little slice of time to bury my own story in the middle of someone else's."

This is the place to do that, they almost all say at once. This is the place to watch us mourn and to prepare to do that yourself, but in a new way. This is also the place, they remind her, to toss back a glass of wine before noon and to laugh all afternoon and just be— just be. It is possible, they insist, because after a few days they feel like letting-go experts. Let go. Stand at ease. Let someone else cut into the dance.

"Annie didn't have many rules for the traveling funeral but we know for sure she wanted us to celebrate her life more than to mourn the loss of it," Laura explained as they inched along in traffic. "We can only talk about the bad stuff for a few hours every day, otherwise the ashes blow up or something."

And there is Marie, they tell Balinda, Marie who is always helping mothers die, Marie who can talk to you on the phone and then who you'll meet in person. Kindred spirits. Shared lives. Just you wait, they tell her.

Laughter propels them through the tunnels and around stalled cars and so many honking horns they all quickly realize that the horns are totally useless because after a while their chorus of beeps blends in with every other noise in the city and they become indistinguishable from the hum of life that in New York is really a roar.

New York.

It slaps them upside their heads the minute they focus on where the plane has actually dropped them. It's no Islamorada, they all agree. It's so different from Chicago or San Francisco or any other city they ever visit or have lived in that they immediately get sucked into the vortex of its charming madness.

"What is it about this city?" Jill asks them all, pressing her fingers against the window as if she were testing the pulse of something alive. "It's like being reborn every time I come here."

They swap New York stories. A quick theater trip. A long layover that turned into a three-day feast of shopping, drinking espresso at sidewalk cafés, and carousing in bars where famous people had kissed their lovers.

"It's partly the history," Katherine decides. "Just about every single major event that changed this country and half the world was launched or born or bred within forty miles of where we are sitting right this moment."

Which leads them back to Annie and wondering what it was she discovered or touched here that was so important to her that she wanted her ashes spread here. They guess.

Love.

Discovery.

Insight.

Wild sex.

A professional milestone.

They are deep in discussion when Katherine suggests it may be a good time to put in the tape from Annie and they might know for certain. The cabdriver warns them that the taxi bill is closing in on fifty bucks, shrugs his shoulders as he gestures at all the traffic, and then slips in the tape for them.

"*Hey*," she starts and her voice seems to still the loud rush of sound around them.

Isn't New York something? The first time I arrived here I was scared shitless. The second time, I remembered where to turn and how to hail the cabbie. Well, I never wanted to live in New York but I visited a lot, especially before my sons were born, and it's where I not only met the only man I ever dared to marry, it's the place where I realized a woman like me should probably never be married—especially to a man like that.

So what was it? What happened to me? Why do I want to spread my dusty ashes in a place where most people who slam into you on the sidewalk will keep right on walking?

You could all figure it out, especially after you check into the hotel and see what I have planned for you, but I'll help you a little bit. Just a little bit.

Think of fun. Think of culture. Think about how our lives are often awash in routine and expectations. Think about making believe you are someone else. Then you'll know.

And a warning: You had better not be sitting around crying in your white wine for a single second of this trip. This is an adventure, ladies!

So? So knock it off with the Kleenex and tell some dirty jokes. Be sure and look out the windows. I'll never forget what it

*felt like to look out the windows the first time and to feel the
rush of the city, its luscious past and the vibrant heart of every
thing and person and experience mingled together like a wild,
throbbing soul.*

There's more to find. See what you can do.

Go kick up your heels. I'm with you, women. I'm right here.

There is a pause as the tape spits itself out of the cassette player
and the women process what they have just heard. It is Rebecca
who breaks the silence, with a very soft "Shit," that makes them all
snap to attention and laugh.

"Shit what?" Jill asks.

"Just shit, it looks like we are going to have to celebrate and have
another wild night on the town. I was not prepared for all of this
vigorous activity. I thought we'd be moping around and crying."

"I've seen more than enough crying to fill up that ocean out
there," Balinda says, gesturing toward the water they have just
passed. "Every time I took my mother to the hospital it seemed as
if there was a new tragedy, young, old, middle-aged—this dying
and grief stuff knows no boundaries."

"It doesn't matter," Rebecca responds. "The pain of loss, for a
baby, an elderly parent, someone who drops dead at thirty, the sorrow and grief doesn't change because of age."

"Once," Balinda begins softly, "when I was in the emergency
room with my mother they brought in a murderer who had been
shot and was dying, right there in front of us. I watched as the
nurse touched his face and reassured him and I could not believe
they were being so nice to him."

"What happened?" Jill asked.

"My mother rose up, took my arm, gripped it as if she was a
weight lifter and said, 'He was a beautiful baby once and his
mother loved him.' "

There is a second of silence when the women imagine the hospital scene and then Laura brushes it all away by saying, "Somehow

the human heart figures out how to move on. It isn't easy but the alternative is a bit much."

Laura's harshness sobers them quickly and no one says anything. There is a tiny rail of tension in the taxi. A bit of tiredness mixed with sadness, that always-present layer of guilt, Katherine's constant in-charge attitude, Balinda's poor-me routine, Laura's impatience, Jill's ache for a new life, and Rebecca's barrel of loss could tip them all over.

While they crawl through traffic, the women begin to discuss shifting roles, and daughters becoming the mothers of mothers, and how they see a rotation backwards, like the old days, when aging parents moved in with their adult children. If there's no money for long-term care, if disability has run out, if you have an ounce of compassion and familial loyalty and love, that's what you do, they all agree.

The taxi driver points out their hotel, which still looks as if it is in the next state, and says, "It's an elegant beauty." Rebecca shares a story about her sister and an aging neighbor woman with a bit of money and the woman's three children who all lived within a mile of her and would not help their dying mother, who was getting frailer with each passing day.

"Maybe she was a closet bitch or something but they came around only once in the four years that my sister took care of Martha," Rebecca shares. "My sister did everything for Martha, who had been widowed since she was forty-three and was eighty-one when my sister started taking care of her."

Rebecca's sister learned only after Martha's death that she had lived with a broken furnace, leaky faucets and a hand-crank washing machine, because she did not want to ask for any more help.

"Damn kids," Rebecca said. "My sister even had the funeral dinner at her house and none of those bastards bothered to send her a thank-you note. But when they split the inheritance, I'm pretty sure they were all in line and right on time at the attorney's office."

"And the lesson here would be?" Katherine asked.

"Always find out if the neighbors have their furnace working."

"Never answer the doorbell."

"Feed your children to wild dogs before the age of three."

"Call my sister if you ever need any help."

There is time for three more stories—stories about neighbors helping neighbors and the real meaning of the word "family" and how terrifying it must be to know that you are ill, incapable of even the simplest bodily functions, to have to rely on the kindness, even if it is paid kindness, of others.

They also talk of Marie and a heart's calling. They decide that there would not have been better hands to hold Annie than the gentle and warm fingers and wrists and arms of Marie from Sonoma County who no doubt at the very minute they are about to enter a new and noisy, tangled unborn jungle is either changing someone's catheter, measuring a dose of morphine, or cradling someone's body in her arms.

"Enough," the cabdriver finally tells them with an accent that is as dark and rich as their morning coffee as he pulls in front of their hotel. "No more dying talk now. This is New York. New York keeps on moving, no matter who dies. That is who we are."

The hotel is a breathtaking elegant step back into time for women who have been around the block but who can usually be found at a sixty-dollar-a-night chain hotel, inside of a tent, or sleeping on a friend's couch while dressed in a well-worn pair of sweatpants, a faded T-shirt and an aging pair of flip-flops.

"Oh, sweet God in heaven," Jill whispers, standing in a lobby that looks as if it has just escaped from a European history book. "Katherine, are you certain we are at the right hotel?"

No one moves while Katherine confirms their registration and they are ushered by smiling men in red suits with tiny red hats to the top of the hotel and two adjoining executive suites. The rooms are an exquisite array of tables, chairs, sitting rooms, and bathrooms that immediately make the women feel as if they have not only been transported back in time, but transplanted into someone else's life as well.

"Do you think Annie stayed here?" Rebecca asks, moving to the window only to discover a view of Central Park that makes her say, "Holy shitski."

"I suppose," Laura says, following her to the window. "She could have had her honeymoon here or she could have met someone here or had a one-night stand. We didn't know *everything* about her. That would be impossible."

Jill discovers a note on the bed and four bottles of champagne chilling on a table. She opens the note, reads it, and then turns to wave it at the other women.

Katherine takes the note out of her hand and holds it out as far as her arm can reach because her reading glasses are stuffed inside of her bag.

Tonight . . . drink every last drop of this outrageously expensive champagne. Do not leave these rooms. Order room service. Take long baths. Have a slumber party. Tomorrow, do the town. Eat out. Go to a bar. You will know where to drop me. Live large. Laugh. You deserve every frigging moment of this. I adore all of you. Love, Annie.

The champagne tastes like gold. They lick their glasses and squeeze their eyes shut while they drink it and imagine it is the stuff kings and queens sip for Sunday brunch. The women quickly claim the space as their own, throw their bags and jackets and cell phones from one end of the suite to the other, and they use the crystal glasses at the bar. They toast Annie and each other and they call home and then they call Marie, who is in the middle of an assessment of a new patient, and Marie orders them to drink faster and call her in three hours because she is also on hold with her travel agent. They jump on the beds, order hors d'oeuvres, and then they draw straws for the whirlpool bathtubs.

The champagne goes right to each one of their heads and they could care less. They lie on the floor and put their feet up on tables that cost more than all of the furniture in their entire living room. They forget about all the parts of each other that drive them crazy. They run their hands along the sides of the long golden drapes, they lean into the windows and watch people—tiny ants below—in the park, they write notes on the gold stationery, and then they push all the chairs together, order dinner and really good wine, and they have a feast of food and words and memories.

Before they fall asleep, before someone finally says, "I cannot have one more sip of wine," Laura asks everyone to be quiet for just a second, which is no easy task. She tells them to close their eyes and to imagine all the voices of the past that were once alive in their suite—the sighs of lovers, the phone calls to Sweden, the lost moments spent gazing into the glittering sky after events like the stock market crash, a huge parade, the end of a war, the Towers' collapse. Laura mesmerizes them with her voice and with what they know that she knows about the past worlds hidden under the thick carpeting and the golden wallpaper and in the lining of the carved mahogany drawers.

"Think of everyone who danced here," she tells them. "The women in long skirts who threw back the heavy drapes and little boys who were told 'hush' as their grandma slept on the divan, and the maid who stood guard, dreaming of the moment when she could race home to hold the hands of her own lover."

Think, she tells them, of Annie. Then make up your own story, she asks. Believe whatever you want of her in this place, this insane and wonderful city. Make it up. Make it real. Hold it in your own hand and dance with it, Laura instructs, dance with it all the way to your bed and all through the night and every time you think of this city and this night.

Before dawn, in that bleak hour when every person, every being wants to stay asleep forever, each one of the women stirs for just a second. Laura, Katherine, Jill, Balinda, Rebecca and even Marie, even Marie stirs and sees or thinks she sees the shadow of someone with her head tilted back and a glass in her hand, laughing so hard that she seems to lose her balance.

Later the following morning and the next day and for years after that, no one speaks of that laughing shadow. They all think it was a dream—this dancing, lovely happy woman who seemed as if she was born to have fun. They think it was a dream, but they never forget.

They never forget.

21

It is just past noon when they finally decide.

They have missed the high tea thingamabob in the hotel rotunda. They have missed breakfast but not the ordering of extravagant quantities of dark, rich coffee and pastries loaded with sugar. They have missed six cell-phone calls and the crack of dawn, and two knocks on the suite door from a maid and the hotel manager, who forgot to deliver fresh flowers the night before.

"Okay, you guys," Katherine finally says. "We need to seize this day or what is left of it. We have a funeral to get on with here, for crying out loud. What should we do?"

Climb to the top and sneak onto the roof? No.

Take one of the funky buggy rides and throw her around in the park? No.

A very she-she or he-she bar? No.

The library. Books. She loved books. No.

All around. A little here and a little there. Fifth Avenue. Alphabet City. Harlem. No.

They think some more. Balinda pages through the book on the desk to find the latest hot and trendy nightspots for dinner.

Katherine paces. Jill stands and looks down at the park. Laura lies very still on the bed.

Balinda comes up with it and she does so as an accident. She is reading the names of the recommended restaurants and places to visit while in the Big Apple out loud and when she mentions the boat tour around Manhattan Island, they all look up at once and say, "That's it!" at the exact same time.

"That's it?" Balinda asks, not really sure but pretty sure.

"Oh yes." Jill moves from the window and claps her hands together. "The boat tour. That's perfect and it's a heck of a lot of fun, if I can remember back that far."

Everyone agrees, even Laura, who looks as if she may have had a wiser thought come into her head. But she doesn't object and they all look at her with gratitude for her silence. So it's decided. Lunch wherever they find it along the way. The last tour of the day. Red shoes all around. Scarves wherever they want to wear them. The ceremony. Dinner on the way back and then they must hit—because of Annie's orders—at least one New York City bar before they can slip in between the perfumed linen sheets again and sleep like drunken babies.

In New York, which celebrates the thin and the fat and the happy and the demented and the joyful and the grieving, they look—well—different. But they could care less, because they are the pallbearers for Annie G. Freeman. The hotel lobby is loaded with dark suits and long skirts as they parade down the set of steps and cross the thick carpeted hall. Several people standing by the desk look at them and stare. Katherine, who is becoming even more boisterous with each passing second, blows them a kiss and then makes certain the shoebox with Annie's ashes is inside her carrying bag along with her water bottle, cell phone, and the funeral book.

The doormen tip their hats and one asks, "Can I do anything, please?" and Rebecca tells them they need a ride to the boat.

"The boat?" quips Jill. "It looks like you just got off the boat."

They ride in a taxi with the windows open and Jill in the front
seat with the driver and with an air of anticipation that makes
everything seem brighter and more crackling than it probably is
but Annie G. Freeman's traveling funeral mistresses are on a mission and they know they are looking at the same streets, maybe
some of the same people, in one of the places that captivated and
captured a piece of Annie and that, for sure, makes everything
beyond just a bit brighter. Their own stuff, just for now, is not allowed on this part of the journey.

"Hey!" Balinda shouts out the window. "Look at that!"

They all look out the window and what they see is another parade. A sudden New York parade where a man dressed not unlike
them in colors that glow in the dark and blowing a silver tuba is
walking down the sidewalk and gathering up passersby who have
formed an imaginary band behind him.

"Do not stop this cab," Jill orders the taxi driver who glances
down quickly at her red high-tops with a polite smirk even though
he has seen worse. He wonders if they are all members of some
new women's terrorist group about to take over the boat tour. He
imagines it even as he thinks it and he does not stop.

The tuba echoes behind them as they swerve down an avenue
where a double-decker green-and-white boat sign proudly announces that it will take them to see three rivers, seven bridges and
five boroughs.

"That should do it," Laura says with confidence as she stands in
front of the sign. "There's plenty of room in all those places for the
ashes of Annie."

Rebecca tells Katherine that Annie has become such a seemingly
live part of her own funeral that maybe they should buy a ticket for
her. Then they imagine what it would be like if Annie G. Freeman
was with them like she was with them just months ago.

Would they be in a different city? No.

Would they talk or drink or laugh less? No—maybe more.

Would they try something new? Yes.

Would they defer to Annie, the know-it-all queen? Yes. Often. Even Katherine.

Would the entire adventure be a revealing, intimate escapade that might be followed by years of follow-up discussion? Oh, yes.

And then, then they wonder why they waited. They wonder why everyone waits to send the note, make the call, say the one thing you know you should say.

"Death," Jill states, "does this to people. It slaps the living upside the head and it makes us ponder and exchange events and feelings that might stay hidden."

"It's like a narcotic, when you think about it," Katherine agrees. "Look at us, for crissakes. We are dressed like clowns and we've abandoned our routines and our kids and our husbands and our jobs to do this funky funeral thing. We'd never have even thought of this unless Annie had died."

The conversation races like the avenues of Manhattan until they see water shimmering at the end of the next block. The taxi driver watches them leave the taxi and hop onto the long blue boat, smiling widely and thinking that "those women are up to something" and he wishes he could go along just to find out what that something might be.

They stake out the entire boat and decide to claim the back seats, perfect for spreading ashes when no one is looking, and then they settle in, wait for the cruise to begin, and share stories of other places and times they shared with Annie G. Freeman.

For a while then there are no lost loves and no overbooked workdays. For a while everyone is safe and none of the children have problems. For a while everyone knows who they are and where they are going. For a while they can set aside remorse and loss and the wider arc of grief that encompasses everything and everyone. For a while nothing any of them says or does will irritate anyone else. For a while they can sit in the moment, sit and not worry or shift a wad of guilt from hand to hand or imagine what it will be like in a week when they are not here in this traveling funeral brigade.

Both Katherine and Rebecca agree that the best times with Annie, the greatest moments, were the quiet ones. Driving in the car, sitting on the back steps and drinking strong coffee or stronger whiskey. Hiking for hours in mostly silence.

"I loved talking to Annie about books," Laura tells the group. "Before I even thought about buying a book, or reading one for that matter, I always called her and she almost always knew something about it or the writer or some far-fetched review. I loved knowing I could count on her that way."

Balinda listens as Rebecca says it was Annie's garage light that made her happy. She said she loved seeing the light on because it meant Annie was home.

"No matter how together we are, how many friends or kids or partners or dogs or goats we have, there are always moments where we not only feel alone but lonely as well. That damn light of Annie's was like my security blanket," Rebecca shares. "It was a light in the darkness, yes, but it was really knowing that I could count on her. Having her to be there for me in a heartbeat if I needed anything is the thing that I miss every goddamn day."

Katherine talks about Annie's voice in such quiet tones it takes everyone a few minutes to realize that she is crying.

"I'm okay," she assures them. "Thinking about Annie's light makes me think about how when I heard her voice, my heart would race, and I could just picture her and what she was doing and that she was close enough to drive to if I really needed her. God, how I loved just talking to her. Sometimes I'd sort of freak out if I couldn't get her on her cell phone or at home or work."

Sometimes, she tells them, she still answers the phone thinking it might be Annie and she forgets. She forgets that Annie has died and that it won't be her on the end of the phone line and then the second she hears another voice, anyone's voice—a telemarketer, her daughter, the phone company—she gets so angry she wants to take the phone and throw it out the window.

"It's just her voice for me that always made me feel loved. That was it."

Balinda cannot speak of Annie except for what she has learned of her the last two days and what Laura has shared with her. She cannot say for sure but she thinks what endeared her to Annie the most would have been her brazen spirit.

"I never met her but I bet she would have told me to find ways to move forward and that I'd still be able to help my mother," she says, rising to move to the railing opposite Jill. "I bet I'd miss her advice and I bet I'd miss some wild-ass adventure, like this, that she'd cook up in between whatever else she did."

Brazen and fun, the other women agree, pretty much would be a good thing to miss and it would be true—that was Annie.

Manhattan looks like a towering mass of concrete from the backside of the boat but it is fascinating and uniquely beautiful no matter how the women look at it. The wind is just a tickle around their necks that picks up as the boat speeds around the first turn and the tour guide begins trotting back through time with the handful of visitors who are on board for the final trip of the day. Annie's pallbearers are not interested in the founding fathers and mothers who set up camp on the island that is such a swirling mass of energy it glitters and seems to move to its own beat. They are not interested in purchasing key rings or cold drinks or in the opportunity to personally rent an entire boat for a private party. They are only interested in figuring out how to distribute Annie's ashes without the other tourists becoming part of the ritual.

"Let's stake out the territory," Rebecca suggests. "We kind of look like a gang with these scarves and shoes anyway. Maybe they'll all be scared of us."

The mere thought makes everyone begin laughing hysterically.

"Look at us," Jill snorts, pulling at her T-shirt and slapping her stomach. "I can see why someone would be scared as hell of me."

They do it anyway because, besides the fear factor idea, it makes sense. Laura stands guard at the entrance, Jill and Balinda stay at their corners, Rebecca rises to stand at the edge of the steps that go upstairs, and Katherine stands in the middle of the back railing holding the shoebox.

There is a slight chance that someone will come to the back of the boat, but the other tourists are huddled around the front of the boat and asking questions of the guide who occasionally shouts up to the captain. Not much chance there will be a raid where the women are.

They guard and then they wait because they really don't have a plan.

"We could just do it all at once, huddle back here, and do it like that," Laura finally suggests. "It would be the one-two-three version of the traveling funeral. We haven't done that yet."

They think for a moment and then Rebecca says it would be better to spread it out.

"I think more than one thing happened to her here," she explains. "I think she had tons of adventures here, had fun, embraced a whole new part of the world, probably fell in love—it would be wrong to assume that New York was just a one-shot deal."

That's true, everyone agrees, but they also agree that it doesn't so much matter how it's done but that it's done and done by them. The boat sways a tiny bit and their red scarves begin to blow and the sun takes a straight shot up and rides as high as possible, dismantling clouds and taking the reins of the day.

Katherine finally suggests that at each turn, one of them spread the ashes and do or say whatever they want to.

"That way," she explains, holding tightly on to the shoebox, "we'll have the entire island covered and we can let our guard down just a bit."

Just as she finishes talking, a couple pushes past Rebecca and says, "Mind if we stand here?" and stops to rest against the railing right in the middle of the traveling funeral. The five women are speechless for a second and then they all want to laugh at what it might be like to try and explain why they commandeered the back end of the boat.

"Oh, we're just having a little funeral this afternoon with our friend Annie," one of them would say. "She's right here, yes, that's here right inside of those cute red high-tops. Oh, no, no don't worry, we won't get any ashes in your eyes and even if we do, it washes out. She was a fun gal. Loved boats and all. We thought we'd take her for one last ride."

They wait it out, ready, each one of them, to say something to get the couple the hell out of there but it turns out their own silence is enough to do the trick. The woman looks around after just a few minutes and discovers that five women are staring at her and that they all have on red tennis shoes and red bandanas and they look, well, they look just a little wacko.

She leans over, whispers into her companion's ear, and then he turns slowly and not so smoothly to look at them—their feet first. He gets it after he does see that the five women are indeed staring at them and that he and his wife must have walked into something terribly interesting but definitely not open to the public. The couple leave without saying a word.

"Close call," Balinda says. "Maybe we should get started."

"Imagine what you will now of Annie and her life here," Katherine suggests. "Imagine it, and throw that part of Annie's life, that passion, that notion for living right back out there when we do this part of the funeral. I'll go first. Is that okay with all of you?"

Of course it is and Katherine has Laura hold the box as she gently removes the cover and opens up the shoes. The women cannot help it. They abandon their posts and cluster around Katherine and they watch as she reaches into the shoes and then holds the ashes into the wind.

Katherine imagines the laughter that constantly freshened Annie's heart. She honors that and then she wishes it for herself, right now, forever, especially the second she gets back to California.

The boat sways and the women take turns making their wishes blend with the ashes into one sweet and soft place that rides behind the boat.

Jill thinks it was the love—when to hold it and when to let it go.

Balinda thinks it was adventure, newness, trying the impossible.

Laura goes for the elegance. Dipping your fingers into a luxurious world and enjoying every last second of what you feel and find there.

Rebecca closes her eyes and imagines screaming fun. The kind of fun you remember your entire life. The kind of fun you have with your best friends and never regret for one single second.

When they dock, the invisible trail of ashes dances in circles in the rising wind. The pallbearers leave the boat, salute the sky, and stand to look at the clouds—in the exact same spot where the invisible ashes are moving apart to be consumed by the entire universe. And in California, just then, Marie has drifted down a long gravel highway near her fourth appointment so she can catch a glimpse of a hidden pond. She stops for a moment, opens the car door, decides no matter what she will fly to Minnesota in the morning, places her hand over the top of her eyes to shade them from the sun and swears she sees a swirling line of darkness—as thin as a thread, ashes in the air, moving across the horizon to the east. She blinks and the line has disappeared.

22

Rebecca wants to sell her house and move into the hotel.

"Maybe they wouldn't notice if we never left," she yells through the bathroom door while she puts on the rest of her makeup. "What if Annie left a credit card with them and that's part of the deal—that we get to live here the rest of our lives and have people wait on us and sheets that feel like heaven and a totally stocked minibar and pastries delivered every morning . . ."

She's interrupted by Laura, who is sick of Rebecca hogging the sink.

"Snap out of it," Laura tells her, laughing. "This is a dream. Get it? A wild wonderful dream. When I snap my fingers, you will wake up and remember nothing and very quickly walk away from that sink."

Rebecca whines. She does not want to wake up. She does not want to think about getting on an airplane or leaving New York or waking up in a new place. She whines that she has no intention of ever using her own washer or dryer again and if her hands ever touch a plastic garbage sack it will be only to set out her clothes for the butler to take to the dry cleaner.

"You are really getting into this, aren't you?" Balinda says from the couch where she is waiting for everyone to finish getting ready for their night on the town. The women have agreed to dress the part for their evening and have lined up all of the red shoes, including the ones containing Annie, along the deep windowsill looking out toward Central Park. Katherine and Balinda cannot bear to part with their scarves even for one evening and they have tied them into each other's hair. They have no idea where they are going, what will happen next, or how in the hell they will get Rebecca out of the bathroom.

"Hey, big mouth, your turn to write in the funeral book," Rebecca says, grabbing the fast-filling book off the desk and throwing it into Balinda's lap. "Write—then we go."

Balinda hesitates. She hesitates and remembers where she came from, what she must go back to, and how she came to be with such a marvelous group of women during a time that goes beyond interesting and fabulous. A time that makes her take the book and hold it under her chin as if she is cradling the baby she will never have. For the very first time in many years she is feeling as if her life may hold some kind of possibility.

She writes slowly and as she falls into her writing the other women become quiet. The banter ceases and they retreat while she writes. They retreat and they watch and their own minds and hearts fold into the turns of fate that have given them a chance of a lifetime because Annie G. Freeman has died.

BALINDA THOUGHT: *When I was a teenager I remember watching my mother sit on the back step of our apartment building while the neighbor women talked. My mother could barely speak a word of English and she fought learning it even though it isolated her. My mother would sit on the step and watch the other women talk while they drank coffee out of white porcelain cups in the tiny slice of grass that served as the neighborhood park. The women were working on becoming Americans, and my* *mother, who was homesick every single day, would not join them. She missed so much because of that and I felt guilty, always guilty, about having my own friends and life. Her choice was not my choice, but over the years that I have been taking care of her I let my own friends slip away because of my mother. I have become what my mother was. This traveling funeral for a woman who died before I even met her has not filled me with regret for what I am doing but regret for how I am doing it. I do not have to be isolated. I can resurrect my world and I think how wonderful this is—how you've given me back something, Annie, because you chose your own friends so well. I am trying to be brazen. I am trying not to worry about my mother every second that I am here. I am trying to fall into this break in my life and hoping that when I leave I will take it all with me and make your traveling funeral part of my life and world. Thank you, Annie, for showing me how to live in the midst of your own death.*

ANNIE THOUGHT: *I don't know you, Balinda, but I think you know now that it doesn't matter. It doesn't matter because my world, my life, was lined with a richness and breadth of experience because I gave in to it. But I didn't always have that. I learned to do that and you can relearn to do it as well. Each one of these women would throw herself in front of a train for you. They are kind, generous souls who have been dragged through the mud in their own lives. Your dance with your mother is a gift of grace. This funeral, as you now know, is about learning how to dance. Dance, Balinda. Just dance.*

When she finishes Balinda feels as if she should get down on her knees and kiss the feet of Laura, Rebecca, Jill and Katherine. She paces her mind back just three days and thinks about how desperate she was and how she could think of no one to call but Laura.

She thinks about the power of that single relationship. She thinks about Laura coming over at two in the morning when her mother fell and she needed help lifting her back into bed. She thinks about Laura making her watch old movies with her and drink tea from wineglasses because there was no wine. She thinks of Laura coming over to turn on the house lights so her mother would not be frightened when Balinda brought her home from the doctor's office. She thinks that without Annie's friend Laura this might be her traveling funeral.

"Laura," she says, rising to find her flipping through a tourist book with Jill. "Can you come here for a second?"

"You okay?"

"I was just thinking about how much you mean to me, Laura. I'm a bit of a sap right now because I just wrote in the funeral book, but I want you to know that I never take you for granted and that I remember everything you did for me and that without you . . . I don't know what I'd do, Laura."

"Oh, honey," Laura answers, opening her arms so that Balinda can walk into them. "This is what women do. This is what you'd do for me. It's okay. I do it because I want to, because you are my friend, because I care for you so very much."

"What we talked about on the boat earlier today, about how death brings out some interesting aspects of life—well, my God, it's so true, isn't it? I never in my wildest dreams imagined I'd be staying at a four-star hotel with a bunch of women who are about to go out on the town in the middle of the week as part of a funeral celebration. I was desperate for a break. So desperate it was embarrassing."

Laura tells her it isn't necessary to apologize. Exhaustion and sacrifice, she explains, are a deadly combination.

"We've all been there," she adds. "It isn't easy to watch someone die, to think that a part of you is dying too. How bizarre when you think about it that dying is as much a part of life as living. Oh, sweetheart, you deserve to be here, and something you should know is that Annie would have wanted you here. She would have. So it's okay and thank you for appreciating me. Thank you, sweetie."

Balinda suddenly feels like a queen. She feels light and free. She knows her mother is resting comfortably and that the nurse has propped up her legs just the way she likes them and left the television on so that a low hum fills her room. She's called the care facility so many times in the past two days they finally asked her to trust them and put down the phone. "Your mother is in good hands, you know that, Balinda," the nurse told her, speaking in Polish so that she would get the hint that her mother was well cared for. "Enjoy the break."

Before the women leave their suite, once again Jill reads them the note from Annie they found on the bed when they'd arrived. She reminds everyone that they are supposed to have a great time, see the insides of at least two bars, and eat at some locally exotic restaurant.

They decide to walk. They also decide not to ask anyone for directions or for a tip on the best restaurant. "We'll know," Jill decides and everyone agrees. That's when Katherine flashes a credit card. She let's them know it was included in the packet with the tapes and that dinner, dancing, drinking and any other disgusting thing they might care to do will be covered. "This night, like all the rest, is on Annie."

"See, we can stay forever," Rebecca shouts as they begin hiking down Fifth Avenue. "The world is ours."

"The world might be ours," Jill tells her. "But my guess is there is a limit on the credit card so we should just buy half the store and not the whole store."

It's early evening in Manhattan and although the hum of the busy day has receded a little there is still a gallery of excitement—taxis jamming the streets, couples dodging traffic to find a place for a drink, live music drifting in and out of restaurants, a sky ablaze with a chorus of lights that blast from earth to clouds 365 days of a New York year.

Annie's traveling funeral is on fire. The women, proud of their mission already accomplished, serenaded by their own blossoming friendships, mourning the loss of a woman they all loved in ways that are new and raw and wonderful, feel anything is possible. They link arms and form a moving pyramid down the street, silently thinking similar thoughts.

How fun this is . . .

How Annie would have loved this . . .

How happy I am at this moment . . .

How in two hundred years I would never have guessed this moment possible . . .

How extraordinary life can be if you take your door off its hinges . . .

They walk in glowing silence until they see a dark shaded patio that is covered in blinking Christmas lights. From a distance all they can see is a forest of green that forms a small canopy around the porch—an oasis—and they hear the very quiet tunes of a woman singing jazz that is probably recorded but sounds real and sweet and terribly beautiful. They all stop at the same moment, exchange glances, and agree without saying a word that this is where they will have dinner.

The restaurant is a cave of modernity that comes with soft purple walls, gleaming floors, white tablecloths, and black-and-white photos of female movie stars—all women. The entire place is women-centered and they wonder if they have not stumbled into a lesbian-favored establishment. The bartender is a woman. The waitresses are all women. The entire place reeks of estrogen and femininity and the wide strokes that only a woman can bring to the world.

"Excellent," Katherine exclaims as they find seats at the bar and reserve a table outside. "If this place was here when Annie was in town I am beyond certain that she spent a great deal of time here. This joint is fabulous."

"Fabulous" quickly becomes the word for the night as the women raise their glasses of wine as a tribute to Annie who brought them to the very spot where they are toasting her, and then to each other. To each other, first for having had the fine sense to know and embrace Annie as a friend, second to have the guts to embark on a traveling funeral with the rest of them, and third to be bold enough to be risking the most valuable commodity available— time.

"And," Laura adds, "for putting up with Katherine's bossy ways."

"And your know-it-all attitude," Katherine chimes back.

"And my cry-baby crap," Balinda adds.

"There's my shitty attitude," Rebecca says.

"And me sitting around and feeling sorry and being regretful," Jill concludes.

"To Annie," they clink, in a chorus of words that mingle with their glasses and create a chime that makes everyone in the restaurant turn their heads. "To us," they add, moving to form a solid circle so that they can touch each other, so that their glasses meet in a wide arch, so that they can freeze this moment forever in their minds as a gift they received and then gave right back to the woman beside them.

Dinner is slow and sweet. They decide that in keeping with the spirit of change and chance and letting go, they must each order something they would not usually order. Fish, meat—a salad made out of something they did not know existed—anything different and new.

And they toast endlessly, falling into their dinner and drinks as if they have been marooned on an island for years and years and were rescued by friends who never stopped looking for them the entire time they were gone. Their conversation maneuvers from where they are to where they have been and back and forth in between both of those destinations. They laugh constantly, pick on each other, and they talk about love.

"Funerals and love—it kind of makes sense," Jill asserts. "It's a terrific time to not only think about how you loved the person who has died but it's also been my experience that funerals make us think about all the still-living people we love—kind of like shuffling through your own life's Rolodex to see if there is anyone you should call or write or go visit."

"I bet every single one of us, though—especially after a funeral—has thought about what we'd do if we knew we were going to die. What if you woke up and whatever superior force you believe in was standing by your bed tapping His or Her finger on Her watch and saying, 'You have twenty-four hours, honey—get cracking.' What would you do? Would you run to the people you love? Would you do what you love? Or would you stay in bed?" Rebecca asks.

No one says anything for a while. It is the longest stretch of silence since dinner started. It is because they are imagining exactly what they would do.

"Well, Annie had that one luxury, didn't she?" Laura asks, motioning the waitress for more wine. "She knew she was going to die and this is what she chose to do. Really, it was a way to spend more time with us even after she was dead."

"That stinker," Rebecca smirks. "She was using us even past the bitter end."

Everyone finally agrees that their first response would be to collect the people they love the most, to touch them, be with them, rejoice in the last few hours of their time with them, time to say whatever it is that was sticking to the inside of their heart before it really was too late.

"That's what people should always do," Rebecca tells them. "We all know it and we try and do it, but it's one of those things that slips away. And then someone dies and there is a funeral and we all get together and say things we should have been fucking saying the entire time. It's always like that. What's with us?"

It comes back to love, they decide. Love and the fear of loss and the even greater fear of opening yourself up in ways that would also leave you open for a bit of rejection and loss if it didn't quite work out the way you had been dreaming.

"What about love?" Jill chides them. "I've told you about my great love, the one I let slip away because I wasn't woman enough for her. But what about your first great loves? Tell."

They all look startled for a moment and then they each fold back into the musty files of their minds where such things are kept buried toward the back of the file cabinet. They look startled enough for Jill to pick up the dessert menu and then she holds up her hands as everyone protests and she quickly reminds them that they are in the midst of a traveling funeral where celebration is the main ingredient. "Besides, the sugar will loosen you up so I can hear your stories," she admits.

And it does.

They switch to dark, rich wine that is alive with a speck of cherry sweetness and as the cakes and tortes are delivered they start their stories which are as sweet and rich in the retelling as they were the last time they were brave enough to haul them out and shine a bright light on this part of their past.

"What you think love is, and how it should be, changes, but I'm still as much a sucker for romance as I was the very first time I thought—let me emphasize the word 'thought'—I was in love," Laura says. "Now I look back on it and smile at my innocence, but that was all part of my own journey. And part, too, of what made all my other loves so much richer."

A college romance, she shares, sipping her wine and then sitting back in her chair as if to open herself up to make the memory larger, more vivid. Her entire senior year in college was occupied with the strains and intermittent joys of luscious sex, romantic interludes in between classes, and the ridiculous notion that the affair was going to last for the next fifty-five years.

"It's amazing how we do that, get so caught up in all that planning and thinking about forever," she confesses. "Sometimes I think I was so busy planning my next fifty years that I lost sight of the moment."

First love is often blinding, they decide as the tables around them fill, as the night begins slipping south and as their stories blend into a chorus that wears the clothes of youth. Think, they all agree, what it would have been like if they knew then what they know now.

"My God," Rebecca moans. "We'd never get out of bed."

Ah, they all sigh, the sex. The delicious fabulous juicy moments of abandonment of time and place and self for the pure and sensuous joy of bodies falling into souls and hearts and the delirious tumble of love that wraps itself inside of something that is often nothing more than a purely physical moment.

"How did we get away from that?" Katherine demands. "The joy of sex. Knowing deep inside that it's beyond okay to crave the release, the pure pleasure of abandonment?"

And then she tells her story. A story that winds itself from her first grope in the back of the high school gym, to a friend's basement, to a college apartment, to a marriage that disrupted her libido for way too many years, and into this place now where she admits that she is afraid of letting go, "just fucking letting go."

There is silence for but a second and then Laura, who has skated through life with a teenage daughter who has all but disappeared as a young adult, and Rebecca, who has experience paddling the same raising-a-teenager boat, agree that sex, in the throes of teenagerhood, is not an easy task. But, they ask, but—could it be that the relationship she is in is not the best? Could it be?

"My God," Katherine almost shouts. "I think you may be onto something here. Alex, the man in my life now, was the first man in such a long time that I never dared to think that it wasn't just that moment, just me getting to that next step. But, well, the sex is good—"

Balinda cuts her off, pushing her chair back and leaning across half the table.

"Good is not good enough. Girl, what are you thinking? I'm one to talk considering the state of my life but I ... oh my God ..."

Balinda slaps her hand over her heart and drops her head onto the table. "Shit, just thinking about this guy gets me more than a little wet. He was a friend from work and we had this chemistry and we flirted like hell and one night, I swear to God, we ended up in the elevator together alone and we both agreed right there to go to a hotel and we made love, I mean *love* and not just sex for like twelve hours, and then we did it again for weeks and months."

The women are spellbound. They are all leaning in so far that their chairs are about to tip over and flip them onto the table. No one can breathe. They are on the brink of panting when the waitress interrupts them with a sentence, just a sentence, that changes the direction of everything.

"I'm so sorry, but there's a man at the bar who just bought you all a drink ... and ..." The waitress pauses because the table smells like sex even though they are just talking about it, and she looks around to see if she has missed anything.

"Who?" they all ask at once, looking inside the restaurant and toward the bar.

"He comes in often and he thinks he knows who some of you are," the waitress says, swooning just a bit from the fumes off the table.

"What?" they all say again as if they have practiced for this moment.

Jill takes over and says she'll go speak to him. They ask the waitress to come back in a few minutes and then they all turn to look at Balinda.

"So?" the chorus demands.

"It was too crazy," she admits, picking up her story. "I was like obsessed and thought about him and sex all of the time and he was the same way. It was like this wonderful addiction that didn't leave room for anything else. But we couldn't stop. I would see him getting out of his car and go pull him into his back seat. But that's all we did. The connection was very physical and I loved him that way but it would have been destructive to go on. So we did something terribly mature. We made a pact that we'd never settle for anything less and that we'd reconnect in five years if we hadn't met someone to fill that place we had with each other and he left. And I never saw him again."

The women forget for a minute that there is a man at the bar who claims he knows them. They forget about Annie and about their own sexual needs and desires and they stare at Balinda as if she has just told them that their faces are on fire.

"Shit," Rebecca says for all of them. "Shit."

Balinda tells them that the five years have come and gone and the man never contacted her and she could not contact him because of her mother.

The conversation moves like a rocket from there. The women admonish her. Call him, they shout. What the hell? Did you make a plan for who would call or who would not call? Did you say we should contact each other anyway in case we are both afraid? Do you think you could love him beyond the bedroom and into every other room of your house and life? Really, what in the hell does your mother have to do with love?

Jill, who had been half standing to meet the man at the bar, sits back down. The women fall into a conversation that they decide later Annie would have loved. She would have loved their yelling kind of discussion and the way they forgot about everything else except that moment, the conversation and each other. She would have loved the way they pushed aside their plates and talked with their hands. She would have loved the way the traveling funeral was moving them to talk and act and live in a way that redefined the way they lived and loved before the door opened, the Bali bra fell apart and the traveling funeral was born. She would have loved how each day of her funeral made them bolder with each other and more open about what they liked and didn't like about life and the person sitting next to them.

Thirty minutes later, after Balinda decides she must locate this wild lover, after Jill recounts again the great love of her life, after they spontaneously call Marie and she talks about Bill, some wild man from the years after her college graduation, and after they think they will not be able to move or walk to another bar no matter what Annie has ordered, Jill remembers the man at the bar.

"Oh no," she says, jumping from her seat and searching the bar for a man, any man. "I forgot about the guy at the bar."

He's left.

The bartender smiles and she points toward the traveling funeral. "He saw that you were having a great time and he said, 'Tell them it wasn't necessary that we actually speak.' "

Jill thinks there is more. Bartenders, she is certain, like beauticians, know everything. They are the world's attendants. They rub your scalp, see you with your hair pulled back behind your ears or your heart hanging in your whiskey glass, and so you will tell them anything.

"Do you know him?"

The bartender smiles. She is terribly beautiful and when she leans in across the bar to talk to Jill, Jill can feel her heart press against her ribs and a sensation of yearning move from her fingers, along the inner part of her skin, deep into her heart.

"He comes in here a couple of times a year, when he visits

from Europe—Italy, I think," she tells her, making certain to touch Jill's hand as she speaks. "He's an artist. He's also in a wheelchair. He's been disabled his entire life, fell when he was a kid, if I remember correctly. He said he was married once to a woman named Annie. He knows she was meant to be alone. He knew it had nothing to do with his bad legs because he told me the sex was fabulous but that marriage was not on his or her Most Wanted list."

Jill freezes in place. She is mesmerized by her attraction to the bartender, to some kind of awakening that has been sleeping for so long she can barely recognize it, and because a brilliant clue to the puzzle of Annie has just landed in her lap.

"What else?" she asks. "What else?"

"He's a gentle soul. Told me he and his Annie spent their honeymoon at a posh hotel here in New York and that Annie sent him a note just before she died and asked him to come here if he was in town this month. Funny thing, though, is that she sent him the note after she died. It was like a very interesting kind of last wish. I'm sure she sent him something else and that there was more to the note but that's all he told me."

"Jesus."

"What?"

"You'd never believe it. Really."

"I'm a bartender. If a bird flew out of your right ear I'd think it was perfectly normal."

"It's almost ridiculous to say it out loud because it sounds like it's something from a movie, now that I think about it. You'll want to throw me inside of one of your coolers if I tell you why we are here and what we are doing and who Annie is and what brought us to this bar."

"Tell me. I might throw you in the cooler anyway because you're so damn cute."

Jill tells her and doesn't even realize that the bartender is flirting.

She tells her the entire story and gets the phone number of not only the bartender but of the beautiful man from Italy who paints as if he can see the inside of the universe and who loved a woman named Annie and who bought her friends a drink, tipped his hat, and then left for the airport.

23

Rebecca cannot believe that she is on her way to a city that she knows absolutely nothing about except that it is mostly always cold there—even on July 4—that it sits on the edge of one of the Great Lakes and the people who live there on purpose, even though they could live someplace warm, like to do things like eat outside in the middle of winter, skate down the frozen highways and wear clothing that is made of wool even in the middle of summer.

"Duluth?" she whines, in the tiny airplane with only seats enough for the traveling funeral members, two short men, and a lone flight attendant who warns them that they don't even have beverage service. "Where the hell is Duluth?"

The two male passengers laugh. They look as if they eat a lot of protein, walk great distances for warm beverages, and would be more at home behind a dogsled than in the seat of an airplane dressed in a wrinkled business suit.

"Hey," one of them jokes, "you are talking about God's Country up here. Knock it off, lady, or you'll make it snow in June. Happens all the time. Not that we'd mind a little snow this time of year. It's been weeks since we've seen any."

Rebecca likes this northwoods giant and she gives it right back to him.

"What good is a lake that's frozen ten months out of the year?" she snorts. "I bet you are the kind of guy who likes to go *ice* fishing, for crying out loud."

"Love it," he answers. "We like to go north for our summer vacations so we can keep up with our snowball fights and stuff like that. I hate it when we get too warm."

This is how it goes as the airplane follows the frozen tundra across the top of Minnesota and the conversation sways like the moving tops of the forest the women can see below them. The plane ride from New York City to Minneapolis was a quiet zoom that included an in-flight call from Marie who is just a few hours ahead of them and already standing at attention in the Duluth airport, a discussion of the New York portion of the trip, a decision to try and get at least one extra hour of sleep because the traveling funeral is beginning to take its toll on the pallbearers, who agree they have never, ever in their entire lives had this much fun at a funeral or pretty much anywhere else for that matter.

And then, just as the plane bumps through some low clouds and it looks as if they are in the middle of a stretch of the world so remote, so green, so filled with trees and the dotted blue smiles of the ten thousand lakes they have seen advertised, the pilot, who sounds as if he is twelve years old, announces that they are ten minutes from landing and "although no one was allowed to leave their seats during the first portion of the flight—don't do it now either."

Charming, they agree, every single thing about this portion of the trip is terribly charming, including the two passengers who want to take them fishing and have no idea that the shoebox is full of the dwindling ashes of Annie G. Freeman. The two guys also do not bother to ask why everyone has on matching shoes; they haven't even picked up on the bandanas and why in the world as they know it these women are traveling to Duluth in a pack. They just can't wait to get back home. They are very happy boys.

The landing is smooth and swift and astounding because the Duluth airport is not the largest banana in the world, and the pilot scoots the plane, like he's probably done a hundred times, into a slot the size of a toothpick without the slightest hesitation. And this is where Katherine tells them, as they are waiting for the itsy-bitsy plane door to open, that there is no tape for this portion of the funeral. No car rental. Just a note saying, *Someone will meet you & you will be off to the White Cap Lodge.*

"That's it?" Jill asks. "The White Cap Lodge?"

"It's up on the North Shore," one of the traveling fishermen tells them, overhearing the conversation because they are all sitting so close to each other it's impossible not to hear every spoken word. "Old place, cute. Nice people."

"I take it that's the North Shore of Lake Superior?" Laura asks. "I've seen photos of it. It looks beautiful."

"It is. Rugged and beautiful. It's where lots of us go to camp and fish and to get away. Some hearty souls live there year-round. You can still hike back into the woods for miles and run into some salty old or young bird who's given it all up and headed into the forest for good."

Katherine recalls that Annie's family, maybe her grandmother, had a cabin in Minnesota. She has a blurry memory of a scattering of stories about a summer trip, a Thanksgiving spent at the cabin or a spring break north when everyone else was going south. Then the door finally opens and they all get off the plane, and know within seconds that they are definitely north of any place they would care to stay for a long period of time.

"Holy crap, it's cold," Balinda shouts into the wind as they disembark. "It must be twenty degrees colder here than it was in New York."

"Something could be blowing in," explains guy number one.

"Usually right before something hits, a day or so, we get a stiff breeze. Don't worry, if you get stranded here we'll have an excuse to get you all out on one of the lakes or we'll put a fly rod in your hands."

The women laugh all the way to the terminal, which reminds them of a small bus depot, and where there is but one lone person in the waiting area outside the front door. He looks just slightly older than a teenager and he's polite and kind as he hoists their bags into a van and apologizes because Lou wasn't able to pick them up.

"Lou?" they all say at once. "Who is Lou?"

Paul, their able and adorable driver, smiles and says, "Lou, she runs the lodge. She's my boss. She's training me to do everything, she says, so she can take a day off once before she dies. But she won't really take a day off. Lou won't ever take a day off unless it's for something like a funeral, but we make believe anyway and I'll be there if she needs me."

"Where's Marie?" they all ask as if they have been rehearsing.

"Is she always like that?" Paul asks.

"Like what?"

"She was here three hours ago and real tired. She called. I came to get her. She seems, well, not confused but maybe she was just tired."

"Marie has a very stressful job," Rebecca tells him.

"Oh, well, Lou will take care of her until we get there. Like I said, she never takes a day off."

The women decide to be polite but they are all thinking about this "funeral" that Lou, whoever she is, would take a day off of work for. Paul drives them out of the parking lot and through Duluth, which they find absolutely lovely. They cross over a bridge that they quickly name "the Golden Gate of the Northwoods" and roll down the windows in spite of what they think is chilly air and stare as two huge ore boats creep slowly from the mouth of a river and under a raised drawbridge on the other side of the bay that has traffic at a standstill. Rolling hills slope toward Lake Superior and they can see that Duluthians have been working hard to try and renovate the old mining city with its stunningly beautiful buildings. The streets were built wide enough years ago for a team of horses to turn around and now for snowplows to do figure eights without having to back up.

Charming, they agree. A bit on the nippy side, but charming.

Paul listens to them and looks into his mirror while they are talking as if they are speaking in a foreign language. He occasionally answers a question and then whips his eyes back to the front of the van where he concentrates on maneuvering past the city limits and out along the shore of the lake. "The Lake," he calls it as if Lake Superior were the only real lake in the entire world and indeed it looks large enough to be a small ocean. He speaks of it as if he were talking about a disciple, a living saint, an admired sports star or the woman who just pulled him out of a burning building.

"I suppose when Annie came here, she probably drove past every single thing that we are seeing right now," Rebecca assesses. "If she did it when she was a teenager there's a good chance she thought she was driving to the edge of the earth or hell or someplace just this side of either one of those places."

"Maybe she came in from the other side or something," Balinda asks innocently.

"There is no other side," Paul says quickly and then puts his hand over his mouth because he's been listening, which it is impossible not to do, but he is a young man filled with manners learned from his northwoods ancestors.

"I never looked at a map," Jill says, "but I'm guessing that's Canada up there, and to the left would be a set of timbers way taller than half the largest cities in the world."

"Yes," Paul answers.

Katherine tears at her memory wishing she could uncover

something that Annie once said about her Minnesota roots but her brain is a dark and dusty spot behind her eyes, she tells them, so they'll have to wait and see what is around the next bend.

The bend is a long one that gives them more than an hour to discuss how the parents of teenagers often forget that kids that age, who are really closer to adulthood than to childhood, develop their own social systems and "families" and have no desire to go up to the cabin or over the river and through the woods once they hit a certain age.

"Remember?" Laura asks. "Remember how stinking awful it was to have to be dragged to some stupid-ass family event when you wanted to stay home and just be with your friends?"

"Was that it?" Jill asks. "Do you think it was some kind of family issue or major mom or dad related event that happened up here?"

Katherine stops them. She has a "feeling" something is about to play out, she tells them, laughing and blaming Laura, the traveling funeral psychic, for having caught her gift of perhaps knowing things before they happen.

"It would make sense for this to be a family place because it's close to Chicago," Katherine says as they round a corner that is so close to the water it looks for a moment as if they are going to be swept out to sea, or in this case, a very large lake. "It feels like family up here, close, warm, friendly and those are the vibes I'm picking up."

Young Paul looks as if he's suddenly seen the ghost of Annie. His eyebrows have gone up into his hairline and he's slowed the van to a crawl. Katherine suspects he knows more than he's saying but she goes on anyway.

"So my guess is that something is about to happen, or we'll make it happen and it will all fall into place."

"Maybe . . ." Rebecca starts and then trails off as if she's gotten lost inside of her own head. "Maybe not knowing every detail about this trip and life is part of the lesson of this funeral. Maybe

Annie wanted us to know that sometimes it's okay to plunge feet-first and fast as hell into something without thinking the whole thing through. Really," she goes on as if she's trying to convince herself. "Think of all the fabulous things that have happened in the world because someone has just *done* it—you know, just jumped off the cliff and worried about the dangers when it's all over."

Rebecca sighs and leans her head into her arm as if she is suddenly exhausted.

"Well, that makes sense, if what I have learned of her is true," Balinda says. "I think sometimes I think too damn much. I worry about this and that and everything else and then I wake up and four more years have slipped right out the back door."

Katherine starts laughing and then puts her hand on Balinda's arm so she knows she is not laughing at her.

"See," she says. "This is exactly what I was talking about. Listen to us. Entire worlds are opening up and we are flinging around some very cool thoughts. It's spontaneous, which is pretty much how this whole thing happened, for us anyway. Annie's the one who had time to plan the whole thing out and here we are riding along in this terribly interesting stream."

They are still laughing twenty minutes later when Paul turns into a gravel road that is arched in branches from birch trees that must have been planted the year Paul Bunyan waltzed through this northern part of the world. A wooden sign painted with the words *White Cap* greets them and then Paul turns and advises them to "hang on." The road twists first left and then right and he tells them that the original owners put the road in this way to save as many trees as possible. "Hasn't changed a bit in all the years I've been alive or all the years before I was alive, from what they tell me," he adds as they round another corner and come to a wide space where a house sits.

"Come on in," Paul says and when he sees them reaching for their luggage he adds, "Leave the bags, please. I'll be taking you to where you are staying in about an hour. There are some drinks inside and Lou is waiting to take care of you. Marie should be in there too."

"We aren't staying here?" Katherine asks, surprised.

"No, ma'am, but it's not far to your place."

"See?" Katherine says as they file into the house that has clearly been converted into a small lodge. "I told you something funky would happen right away."

They enter a small lobby that reeks of a gentle, warm, "up-northness." There are wool jackets hanging on wooden pegs, throw rugs placed up and down the hallway, and old photos hanging haphazardly on the wall as if someone had been dancing up and down when they placed them there. Before they can get close enough to examine the photos they hear a voice.

"Yo-ho," a woman calls from somewhere inside the house. "Keep walking, gals. You'll run right into us."

Which is exactly what happens as they move forward and enter a living room that looks as if it could be the inside of a small cathedral. The room is a cavern of greatness that stretches out to the edge of Lake Superior, so close to the shoreline it looks as if there are wave marks on the windowpanes. The view, a kaleidoscope of trees, water-washed rocks pushed flat by years of crashing waves so that the beach looks as if it is layered in colored pancakes, and windows that float into the clouds, takes everyone's breath away.

"Oh," they say in a succession of gasps that obliterate every other thought from their minds, including the not-so-soft voice of Lou that bounced through the house just a moment ago.

When Lou, all 232 pounds of her, comes around the corner and sees the women standing in a row like the wild ducks she loves to watch each morning as they seem to be discussing the weather on the beach, she starts laughing.

No one can say anything. Lou is a vision. She bounces when she breathes and her well-stocked frame is poured into a pair of jeans that would be tight on the Jolly Green Giant. Her gray hair, braided into two long strands, swirls down like snakes. This Lou woman has her hands on her ample hips and a smile that could knock the lights out in a football stadium, and to Rebecca, Jill, Katherine, Laura and Balinda she looks stunningly beautiful and confident.

"Come here, girls," she commands, opening her arms and the women walk into her as if they have just been hypnotized and begin a kissing and hugging frenzy that they will later remember as terribly wonderful.

Then they stand back and they ask her who she is and why they are there and what in the living hell is going on.

"Oh," Lou snorts, laughing again. "Annie told me you'd all be like this. I bet you are about going crazy wanting to know why this part of your journey has landed you in Minnesota."

Then she holds up her hands as a woman who can only be Marie comes around the corner and says a simple "Hello." The women move to meet her and then stand back to size her up as if to say, "Let's see if she fits in." Marie does the same thing. It laughingly looks like a face-off for a few moments, with Marie and Lou on one side of the room with their hands on their hips, and the rest of the funeral brigade on the other in the same position and then they embrace, moving together to form a mass of genuine warmth.

Marie looks nothing like any of the women, except those who know her, have imagined. She is the opposite twin of Lou—a tall, very thin willow of a woman who has let her hair grow gray and lets it twirl however it cares to around the tops of her breasts like dancing strands of corn silk. Her dark eyes are alive and bright and the laugh lines that move in circles from the edges of her eyes in every direction come from a place, so it seems, that is much deeper than the skin that holds it in place.

The line closes, they all embrace again and because Marie has been talking to them constantly since the funeral began, she hops into the traveling funeral, into the day, into this phase, as if she has physically been there all along.

"So?" they all ask Lou. "Tell us."

She will tell them, she promises.

But first they must wash up. Then they must sit around a table that looks as if it has been dragged in for the largest family that has ever existed. The table seats sixteen and is tucked into a dining room that was designed for a table that seats eight. Then they must drink coffee and tea and eat huge quantities of home-baked sweet rolls, sweet breads and some northwoods pastries that do not need to be chewed because the moment they sit on a tongue they disintegrate and make anyone who inhales one sigh with joy. They must wait. They must wait while Lou asks them about their trip and who they have met. She claps her hands as they spill out the history of the traveling funeral. "We met the father of Annie's children." "We were seconds away from meeting her husband." "We met this young woman in New Mexico who is about to move in with Jill," or "Balinda flew into our lives at the last moment because she put her mother in a facility that has a Polish-speaking attendant for only three more days," or "I finally just said to myself that if I didn't go now, if I didn't just leave, the entire funeral would be over and I'd still be sitting at the nursing home filled with regrets."

All of that and then Lou leans into the table, which only means about half an inch of leaning, and says, "I'm Annie's grandma's sister, which means I was sort of Annie's grandma as well. I watched that little thing grow up."

The women gape at Lou as if she has just told them she pulled the winning lottery ticket out of her right sock twenty minutes ago. Why this news is astounding is unknown but it's not what they expect. They pelt her with a verbal collage of who's, what's, why's and when's that immediately bring Lou right back to her originating point of laughter.

"You are all something," she exclaims, slapping her hands on the table. "Let's clean up this mess and go sit by the big window and I will tell you what you are in for. Did you bring the ashes?"

This woman knows everything, they think. She even knows we

have Annie in the shoebox. She's a wizard. A large, gracious, and absolutely lovely wizard.

First they brief Marie, who knows just about everything anyway from all of their phone conversations, and then Lou tells them what she knows of Annie. The steam from their coffee cups forms a ribbon of warmth around their faces as they gather around Lou as if they were watching a campfire or the last movement of a symphony or the chorus line of a Broadway musical. This they absolutely have to hear and Lou tells it all as if she is on stage, moving her hands in ever wider circles as she tells them a series of stories from front to back.

Annie called her every day the last week before she died.

Annie let her know about her funeral plans and talked to her about every single one of them—in great and glorious detail.

Annie wrote and stayed in touch with her, especially after her grandma died.

Annie spent two weeks, almost every summer, at the family cabin.

Annie once nearly drowned off Gopher's Point when she swam out too far because she wouldn't listen to anyone.

Annie once had such a horrific crush on a neighbor boy she almost quit school and moved north to this fine wilderness.

Annie used to sneak outside, under the roof of the back shed, to smoke cigarettes and drink beer that she stole from the grocery bin behind the kitchen table.

Annie loved watching the water here, started writing poetry when she was ten, and had a special place where they would often find her asleep or just sitting but mostly always reading.

Annie's grandpa died tragically, when his truck went off an icy cliff. Two years after he died, a photo of Annie, the one that was clipped to the visor of his pickup truck, was picked up on a beach by a stranger who spent two solid days trying to find Annie and he did.

That's when they finally stop her.

"You have got to be kidding!" Laura shouts, unable to be silent any longer. "Are you making this up?"

"Honey, the last time I lied is when I told a man I loved him. This is the real deal."

Marie, who is far from quiet, is mentally jotting down the synergy of her fellow funeral women. She is smart enough to realize that her absence up to this point has given her a bit of an edge. She knows she can ask spicy questions. She knows she is a new set of eyes and ears and she also knows she won't hold back for a second. Marie can barely breathe from the excitement.

Katherine scoots in closer to Lou because she thinks that she is acting so much like Annie that maybe this is her real grandmother. The way she is so sure of herself, her extraordinary sense of humor, her graciousness. Everything but the hips.

"Are you sure you are not her real grandma?"

"Oh, honey, no, like I said, I was her grandma's sister, but we are a close bunch up here. It was, up until a few years ago, kind of like a big old commune what with everyone coming and going and kids here and there and everything all commingled," Lou explains. "But as you know, things change. People die. Everything changes."

There is a moment then when everyone recalls why they have come to this house by the big lake. They remember that what is left of Annie, their tie to this corner of the world, is resting on the table right behind them and that their red shoes and tattered funeral book and this very conversation is leading them to another moment when they will have to tear open whatever emotional package Annie has left here for them.

Lou turns from her chair as if she is judging a beauty contest and she looks at Katherine, Marie, Laura, Balinda, Rebecca and Jill with such seriousness that they are expecting a great announcement.

"How are you girls doing? I know you all loved Annie so much and played a very special role in her life. This isn't all easy. Are you okay?"

They tell her. One by one they tell Lou about each ceremony and about the secrets of Annie's life that came with each location and about their own personal revelations. They tell her and Lou listens as if she has known each one of them her entire life and she looks like she wants to grab each one and put her in her lap where they will talk about the hard parts and rest their heads against her chest. She wants to do that and they want to let her. The women, Annie's pallbearers, feel as if they have fallen into the womb of something warm and wonderful and they never want to leave.

"It ain't easy," Lou says, slapping her knees and standing, when they have finished. "I've had a world of loss dropped into my hands, including our Annie, but we're women and we deal with it and we do it in a way that somehow becomes a gift. Isn't that something? Isn't it something how we can take something that is so painful it makes you drop to the floor and turn it into a life lesson that makes you actually glad it happened? That's what women do. We get on with it. It sure is something."

The women know it's something. It's been something since the moment they met Annie. It's been something since she became ill and then really something since the box of ashes arrived at Katherine's home and then something even wilder after that when they were assigned the duties of the official pallbearers. And now this.

"What about the photo and the guy who found it?" Marie begs Lou. "What happened?"

Lou smiles. She's got them eating out of her hand and she loves every second of it.

"Here's the deal. I'll tell you but I'll tell you this evening because I have to get back to work and you have to get over to the cabin and get settled and figure out what to do with those ashes in those red tennis shoes, which are hilarious by the way. Annie loved those damned things, didn't she?"

Lou tells them that Paul is about to take them over to the Freeman family home, a cabin more isolated than the lodge, further into the heart of the North Shore. The kitchen is fully stocked, she tells them, there's wine on the counter, she explains, winking, and she'll be over to share dinner with them—they have to cook—as soon as she's done preparing for the group of lodge guests who are due within the next few hours.

While Paul drives them to the cabin they wonder if they could just keep going like they are—moving from place to place, from adventure to adventure for the rest of their lives. Chicago, Toledo, some tiny town in the plains, someplace way north. Just drive and fly and travel, call home occasionally, drink wine every night, talk until dawn, spread ashes from one corner of the world to the next.

"I should have come sooner," Marie sighs, sticking her long legs in between the front and back seat. "I feel like I've missed most of my own life. I feel like I could have left sooner but needed to stay and help another dying patient or a dozen of them, but I should have come sooner for Annie and for me."

Paul listens as if he's an undercover agent. He likes these women who apparently are unafraid to say anything, go anywhere or do anything, and he wonders, as he listens to them, what it would be like to just pick up and go and have a life that does not revolve around the shifting tides of the big lake and the changing seasons. He wonders but then he thinks about how his heart feels every morning when he wakes and looks through the bathroom window at the lake and isn't sure if his heart would survive the separation.

"Annie would be laughing now," he finally tells them, shyly. "She'd love what you are talking about and you know she'd want to go along. That would be Annie."

"You knew Annie?" The women never thought to ask him.

"Heck, everyone knew Annie. We had a big ceremony up here last week for her. About a hundred people came and we had a party out on the beach and it was a wonderful thing. Sure, we knew Annie."

The pallbearers think, "My gosh," just "My gosh" as Paul turns into an unmarked driveway and the van bumps across a small bridge spanning a stream that rushes under them like the fine wind of Annie's laughter that seems to be getting louder every single day.

24

Paul wonders if he will ever see anything like this again the rest of his life.

Before he can stop the van the women have opened the side door and are jumping from the vehicle as if they have just spotted a ghost. By the time he parks the van, gets out and takes two steps, he can see them all running through the cabin and he can catch bits and pieces of what they are saying through the windows they are opening and because in their excitement they have left the front door open.

"Holy crap," "Cool," "Come look at this. . . ." Their words make him laugh softly and he imagines this is exactly what it must have been like every time Annie and her family pulled into the driveway and the doors were flung open and the kids ran to claim their favorite bedroom.

After he sets down their bags in the kitchen he calls them together, shows them how everything works, and hands them his telephone number. "Cells don't like the north woods," he explains, and tells them that Lou will be back by six P.M. and they better have dinner ready or she'll kick them out.

"All set, kids?" he teases them as he backs out the door. "Go check out the beach. You will love it."

The pallbearers are beside themselves with excitement and not just because the cabin is actually a fabulous and very ancient log home that has been added on to, updated and taken care of with what appears to be more than loving care, but because this was Annie's home, because they have discovered yet another part of her world, and because they know, without hesitation, that they are about to discover even more of her.

The women gather in the kitchen to make plans. Marie, who is used to a fairly fast-paced life, with teenagers and a sixty-plus-hour workweek, is about breathless with the activity. She's also jealous as hell because the women have been together for days and have a friendship that seems about ready to combust. First, they agree unanimously, before they go to the beach, look in the refrigerator, before they do another thing, they must first figure out which bedroom was Annie's favorite.

"There could be some clue, something fascinating," Laura laments as if she's the one who has hidden something there. "She could have been back here after she found out she was dying and she knew we would not be far behind."

Marie stops them.

"Wait," she demands. "We've all talked on the phone for hours but I need a once-over. Give me something here before we take another step."

Marie points, which Katherine finds hilarious, and demands that each one of them give her a synopsis of their individual life's challenges.

Laura: "Kind of psychic. Have this missing-daughter thing. Not happy in Chicago. Husband stuff okay."

Rebecca: "You know me, Marie. Stuck in reverse. Filled with loss. Tired of people dying. Feel as if the world has betrayed me. Have not been laid in way too long."

Jill: "You know me a little bit, too. A professor. Wallowing in self-pity. Closeted lesbian—My God, Marie. That's enough. I've never even said that out loud before."

Balinda: "Tired. Tired of sacrifice. Have also not been laid in a very long time. Desperately seeking my own life."

Katherine: "I'm going to laugh, Marie. Let's see . . . Supporting the entire world has ruined my back. Missing my dead mother. Settling into life when nothing should be settled. There. That's enough. Are you happy now?"

"That was terrific," Marie jokes. "We'll have another session later this afternoon."

"Wait," Katherine commands. "Your turn."

"Damn it," Marie says. "I was hoping you wouldn't notice."

"We're waiting," Laura tells her.

Marie: "Obviously always very late. Can't let go. Too hard on myself. Need to take a course in spontaneity."

"Now can we?" Jill asks. "Can we please?"

They explore. They move from the kitchen and through an attached dining room that opens onto a porch that takes up the entire front of the house. The porch slopes toward the water and is large enough to hold a high school band. The living room has been enlarged and includes an old piano, five chairs circled around a huge fieldstone fireplace and three couches placed together to form a U at the far window. Every single window has a view of the water. There is one downstairs bathroom, and a back room that has a desk and looks like it must have been used for an office or as a writing studio by someone—maybe Annie, they think, as they race up the steps again and examine the six bedrooms, three in front and three in back, and wonder which one was Annie's.

They agree that it's probably the middle room in the front that has an unobstructed view of the lake and a bed that's been positioned in the corner which at first doesn't make sense until Laura lies in it and discovers that she can see a wonderful blend of forest, water and sky.

But then they head around the corner and they discover the last bedroom. There are books everywhere. They are stacked on top of the dressers, tightly packed into three bookshelves, lying on top of both windowsills and when Rebecca opens the closet she discovers more of them. They discover lots of things.

"My God, look at this," she says, from inside the closet. "I think these are Annie's old notebooks. Look, doesn't this look like her handwriting?"

They all look, shoulders touching, at stacks of spiral-bound notebooks that indeed once belonged to Annie G. Freeman. Some of them are obviously old school notebooks, but many of them are also filled with notes, her compulsive drawings and doodles—long lines and flowers and intricate drawings of buildings and whatever else was inside of her head when she was sitting in front of the pages.

"I think we should take them all out and read them," Jill announces.

The rest of the women hesitate but only for a moment.

"She wanted us to come here," Katherine says. "She knew what we would find, she wanted us to read these, to read about this other part of her life."

Laura reaches in back behind the books and finds other boxes filled with clothing. There are shoes too, an old sleeping bag, things—Annie's things—and when Laura discovers a bucket of rocks she knows for certain that this is, without a doubt, Annie's favorite room.

"Did she ever tell anyone else about how obsessive she was about rocks and picking up things and doing this one funky thing every time she left a place she loved?"

Of course, the women laugh—especially Rebecca, who tells them she carried more than a few rocks from Annie's car trunk and into her backyard.

"She told me once," Laura shares with them, "how every time she left a place she loved she'd do something like put a stick someplace odd, or leave something special under a tree or in a drawer because it would be like a part of her was still there. I bet she did it here. . . ."

Before she finishes, the women have scattered to every corner of the room as if they have been shot out of a cannon and they begin opening drawers and peering under the mattress and tossing back the curtains. It is a scavenger hunt into the past and they find pieces of it everywhere.

"Here's a rock. . . ."

"There's a bird's nest in this drawer. . . ."

"Oh, look at this . . . there's at least a dozen magazines under the mattress that have leaves pressed inside of them. . . ."

"Look at this . . . what is it? Shells . . . and a silver bracelet . . ."

Inside this snug room, they find an entire slice of Annie's life. Sticks and stones and bird feathers. They pile the treasures onto the bed and kneel around it, touching everything as if they were bowing down before an altar. They pass around her stones and they make certain that the leaves stay pressed in all the right places. They fence with the sticks and each one of them admits that they did the same thing—saved and savored special places with notes or treats from the earth.

"I used to bury notes," Balinda admits.

"I would sing goodbye songs very quietly to places I loved," Laura shares.

"I would write something, just a word, and put it into my pocket," Jill tells them.

"I would leave tears if it was someplace I truly had a connection to," Katherine reveals.

"I'd say something remarkable and think that I would always remember it the next time," Marie admits.

"Pennies. I always left pennies under rocks. I would say to myself that I would come back, remember the exact spot and get the penny back one day," Rebecca confesses and then tells them she never ever found one hidden penny again.

Kneeling there, around the twin bed that must have been Annie's as she grew up, the women pull back the covers of their own lives and fall into a discussion about the tumultuous years when the simplicity of childhood gave way to the perilous passions of adulthood.

They rest their elbows on the bed, tuck their hands under their chins, and they imagine all the dreams Annie Freeman designed while lying in this very bed and looking out into the often stormy skies of the lake. Did she see her life splayed out in the way it actually unfolded? Is this where she went into her horrible despondent spin and crashed before trying to take her own life? Could this be where she dreamed of boys who turned into men and danced with her under the canopy of trees that arched their way across the driveway? Did she sit in that chair and read herself into oblivion? Did she scream at her mother when she was called down to dinner or asked to go pick up the toys scattered across the beach?

They wonder as they select a small rock for Marie's growing collection and then agree to put everything back just the way they found it—except the notebooks, which they will share as they sip their wine on the beach.

Downstairs they discover an entire world inside of the refrigerator and a clearly defined dinner path. Fresh whitefish, rice, salad, rolls, drinks, vegetables, breakfast food—the refrigerator is filled to the brim and Lou has filled at least a dozen vases with fresh flowers and placed them on tables, in the kitchen window—just about everywhere they look.

"Fabulous energy," Laura reports happily after she riffles through the house with her magic mind. "Lots of good stuff happened here."

"Let's keep it up then," Katherine commands as she cracks open a beer for each one of them, pushes a piece of fresh lemon into the opening of each beer bottle, and orders them outside for a hike to the beach.

They exit onto a wide piece of grass that has been left to go wild. Tall grasses wave to them as they walk straight down a path that is lined with rocks and heads directly to the beach. And it is a real beach. Here, at the Freeman northwoods home, they find a stretch of sand that is long and white and as seductive as anything the women have ever seen.

"It's beautiful," Balinda says, dropping to grab some sand in her left hand. "I've never seen anything like this. Actually," she adds, standing and turning toward the women, "I've never seen much. Chicago. If I try really hard, I can actually remember what Poland looked like when I was a little girl."

"This ain't no Poland," Laura shoots back as she sets down her beer and runs to see how cold the water is.

Minutes later the women turn as she screams at the top of her lungs, "It's frigging freezing! Do you think they ever actually *swam* in here?"

Of course they swam, Balinda tells them. She's a Chicago girl and she knows that men and women and boys and girls who are raised in places where it snows think that it's warm when it's 50 degrees and there is no snow on the ground.

"Those guys on the plane weren't kidding, this is hearty heaven up here," she tells them.

They walk and talk. They watch the sky consume itself and fold small clouds into bigger clouds until the sun comes back and blows everything apart. It is a beautiful, warm and rare day in early summer along the shore and they decide to set up camp in front of the home, assign some cooking duties, read Annie's old notebooks, and catch up on writing in the funeral book.

Then they sit.

Marie needs to let her limbs relax, she tells them, and perhaps her mind will follow. She admits that it has been months since she has taken more than half a day off.

A parade of changing light covers them as they turn pages, drift into conversations that float as wide and as high as the sky that seems to stretch from one end of the world to the next. They doze in the sun, they read Annie's high school poetry, they fight over who will cook dinner, and they add another page to the funeral book, there on a beach where Annie roasted marshmallows, went skinny-dipping, and threw sand into her cousins' eyes.

KATHERINE THOUGHT: *How lucky you were to be here, Annie. How lucky am I to have known you so that I can now be here too. Thinking, I am thinking, about the unopened gifts of life. About how some people try so hard to give us gifts—not the physical ones—but the real gifts—you know, time and energy and love and all of that—and how sometimes we ignore them and what a mistake that was. You were always remarkably generous with your gifts, Annie. Thank you.*

LAURA THOUGHT: *The energy here is an astounding blend of fun and intensity. I can dip through this house, this summer palace of your past, and feel you in every single room. I imagine yelling matches by the fireplace during Monopoly games, snowball fights outside in the yard when you came up for Thanksgiving, and the enviable time you must have spent with your mother in the kitchen. And something else, Annie. What was it? What did you struggle with here? Is this where your teenage demons were hatched? Is this where you danced with the dark shadows in your mind? Maybe the stones in your room fell from your heart. Maybe you healed yourself every day at this beach when the sun rose and the water rushed over your bare feet and you started again. Maybe . . . Maybe . . . Maybe.*

REBECCA THOUGHT: *It doesn't matter where I am or what we are doing, Annie, because when I breathe or talk or look up I still expect you to be walking into the room or singing in the yard or driving up the driveway. I've done this before. I know how it works but I cannot get used to it. Not yet. You just piss me off. I love you.*

JILL THOUGHT: *How fun, Ms. Annie, with all the books. You had it bad for words, all those years ago, clawing your way to adulthood. Did you dream about teaching and shaping the minds in that cute little bed of yours? The bright wings of words were a way for you to fly away from here but I bet you always came back, in your mind and heart, for how could you ever leave, oh Annie of the north woods? How could you ever leave?*

BALINDA THOUGHT: *The sand on my hands, the wind in my face, that freezing cold water washing across the tips of my toes—how wonderful this is and how wonderful you must have been and how lucky to be in this place and to have what you had here. I see you dancing across the waves of this lake, laughing at the bouncing sky, and at me, too, for feeling guilty because I am here and not with my mother. Thank you for this, Annie, and for sharing your friends and for dancing slowly enough so that I can follow your steps.*

MARIE THOUGHT: *I'm here. I'm exhausted and I should have come sooner. These women are a jumble of fineness. I close my eyes, even after these few short hours, and I see you with each one of them. I miss you too, Annie. I miss you.*

Lou could almost feel the house vibrating as she turned into the driveway just ten minutes this side of six P.M. She smiled all the way from her lodge to the Freeman house, which was 50 percent hers, which she protected from the county foreclosed bin and into the hands of the assorted cousins, one lonely uncle, herself, Annie's boys and a handful of mismatched relatives who had all taken their summer turn at the house and who agreed with her that come hell or high water the house should never be sold.

She smelled her groceries cooking before she got out of the car, and she paused before she slammed her car door, before they heard her and ran outside to greet her. Lou paused with her hand on her heart to listen to the voices of Annie's friends reverberating throughout the cabin and into the forest and out across the long sweep of lawn onto the beach.

Closing her eyes, she could remember a time when the sounds lasted for months with the comings and goings of uncles and aunts and cousins and Annie's family, who refused to deny anyone who was even a remote relative from coming and staying for days or weeks at a time. She remembered beach parties, and winter skiing trips and Thanksgiving dinners that lasted for hours and often turned into weekends of fun because they all got snowed in. And she remembered Annie.

Lou, who claimed Annie as the granddaughter and the daughter she never had, Lou who always stayed behind when one and then another and then another after that left, Lou who filled her own houses with guests to keep her company and to keep the family house as vibrant and whole as possible, already knew what she was going to do as she patted her pocket, took in a deep breath, and shouted her "Yo-ho" from the drive.

Dinner was a delicious whirl of food, conversation, laughter, and wine. The women jostled around the kitchen as if they had been maneuvering in tight quarters together their entire lives. Laura, Marie and Jill were in charge of the dining room and had gathered pieces of driftwood and rocks from the beach and combined them with the flowers into a centerpiece that would make Martha Stewart blush. They had discovered a set of china and had scavenged through the house for candles. They flung open the windows, plugged in a CD, and were standing at attention in case Balinda, Rebecca and Katherine needed any assistance in the kitchen.

Lou sat at the head of the table and could not stop smiling.

"This," she told them, "is why this house was built by Annie's great-grandpa and this is what is supposed to be happening here all of the time. You gals have done a fabulous job. Another week, and the place would look like one of those Pottery Barn furnished joints."

Thus began dinner and several hours of talk about Annie as a girl and Lou's life path that took her through three marriages and so many damn funerals—all three husbands died—that she decided it was time to hang up her wedding bells and settle down like a good girl—alone. That's when she turned into the full-time caretaker and nursing assistant as Annie's real grandma and uncle and so many other people that she can't even name them became ill.

"They were all too damn thin," she laughed as she drank her wine and told her stories and laughed more than she had laughed since the day Annie had called to tell her that she was terminally ill.

"My God," Marie whispered. "You were a hospice nurse too."

No one meant for three and then four hours to pass but there was plenty of wine and absolutely no one wanted coffee and the party eventually moved to the porch where they settled in to ask the questions that were quickly becoming muddled by alcohol and the blinking stars and a moon that was so close to being full it could hardly keep itself in the sky.

"Shit," Rebecca finally says. "This is so peaceful, Lou. I can see why it would be hard to find someplace better."

"Yes, shit," Marie agrees as they focus on Lou, who is rocking in the porch swing and watching them as if she is enjoying the best movie ever created.

"You are a wild one, Marie," she chuckles. "I bet you keep all those dying people alive for lots of extra weeks because they are afraid to miss something."

"Maybe," Marie answers. "Most people are afraid of dying. Really."

They ask her then. They ask Lou about Annie and what magical moment could have possibly occurred, besides the dozens of events they have already discussed, that could have possibly changed or imprinted Annie's life enough to make this spot part of her traveling funeral. And Lou begins to cry.

The women all reach for her at once and Lou puts out her hand and tells them that she is "better than fine" and that what she has to say is only sad because Annie is not here to tell them herself.

"Let me cry," she asks. "Just let me. I need this."

The story is as simple as the spontaneous yet unpredictable ripple of the waves that roll out across the beach stones just the way they have for hundreds of years. It is a beautiful tale that rhymes with the very foundations of life and beginnings and coming to find a place that you can always touch no matter where you are.

"You think it would be something grand having to do with that washed-up photograph her grandfather used to carry," explains Lou, rocking and crying softly. "You think it is something magical that Annie wanted you to know but I am thinking that you already know it. Just listen. It is no secret. It is not a large and mysterious story. It is just a story of Annie's coming to know how she was formed and where she could go and what she always had."

They listen. They listen as Lou stops crying and looks out across them and tells them a story that is as beautiful as it is simple. They listen as the moon, full as it will ever be, dips into sight and lingers for so long it looks as if it has been painted across the dark sky that connects this one spot to the rest of the world. They listen as the waves crash and they breathe in air that is pure and clean and safe and strong. They listen as they reach for each other's hands and occasionally close their eyes and see the face of Annie G. Freeman.

"Annie had recovered from her suicide attempt," she tells them, "it was years beyond that, and those demons that haunted not only her but so many members of our family had retreated. She was at the end of her college years, I think, maybe even past that and moving into this open, wild and wonderful place that she came to embrace as her own."

Lou talks in a whisper. She rocks and talks and the women, Annie Freeman's pallbearers, do not want to miss one word, one movement, one second of this story.

"The man who found the photo had lost a daughter the same age, size, and shape of Annie," Lou recalls. "It was one of those horrible, tragic accidents where a car came out of nowhere and struck Isabelle as she was getting off of her school bus and while her mother watched from the kitchen window. God, I can see it like I was there," Lou says, stopping for a moment to clear the image from her mind. "It was nothing more than fate, an accident, but as this always does, it devastated the family."

The father lost his job, and eventually his wife and every single thing that he had, and he clung to this notion that his Isabelle was alive, Lou continues. Isabelle was Annie's double. They could have been twins. When the photo of Annie washed onto shore, the father thought he knew she was alive and that the last six years of his life had been a dream and he searched the entire area with the photo clutched in his hand looking for his Isabelle.

"He found Annie instead, thinking she was his dead daughter," she told the women. "She was sitting right there, at the kitchen table, when he came in and fell to his knees and sobbed out his story and called her Isabelle."

The women cannot move. Their internal and external functions have become frozen inside of this story and if a bomb were to explode or the brilliant moon were to fall from the sky they would be trapped in this position forever.

"What happened?" they ask.

"My sister, Annie's grandmother, was right here in this room and she took the man in her arms and let him cry and she told him the truth," Lou continued. "She told him that his life was not a dream and that his baby was dead and that he needed to move on and find his life again because that is what Isabelle would have wanted."

"What did this do to Annie?" Katherine whispered, mesmerized. "What happened to our Annie?"

There is a break in the movement and talking that puts everyone into balance. A balance so that they can see how simple, and yet how complicated, that photo washing onto shore became.

"It changed everything for Annie because she saw in this man the power of family love," Lou says, moving forward so that her face is just inches from the women. "She had been through her own kind of hell but she had never seen that same kind of hell cross over into someone else's life. She saw from those moments when that man bared his grieving soul what it might be like to lose everything and understanding his loss made her embrace things that are seemingly simple yet absolutely exquisite because of their truth and sincerity."

The sound of the waves.

Her mother's voice at the end of the phone.

The way her grandma sang while she cooked.

The reliability of the seasons.

How resounding and concrete tradition can be and become in a life.

The comfort of familiarity.

"She'd bucked against family until that time, she did not get how it is okay to celebrate your beginnings and hold them close to your soul and keep them there and then move on," Lou said. "But that night she fell into her grandma's arms and they talked for hours about the power of love that never changes color no matter what happens. They shared secrets and held hands and came to a place of understanding about the boundaries that are created and then relinquished in hearts and lives that are born from a family— no matter what that family looks like.

"Her life, as you know, took so many twists and turns but she always came back here, she always remembered to take care of us, she always, after that night, honored her beginnings," Lou shared. "That is why she wanted you to come here. That is why a part of her will always be here."

That is why.

25

The air is a narcotic vibration that reaches inside of the Freeman house and corrals Katherine, Jill, Laura, Marie, Rebecca and Balinda into a place where dreams jump and swing and rumba as if they are trapped inside of a wave that rolls on into eternity.

The women, tucked into beds from one end of the house to the next, dream about riding naked on motorcycles, dancing with dogs, reading books that weigh as much as an entire truck, and speaking in foreign tongues in the middle of a cattle drive.

Breakfast begins at 12:30 P.M. as they stagger to the kitchen and share their night terrors while dressed in an assortment of clothing that would make the boys on *Queer Eye* collapse in shame and disgust.

"What the hell," Katherine exclaims as she flops into a chair praying that someone else has made coffee as strong as tar. "Was it the wine? The story? The ghosts coming out of the closet? What?"

What indeed, they agree. In a matter of days, Jill explains, they have embraced not only the death of a friend who meant the world to them but discovered parts of her world they never knew existed and parts of each other's worlds that they most likely would never have even seen if this traveling funeral had not existed.

"Think about it," she says, swaggering over to the counter to make yet another pot of coffee. "Add a ton of wine and this emotional liquidity to the mix and we are one group of loose-limbed women."

Without thinking, Laura suggests the ultimate in morning salutes. She stands up, throws down her coffee cup, and says, "Let's all go jump in the lake."

They look at her as if she's told them they are all going to stand on the kitchen table and pierce their navels with a wooden toothpick. No one says a word.

Laura doesn't wait. She's a woman possessed.

"Babies!" she taunts as she turns and walks out the door and toward the beach.

They all follow. They could not stop if they really, truly wanted to.

Within five minutes there is a screaming concert of female voices that collides with the oncoming waves as one after another of the women strips off all of her clothes and jumps naked into the coldest water she has ever felt in her life. They each go under once, and then twice, disappearing inside of sluices of water that feel as if they were ice cubes just moments before.

"Oh my God," Marie screams, running from the water so fast she trips and falls and ends up going under one more time. "Do people who swim in this water ever have children?"

They emerge as moving dots of red, their skin raw and numb, and their senses as alive and fresh and keen as they have ever been. Back at the house they wrap themselves in blankets, begin making coffee as if their very lives depended on it, and they stretch out in the great room and laugh at what they have just done, where they have been, what they have accomplished.

"This is something." Balinda smiles, realizing in that exact moment that it has been hours since she has worried about or even thought of her mother. "I cannot believe how absolutely wonderful and alive I feel at this moment."

"Who would have thought that this would happen in the middle of a funeral?" Rebecca asks. "I feel the same way, Balinda. I suppose Annie thought about some of this, imagined it even as she was pushing that pen across the pages, but I also suspect that she made room for the spontaneity that we all seem to be getting the hang of as each day of this traveling funeral passes."

Jill thinks about that and about the spaces in her life that she tried to fill up with routines, never letting things just happen, always making certain she checked off her boxes, followed her plan, was in control of every second.

"It's something," she finally says, shifting so that her frigid feet are tucked under Katherine's rear end. "How you think most of your living might be done and then you look up and see a new way to do something, really, a new way to live."

Katherine puts her hand out fast and grabs Jill's arm.

"That doesn't take away from any of the past living," she tells Jill. "That doesn't take away from how you lived or what you did but obviously this, this day and this week and being with these wonderful women, has shown you and all of us that living, *really* living, needs to be spontaneous at least some of the time."

Marie tells them that she feels as if she has the most to gain.

"Annie told me I work too much and that even though I am doing the work of the saints that it's wrong to lose yourself so much that you don't live either," she tells them. "That's all I thought about since this started. I've thought about Annie, of course, but for all those miles between here and there I've thought that maybe I've given away too much."

Balinda cannot speak. She feels as if Marie is speaking for her. She thinks that maybe her mother would not have wanted her to give up quite this much.

The women who are mothers dip into the conversation as if they are being punished. They tell stories, with their heads lowered, about washing diapers and making beds and picking things up, when all that "shit," as they call it, could have been saved and replaced with a spontaneous moment that might have been something as simple as sitting still and singing a song.

"I'd be in the middle of it," Laura admits, "saying something like 'No, you pick that up now,' and would be knowing the entire time I said it that it really didn't matter if it got picked up now and that we should just cuddle or eat a goddamn Popsicle. For some unknown reason I almost always kept going instead of just, well, stopping for a moment."

Stopping for a moment.

The women look at each other, eye to eye, making the rounds from one face to the next without saying a word, and they realize, in those quiet seconds, that Annie wanted them to have this conversation. She wanted them to sit naked under blankets, sipping coffee on a summer afternoon at the home where her roots were. She intended for them to discuss the importance of just simply doing precisely what they were doing.

They know, each one of them, that they don't have to say another word. They know that they could just sit there, they know that they could get up and do the tango or recite some interesting Annie story, or walk to town in their bare feet for more beer or coffee, and that would be okay also.

"Damn," Laura finally says. "Annie really was something."

"She was and so are you and so are all of us," Katherine adds.

"I'm thinking," Balinda says, smiling so widely that she starts laughing, "that if word of this catches on and people realize how much fun they could have at funerals, people would be dying to try it."

They all throw something at her—pillows, shoes, socks and books go flying and then Jill turns the conversation into something more practical than serious but serious in a way that makes them all turn and look at her.

"The ceremony," Jill asks them. "Does anyone want to focus on that for just a second?"

Yes. They all want to focus on it and not as a chore, they agree, but as a wonderful part of the entire "up north" experience that has already changed how they think about the benefits of spontaneity and how they will forever feel about cold water.

"Ideas?" she asks them.

"Well, outside," Rebecca says forcefully.

"I've already thought about it," Balinda says next. "Is it okay if I say what I was thinking about this even if I am not part of the original group?"

The women look at her as if she has just told them she's got a hidden camera under her armpit and they will be on the ten P.M. news swimming nude in Lake Superior. No one says anything and she gets that point just as much as if they had yelled into her face.

"I was thinking about a campfire, one on this little bluff I found this morning before you all got up," Balinda tells them. "I went for a walk because, as you know, I was the one who was drinking the least amount of wine, and right off to the left of the house there's a trail that winds to a bluff and there are little chairs made out of trees and a place to build a fire and I was just thinking that the whole setup looked like Annie even though I never knew Annie."

Before she even finishes they all know that is where they will be holding the second-to-the-last phase of the traveling funeral.

"Can you see the lake?" Katherine asks Balinda, just to be certain. "We'd have to see the lake."

"Of course. And if you turn your head just a bit you can see the cabin and off to the side it is nothing but solid trees. From what we've discovered it seems like that would be the perfect combination of this part of Annie's life, what she learned, what she was trying to share with us."

It's settled and they also agree that Lou must be called with the details in case she objects, which she does not. She does not, however, want them to cook dinner as she is making a huge pot of soup, which she will bring over at four P.M.—"on the dot"—and when she finds out how they have spent part of the day she laughs so loud that Rebecca has to hold the phone away from her ear. "You girls," they can hear Lou say through a laugh that barely needs the telephone. "Oh, you girls."

They sleep and walk and call their children and a neighbor or two, their lovers and husbands and the nursing home and then they just wait in a way that leaves them ready for not only the spreading of Annie's ashes on the shores of Lake Superior but anything that might happen—anything at all.

The moon does not appear near the Freeman homestead until it is past eight P.M., and Lou explains to them that by the middle of summer it stays light very, very late and the long days help some of them make amends for the terribly long and always cold winters.

"In another few weeks we'll be out here reading on the beach at ten P.M.," she explains as they put away the last of the dinner dishes and begin slipping their tennis shoes on for the procession to the campfire zone.

Lou is not surprised when they tell her where they have decided to have the up-north funeral. She wondered if they had discovered the family fire pit where generations of Freemans have been holding court, deciding the fate of each other, the world and whatever else they felt like deciding as they burned trees that had succumbed to the perilous Lake Superior weather, sat close enough for their knees to touch, and soaked in the miraculous healing rays of the northern lights and a sky that seemed to grow more enormous each year.

"The parties we have had up there," Lou recalls, slapping her knees. "If the trees and sand and sky could talk, it would pretty much be an endless tale of Freeman fun and frivolity. And some seriousness, too, because I can tell you lives were changed around the campfires that we had up there."

Before they leave the house, the women want to know. They want to know about the changed lives and if anything more re-markable than what they have already discussed happened to Annie. Was she always alone? Who came with her? Were there ar-guments? Did people fall in and out of love?

"Whoa . . ." Lou stops them by putting her hands up as they stand around the kitchen. "All of the above. Annie brought a few friends now and then. Katherine, I am surprised you never came up here, but if I remember correctly the timing was always off. That young man from Florida who you went to see, he came twice actually. Never her husband, but then again that only lasted about twenty minutes."

After that, Lou tells the women, Annie disappeared from the shore as she kick-started her professional career and began having babies.

"You know what those years are like," Lou says. "Too busy to breathe. But she occasionally brought the boys up. I think those two boys were here about five or six times over the years and they absolutely loved it every time they came, and hated to leave," she said. "They know they are welcome and I imagine when they clear away the sorrow surrounding Annie's death they will return to re-connect with her past—their past as well."

And yes, there were romps in the bushes and some uncles fling-ing whiskey bottles into the rolling waves during particularly heated discussions and of course even the glorious surroundings of a place like this don't erase the realities of real life, real emotions and the very real people behind all of those things, Lou said.

"Well, you don't really forget the crap, do you?" she asks. "You might put a blanket over it and push it to the back of your mind but that doesn't really make it go away. Like Annie's suicide at-tempt."

Oh, that, the women nod. The suicide attempt.

"We talked about it after it happened. And we all agreed that the next time Annie came to visit, we would not bring it up, but we wouldn't shy away from it either," Lou remembers. "It was there. It was always there, but it got dimmer and I know some of us were brave enough to ask her questions and I know that as she grew older and wiser herself those questions were always easier to answer."

"Such wisdom," Rebecca tells Lou. "We should have just come here and done the whole ash-spreading right in one spot."

The one spot is definitely the correct spot for this segment of the traveling funeral, they agree. The women wind their way through the trees and end up yards from the house carrying the mixings for s'mores that Lou gave them when she found out there was going to be a fire. Paul had already stacked an entire cord of wood on the hill and Lou (Who would have thought! the women joke with her) has snagged a bottle of brandy and plastic cups for a toast or two as they tend the fire and stretch out the traveling funeral into a night of long discussions.

The fire becomes a roaring blaze and Annie has a place of honor, far enough away from the snapping flames and poking sticks, resting in the shoebox that rests atop of the largest log.

Lou, who is used to taking charge and monitoring the cadence of those around her, becomes the proverbial program director. She tells the women it's okay to cut some sticks for poking and roasting and she tells them water stories and tales of her own life growing up in a place that was even more remote sixty-eight years ago. Stories about ore ships sinking and storms that whipped across the lake and grabbed babies and grown men in singular motions of violence that rocked the small communities who clung to its shores.

"This is the kind of place you either love or hate very quickly and those of us who were born here, who came to this land from inside of our mothers, have some kind of magical connection to it," she tells them, standing in front of the fire so she can look out into her beloved "northern ocean." "It's funny how many of us try to leave and then end up coming back to scrape a living off a land that seems to reject us every chance it gets.

"Stamina," she informs them, is the key word for survival in the north woods, and Annie, she quickly adds, had stamina in spades.

Lou passes out her plastic cups and offers a dab of brandy for anyone who wants to join her in a toast for what is apparently the kickoff of the Lake Superior portion of Annie Freeman's fabulous traveling funeral. They sip the bitter alcohol that warms them quickly from the inside out as they all sense a shifting in the air, a subtle increase in the wind, and a movement of clouds that Lou immediately tells them means something is about to blow in.

"Reading the weather up here is like reading the newspaper in the places where you gals live," she says, sipping her drink and turning her head into the wind. "It can mean everything, just everything, if something moves in fast and you happen to be in the wrong spot.

"So," she continues and then stops as her voice catches in her throat.

The women freeze for a second and both Laura and Jill, who are standing next to Lou, reach to put concerned hands on her arm.

"So, I know we are here to spread some of Annie's ashes in a place that meant a great deal to her throughout her life and especially as she grew older and wiser. But before we do that, however in the world we do that, there is something I would like to do," Lou tells them.

She reaches over to set her glass on a log behind her and then straightens and puts her hand inside of her front pants pocket. When she removes it she is holding six keys in her hand. They point toward the water and glimmer and shine in her palm when the flames flicker and soar.

"Annie did not ask me to do this. In fact, she only sent me a fairly short note that didn't detail this portion of the adventure at all," Lou explains. "But this is something I know that she would love. And it is something that would mean a lot to her and to me."

The quiet, she told them, sometimes consumes her. The absence of laughter and the slamming of doors, and feet on the stairs, and kids throwing balls onto the roof. The clink of ice cubes in glasses filled with gin before noon and a dozen people talking around the dining room table, and sandy footprints across the wooden floors.

"I fill my own house with guests to help pay the heating bills but I also do that because I like people and what the familiarity of family brings to a life," Lou tells them, closing her hand over the six keys. "Family does not mean people with the same last name or the same DNA. It means people who care about you, who you trust, who you care about—people you can count on."

Like Annie counted on each of you, she shares.

Lou tells them that she is giving each one of them a key to the Freeman family northwoods home. She is giving each woman a key and clear entrance into her life as well. A place to vacation, a way to stay connected with this part of Annie's life, a chance to explore a part of the world that is as fine as it is frigid.

"Oh, hell," she tells them. "I'm a lonely old bat up here and those damn cousins of hers never come up and I keep the heat on and the refrigerator stocked and Annie and my sister made certain that I was taken care of and her boys will help me too so it would mean a lot to me for you to take these keys, use them, call me sometimes, become a part of my life the way that you were a part of Annie's life."

The women are astounded by her generosity and as she walks around the fire circle and places a key in each one of their hands, they rise to hug her and thank her.

"This is something," Balinda says, holding the key up against her heart. "No one has ever done anything like this for me before."

"Oh, honey," Lou says. "You, more than anyone, need this. You are close enough so that you can come visit anytime and if your mother ever gets mobile you just throw her in the car and bring her right along with you. Do you hear me?"

They all hear Lou who has a heart of gold so thick that it glimmers under her skin as if she is a walking mine. Lou who hiked with Annie up to this very spot and listened to her sorrows and joys and held her like a baby when she came back from the hospital and then the New Mexico desert after her suicide attempt. Lou, who they know looks out across the ocean of her own life to recapture the times of sweetness that they all know can come back to her in the form of the new faces she has now embraced.

"We'll make a kind of schedule," Jill announces. "Oh my God, could I like come and stay for *weeks* at a time?" she wails.

Lou laughs because Jill finally realizes what this might mean even if she has a new housemate and suddenly the entire world has changed for both of them.

"Of course you can both come and stay as long as you want," she tells her. "Anyone brave enough to come in the winter gets bonus points too."

They imagine that, all of them at once, in a swirl of energy that almost makes it snow. Frozen water for miles and miles and icicles hanging off the gutters that need to be kicked down to save the roof. Paul shoveling until his arms ache and mountains of snow that grow deeper and wider every week. Brave birds wintering in the trees and the hungry deer loping down from the hills who search for tiny buds to nibble.

Then when the imagining stops it is time to dip into Annie's tennis shoes and spread her ashes across all of those thoughts. Across the years when she was an innocent player in the sand and lay in the back bedroom at night drawing stars and hiding stones under her pillow. Across the walks in the forest along paths that led for miles into the back country and the fort she built against the rock cliffs with her cousins and the nights she stayed up until dawn drinking beer and skinny-dipping herself back into a sober state so her mother wouldn't know she was the one who drank all the beer. Across the years when she did not come home because she thought it was a simple place and that she was done with her past and she turned her back on the people who had held her hands and helped her roast her first marshmallows and sang to her when she could not fall asleep. The years when she was busy at school and would drive all night with her sons in the back seat so that Lou and her grandma could cook and take the boys fishing and show them how the long boats disappeared off the edge of the water that was what they called "the horizon of tomorrow." Across the days when she could not leave her job and when she became caught up in the swirl of business that comes with children and life and work and loves. And then the last visit—not so long ago—when she sat on the porch and rocked for hours and asked someone to help her walk to the beach where she lay in the cool sand for three hours and fell asleep with tears in her eyes and her hair full of sand that she refused to wash out for an entire week.

And then now.

Now when they each take Annie's ashes and cup them in the palms of their hands and then count to three and toss them into the northern air where they are swiftly consumed by the breath of the millions of stars that shine through the increasing clouds and into the air that grows colder by the second.

"Goodbye, Annie," they say one at a time, except for Lou who manages a very quiet "Welcome home, honey. Welcome back home."

26

"Holy shit," Rebecca is yelling from the back of the dipity-do-dah plane that is rolling and rocking them toward Minneapolis.

Holy shit indeed, as they are about to discover, when the same baby-voiced pilot who took them to Duluth struggles to get them back to Minneapolis in the middle of a storm that has gained speed as it has cruised across the country. He gets on the intercom and says without hesitation, "Folks—well, you women anyway—this is one hell of a ride. Don't get up. As you recall from our ride the other day, this plane is a tiny thing and today's wild weather has us at a bit of a disadvantage."

"Disadvantage my ass," Marie, who does not care for small airplanes in large storms, seethes through her clenched teeth. "We'll be lucky to land."

As if he is reading her mind the pilot buckaroo says, "I'll get her down, ladies, don't worry. I've flown through worse than this. Be patient. We'll be in Minneapolis before you know it."

I hope so, they all think mutely as they drop a few hundred feet and the pilot wrestles the plane into a small pocket of quiet air.

The storm, they read in the newspaper they found lying on a seat, has pretty much paralyzed half the country. There's snow in the mountains, rain in Seattle, and a pattern of moisture that is barging across the United States as if it's been kept in a holding pen for the past fifty years.

Airports from San Francisco to Kansas were backed up, and if they had thought to check the weather, made a phone call or come down from their campfire high, they would have stayed at the cabin until the skies cleared and it was not only a bit safer to fly but possible to get from one end of the country to the other without spending part of the day spinning in an airplane like a top.

"Once," Laura shares with them at a moment that makes Marie want to take off her shoes and fling them over the back of the seat, "my husband and I were flying back into the States from Mexico and we kind of got sucked into this horrible storm that left us totally in the hands of the airplane pilot and at the mercy of the weather gods."

"Is this story necessary?" Marie shouts back to her.

"It's got a happy ending."

"But is it *necessary*?"

"Yes!" everyone else votes. "Tell us the happy ending!"

There was not enough gas, Laura explains, for the plane to go anywhere else but into Chicago even though the airport was mostly closed—except for one solitary runway that was being held open for renegade airplanes. She told the women that just as the plane neared the airfield it almost dropped out of the sky because it got sucked into a wind sheer.

"We were going sideways down the runway," Laura recalled, closing her eyes as she told the story. "I could see people inside drinking coffee as we cruised so close to the terminal I swear I could feel someone's breath on my neck."

"Well?" they all demand, beyond breathless for more than one reason.

"Just as I thought we were about to die, and people were screaming, and the stewardesses were on the floor, the pilot pulled us up
out of it, but that wasn't the last of it."

"What happened?"

"We had to circle and come back and do it all over again."

"How in the world did you ever get on an airplane again?" Jill
asked her.

"I didn't for three years and it took me three years after that to
do it sober. I used to take my water bottles, fill them with vodka,
and get totally buzzed the entire time I was flying."

"Thank you for sharing," Marie shouts back with a face that is
the color of the snow they imagine flying into the high mountains
of Colorado. "If Annie was here right now, I'd *kill* her."

Exactly eighteen minutes later they land, not sideways, but
surely not in the most gentle and professional manner ever seen at
the Minneapolis airport. They are greeted by a fine thank-you
from the pilot who also informs them that they should be proud
because their little airplane is going to be the last one in or out of
the airport for what looks like more than a few hours.

While they file into the main terminal that is already churning
with restless travelers, they cannot stop talking about near-death
experiences and the sometimes taken-for-granted gifts of safety
and the bliss of second and third chances. They join a long line
outside the agent's desk and the talk escalates in gusts, like the
winds they just rode across the state of Minnesota.

"Nothing is leaving."

"Airports backed up across the country."

"Impossible to tell what will happen."

"What do you think?" an elderly woman asks them as they stand
in line.

Katherine laughs because asking this group of funeral-goers
what they think could unleash a storm all of its own. We, she wants
to say, think about everything and have discussed just about everything during the past week. We've hashed out Annie's life and our

lives and the fascinating intersections where the past and present and future cross. We've cried and swum naked and tossed back more wine than some of us—that's just some of us, she laughs to herself—drink in a year. We've danced in the desert and dipped our feet into the other side of the ocean, tossed Annie's dusty bones in more places than some people ever get to see in a lifetime. It's not over either, she adds in her mind. Something beyond the weather, beyond what has happened or what Annie planned to happen is apparently brewing at this very moment.

"We have no idea," Marie tells the woman. "We just fell out of the sky moments ago. What's the weatherman saying, do you know?"

Not so good for today, the woman tells them all.

Katherine decides to check at the desk anyway. She can't help herself.

"It's not like we can do much," Jill says with a shrug. "Apparently we've lost touch with the rest of the world in such a lovely way we never bothered to pay attention to the winds that whisked around our embers last night."

"That sounds a little dirty," Laura laughs, not caring that she's twenty-third in line and looking at an evening on the terminal floor, a long night in an airport hotel, or hitchhiking to Seattle in time to make the last portion of the funeral and catch the plane out of Seattle and back to San Francisco.

They wait.

They wait as other airplanes fall out of the sky.

They wait while they drink the dwindling supply of airport coffee.

They wait while the terminal television screens blink "canceled."

They wait until there are no more planes moving from east to west or west to east and then cruising to the Minneapolis runway so that 50 or 60 or 170 more men, women, and children can be dumped into a building that may explode if one more airplane descends upon it and opens up its doors.

Laura has cleared a spot for them. Their carry-on bags and Annie's shoebox are under a huge window that is flanked by chairs, newspaper stands, and ever-increasing hordes of travelers who begin setting up their own camps. Within an hour, it looks as if the Minneapolis airport has become a refugee-holding center.

They sit on the floor, place Annie in the middle, cross and un-cross their red tennis shoes, wait out the tempest and observe the storm of humanity that has clustered near gate B-46.

"We must look like we are sitting around a campfire at Girl Scout camp," Jill says, as she stretches out her legs behind her, rests on her tummy and puts her chin on her elbows. "Who would think we'd get stranded in Minneapolis this time of the year in the mid-dle of a traveling funeral?"

"I bet there isn't a contingency plan for this in Annie's papers," Marie says. "This probably doesn't happen much if it isn't the dead of winter."

"There's that word again," Balinda growls, rolling over to put her head on Jill's rear end. "Dead. I've been thinking that I'll have to take care of my mother's funeral sooner or later. I'm not sure I'll do this traveling funeral thing though, because I'll have to go back to Poland to do it. That's the only place that she loved, really loved."

"Why not?" Rebecca asks.

"Why not?" Balinda responds. "What do you mean?"

"If the place was important to your mother, if she grieved every day for it, why not take her ashes back there and have your own traveling funeral for her? Hell, I'll go with you. Poland isn't exactly on my must-see list, but then again why not? We'll all go."

Everyone leans forward. They are thinking, "Poland." They are also thinking how Balinda has woven herself into their lives and how, if they could, they would surely go to Poland or China or Ohio if they could help Balinda, Marie, Laura, or those cowboys from the bar in New Mexico.

"My friend Gracie flew over Germany on her way to Bosnia

several years ago," Katherine begins. "She said once she got past the terrifying thought that she was flying into a war zone she started looking out the windows as they flew over Germany and she felt as if she were flying over Wisconsin. That's why so many Germans and Poles settled in the Midwest. It looks just like their homeland. I suppose it would be kind of neat, Balinda, for you to go back and find all your cousins and great-aunts and to look into the face of your own past."

Imagining an international traveling funeral takes its own twists and turns as the six women joke about being stopped by border guards who want to sniff the ashes and make certain the girls are not smuggling drugs, questions about the matching shoes and bandanas and the funeral book which could be filled with code words for international espionage.

"How are the Polish jails?" Laura asks. "Maybe you'd meet some handsome soldier, fall in love and—"

"Love and funerals," Balinda interrupts. "Not a good mix."

The women are suddenly joined in conversation by a man who is sitting so close to them Laura could knock his teeth out if she moved in the wrong direction at the correct speed.

"I'm sorry," he said, bending at the waist to get even closer to them, "but it's impossible not to hear what you are saying in these cozy quarters. May I say something?"

He gets to speak following a unanimous vote by all the members of the traveling, and now stranded, funeral, mostly because he's polite but also because Laura, Ms. Know-It-All, feels that he has something important to say. She's looked past his eyes, she whispers to Rebecca, and can tell he's got a bowl of knowledge that he'd like to pass around.

He wedges himself in between Jill and Laura and tells them he's an anthropologist who has done a ton of work surrounding death-and-dying issues. He's mesmerized by the bits and pieces of information he's picked up from the women's conversation but he also has a story to tell.

"Death, as most of you know, really gives new life to many relationships," he begins. "Families reconcile, people forgive each other, they say things they have kept hidden or buried or were afraid to say when someone was alive. . . . It's like something springs loose beyond the grief and sadness and those feelings of loss that make you want to die yourself," Dr. David ReNould tells them, speaking with his hands as if he were giving a noon lecture.

The women are focused on the professor and his lecture and they do not see that one and then two and five and then fifteen people have gathered to listen. The original circle, centered around Annie's shoebox—which now has tattered edges and coffee stains and flowers drawn across its side—has grown so that it looks as if the women in the red shoes are holding court, preparing for a séance, ready to pounce.

"There are remarkable stories that drift from generation to generation and that cross cultures, having to do with astounding instances of the living having experiences of connection and transformation at funerals and during the grieving period that are always explained by giving power back to the person who died," he tells them, focusing in on his own words in a way that makes the women realize he has had personal as well as professional experience.

"Tell us your story," Jill, the professor, asks him. "You have something very personal to tell us."

David studies her and smiles. His smile says, *She knows. She's got it.*

"It's a love story," he answers. "I was in college and had already decided on my professional path. I had been dating a woman, who by the way was and is still named Ann, isn't that one hell of a coincidence, and we broke up, mostly because I was an ass."

"Well, you are a man," Rebecca interjects.

Someone in the third row back says, "You go, girl," and it's the first time they all turn to look and see that their circle has spread like a rising tide into the chairs and past the end of the windows.

Rebecca smiles, does a quick eye check with the other women to make certain what is happening is okay, and then nods as if to say "Thank you." She smiles at David, blows him a kiss, and he continues.

"Then my grandma died and Ann, who happened to be in town, phoned on a whim to say hi to my mother and discovered the funeral was the next day," he said. "My mother mentioned to Ann that the weather was horrible and they anticipated a small turnout because she didn't expect elderly people to come out in a storm," he recalled. "When I found out that Ann had called I could not sleep. I was still very much in love with her and all night long I hoped that she would show up the next day."

He hoped, David said, so much that he waited in the parking lot of the funeral home until Ann's car pulled in, and they were cordial to each other and she was one of ten people who showed up for the funeral and then he invited her to come back to the house where she ended up being stranded and they talked all night.

There is a pause, when David shifts his weight and when the crowd pushes in, and Jill reaches over to pat the shoebox, and then he continues.

"We've been married twenty-seven years, Ann and I, and there is not one person who knows us who doesn't think that my grandmother had something to do with our getting back together," he says. "Things happen at funerals. It's some kind of cosmic, absolutely cosmic, spiritual process that helps maneuver fate and challenges the hearts and souls of people to step up for crissakes, step up and get on with it."

The crowd goes wild and people begin raising their hands as if they were in class. "Oh, oh . . ." some of them are shouting, softly, but they are shouting. There are suddenly funeral stories fanning out in the crowd three rows back, like a sail that has caught the wind and moves from top to bottom in a gentle push.

"Let's go," the women all seem to say at once as they widen the circle, leave Annie in the center and listen. Katherine, the consummate leader, the funeral director, the one in charge, selects the speakers.

Marie, who completely understands this rich connection between the dying and the living and then the dead and the living, sits back and listens in wonder. She listens with a small piece of her mind rotating back just a few days, before the funeral, and it makes her wonder while David speaks what else she has missed by feeling she needed to be so tied in place.

There is a woman toward the back who rises when she speaks. She has on a dark blue business suit and she's kicked off her shoes and undone her hair. Her story unfolds in a way that keeps everyone spellbound and she cries as she tells it. Her brother was killed in a car accident when she was fourteen years old. She said the tragedy devastated her parents so much that she ended up living with her aunt and uncle because her mother started drinking and her father left. She said from the time she was fourteen she attended a succession of funerals that were like stacked blocks that fell one after another after her brother died. Brother. Grandmother. Mother. Another grandmother and then her father. Funerals, she told them, became a part-time job.

One day, the blue-suited businesswoman drove herself to the cemetery where it seemed as if her entire family filled half of the space, and was strolling from one gravesite to the next when she literally walked into a woman who was kneeling in front of another marker. The woman was grieving for her daughter, who died the same week as the woman's brother. The two women talked, standing in the shadow of a mausoleum that was covered in ivy that scratched them as they leaned into it. They talked for five hours, exchanged phone numbers and then left.

"She became the mother I always wanted and needed," the woman, who finally identifies herself as Sally, shares with this crowd of strangers. "I moved in with her, she and her husband put me through college, and I owe them everything, everything."

The women sit up after Sally's story and like the crowd around them, quickly become mesmerized by what is happening. Another woman from the group, which is still growing, rushes off to the concession stand and buys coffee, beer and water, and has her children deliver the drinks to everyone sitting in the circle that now stretches out into the walkway where no one is moving anyway.

"Oh sweet Jesus," Laura whispers into Jill's ear. "What has Annie done now? Look around. This is totally amazing."

Jill looks around and sees a sea of faces hungry for more funeral stories. Hungry to listen and talk and funnel something—whatever they have been keeping in their own personal casket—back to life, back to *now*. Everyone needs some life food.

David has hauled out a notebook and is busy taking down notes. He looks as if he has discovered gold. Jill winks at Katherine, who mouths "Oh my God" across the circle, and she and Jill turn to look at Balinda, Laura, Marie and Rebecca. They feign innocence but they all know that Annie's funeral, their constant energy, the closed tarmac, and cosmic forces that have aligned to bring this fine group of travelers to their knees have helped to create this sacred and beautiful slice of time. Their smiles and nods encourage the storytellers; the courage of sharing rises like heat on a Miami Sunday.

And thus the stories go on and on.

I met my husband at my best friend's father's funeral. . . .

When my girlfriend was killed in a car crash the year I was sixteen, my whole life came into focus. I became a minister and now when someone dies, when there is a loss, a hollowing out of that place, that deep long tunnel of sadness, I feel as if I can go back and help in a way I might never have been able to help if I had not experienced death and grief at such a young age. . . .

My mother turned to me while we were sitting in the church just as my grandpa's funeral was to begin and said, "You are adopted." I was twelve and I looked at her as if she had just told me she was going to run off and join the circus. Why she picked that moment I will never know. Later, she helped me find my birth mother and we discovered that she had been at my grandpa's funeral with her husband who knew him from work. She looked at me, knew instantly that I was the daughter her parents had made her give up in high school, and she followed us home and then waited. Funerals are something that I am never afraid of and my life was never the same after that day. . . .

Sometimes, when I feel so lonely I could roll up and die my-self, I pick up the newspaper and then I go to a funeral where there are very few survivors listed. I pray for the deceased and the living. It makes me feel good and I think it makes the other people who are there happy. . . .

I know lots of people who have gone to funerals and met someone—a former girlfriend and they get back together—or someone from high school's mom who was really nice to you and then you meet someone there. I did that. When my old coach died I went to the funeral parlor just before the service at church and his daughter came up to me, we were both married, but later when we were not married we got together because after the funeral I kept her phone number in my wallet. I guess I always loved her. . . .

Someone else gets up to get more drinks and finally a well-dressed man at the edge of the crowd whispers to the man behind the bar at the concession stand and an entire drink cart is wheeled out and placed at the edge of the widening traveling funeral. It is like a private party that really isn't private at all.

Katherine turns to face every person who speaks and as she moves, her shoulder brushes against the box of ashes and reminds her why they are on the floor of the airport and where they have been and what is actually for real and true and happening at that very moment, and the nudge from the box feels like Annie's hand on her shoulder and it makes her smile.

It makes her smile and remember her frayed bra and the morning just two and a half weeks ago when she answered the door that now seems as if it was a year ago, a decade ago, something that happened before she was born. This thought passes through her mind when a little girl climbs on what Katherine presumes is her dad's back and says: "If my mommy dies I'm not going to the funeral."

Everyone laughs but then a whole new discussion breaks loose. A discussion about the place where funerals are held and how we honor tradition, and why—with so many of our parents and friends and selves on pause and in a position to be ready for a personal funeral—it took Annie G. Freeman for so many people to see there are so many fine and glorious ways to honor the dead—yes—THE DEAD—such a horrible, terse and final word but it is what it is—outside of the curtained walls of a fine but remarkably dull funeral home.

And Marie tells her story. She talks with such compassion about the months and days she spends with her ill patients and how she can see the lives of her patients flash like short films through their eyes. She talks about the importance of forgiveness and of letting go and for being a presence that does not intrude on a very important process.

"It's tiring," she admits maybe for the first time out loud in a very long time. "It's tiring and you have to be careful so that part of you does not die too."

There are a few more stories, really just two, from the crowd that has frozen itself to the Annie G. Freeman gate at the Minneapolis airport.

One man who has a face that radiates kindness has been waiting to speak. He is sitting close to the circle on a chair, lined up to see the television screens and the sky where there is not one plane in sight. The women all guess him to be close to eighty years old and he has a habit of pushing his hair back from his face with his hands every few seconds, and then nudging his glasses up onto his nose when they slip down.

"I've never told anyone this," he begins slowly, "and I have no idea why I am about to tell you now except maybe it's because you all seem so nice and we are stranded here and there's no place to go."

He hesitates as if he is trying to decide at the last minute if he should move forward or stay right where he is and when he looks up in that moment of hesitation and sees a small sea, a tiny lake really, of asking eyes and hearts wondering what he could have to say to them about death and dying and funerals, he decides he has absolutely nothing to lose with this crowd of traveling funeral-goers.

"Well, some might think this is silly, but my wife—my wife Pauline—she's been dead for six years now and every single night I sit down in our living room, just like we used to sit down, and I have a glass of wine and an entire conversation with her just as if she was sitting there and we were talking." He closes his eyes as he speaks so he can put himself right inside the living room. "Oh, we loved to do that. We loved to sit and have our wine and talk and share every night and I miss that so much and that is how I re-member her and what we had."

There is a quiet moment and then the group claps softly, not loud, just the gentle tapping of fingers against the palms of hands slowly while the words "That's lovely" and "How beautiful" parade from the floor to his ears.

A young woman across the room smiles at the kind man. She waits for the applause to stop and then she says that being stranded at the airport like this is the best thing that's ever happened to her. She's sitting on the floor with her long legs crossed and tucked up under her, and she's crying. It looks as if she has been crying for a very long time.

"I'm on my way to my mother's funeral," she tells them. "She died just last night, before I could get there, before I could say goodbye, before I could just look into her eyes one last time and tell her something, tell her maybe just one thing that I have needed to say for a very long time."

The woman sitting next to her reaches out to put her arm across her shoulders and everyone can hear her say, "Oh, honey, I'm sorry. I'm so sorry."

"I'll say it anyway when I get there," the young woman continues, looking up and into the eyes of everyone who is listening. "I'll tell her I love her, and why I was never able to say it when she was alive will be part of the traveling funeral I take with me until I can figure that out."

Enough, Katherine finally decides.

She stands with the shoebox under her arm and directs the group toward celebration. Waving her free hand across the room, she orders everyone to their feet and to their drinks and to a junction where they can hold their lost loves in a place of honor and delight.

"Our Annie could only take so much sadness," she explains. "On your feet, dance if you must, celebrate the life that was before the death and what it gave you and what you have even now."

Then the Minneapolis airport does just that. While a staggered line of airplanes waits under dark clouds that serenade an entire afternoon, a rumba line snakes through one concourse after another driven by one woman wearing red high-topped sneakers, with four wearing identical shoes scattered throughout the line, and one hanging on to the back end with the ashes of Annie G. Freeman bouncing gently under her right arm.

27

It is 6:30 P.M. and four hours past the time when the traveling funeral should have touched down at the Seattle-Tacoma airport and departed for a small road trip to the ferryboat dock and a ride to an island not far from the last boat landing.

"What are they saying on your end?" Marie, who is standing with her hands over her ears because the entire airport seems to now be engaged in dancing, drinking or some other fancy form of waiting that has spun off from the funeral discussions and the brazen talk just a few hours before, asks her husband.

"You may never leave the airport," he tells Marie, laughing before he hangs up. "From the news reports I have been hearing, all the airports are a mess from here to Minneapolis."

Katherine confirms this news and says that airport officials are hopeful that as soon as the storm passes they can begin sending planes out and receiving them from the West Coast but the snarl of backlogged planes could mean delays for hours and hours—maybe even a day.

"Look through those papers Annie sent you," Marie orders. "Is there any kind of contingency plan in there?"

"I think that's what she wanted us to figure out," Katherine replies. "We'll have to make some kind of decision soon about what we do next. I bet Annie wasn't focusing on one more thing messing up her plans and I'm thinking that we can probably hang just a bit longer and then decide. What do you think?"

Marie wants to say that she's tired of thinking and even more tired this moment of doing. She'd like to say how the funeral break was this huge beaming light at the end of her week, the week before and two years before that. She wants, right this very second, to lie down right where she is and have someone put a blanket over her. She'd like to have her feet tucked in and a warm drink right next to her right hand. She'd like to take a really long nap and know that it doesn't matter when she wakes up and she'd like her entire family to be locked inside of the house while she dozes so she knows they are all safe and she won't have to worry about them.

"Marie?"

"Sorry," she answers. "I was dreaming that I had nothing to do but eat, drink, sleep and be, well, Marie."

Katherine laughs and asks her if she's tired.

"Like the rest of the women in the world, yes, I am tired but it's not anything this break in my routine can't take care of for a while anyway," she explains. "So?"

So, they decide to wait just a bit longer and see if they can get a flight out or if they should find a bus or take the train or maybe just walk.

"I'm a good waiter," Marie tells Katherine. "In a way it's kind of exciting not to know what is going to happen next. So many parts of all our lives are predictable."

"Absolutely, especially the past few weeks," Katherine agrees as they decide to just wait it out a bit longer.

Marie leaves to tell the others they are just hanging for a while and Katherine finds a chair by the window and sits, alone, with Annie's ashes on her lap and her ankles crossed so that her red tennis shoes can bounce against each other. She knows she's guarded the ashes and Annie's place in her life with what she hopes has been a fine mix of seriousness and frivolity up to this point and she decides, just then, at that moment that she is also tired and yes, Marie, it would be wonderful to lie down and take a nap.

Which is what she does suddenly and without any thought beyond the tiredness that has grabbed her by the back of the neck and seems to push her down into the next seat. Katherine rolls her hips into the most uncomfortable chairs ever designed, pushes herself against the shoebox and falls asleep so fast she does not feel her left foot drop or the blanket from inside the bag of the mother next to her slide gently around her shoulders.

She dips into a place of dreams so fast it is amazing that she was able to walk to the chair and sit down without falling into a coma. Her legs jump, and the woman—the mother next to her who was a witness at the recent airport funeral and who wept when everyone told their stories—touches her as gently as she touches her own babies when they dream and move at night so that they will know they are safe and they can feel the anchor of her arm holding them.

Katherine goes far away and she travels past faces that are familiar and into a zone that is a dark tunnel of strangeness. She is trying hard to find someone. Who? She doesn't know who. And as fifteen and then twenty minutes pass, her leg movements become stronger and she starts to move her hands so that the shoebox begins slipping and very nearly falls to the floor.

The woman, Gretchen Smith, a pediatric nurse from Seattle who will eventually end up on the same plane as Katherine and the others and who will ask for help during the flight when her daughter gets ill and who will also slip a book into Katherine's carry-on bag that is her textbook—the one she wrote on death and dying when the patient is young—so damn young—catches the box,

Annie's ashes, and then holds them just as gently as Katherine would have as the next forty-nine minutes Katherine sleeps and searches for the mystery person.

In her dream, Katherine has to climb up something very tall and she cannot rest. She moves as fast as she can and even though she does not know where she is supposed to be she's desperate to get there. Later, when she is also on the plane and she finds the book tucked into her bag and the note that says: *Letting go does not have to be just because of a death. People lose many things they once believed they would have forever. I am certain, without ever having met her, that Annie would have told you the same thing and she would have been there when you let go of the rope. Let go. I guarantee that you will not fall. Your new friend—Gretchen,* she will remember the dream and will jump back inside of it to see what she is supposed to see and what that will bring her is something new, something that is not yet even a thought, something that might never have come to her if she had not been on a traveling funeral and asleep in an airport in Minnesota.

It will come to her months later when Gretchen calls and when they meet for lunch and when they become friends who connected during a traveling funeral and when Katherine finally realizes that she is ready to discover entire new parts of herself and to dust out all the corners of her life and see what's back there, what she tossed in the closet and why she was sometimes afraid to turn on the light to help her find a new direction. They will wonder, then, these two new friends, if Annie was not at the Minneapolis airport and if the man, David the professor, did not predict yet another cosmic happening because of all the lives that crossed for just those few hours when the clouds drifted into each other, the planes took a nap, and the world waited for the skies to clear.

But first Gretchen spies Jill, Balinda, Laura, Marie and Rebecca looking frantically for Katherine who, they are certain, must be reorganizing the management plan for the entire airport. Gretchen points toward the seat next to her, puts her finger to her lips, and silently invites the women to sit.

Jill wants to wake Katherine because Balinda thinks she has decided to take a bus back to Chicago. The wild winds from the west have changed everything.

Balinda has twenty-five minutes to make up her mind for certain, get a seat, and get out of the airport before everyone else tries to get on the same bus and get back home before the end of the decade, before George W. Bush ends a war or starts another one, or before women are finally allowed to do whatever in the hell they want with their own damn bodies.

The women funeral warriors watch Katherine sleep for a good five minutes before anyone is brave enough to wake her. They watch her because she not only looks beyond adorable curled up in the plastic seats with just a small trickle of saliva running down her lips but because every single one of them realizes they are going to miss her fine wit, penchant for organizing and for telling people what to do in a way that is sweet and usually very thoughtful, and her kind heart.

"Damn it," Jill says and in the back of her mind, way far back as she is searching and grabbing for whatever it is she is looking for, Katherine hears her and shifts her mind toward the light.

When she opens her eyes it takes her a moment, blinking under the lights, to realize where she is and what she is supposed to be doing.

"Annie," she says instinctively, searching for the box.

Gretchen puts her hand on Katherine's leg, hands over the box, and says, "Here she is. You fell asleep."

"Thank you," Katherine says and impetuously leans over to plant a kiss on Gretchen's cheek. "I must have drifted off."

"Just a bit," Gretchen tells her. "You were dreaming like crazy. Was someone chasing you?"

"I don't know. I kind of feel like I'm drunk. Do I know you?" Katherine asks, looking blankly into her eyes.

"Not yet, but sort of. I just tucked you in, stood guard over Annie, and came to the funeral you just conducted in the airport terminal. That should get me past the door."

They all laugh and Balinda bounces forward and tells Katherine she thinks that she must leave. She said it looks bleak for anything happening in Seattle—this day, at least—and she's worried about her mother.

"It's time," Balinda explains. "I can be there before midnight if I hop on the bus. I think my mom needs to see me even though she can barely talk when I call. I think she needs me and I feel charged up and ready to go back."

"Of course she needs you," Laura tells her. "You go. We'll all walk you to the pick-up spot."

Balinda wants to go and she wants to stay. She tells them this as they press through groups that have formed at various points throughout the airport. There is a herd of people in front of every bar and they watch as one group has formed a fascinating process for a drink to get from deep inside of the bar to someone on the outer edges—it's a dancing line of humans who stop whatever they are doing when someone shouts the word "Another" and a drink on a serving tray goes one way and the money for it on another tray goes the opposite way. Some are playing cards, a few kids are kicking a soccer ball up and down the escalator steps, and there are dozens of small squabbles and loud phone conversations going on everywhere.

"Awesome," Laura decides as they gather around Balinda by the bus stop. "It's like some third-world country or something in just a matter of hours."

The women, Annie's pallbearers, stand under the long overhang at the side of the airport because rain is blasting into the building from every conceivable angle and they plant Balinda in the center, protecting her, covering her with their arms and hands in a group hug that brings her to tears.

"This has been wonderful for me," she tells them. "Thank you for letting me barge in, for talking to me, for making me feel as if I was meant to do this from the beginning. Thank you for letting me believe that I was a real part of the whole traveling funeral."

The women tell her to stop it. They assure her that Annie would have had it no other way and neither would any of them. They tell her to call and write and Laura promises to bring her luggage when and if she makes it back to Chicago.

"I feel ready to open up the boundaries of my own world," Balinda confesses as she leans into Laura's arms. "It hasn't been just my mother. It's been *me*. There's also something I want to ask you, something that would mean a lot to me."

"What?" the women all ask at the same time.

"When it's time, when my mother dies, will you all help me with a traveling funeral? Will you start to save your money so we can go to Poland and spread her around and dance along the rivers, drink dark beer, and see what it was that made her love it so much?"

Right there, at that very moment, Jencitia Chalwaski's fabulous traveling funeral is conceived and the women close their eyes and see flocks of foreign birds drifting toward the center of a large lake, they can smell sausages cooking at roadside cafés and hear whistling barmen swishing beer into glasses the size of mixing bowls. They all fly to Poland, just then, and hear the whispers of Jencitia's own mama saying, "Welcome home, baby girl," and they feel the fingers of the past wrapping themselves around their shoulders so that they know, they really know, the connection of a place—Jencitia's place—that has driven itself into the center of the dying woman's heart.

"Oh . . ." Balinda sighs. "This makes me so happy. I am going to tell my mother too. I'm going to tell her that we will take her home."

Marie and Balinda spend a quiet moment together alone before Balinda gets on the bus. Marie presses her phone numbers into

Balinda's hand and they both say, almost at the exact same time, "You are not in this dying business alone." And then Balinda whispers, "Thank you," into Marie's ear and Marie whispers, "No, thank you," into Balinda's ear.

Jill, Marie, Katherine, Laura and Rebecca huddle together, arms crossing shoulders, hand in hand. They stay outside until the bus pulls away and all they can see are the vanishing taillights that blink at the turn and then disappear into a stream of water that resembles a sheet of white glass. Balinda stares out the back window of the bus for hours. She watches the wet skyline fade into fields of corn, suburban subdivisions and roadside gas stations and she imagines the women waiting at the terminal and honoring, until the very end, the spirit of Annie G. Freeman.

Six hours later when Balinda gets off the bus and takes a taxi straight to the care center where her mother is resting against a stack of pillows that have been strategically placed to help support her bad back, she stands in the doorway and places her hands across her mouth to suppress an emotional cry. It is a cry of love. She wants to run and throw herself on the bed and ask her mother to forgive her for every harsh and horrible thing she has ever said or thought. She wants to hold her mother in her arms like a baby and promise her—again—that she will take care of her until the day she dies. She wants to sing her mother a song in Polish and vow to her that she will take her home.

Balinda does sing and she does promise and when her mother wakes up two hours later and sees her there she reaches for her hand, grabs her wrists and pulls her right onto the bed and for the very first time in her life says, "Come here, my baby," to her daughter in *English,* and the two women huddle together as the storm floats to a halt, tired as hell, just the other side of downtown Chicago.

———

By ten P.M. Laura, Rebecca, Marie, Katherine and Jill have been at the airport for 12.3 hours and it is beyond obvious that there is no way in hell they are going to get to Seattle that day or maybe even the next day. The airport is still loaded with people who have now tired of drinking beer, playing cards and being happy about the odd sensation that comes with uncharted free time and being frivolous with what you share with total strangers, and they have descended into a grumpy aisle of tiredness that has many of them sleeping in places that make the entire terminal look like a war zone.

Marie has long since given up hope of watching the sun rise over the ocean islands. In her world of in-your-face reality, she has decided to make the most of the moment and throw down her cards first.

"Well, ladies," she says. "Apparently we are going to have to come up with Plan B for this segment of the traveling funeral. What say ye?"

"We don't know what to say," Jill tells her. "We stink, we're full of cheap-ass bagels and light beers and we've stumbled into that dangerous place of exhaustion called 'Who the hell cares?' "

"I see," Marie responds, standing with both her hands on her hips. "I'm a helper. So now I am going to help you by sending bold Katherine over to that desk, where she will ask for a room, travel vouchers and anything else she can get out of the almost bankrupt airlines people."

Katherine is all set to be a hard-ass attorney but when she gets to the front of the desk, thirty minutes later, and sees the haggard attendant, stacks of paperwork, piles of coffee cups, and the line of furious people behind her, she cannot do it.

"People don't realize we can't control the weather," the attendant confides as she stamps out a voucher for a room at the Sheraton. "I appreciate you being nice. I've got to get a new job."

Katherine laughs, finds out that they will be booked on the first morning flight to Seattle, unless the storm changes its ugly mind and wakes back up, and—because she's been so nice—they each—even Balinda—will get a round-trip ticket anywhere in the United States as a thank-you for not being jackasses.

"Whoa . . ." Katherine says, giving the woman a high-five. "Anywhere?"

The woman motions for Katherine to lean into the desk. She whispers to Katherine that not many people realize that for just a few hundred dollars the tickets she is handing them can be changed for use in international travel—round-trip.

"You are kidding?"

The woman smiles and says no, she is not kidding.

"Could we fly into Poland?"

"You'd have to go to Germany and then take some little bump ride over there but yes, you could work it out."

Katherine hugs her so tightly the woman winces and then points to her shoes and asks if she was with the group holding the traveling funeral. "We were and are," Katherine shares. "It ain't over yet."

"What a fabulous idea," the woman says. "You all really helped a mess of people today. The entire airport is talking about traveling funerals. Here, honey," she adds, pushing dinner coupons toward her. "Take your friend in the shoebox out for one last fling on me."

They do.

The looming end of the traveling funeral turns each one of them into manic mamas. They check into the hotel, take ten-minute showers, put their same clothes back on, brush off their red tennies, then head downstairs to the pub and dining room where they clear the center of the table, make room for Annie, and order appetizers, shrimp, steaks, salads with names they can barely pronounce and several bottles of the wines that they have been dying to try for the past five years.

The bar and restaurant managers decide to stay open an extra two hours, not only because the hotel is suddenly full and people are still ordering main courses at midnight, but also because a mysterious man—also stranded in the storm—has given them his Visa card, pointed at the group of red-shoed women who have placed a shoebox in the center of the table, and said, "Make sure they have whatever they want for dinner, for breakfast, in their rooms . . . anything."

Anything.

The night flies into its dark self then and the storm flows into a small circle until it retires and lets the world get back on course. The women toast and eat and drink. They sing at the bar and buy other stranded men and women drinks. They tell stories to these strangers about Annie and who she was and what she did and then later, so much later that it is already getting light outside, they stagger back to their rooms to find flowers on the bed, boxes of candy, bottles of champagne, and an absolutely beautiful note from the man.

The man.

You do not know me but in this absolutely brilliant world that was once inhabited and changed by Annie G. Freeman something happened to me that changed the direction of my life. My son was despondent and on the verge of committing suicide when he was in high school, and Annie's work, her writing and her program saved my son's life and mine also. I never met Annie, but I find it utterly fascinating that I was at the airport today and you were at the airport today. Annie would have loved this, I am certain of it, and even though I did not know her I know her through the vibrant force I felt coming from your friendship and love for her. Thank you, Annie, and thank all of you. I was in Minneapolis because my son graduated from his master's program this week and is now full of the same pieces of life that Annie passed on to so many people. I salute you as I salute her every single day of my life.

There was no name on the note, just the fine scent of generosity and thankfulness that carried each of them into her bed for three hours of sleep and an exhaustive discussion about believing in the magic of life, the power of hope, the cosmic sanity of chance and change, and the unmistakable power of love.

28

There is absolutely no ending Annie Freeman's traveling funeral quietly, with moderate grace, with anything but the wild gusto and the enormous attitude that Annie brought to almost every moment of her own life.

This is what the five surviving pallbearers discover when they awaken to a full slate of room service, morning massages from the hotel spa compliments of "the man," a fast and complete cleaning of their only set of clothes while they lounge in thick terry bathrobes, and a message from the airline saying they have been upgraded to first-class for the flight to San Francisco.

San Francisco and not Seattle because they have decided that Washington and those luscious islands off its coast need more than a twenty-second spreading of ashes from a taxi that is moving at the speed of sound.

San Francisco because by the time they arrived in Seattle they would have but a handful of hours to fulfill the desires of Annie. San Francisco because Marie deserves more than twenty minutes. San Francisco because it is time, because if they go to one more airport and create one more traveling funeral mess that seems to attract crowds from nowhere, they may all end up in a penal institution and Annie might not like that—heavy emphasis on the word *might*.

The San Francisco decision is hours behind them and leaves nothing but four hours of total debauchery, including facial treatments, breakfast pastries that have been baked with so much butter they can barely stay on the plates, Bloody Marys, coffee that smells as if it was just brewed in Costa Rica, and a wish that "the man" was there so they could each kiss him.

"Just when you think the entire male race is full of wild farm animals, go figure," Rebecca says as she sits with her feet up reading the morning newspaper and sipping coffee that makes her push out of her chair and grin each time she takes a sip.

"Look at the fascinating turn this entire funeral has taken because of one lousy storm," Jill points out.

"It wasn't like a tiny little storm," Marie interjects. "Look at this."

She holds up the front page of *USA Today* and shows them photos of flooded streets, people peering out of homes without power, and airplanes lined up for blocks and blocks at the Chicago airport.

"It was a pisser," Marie reports. "One of those once-in-every-twenty-five-years kind of storms. You know, I think we should find that pilot who got us here from Duluth. We could have been killed."

Jill and Laura stare at her as if she has just told them something unimaginable. Katherine, who at the very moment is getting a massage that has made her weep with pleasure, would agree. They are absolutely certain of it.

"Look," Laura suggests. "If anyone could control the universe it would be Annie. Maybe she planned this whole thing. Maybe she sent this man up here and created the storm and had us all placed in perfect alignment so that all these funky things would happen to us."

"Maybe not," Jill says, laughing. "That's not her style. You know that. But really, if you think about it, that's exactly what she did."

"What do you mean?" Laura asks.

"Well, what she did and who she was created a kind of funky motion that sparked a whirlwind. It's like people changed because they knew her or because she touched their lives in a certain way."

"She wouldn't see it that way at all," Laura says, kicking off her white slippers and swinging her legs off the chair. "She'd say that she just did what she did and people changed *themselves*."

"I think it was both," Jill answers her back. "They might not have been moved to change unless they had met her, so it's kind of a Catch-22. Were they changing anyway? Would they have moved in a new direction? Fell in love? Driven to the airport in a storm? You know. It's kind of a little bit of both."

"You're probably right. And she'd also say, 'What the hell difference does it make?' "

The four of them laugh and decide that whatever any of them thinks about who she was or what happened or why people do what they do is just absolutely fine and dandy as long as they have a good time, do it with a kind heart, and pay homage in a respectful way to the goddesses that have gone before them.

That's when Katherine flings open the door, puts her hand on her forehead, moans as if she has just risen out of a bed of extreme sexual pleasure, and declares, "Take me. Take me now. Nothing else will ever be the same."

"See," Jill says, pointing toward Katherine who has obviously had an experience that is a combination of fun and total pleasure. "Fun at all costs. That's what she would have said."

"What *she* is the center of our world?" Katherine asks.

"The Anniemeister. Who else?" Marie responds. "We've been having a fascinating discussion about the power of Annie. The cosmic relevance of everything that has happened and continues to happen. The power of death. The enlightenment we can harvest from grieving. You know, just a typical morning discussion on what might just be the last day of a terribly marvelous traveling funeral."

Katherine sits because her legs are suddenly made of rubber, orders Rebecca to the massage room, then throws herself on the long couch as if she is the queen of the world.

She tells them what she knows is that Annie struggled just like the rest of the world. She tells them that Annie reached some kind of interesting magical moment in her world or a combination of moments—moments in California, Chicago, New Mexico, Florida, New York, Minnesota, and Washington—that helped her tone and define her own life process, who she was, who she became.

"I won't deny that she had a terribly powerful presence and that I loved her beyond what some people would consider normal for a relationship that does not cross into something physical. But when I pull it all away, when I get down to the bones of who she was and what she gave us, it's all very simple," Katherine explains.

No one says anything. The women, including Rebecca who has not yet left the room, snuggle into their chairs as if they are listening to a bedtime story.

"Annie had her stuff," Katherine goes on. "She had the suicide thing, the depression, the stalking, the loss of her first great love, raising kids alone—by choice—but nonetheless we know that was no easy chore," Katherine explains, drawing from the mental notes she has managed to keep filed during the past week. "She was occasionally a pain in the ass too."

This stops the conversation. They laugh and then each one of them launches into an Annie story that makes Annie normal and honest and puts the skin back on her bones and makes her *real*. So very fucking *real*.

They get into it in a big way. She has to be real to them, always and forever real to them, even though each one of them knows that she is dead, that the remains of her ashes are sitting right in front of them, that they will never be able to touch her hand, lie in her lap, have her call them on the phone in the middle of the night, or walk with her along the beach, listen to her bullshit about the economy and politics, drink endless bottles of wine on a wild women-only weekend.

They know it and they launch into the realness of Annie as if they have just picked up the hotel carpeting and discovered an opening into an undiscovered world where women are always in charge and where men have babies and wash dishes and never make the same amount of money that women do who have the exact same jobs.

"It pissed me off, totally, when she would call and say she was coming over and then she would never show up," Laura says. "I'd be waiting, and then she'd never come and a week later she'd call and not even remember that she'd called. It drove me out of my mind and I'd always say, 'That's it,' and promise myself I'd never change plans for her again but I never did that either. That was Annie. It was just this thing in her head that took her away and made her stay on her path no matter what."

Katherine understands. She tells them that because she was Annie's oldest and longest friend that sometimes she felt taken for granted even though she knows it wasn't true and that Annie loved her.

"But, you know, there were a few times when I needed her and she would just not be available and it made me sad," she tells them. "I understood, but it made me really sad and I always wanted to tell her that but then she'd show up a few days later and we'd do something like throw water balloons off the roof with the kids and I'd turn and look at her and think that it was just Annie and here she was and it really didn't matter."

Laura said she absolutely went crazy when Annie would obsess about something, like the way the Democrats never quite get it right, and then hang on to that one thought so long it would get moldy. Obsessive, Laura said, Annie was obsessive but that's what made her so attractive to so many people.

"Sometimes she just would not hear." Laura moves her hands so fast it would be impossible to follow them with the human eye. "The Democratic thing sticks in my mind because of the last damn Bush election and she'd go on and on for hours about how the Democrats were always like party planners who fucked up the details. They'd get a big band but forget to host the event at a place that had electricity. Annie would not stop and sometimes, well, shit, many times that was so maddening I wanted to strangle her."

Once, Laura goes on, she did strangle Annie. After a particularly long conversation—totally one-sided—Laura said she reached over, put her hands around Annie's throat, and very loudly said, "So shut up and do something about it." She said Annie just looked at her and laughed.

"She laughed and laughed and then I put my hands down and that was the end of it but like a month later she wrote this huge article that was printed on the editorial page of the *San Francisco Examiner* and it was about what we had talked about. Annie did something, but I had to strangle her first. Maybe I should have done it more often. . . ."

Rebecca takes a long sigh, she almost sounds like a horse who has walked through the desert and has finally come out of it and is drinking from a lake, and then she looks from Jill to Laura to Katherine to Marie and asks how much time they have.

"Don't laugh," she says, moving forward in her chair as if she is about to shout. "I lived next to her, closer to her than any of you have in a long time, and so many things about her drove me crazy too. My God, do you know that she never, ever once took out her own goddamn garbage?"

They all roar because they, each one of them, has lived with a variety of people and in a variety of places, including each other for the past few days, and they know how often it is one small, tiny, minute thing that pushes a relationship over the edge. Sometimes it is the way someone parks a car, just too close to yours, or the way they make the bed or the ridiculous way they line up cans of soda and water in the refrigerator. Sometimes it's their favorite hat or the way they always have to buy gas on a Friday night. It's always just one hellish little thing.

"There were tons of things," Rebecca says as if someone has finally given her permission to let it all fly. "I had to get her damn dog so many times from the pound I was thinking about running the pup over myself but I loved the poor thing too much."

Little things.

"Well," she sighs, "I never let it ruin anything and I always told her she pissed me off with this little shit but it feels pretty damn good right now to just throw it off my skin one more time."

One more time, they all agree, is good.

Good for keeping them all safe and for making certain that above all, above everything else—above the writing and the workshops and the tragedy that Annie overcame, above the fine boys she raised who turned into men who are disciples for everything their mother taught and showed them and the way she shared her heart and love and life with so many people, above the way she cared mostly how she felt and not what others felt who might try and stop her because she was not doing or being what *they* thought but what she thought and needed, above the way she would have thrown herself in front of a truck or train or car or boat or bus for someone she did not even know let alone love— Annie G. Freeman was human and she had failings and she struggled and she sometimes lost—but, goddamn it—Annie G. Freeman never gave up.

She never gave up except for that last time. The time when no matter what she did or said or how hard she tried the cancer would not leave her alone. And even then, even in her dying, the very human Annie G. Freeman struggled and made her presence known and felt after her death in this traveling funeral and in all the lives that she has touched because of that and because of them.

"I can't really add anything to this," Marie reminds them. "I knew her in a different way, when she was just totally perfect."

"Damn it," Katherine says, throwing her newly manicured feet onto the floor and clapping her hands together. "I guess this means we have to forgive her one more time. If she is listening, she is laughing like hell. I can guarantee that."

Of course, they all agree, of course they have to forgive Annie and they have to remember this conversation that they will probably have many more times over the course of the other traveling funerals and reunions and trips to the cabin in Minnesota. Of course they will forgive Annie when they look out across the Pacific Ocean and think of the time they all went swimming on the coldest day of the year and then stumbled back to the car and drove half-baked to the cabin they had all rented in a town the size of a postage stamp that did not sell wine that came with corks and not screw-off caps.

Of course they will forgive Annie again when a note she wrote falls out of an old book and they read it and it says something remarkable and they want Annie to say it to them in person and they cannot do that because she is dead. Of course they will be pissed off.

They will be pissed off when it's the anniversary every year of the traveling funeral and they remember how they came together and learned new things about a woman who will always be remarkable and wise and strong in their hearts.

Of course they will be pissed off and angry when they occasionally reach for the phone to try and call Annie because they want to tell her something simple like "My daughter got into a great school" or "I just had the greatest sex I have had in ten years" or "Can you come over and watch *The Big Chill* with me for the fiftieth time?" and they realize as they are dialing her phone number that someone they have never met or known will answer the phone because Annie is dead.

Of course they will be pissed off and then forgive her for dying when one of them falls out of love and needs help. Needs help to realize it's okay to fall out of love and to move on and that there is a way to do that with great dignity and compassion. Annie would have helped them through that with her own stories and with a walk in the park and a night on the town and with the way she would fan her hand out across the horizon and tell them that life has so many pages to turn and that this page does not mean the story is over.

The story is never over.

"Shit," Rebecca says. "Shit. Shit. Shit."

Katherine says "shit" and then Laura says it and then Jill and finally Marie. They say "shit" singularly and they all stand up and hold hands and they say it together.

"Shit."

Then they say it again.

"Shit."

And then they cry. They don't want to cry because they are sick of crying and missing and wishing for something that will never come again, but something they also know is as real and large and as wonderful as the legacy of kicking ass that Annie G. Freeman left them.

They don't want to cry but it is an emotion that washes over them and covers their hands and arms and fingers and feet in a cleansing movement that is a bonding element that guards and keeps them tied together as if they are in a club for women warriors where teardrops, golden pure and sweet teardrops, come from a common river that runs through all women and holds them together in a way that Annie G. Freeman helped them to see and to live.

They huddle in their bathrobes, the pallbearers for Annie's fabulous traveling funeral, and they just let it go. They cry for how pissed off they are because Annie has died. They cry because they love her and now they love each other. They cry because there is an ache inside each one of them that is raw, new, fresh and a wound that needs tending now and for many days to come. A wound that will never quite heal but a wound that will allow them to run their fingers over the top of it, feel it, know that it is there and will always be a part of them until they are designing their own traveling funeral and about to meet Annie again in a place they imagine is a glorious paradise of freedom, wildness and fun. Always fun.

They cry and hold each other in a solidarity stance that says without having to utter a word that now they have Annie, they have this, they have their memories and they also have each other. They have phone numbers and this unique spread of time and they have a glimpse into each other's souls that no one else has. They have the warmth and security that comes from knowing you can trust someone, that the woman next to you will not call her sister and tell her what you look like running naked from a freezing body of water or sleeping with your mouth open after consuming several bottles of wine, or sobbing on an airplane while a piece of bread is stuck to your front tooth.

They cry because they are raw. They are raw from an openness that has been like an emotional surgery that has ripped them open and exposed a love for a woman, their friend, that is vital and secure and that they know will go on long after the last of the ashes have been spread.

It will go on for years and years as they remember bits and pieces of not only this traveling funeral but of the times they shared with Annie and with each other. The times when they knew Annie could not be replaced but that she had left them this great gift of each other and the freedom to launch ahead with whatever became exposed during the traveling funeral.

The funeral where they laughed and cried and danced and sang and saw parts of the world and of Annie that they should have known existed but had never bothered to visit, not because they didn't care or didn't want to, but because they were consumed by the real parts of living and loving that mattered more than going to confession over the little things. The funeral that gave them a chance, a chance to live in a way that was not necessarily new but definitely larger and bolder and more satisfying then the worlds that they had spun around themselves, their lovers and families.

The funeral that gave them a chance to say things about Annie and to Annie that most of them said when she was alive but not everything—not every damn thing.

And so they cry and they say things to each other in a practice session for what they will take with them and what they will say to other people whom they love and honor and cherish. They say how they loved being themselves and how they loved knowing they could make a stinker after lunch and no one would say anything. They say how they were scared about losing Annie because she was so much a part of them and who they were and eventually became. They will say how they appreciated the openness and every little kind gesture that was passed around as if that is just how it is supposed to be.

They say how they loved being with women—women—who knew what they needed without asking and who got their shit. They loved not having to worry about what was for dinner and how someone would react if they told a secret. They said how wonderful it was to be gracious to each other and realistic at the same time and how whatever happened, every single thing, had given them a new face to love and hand to hold and how Annie's greatest gift to them had apparently been each other.

Katherine, Marie, Jill, Laura and Rebecca cry for a very long time and they wipe their noses on the edges of each other's bathrobes and Jill goes to get them all glasses of water, and then they cry just a little bit more until they realize that it is two P.M. and that they have less than an hour to get their shit together, get to the airport, and fly into the rest of their lives.

Then they move like hungry lions.

The women pack and prance around the room and they take the three extra bottles of champagne so they can continue the funeral on the airplane and then they take turns kissing each other and they throw a kiss to "the man" and then they run to get into the limousine and on the way to the airport they make believe that they are movie actors and that they are on the way to a premier in California that is about to make them stars.

Stars.

Glorious, brilliant beautiful wise female stars.

29

Just before they get out of the limousine and double-knot the red high-tops for the last leg of the traveling funeral, Laura, Marie, Rebecca, Katherine and Jill decide to wear the red bandanas—which (thank the heavens) have been washed and pressed into neat four-square sections like they remember their fathers' handkerchiefs being folded—tied into their hair so that they look red from head to toe.

"Hey," the driver tells them as he pulls in front of the airport that had been their home just the day before. "You dudes look pretty cool."

"Yo," Jill says, laughing.

"Dudes," Katherine laughs back. "Isn't it something that women can be dudes these days? You should hear my daughter, she's constantly 'Hey duding' every single person, especially her girlfriends. It used to drive me nuts but now I think it's a tribute to the degender modification that has been cranking for more than a few years."

"My daughters do the same thing. What's with that?" Marie asks.

" 'Dudette' just doesn't seem to sound quite right," Laura agrees. "When my daughter was around she was into the same thing. If this dude thinks we look like cool dudes in our bandanas I am surely not going to dismiss this modern and very fine compliment."

"Yo," the driver responds, which sends them all into a round of laughter that carries them to the check-in counter where they have major déjà vu.

Everywhere they look they see the same people from the day before. The woman from behind the counter, half the people from the waiting room, and, they suspect, somewhere lurking in the crowd is "the man." They look for him to see if they can decide who he is but then give up when they realize that just about every single person in the airport knows who they are and is smiling and waving at them.

"Hey, you look fabulous," their airline friend behind the counter tells them. "Did you have a good time last night?"

"Last night and this morning and every single second since our plane was stranded," Katherine shares. "We were kind of hoping for another storm. We spent the morning looking for apartments in Minneapolis."

"You kill me," the woman tells her and then says, "Oops, sorry," and points to Annie's ashes.

"She'd love that, sweetheart," Katherine assures her. "Don't worry. We are all in good hands."

"Listen, you were already booked into first class for this trip, by that Annie woman, which I find amazing considering she's in that shoebox under your arm, no disrespect intended, so what I've done is given you a free upgrade on those other tickets you have from yesterday."

Katherine looks to the left and the right at her friends and wonders in amazement if things could get any better.

"I don't suppose one of us won the Pulitzer or a Guggenheim or a Nobel Peace Prize this morning while we were getting our nails buffed?"

"Not that I know of," the woman says, laughing. "But I am imagining this will be another interesting part of your journey because just about every single person on board has stopped to ask if the 'funeral women' are on their flight. It ain't over yet, apparently."

"Let us at them," Laura shouts as she turns around. "If we can stay awake we are all theirs."

Balinda calls Katherine just as they are about to board to let them know her mother appears to be getting better and that she arrived safely back into the womb of her own world and misses them terribly.

"It's strange," Balinda says. "She's started eating a bit and when I was gone this Polish nurse got her to start speaking in English."

"You should never have gone back," Katherine tells her as she waves the other women onto the airplane. "Maybe she'd be speaking French by the end of the week."

"I'm stumped," Balinda tells her. "Maybe she needed to get out of the house as much as I needed to get out of the house. Sometimes you just don't know until you do it, try it or, I suppose, be it."

Katherine rushes onto the plane just before they close the doors and is not at all surprised to see her "dudes" already holding court during the last few hours of the traveling funeral as they lean over their extra-wide seats and across the aisle to talk to a group of women who seem to be fascinated by the red tennies, the traveling funeral and where they can get a copy of the program so they can begin designing their own traveling funerals.

She is not sure as she walks up the aisle if she wants to get into it for the next four hours, drink the champagne, or sit quietly and prepare herself for the jump back into reality. She decides before she sits down to combine all four.

And she begins by also deciding that they all need to add one more note in the funeral book, without Annie's thoughts, just their thoughts, as they descend from the happy and sometimes sorrowful high of the last nine days and into the arms of the days and nights that lie in front of them.

Work. Kids. Husbands. Lovers. Schedules. Life without Annie in her physical form. Changes. Letting go and holding on. Whatever it takes. Here it comes. Ready or not.

She begins writing as the huge plane picks up speed and Minneapolis becomes a palate of green mixed in with blocks of the whites, grays and blacks that are the colors of cities, every city, from the air. Her eyes linger for a moment on the diminishing skyline of a city that turned into an adventure, a quick stopover that changed lives, a thirty-minute blip that turned into almost two days.

That is what grabs her mind as Jill, Laura, Marie and Rebecca quietly succumb to the few quiet moments when it is hard to talk, when they climb into clouds and fly—which still amazes her—into an hour that has already passed in the time zone they are just leaving—which also amazes her—in a place that has now become an important stop on her memory chain, in her life and especially in her heart.

KATHERINE THOUGHT: *We are heading back home, Annie, and there is just a tiny bit of you left in this box, enough for one more drop into the wind, enough for one more encounter with whatever it is that helped form you. We are tired and grateful and more alive, I think, than any of us have ever been before. I want to lie down in this seat and open my eyes and look across the aisle and see you reading and writing in your notebook. I can't help it. Sometimes when I think of you and then remember that you are gone, my stomach rushes to my throat and I have this spontaneous reaction that makes me wonder how I will ever be the same. Then my analytical side grabs me, Annie, it grabs me and I realize that I will never be the same and how wonderful is that? I realize that this traveling funeral that you designed is what I needed to help me in so many ways. I know this:*

I love you and will always love you.

We gave each other the world in a way that the other could not always see.

Something happened to me on this trip—a break in the link of my planned and paced life that is going to change everything.

I cannot wait.

You have shared your best and most important friends with me and for that—oh, Annie—for that, my heart aches in gratitude.

We are done.

And we will never be done.

The funeral book passes from one set of pallbearer's hands to the next as the plane levels off, as the hundreds of people who are flying into their own futures stake out their temporary place on the plane and in each other's lives and as the traveling funeral dudes get ready for what is left of this day and this terribly important part of Annie's funeral.

LAURA THOUGHT: *Sometimes I am so pissed that you are gone I could go blind with anger and then I realize that not once, not even once, in my life has anger given me anything positive or taken me to a new place. Well, once it got my daughter to stay home and the party she was supposed to go to got busted but that really didn't change anything. Gliding back, I am ready now to share our secret, Annie. I have saved it for the end. I have honored your idea that we should let it ride so that it would not color anything that happened after your death and I have managed, with great difficulty, to keep my big mouth shut. And, oh Annie, I have seen so many new possibilities in my life and with this chance that you have given me. You think that I saved you all those years ago but I think you are the one who saved me. You spread choices like a roving parade that included the banquet of life in front of me. I'm not scared anymore. I am excited and ready to land—so damn ready to land and then take off again.*

JILL THOUGHT: *I could have stayed home and taken up knitting and sat on the back porch with my cooler of water and this longing for the past and my lost world and the touch of academia that I so need to help me breathe. I could have lapsed into a coma on that porch and the swallows could have picked out my eyes and laughed at me as they carried off my chairs and the car and the lawn mower. I could have skated through another week and a month and the year after that with this grieving force and this burden of loss from you and my former life and with the things— and I mean things—that I thought I need to stay alive. Then came this funeral and these women and the chance to look into the mirror and see myself and my life and the possibility that comes when there is a sudden change. I am even more grateful now for knowing you and for touching your life than I have ever been. I'm pissed that you died, but I rejoice in your gifts, in your grace, in the way that you linger in my life, our lives, even now as we cruise toward home and the rest of our lives in a way that I could never have imagined just a short week ago.*

REBECCA THOUGHT: *You are such a bitch. Do you have any idea how hard this has been? How wonderful? Here is what I know:*

    I will miss you every day for the rest of my life.

    I loved you in a way that I have never loved anyone else.

    Your patience and persistence helped me plow around some new corners in my own life.

    The gathering together of these women has created a brigade of friendship.

    No one else who meets us will ever be the same.

    I am learning to mix my sorrow over this great loss along with the remembering and the honoring of what we had as friends, neighbors and women on the run. I am learning how to temper my anger at the seemingly unending numbers of deaths I have to embrace with the realities of life, happenstance and circumstance and I am doing all of that while I hold on to my own heart, my own self, the person I was. I don't want to let that slip away and I am trying hard to honor everything and everyone in the process.

*I cannot imagine ever not missing you, not instinctively turn-
ing to see if your bathroom light is on, not listening for the crunch
of your tires on the gravel driveway, not longing to talk to you, see
you smile, put a cold drink in your hand in the middle of July.*

*I miss you, Annie G. Freeman, and even as I believe and know
I will see you again, I also believe and know that in the midst of
all your humanness you were a golden glow that filled my life in
ways I will always and forever appreciate.*

Marie Thought: *I should have listened to you and embarked
on this adventure sooner. I should have known you were dishing
out advice about my own life even as you died. Here I thought
this was a funeral—your funeral—and it's turned into something way beyond that. Your friends are grand and you were a
spirit of inspiration and knowledge to me even for the short period of time when our lives touched. Our lives are still touching,
Annie. They will always touch.*

When Marie closes the funeral book, places her hands over the
top of it and turns to Katherine, she asks, "Now what?"

"Apparently we will also be going to Poland," Rebecca says.

"It also sounds like Jill will be getting a new roommate," Marie
says.

"I'm thinking of chucking half of my life, maybe reevaluate the
passion I have for everything I am doing, figuring out what I
want to do beyond all of this lawyering and schedules and working
weekends that I've done for way too many years," Katherine says.

"Really?" Marie asks.

"I'm tired of keeping all those balls in the air, you know?"
Katherine pushes her back into the cushion and closes her eyes.
"The immense court calendar, schedules, my damn boyfriend—
who seems to be more bother than he's worth some days—taking
care of the house. Maybe it's time to simplify my life."

. "Whew, all this from a traveling funeral?" Marie says.

"It's all been swirling around me, I think," Katherine explains. "We've been talking about it all week. I've just not bothered to sit still long enough and link it all together."

"Another gift from Annie."

"That's not all," Laura says, leaning over from the seat across the aisle. "There's one more thing—well, probably more than one more thing—but something else that's going to be a big change for me and probably for Rebecca too."

The women look at her, waiting, wondering, as Jill leans in across her seat to listen and says, "What the hell?"

"I'm really going to seriously consider buying Annie's house and moving there."

No one but Marie, who has not been on board long enough to hear the earlier discussions, seems surprised. Laura explains to Marie how she and her husband have been considering moving for several years and how Annie talked to her about buying the house before she died.

"For a long time, when our daughter took off, we kept saying how we couldn't leave because she might come back at any moment," Laura tells Marie. "But this is just how she is. She'll be fine. She just can't stand still and remember for months and months that there's anyone but her in the entire universe. We've both been tired of the city for a long time and we are both pretty transferable."

Rebecca can barely imagine it. "Really?"

"Really," Laura responds, smiling widely.

"Do you take out your own garbage?"

"Never."

"Then you have my vote," Rebecca laughs.

Laura said that their modest Chicago bungalow had been appraised way higher than they had imagined and that Tom was prepared to transfer to a smaller company in Sonoma County, where the cost of living was actually cheaper than in Chicago and much closer to the vineyards, as Tom liked to say. They had decided that their roving daughter would be able to find them if she ever chose to come home.

Her work at the women's center, Laura says, can transfer to numerous nonprofit agencies in one of the cities or towns near Annie's house that are always looking for someone with lots of experience who is willing to work long hours for low pay, and with little or no hope of advancement or a salary increase.

"Perfect for me," she says, laughing. "That's where my heart is anyway."

"Laura, this is unreal, fabulous, perfect news," Rebecca says, trying to get out of her seat to embrace Laura. "Do you have any idea what this means?"

"Well, if this trip is any indication, it means we could be in really big trouble."

"Balinda?"

"She'll be okay. Actually, having her on the trip and seeing that she is getting ready to fly again, without an airplane, helped make my decision become even more clear. We have sort of been taking care of each other, even though Balinda thinks I have been taking care of her. I think this traveling funeral helped her get her life back."

"My God!" Jill exclaims, slapping her hands against her thighs. "All we need is Barbra Streisand to come up the aisle singing and I think we've got ourselves a musical."

Their words become a kind of musical as they sing through the days they have just shared and the messages that cradled them through hours of grieving.

"It's so odd, isn't it," Jill asks, "that we know we are all going to die and that we have these difficult passages to go through with our parents and friends and other people we love and care about who are also going to die. And yet it's almost as if we are never really *ready*. Does that make sense?"

"Well," Laura tells her, "it's one thing to think about it but then the reality of it, when it really happens, is like a breathtaking and almost frightening experience. We all knew Annie was dying but when the boys called us to tell us that she really had died, it was as if that was the first time we even knew she was sick."

"Nothing can prepare you," Rebecca says quietly.

"Exactly," Laura agrees. "And it will happen again and again. Balinda's mom will die, my mom will probably end up living with us, one of your friends will die of breast cancer . . . it is sort of endless."

A luscious moment of silence slips into the conversation for just a second, not longer than it takes for a true thought to climb its way into the minds of each one of the women.

"I'll say it," Rebecca says. "Annie's thing was to concentrate on the living. To honor every day and every person in some interesting way because that's what you had, just that one moment."

"True," Katherine adds. "I think she thought it was important to honor a life, the way it was lived, the potential it had to grow and change. But she also wanted us, and now all the people we have touched, to see that saluting someone after they die can be done in a way that allows us to grieve and to celebrate. Does that make sense?"

Of course, they agree.

Of course Annie was one of the most alive and vibrant people they had ever known and her ability to reach places in people through roadblocks and long tunnels and sealed off passageways was remarkable. It was also remarkable that she thought they saved her and how they think she saved them.

Of course there are many ways to celebrate death and life and of course as they bounce into their forties and fifties and sixties the fingers of time grow a bit longer and yet, they agree, and yet life does not stop. Life does not stop or wait even if you do. Pause if you must, the women agree, but then catch up fast, run with the wind, slide down the hill tumbling headfirst so that you can fall into the hands of now—today, every day, every minute, every second.

Of course it is also okay to hold on to your grief and ride it as if your own life depended on it through a sea of rough water, waves as high as heaven, through the thunderous barrage of emotions that are the very heart of loss—any loss—love, death, job—a slice of a segment of your life that made up the whole.

Of course they also agree—the whole damn world needs to have more fun. A hell of a lot more fun.

Which is what they decide to do during the last two hours of the plane ride once they have called Marie's husband on the fun in-seat phone to make certain he will be at the airport to drive them all to Rebecca's house before they scatter back to their own worlds with fresh wind under their wings. First they tap the edges of Annie's shoebox as a concluding salute and slip the funeral book inside it for safekeeping during the last hours of the traveling funeral and once they have agreed to celebrate with as many people on the plane who want to celebrate and share the secrets of the formation of a traveling funeral and the life of Annie G. Freeman.

Before they can leap into more conversations or walk to the bathroom or have an engaging session with all the fine folks on the plane who have been sending them notes and trying to buy them drinks they hear a tapping on the intercom system. They think it's a weather report but it isn't. It's not a weather report at all.

"Ladies and gentlemen, and you too Frank," a woman laughs into the intercom. "Sorry, I had to say it. This is Beverly, the head flight attendant again, but maybe not for long after this. My wonderful friend Frank, who everyone on the plane knows now, has something he'd like to say, so sit up, get your head off the tray and out of your horrid dinner and listen up."

Who wouldn't be listening up? The women look at each other, laugh out loud and yes, right into their horrid dinners and wait for whatever in the heck Mr. Frank has to say.

"I should throw you out the window," he tells the attendant, "but as most of you know, we have more important things to do."

Something has obviously happened that Annie G. Freeman's

pallbearers know nothing about because the entire plane, without them, is clapping.

"Katherine, can you come up here for a second?"

Katherine looks around and realizes Frank is talking to *her*. Laura pushes her to her feet and Katherine swaggers to the front of the plane where Frank is waiting for her.

He begins by telling her that every single person on the airplane, all 289 of them, was stranded at the airport at the same time as Katherine and her friends. He tells her he is a minister but before that he was a real person, just a man, and that the entire planeload of passengers has been touched by the traveling funeral, by what they know and have learned about Annie G. Freeman and the friends she has, who have been whooping it up across the country to honor her life.

"This isn't about religion or anything more subtle than us, every single person on this plane, wanting to let you know and Annie if we could, that we agree there is more than one way to live and more than one way to celebrate a life after it's over," he tells Katherine, wrapping his arm around her shoulders. "We passed the hat and collected fourteen hundred dollars that we want to donate in her name to one of the scholarship funds for Annie's programs we found online that help kids who need just a bit of a push to the next truck stop."

Katherine is astounded.

Laura is astounded.

Rebecca is astounded.

Marie is astounded.

Jill is astounded.

"Before you say anything," Frank goes on, "we also want you to know that you have given us a fine glimpse into the heart of uncommon friendship, the spirit of grieving—which we all do and have done and will do again—and a notion that having a great time, of grabbing a moment even if it's just a stranded moment at the airport, is just as important as turning off the hall light before you go to bed. We think you are all terrific."

The noise from the clapping is just as loud as the engines and then the pilot comes on and tells Katherine that any time her girls need to go on another traveling funeral they should give him a call and he'll make sure they get a smooth ride.

Katherine hesitates for just a second and then she takes the microphone and tells them all, "Thank you." She hesitates again, and then says:

"We thought this was going to be an intimate celebration for a woman, a friend who was a very important part of our lives, but as many of you know, as we rolled into one day after another we realized that not only are there many ways to grieve but that sharing sorrow, reaching out, being honest about your loss is as important as anything," she tells them. "If someone had told me a month ago that I'd be standing up here and lecturing an airplane crowd, I would have checked them in to the nearest hospital. I know Annie would have said go kiss someone, go swim naked, go quit the job you hate, go celebrate your own life before it's over. Go. Do something and do it with gusto and gratitude and with a laugh at the back of your throat, a laugh that never ends."

Holy shit.

"Holy shit" is what Annie G. Freeman's fabulous friends think and say as Katherine sits back down and the plane circles toward San Francisco and dips its wings to the ocean, a salute, a homecoming high-five, and then lands into a world that will never be, should never be, the same.

Hours later, when Rebecca, Katherine, Laura, Jill and Marie are sitting on the back steps of Rebecca's house and have watched the afternoon sky float in circles—darkness chasing light in the nightly ritual—the women each take a breath, the wind stops for just a second, there are no birds winging across the line of trees searching for a night nest that will cradle their wings, the sound of traffic echoing from one hill to the next disappears and they all lean forward as if someone has gently pushed them from behind.

They lean forward and they look around the corner into the

next day, that tiny sliver of light that never really fades, that stays glued to the edge of the world no matter how tight the darkness descends, and they catch the scent of something that they remember as earthy, sweet, bold and warm. It is the scent of Annie wrapping her arms around each of them as they move forward in directions that a great cartographer would need a new map to follow. It is a scent that will always stay with each of them. It is the fuel each needs to remember, to move forward, and it will never ever go away.

Epilogue

The women all decided to spend the night at Rebecca's and they spread out with blankets and old sleeping bags from the porch to the living room and upstairs into the two back bedrooms. During the night, just three hours after they finally gave it up and no one could utter another word, a small rainstorm—the last bark of the mega-storm that stranded them in Minneapolis and left a wide slap across the nation—sprinkled its footprints on the lawn as if someone had been tiptoeing to try and get into the side windows.

When they gathered for breakfast the following morning, slumped over coffee and scrambled eggs and a huge bowl of fruit that Marie had purchased at the roadside stand, they began sharing their night's dreams.

"My gawd," Jill drawled. "I was on a boat with a mess of people I did not know and all of a sudden there was a parade. A parade on the water. Boats with lights and people dancing and dogs barking. It was awesome."

"What?" Laura asked just about the same moment as Rebecca, Marie and Katherine.

What, because every single one of them had a dream that featured a parade and water. Waterfalls, a lake, Marie swimming toward some fireworks after a parade, a canoe ride up a river that ended up being part of an annual festival. The women looked at each other, shook their heads, said, "Annie," and then kept going as if this kind of cosmic similarity had become a routine part of their lives.

Laura stayed with Rebecca for a week and the two women spent a great deal of time at Annie's house sorting through her personal effects with her two sons and then working out a final arrangement for Laura and her husband to purchase the house. After Annie's sons took what they wanted—a few pieces of furniture, most of her books, and family treasures like photographs and the back porch swing where Annie loved to sit and talk to her boys— the women held a huge rummage sale that quickly turned into an Anniefest and a grand yard party for the entire neighborhood, the university community, and what seemed like half of California.

Laura and Tom moved into Annie's house three months later. Tom found a job at a small company as the business manager, and when the county restructured its facilities management plan and the director of emergency services retired, Laura applied for the position and got the job. It took her less than a month to reorganize the entire department and to design and apply for a grant to offer special programs for teenagers at risk that was quickly funded in full by an anonymous donor, identified only as "the man from Minneapolis" who only asked that the program be named after Annie G. Freeman.

Tom's brother, an English teacher from a small college in the Midwest, spent a week helping Laura and Tom move in and unpack and by the end of the week had spent most of his time trying to seduce Rebecca who was just as smitten as he was. He made it into the bedroom on the last night, sent her a plane ticket for a weekend visit, and at this very moment is flying back to visit her for the third weekend in a row.

Rebecca, happy to the point of making everyone—including her new neighbors—nauseous with the romantic turn of events in her life, threw herself off the cliff of love and also managed to design several new marketing programs for her office that made them forget all of the time she had taken off to care for her dying relatives and to go on a traveling funeral that was now and forever part of the legend of Sonoma County.

Laura and Tom never locked their doors, Rebecca never locked hers and as her neighbors gradually turned Annie's house into their own, a wonderful synergy of give and take, a kind of communal living that made way for the traveling brother, Annie's boys—who are really men—and Marden, Rebecca's daughter, began to unfold and new stories and parties and memories were formed before the boxes were even unpacked.

Balinda called not long after Laura and Tom's old house sold to a family from Poland, who took over not only her yard to plant a garden but half of her mother's life as well, to tell Laura that her daughter had just pulled up in a convertible looking for her.

"I gave her your new address and she said to give you a call and let you know she'd be there in a few days unless she found an interesting side road that she needed to explore," Balinda told her.

The wayward daughter, Erin, who was really a fairly successful web designer who simply had the blood of a gypsy inside of her and could do business from the back of her car, a gas station bathroom or an eighty-nine-story building, did show up at Laura's new home but it took her nine weeks to get there. She stayed for a very long time, which for her was more than two weeks, and when Annie's son Donan came for a visit, the two hit it off like only opposites can.

Donan, who drove a restored Dodge van and dressed like the world's stereotypical image of a computer geek—button-down shirts, actually buttoned to the throat, khakis and loafers—loved the creative flow that he harnessed with Erin's laughter and he offered to partner with her in a business that would allow her to live exactly how she wanted to live. She agreed but only if a certain percentage of their work was pro bono and if they did not accept work from ultraconservative groups or anyone who had ever spoken to, voted for or said one good thing about President George W. Bush. He reluctantly agreed and within three months the two of them—Donan, from downtown San Francisco, and the wayward daughter, when last heard from in an adobe cottage in southern Utah—were on the verge of becoming widely successful.

Balinda was beside herself with more than the good news about what she called "her new world." Something remarkable had happened to her mother in the assisted living facility. She was not only speaking entire sentences in English, she had three new and very fine women friends and was proclaimed well enough—well, sort of well enough—to move back home if she wanted to. But she didn't want to.

"My mother wants to stay where she is and she wants to go to Poland before she dies, not after she dies," Balinda told them. "Will you all still go?"

They did.

This time they extended the Poland trip to lovers, kids, boyfriends and husbands because they had so many free tickets and a place to stay with about five thousand Chalwaski relatives. Fourteen of them flew to Poland and they had so much fun they almost got kicked out of the country. They toured, danced in the streets, drank homemade beer and wine, went hiking, and watched Jencitia Chalwaski's eyes light up and nearly set the country on fire when she saw friends, relatives and a place that she had held in her heart and memory for a very long time. She could never travel after that but it did not matter to her because she had been home.

Balinda started to date again after she joined a dancing theater troupe, a decision which pretty much came out of nowhere, because she didn't even know she wanted to dance. At last count, she had tap-danced her way into the hearts of four men and two women, but she had decided to keep her tap shoes, so far anyway, under the beds of only the men. She was also in the midst of a nationwide search for the sexy man of her dreams.

Jill's life was never and would never be the same following the traveling funeral. She barely had time to sit on the back porch and mope, and feeling sorry for herself was never an idea that entered her mind. Melissa—the waitress from New Mexico—and her family, with the help of maps, gas money and no clear picture of what to expect when they left Bernahillo, came for a visit. Melissa fell in love with the campus the second they pulled into the parking lot at the university and got a job at a swanky local restaurant about twenty minutes after that and traded in her cowboy boots for Birkenstocks.

The quiet house on the edge of town quickly became a thriving center of action and life, the likes of which Jill also saw a lot of on her own side of the house. The classy bartender from New York, Nina, called her and just happened to be a two-time author and a therapist who loved interacting with people as a bartender because they did not have a clue what she did to pay her mortgage. They corresponded. They stayed up all night talking on the phone. They flirted like mad just like they did the night at the bar when they stayed at the hotel in New York and then Nina, without telling Jill, hopped on an airplane and showed up on her very doorstep, just like in the movies, with flowers, champagne and the most unbelievably beautiful smile Jill had ever seen in her life.

Katherine went back home, made sure her daughter's grades were still good and the flowers were watered, and very quickly downsized her entire life. She told her boyfriend, who really wasn't that bad, that she needed a break, put the house that she had slaved to buy, remodel and finance on the market, and found a very small, two-bedroom home right in the heart of the city but close enough so that her daughter could finish her last year of high school with the friends and teachers she knew and cared for.

Two months after moving, Katherine literally bumped into a woman in her courtroom who was rushing to file papers for an addition onto her restaurant. The women talked for twenty minutes, Katherine accepted a dinner invitation, confessed over a bottle of fine red wine that she had always wanted to learn how to cook at a "real joint," and became a part-time apprentice to one of the finest chefs in California. After figuring and refiguring her finances she was able to quit her assistant district attorney position with a small pension and work full-time (and then some) at the restaurant with the hope that her daughter would get some big-ass scholarship to pay her way through college. She loved her new life so much she sometimes cried on the way to work because she was so damn happy.

Marie kept her job as the hospice nurse because she could not imagine her life without the Annies and Willards who depended on her to ease their final days and to do what was right—no matter what the rules said. Her experience with the traveling funeral helped her develop a series of workshops, which she called celebrations, to help people with issues of death and dying and to engage in discussions with family members who were terminally ill and wanted to plan their own funerals before they died.

Her husband surprised her by building her a beautiful cabin on the back side of their property so that she could hold her workshops there and so she could have a place to mentally detox without a ringing phone, the pounding feet of her family or the distractions of a world that she needed to put on pause after her terribly emotional days and nights. He planted a tree outside of the window he was certain she would sit near and made a family rule that no one could go inside the cabin unless they were invited.

Then Marie drove to the Harley dealership, signed up for a class, and started shopping for a used bike that she dreamed would carry her into the wind, past twelve clients' homes and into a world where she could catch every dream she'd ever had. She also began taking regular days off, was rumored to have actually used one sick day, and is now planning a trip with the entire family to Annie's family home on Lake Superior.

It took the women a year to finalize plans for the last leg of Annie Freeman's fabulous traveling funeral. All of the women, except Balinda who had a very large role in a small play, flew to

Seattle on a Friday afternoon. They followed Annie's directions right down to the rental of a red van, picking up the six P.M. ferry to Bainbridge Island, and just waiting at the dock for a nice woman who would have them follow her to a cabin on Little Manzanita Bay.

This cabin was a world away from new loves and old dreams and the ever-quickening pace that they had all fallen into following their return a year ago from the wild days and nights flying from one end of the country to the other with Annie's ashes. When the five women got off the boat and met the woman on the dock she laughed out loud to see them in their red high-tops and bandanas and said, "This makes total sense" as she whisked them off to the cabin by the sea.

They had two nights and a day to figure it out but it didn't take that long. Annie's last note to them had stayed inside of the red tennis shoes for all the months when the box had been tucked away inside of Katherine's underwear drawer. They had their glasses of wine on the long deck with their feet up, tennies pointed toward the water, when Katherine pulled out the final note and read it.

Just pause and remember. I came here several times just to do that, and to feel that salty air on my face, to be by my water, to just sit down and let the world I live in pass right through me. It was an important lesson. I should have done it more. Just pause, my loves, remember me, and then keep going. Love, Your Annie.

The next evening they each dipped their fingers into the ashes and cupped them in their hands and then they went in five separate directions. They did not plan anything after that, they did not time the release of what was left of Annie, they did not sing or toast or cry, but anyone watching, anyone hovering above the bay would have seen a swirl of ashes, tiny particles of matter, released at the exact same moment by the beautiful fingers of five of the most wonderful women ever created. Annie's friends, her female family, the women she loved, tossed her ashes into the summer wind, they each caught a sob in the back of their throats, and then each, in her own special way, said goodbye.

Later, Katherine threw her old Bali bra into the fire they made on the beach and they relived every moment of Annie Freeman's Fabulous Traveling Funeral and her totally fabulous and ever-present life, and they did exactly what Annie would have wanted them to do: they paused and then they kept on going.

About the Author

KRIS RADISH is an author, journalist, and nationally syndicated political and humor columnist. Her Bantam Dell novels, *The Elegant Gathering of White Snows* and *Dancing Naked at the Edge of Dawn*, were both Book Sense 76 bestsellers and appeared on national bestseller lists. She is also the author of the true-crime book *Run, Bambi, Run* and a psychology book, *Birth Order Plus*. Her speaking engagements take her across the country to talk about writing, and women's and feminist issues. Her Elegant Gatherings and Dancing Naked Workshops have set more than a few women on fire.

She lives with her two tall teenage children and her partner in Wisconsin, where she rides her motorcycle—usually fully clothed— loves to swim, hikes with her writing tablet in her back pocket, and often scares unsuspecting neighbors with her wild laugh. She is working on her fourth novel, *The Sunday List of Dreams*, and several nonfiction projects.

If you enjoyed Kris Radish's
**ANNIE FREEMAN'S FABULOUS
TRAVELING FUNERAL,**
you won't want to miss any
of her beloved novels.

Look for the bestselling
**THE ELEGANT GATHERING
OF WHITE SNOWS**
and
**DANCING NAKED AT THE
EDGE OF DAWN**
at your favorite booksellers.

And you won't want to miss Kris's next
heartwarming, inspiring novel,
**THE SUNDAY LIST
OF DREAMS,**
coming from Bantam Dell in 2007.
Find out why so many readers have fallen
in love with the novels of Kris Radish!